1/12

WHAT'S IN
A NAME

WHAT'S IN
A NAME

•

Karen Frisch

AVALON BOOKS

NEW YORK

Published by Avalon Books,
an imprint of Thomas Bouregy & Co., Inc.
New York, NY

Library of Congress Cataloging-in-Publication Data

Frisch, Karen.
   What's in a name / Karen Frisch.
      p. cm.
   ISBN 978-0-8034-7616-5 (hardcover : acid-free paper)
   I. Title.
   PS3604.E5858W47 2011
   813'.6—dc23

                              2011025770

PRINTED IN THE UNITED STATES OF AMERICA
ON ACID-FREE PAPER
BY RR DONNELLEY, HARRISONBURG, VIRGINIA

To Carolyn Sullivan, world's best goals partner,
for pestering me when I need it most.
You're always there with patience,
understanding, and humor.
Thanks for being such a good friend.

Chapter One

Boston, 1871

Juliet Halliday stared in disbelief. Her gaze wandered from the rotting lintel above the boardinghouse door to a broken step that seemed too insubstantial to support the weight of a mouse, much less her own. From the look of it, there were probably plenty of mice, and worse, beyond the threshold.

"This can't be the right address, Clara. Can you imagine Cordelia having lived in this neighborhood?"

Convinced they had taken a wrong turn, Juliet withdrew her sister's letter from her reticule. The brass numerals over the door, while scratched and bent, proclaimed this to be 23 Methodist Alley. Cordelia's last letter had been mailed from this address in April, just two months ago. Behind her, the woman who served as Juliet's housekeeper and traveling companion cleared her throat, startling her.

"Considering this is supposed to be Methodist Alley," Clara Crabtree said, her voice uneasy, "I don't see any church. The neighborhood certainly seems in need of one."

This was the street to which the conductor had directed them, Juliet reflected. During their ride through Boston's privileged neighborhoods, she had expected the horsecar to pull up before one of the stately brick mansions where she assumed her sister and nephew had lived. Instead, she watched with dismay as they passed one imposing home after another until the elegance disappeared and the view became one of tenements with threadbare sheets blowing on clotheslines. They had disembarked near a familiar address in an unfamiliar neighborhood.

What were they to do now? Juliet set down her valise, studying the crumbling brick row house, with its shuttered windows, before her. The alley where they stood was so narrow that neighbors across the way could have heard them whisper. If Cordelia had lived here with Marcus, Juliet thought, her life had been harder than she'd admitted. From around the bend in the alley, two boys in stained shirts and tattered trousers peered at them.

"You ought to be in school," Clara scolded loudly enough to send them running, their feet clattering on cobblestone.

"I suppose it's time we announced ourselves," said Juliet.

"I think I feel safer out here," she heard Clara mutter before the housekeeper tugged at her sleeve. "Are you sure you don't want to turn back? It isn't too late to change your mind."

Juliet turned, surprised by the urgency in Clara's tone. Clara was shorter by six inches, but Juliet couldn't help but see the uncertainty and fear in her eyes.

"Why would I want to turn back after coming all this way? We need to get my nephew and bring him home."

Summoning her courage, Juliet mounted the rickety steps. As she raised her fist to knock, the door was opened by a woman with hair as white as Juliet felt her own face probably was.

"You must be Cordelia's sister, along with Mrs. Crabtree," the woman said in a cordial tone, reaching for their bags and leading her visitors inside. "Here, let me help you. I'm Lillian Wetherall. I made tea, knowing you'd be exhausted after your long journey from Maine. I hope it was pleasant."

"That's very kind of you," Juliet replied in confusion.

"Please sit down. The refreshments will just take a moment."

The woman indicated chairs by the fireplace before she left them alone. Juliet edged into the crowded parlor with Clara close behind her. Old lace and worn bric-a-brac on a nearby étagère met her gaze, a welcome surprise considering the home's shabby exterior. A sampler stitched with garden herbs bright-ened the faded floral wallpaper, and gilt-framed photographs lined the mantel.

Juliet moved forward to study the faces. Unable to recognize anyone, she found it hard to picture Cordelia living in this house. In Mrs. Wetherall's absence, Clara traced her finger along a dusty sideboard until Juliet stopped her with an admonishing glance.

When their hostess returned moments later, they were both settled in comfortable wing chairs beside a cozy fire. Juliet tactfully avoided glancing at the crocheted doilies that hid the bare spots on the upholstery. Gratefully, she sipped the spiced tea Lillian Wetherall put before them.

"There, that's better." Setting the teapot on a mahogany side table, Mrs. Wetherall took a seat opposite them. "I'm very sorry for your loss. Your sister and I were close friends."

"Thank you." A familiar knot tightened in Juliet's throat. "It's Marcus I worry about. I haven't seen my nephew in four years. If not for you, Papa and I wouldn't even have known of Cordelia's death. I'm glad she had a friend." She drew comfort from the thought that her sister had not been alone at the end.

"I only wish I'd been able to reach you before the funeral," the woman lamented. "It took time to track down your father."

Perhaps Cordelia would have preferred it that way, Juliet thought. Her sister had been private, secretive even. Still, with Marcus on his own, she couldn't understand why their solici-tor hadn't sent word. She tried to focus on the present. "I know you must have concerns about what will become of this house. I'm sure arrangements can be made for you to stay on until Papa decides to sell it."

"I don't think you understand, my dear." Mrs. Wetherall gave her a smile that seemed at once gentle and ominous. "I let Cordelia live here. She had no money, you see."

Juliet exchanged a look with Clara, whose face registered her own bewilderment. "We were under the impression this was Cordelia's home."

"She would always have been welcome here," their hostess

assured her. "My husband left me the house. He died young, just as Cordelia's did. Perhaps that was why we had so much in common."

Juliet felt light-headed. Something was dreadfully amiss. She had hardly adjusted to the idea of Cordelia living in such squalid conditions. To realize she'd been allowed to remain here out of charity was beyond imagination. Juliet's face must have revealed her shock, for her hostess reached for the tea.

"No, thank you." Juliet rose shakily, forcing a smile. "I'm afraid I misunderstood. It might be best if we collect Cordelia's belongings, take my nephew, and find a hotel."

Mrs. Wetherall's features grew grave. "There's nothing left, I'm afraid. Cordelia pawned most of her family heirlooms to make ends meet. I used what was left to give her a proper burial."

"So that's why no solicitor contacted us. I shouldn't be surprised, I suppose. Daniel probably didn't leave her much when he died." Juliet felt her heart pound as she tried to come to terms with the unexpected realizations. "Is Marcus at school now?"

"Marcus doesn't go to school." Mrs. Wetherall used that maddening tone again, as if Juliet were slow-witted. "They were facing such hardships, he quit school to go to work."

Juliet felt as though she'd been struck. At home in Maine, where she taught school, the idea of a nine-year-old working for a living was unthinkable.

"Children shouldn't have to work at such a tender age," Juliet objected, her voice faint.

"Yet some must." Mrs. Wetherall's tone was firm but sympathetic. "Is there a reason you couldn't stay here with Marcus, at least while he adjusts to the loss of his mother?"

Juliet dropped back into her chair, unable to comprehend the idea of her nephew going to work each day. Like her Shakespearean namesake, Cordelia had loved their father, but she also had been headstrong and had married against his wishes. *Yet, if she and her son were forced to live in poverty, why hadn't she turned to Papa for help?*

It was pointless to leave now, Juliet realized. Even without an estate to settle, she had to learn why Cordelia had lived a life so different from what she had led her family to believe.

"Very well," she agreed. "Once we're home, Marcus can resume a more traditional routine. Now I'd like to visit him at work."

The landlady's face puckered with distress. "That's just it. When I went to the fish market on Salem Street earlier, Mr. Santilli said Marcus didn't come to work today. It isn't the first time," she added with a hint of disapproval.

"You mean Marcus isn't there?" Juliet tried to calm her consternation. "Young boys don't simply disappear."

"These city streets hold many distractions for children. I've often seen Marcus on the corner during the day."

"Where we come from"—Clara spoke up indignantly—"we make sure children don't have such distractions."

Juliet opened her mouth to advise Clara to speak prudently, then closed it. It was nearly suppertime, and no one knew her nephew's whereabouts.

"Cordelia wrote such glowing things about Boston," she said slowly. "After her husband died, she said she would let out rooms. I expected to find Marcus living in comfortable circumstances."

"He did once." Mrs. Wetherall's voice was kind. "But since Cordelia's death, his habits have changed. He hasn't been here the last two nights."

Juliet felt the blood rush to her cheeks. Was it possible that a nine-year-old boy was sleeping on the streets at night? Frantically, she sought to make sense of Marcus' absence.

"He can't have run away," she protested. "I wired him to say I was coming to take him home."

"Maybe that's why he's running," Mrs. Wetherall said softly.

Juliet took a deep breath. The tenderhearted young boy she remembered was motherless and in desperate need of nurturing. But before she could help him, she had to find him. She turned to see Clara looking as mystified as Juliet felt.

Juliet tried to convince herself everything would turn out

fine, even if it didn't feel that way now. She had grown up in a seacoast town where she knew the rise of every hill, the curve of every lane, and the shortest distance between them. It could not be that different for Boston residents. Marcus knew the city and would find a way to manage. Her nephew was in God's hands, as they all were. Yet, she needed to find him soon to put her fears to rest.

She fumed to think he was growing up this way. *What kind of person hires a boy to do a man's job?* Juliet intended to find out.

His hair damp with sweat, Antonio Santilli wiped his brow with his sleeve and stepped into the shade that the awning over his fish market provided. Relieved to be out of the sun after a lengthy but unsuccessful search, he tried to stem his mounting frustration at his failure to locate his younger sister. While he would gladly endure June's heat to find Maria, he decided he needed a better plan.

Looking up to see Antonio had returned, his brother Giorgio stopped sweeping the sidewalk.

"Any sign of her?" Giorgio asked, his tone anxious.

"None," Antonio said tersely. "I walked every street in the North End. If she's hiding, she's staying a step ahead of me."

Not only had that scalawag Marcus Malloy vanished, but Antonio's sister had disappeared right after. Maria had been missing since yesterday. While she was stubborn and prone to outbursts, she'd never run away from home before. It was all Antonio could do to keep their mother from succumbing to hysterics.

"Maybe she'll come back on her own," Giorgio suggested.

"I won't rest until she's stealing *guanti* from the kitchen table like she usually is." Antonio shook his head, picturing his sister reaching for the wafer-thin, powdered-sugar-coated fried pastries as soon as their mother's back was turned. "I didn't expect to be gone all day. Anything urgent going on?"

"Only Maria's disappearance. I still haven't unpacked that shipment of olive oil." With one hand on his hip, the other clutching the broom, Giorgio turned to his older brother for guidance, his expression uneasy. "What do we do next?"

"Why don't you go indoors and finish unpacking?" suggested Antonio. "I'll take over here while I think about our next step."

Giorgio returned inside, leaving Antonio to continue sweeping while contemplating Maria's absence. He kept a sharp lookout while he greeted passing customers, briefly updating those who stopped to inquire about Maria. Feeling conspicuous as he paced, he saw that Giorgio had cleaned the street with a dustpan, as Antonio had requested, until there wasn't a trace left of the waste from passing horses.

Restless, he tossed the broom aside. The sidewalk could wait. He had only one concern at the moment. The clatter of footsteps from their apartment upstairs warned of Mama's approach. Her apron askew, dark hair feathering out of its tight bun, she gave him a look of dread as she read the answer to her question in his face.

"Maria has not returned," Theresa Santilli lamented in Italian, her voice quavering. "I was so sure you would find her."

"I haven't finished looking, but wherever she is, I'm sure she's safe," Antonio reassured her. "The police told me children often run away. Maria was angry before she left. She has a strong will." He tried to hide his worry with a smile. "Like you."

His mother shook her head gravely. "That was long ago. Always, before this, she's a good girl. Now she has vanished into thin air. What did I tell you? That boy is a bad influence." A wail punctuated her words. "We should never have come to America. If we had stayed in Italy, we would still have our little Maria."

With wrenching sobs loud enough to wake the tobacconist who dozed outside his shop across the street, Antonio's mother ran upstairs before he could placate her. As he watched her disappear into the apartment and heard the door slam, he muttered with chagrin. Mama forgot that if it were not for God's grace in bringing them to America, they would still be living in poverty in their ramshackle cottage in Abruzzi, his father's grave on the hillside behind their home a reminder of his sacrifice for his country.

Antonio had been happy to leave Italy. Here in Boston, he had earned a solid reputation with his hard work and built a business that provided comfortably for the needs of the family. He'd done both before the age of thirty. But Mama missed the Italian countryside, the olive groves, the gentle climate. She missed being able to grieve at the graves of her beloved husband, Lorenzo, and her son Carlo, Antonio's older brother. Antonio needed no reminders of the past.

In exasperation, he kicked the broom, wondering where he could look for his rebellious sister that he hadn't already. Maria had been in a temper of late, and yesterday's shipments of lobster and mackerel kept him from paying her the attention she needed. Mama was right. Marcus Malloy was a poor influence. Antonio had hired the boy because he felt sorry for him and his widowed mother. They were proof it wasn't only immigrants who struggled to get by in this city.

Poor Mrs. Malloy was dead now, her son orphaned. Antonio would not allow sympathy to blind him. Since his mother's death, Marcus had turned to crime. Antonio wasn't the only shopkeeper on Salem Street who'd noticed items missing from his stock. The boy would need a firm hand if he were to succeed.

Antonio was about to go upstairs and check on Mama, but he paused at the approach of a tall, slender woman. Even from a distance, the elegance in her step indicated she came from a life of privilege. Her black mourning dress was more fashionable than he usually saw in this neighborhood. Hadn't she sense enough, he wondered, to know its ruffled hem would get dusty dragging in these streets? Beneath the brim of her hat, he caught a glimpse of hair so red, it was nearly the shade of a cooked lobster, incongruous with her dress.

Noting her purposeful stride and the intent gaze that seemed to be fixed on him, he realized she was headed directly toward him. Three feet from him she came to a stop. A smattering of freckles contributed to her sweet, youthful appearance, but the hardness in her eyes and her harsh tone quickly changed his opinion.

"My name is Juliet Halliday," she said hotly. "I am Marcus Malloy's aunt. You, I believe, are the owner of this market."

With eyes so green they reminded him of the olive groves back home, she looked enough like Marcus to be his mother. But with that shock of red hair she did not look like any Juliet he had ever envisioned. Her upswept tresses gave her face a pinched look, yet her expression was sincere. While he disliked the criticism in her voice, he bowed courteously.

"Antonio Santilli, at your service," he said evenly.

"I understand you hired my nephew to work for you. Now he is missing." Her tone was accusing. "Have you any idea where he's gone?"

"So you're Marcus' aunt. Yes, I hired your nephew." Antonio bristled at her implication that he was somehow responsible for the boy's absence. "As for the boy, he could be anywhere—anywhere but work, that is. He spends more time on the street corner than in the market. Fancies himself an entertainer. Too bad he wasn't entertaining customers."

His resolve did not waver as he saw her lips tighten. "He shouldn't be working at all. Where I come from, in Maine, it's customary to educate children."

"Where I come from, in Italy," he announced, "children stay home and help their families. I hired your nephew as a favor to his mother. Maybe you did not know." This country woman clearly understood little of the demands of city life. Perhaps an attempt at charm would check her anger before it escalated. He gestured toward the storefront. "Shall we sit inside and talk?"

"About your hiring practices?" she demanded. "How do you expect a child to succeed without schooling?"

"Through hard work and determination. That's how I came to own the largest fish market in Boston's North End." Antonio crossed his arms on his chest. He despised the pride he heard in his tone but knew he'd earned the right to boast. "A child succeeds through effort and honesty. Your nephew would rather juggle tomatoes than cut fish. He is a thief, just as shifty as Mr. Dickens' Artful Dodger. He stole from many shopkeepers."

He swelled with satisfaction to see her face turn as red as her hair. "My nephew is no thief. How dare you compare Marcus to the Artful Dodger and refer to him as if he were some street urchin? If you are so opposed to schooling, what do you even know of Dickens' works?"

Impatient with this woman, who probably suspected he was illiterate, Antonio carried the bucket of water indoors before anyone could trip. He had first heard of the Artful Dodger when a customer compared Marcus to Dickens' young thief. Newly introduced to *Oliver Twist,* Antonio had devoured every word of the story, fascinated by the language and the characters.

Returning outside, he turned back to Marcus' aunt. "A child is still able to learn while helping to support his family. At least, an industrious one can."

She shot him a dark look. "I have no doubt my nephew ran away because he was unhappy at work. I'm afraid of what might happen to him on these streets."

Antonio worried more about what Marcus might do to those he encountered on these same streets. He was tempted to tell her the boy was distracted these days, too irresponsible to earn an honest day's wage. He was stopped only by pity for this woman who was unable to face the truth about her nephew. Marcus' behavior had worsened upon his mother's death. While Antonio had witnessed the consequences of his bad side firsthand, his aunt undoubtedly saw only the good.

Recognizing his affection for his siblings in her concern for the boy, he let her speak. Blood might be thicker than water, but this woman was too naive for her own good if she believed what she said. He chose his words carefully.

"Your nephew will be fine," he told her, "and he will return when he's ready. But do not blame me for his disappearance."

"I blame you for hiring him." Her voice edged with resentment, she wrinkled her nose in distaste as Giorgio walked by, giving her a curious glance as he left to deliver a parcel of oysters marinated in garlic. "Did you notify the police?"

The blue blood incensed him so much that Antonio forgot the English translation of what he intended to say. He prided himself on his linguistic fluency. After seven years in America, he rarely made an error. Embarrassed by his momentary lapse, he stumbled over his words.

"The police think the children are playing—how do you say?—hide-and-seek," he said impatiently. "This isn't the first time Marcus has run away. And he isn't alone. He took my sister with him. Maria is eight. Do you think I feel any easier knowing she has only a nine-year-old to protect her?"

Juliet Halliday's mouth parted slightly before it snapped shut. Her enormous green eyes took on a slight blue tinge from the sky's reflection. She studied him with an intensity that convinced him she took him seriously at last.

"How are we supposed to find two children in a city the size of Boston?" she asked, her voice tremulous.

A surge of compassion made Antonio hesitate. This stranger, unfamiliar with Boston, had made the long journey from Maine only to find her sister dead and her nephew missing. Noting the sky's waning light, he suspected similar fears would be filling Maria's head with another night about to fall. His sister had never slept away from home before. Her absence worried him, but he would not admit it to this woman, who had trouble enough.

"The children know this town better than you," he told her gently. "They know how to get by. They also know where to hide."

"It's almost dark," she said, alarm in her voice. "We have to find them soon."

He watched her gaze up Salem Street with as much recognition as if she were viewing his hometown in Italy for the first time. He knew at a glance that Marcus Malloy's aunt would be more of a hindrance than a help. If he hoped to track down the children, he would have to rely on his knowledge of their habits. The words he expected to hear came next.

"Maybe we should hire someone to find them," she suggested.

"No one knows the children as well as I do," he said. "I know all the places they like to play and hide. If I don't find them tonight, I expect I will tomorrow. Why don't you go home and rest? I don't think they've gone far."

"I hope not," she said curtly, turning away, "for your sake. I hold you responsible for Marcus' well-being. It appears I shall have to find my nephew myself."

Forcing himself to remain silent, he watched her walk slowly down the street. If she insisted on endowing her nephew with imaginary virtues while ignoring the fact that Antonio had hired him out of kindness, the woman couldn't have much insight. In disgust, he turned back to the stairs that led to his apartment.

He would help Juliet Halliday, all right—but only to find and punish the young thief who had robbed him and run away with Maria.

Chapter Two

Alone in her room at the boardinghouse the next morning, Juliet laid out Cordelia's remaining possessions on the flowered quilt that covered her bed. She'd been disappointed to learn that the pawnshop had sold the most valuable items by the time she called on the proprietor yesterday, but she felt a sense of triumph at being able to retrieve some of the more sentimental pieces.

She studied what she had salvaged with a mix of nostalgia and regret. Tenderly, she fingered Mama's silver filigree brush and comb, a spaniel figurine that reminded her of her favorite pet as a child, and a small trinket holder. A handful of knick-knacks was all that was left from Cordelia's life. Juliet hoped they had brought her solace in the time she'd had them.

Dabbing at her eyes with Cordelia's handkerchief, Juliet felt a wave of relief when a knock at the door drew her attention. She put away the handkerchief and opened the door to find Mrs. Wetherall waiting with a breakfast tray and a smile.

"We missed you this morning," she chided Juliet gently. "You should have eaten a little something before going out like that."

The enticing scent of tea, biscuits, and blueberry jam wafting from the tray reminded Juliet of home. She hadn't wanted to go out on an empty stomach, but her determination to pursue every lead in her attempt to locate Marcus made her unwilling to waste even a moment. But she had made minimal progress at the docks on her visit early this morning, and she felt ravenous. Another day of searching would require all her strength. Dietary fortification would be far easier to come by, she figured, than the emotional kind.

"You're right, Mrs. Wetherall. Please, won't you join me?"

"I hardly need a second breakfast," the woman said, rubbing her ample midsection, "but I'd enjoy your company. Mrs. Crabtree, by the way, is reminiscing with the boarders about Cordelia."

Juliet wasn't surprised that Clara had taken advantage of the chance to get to know the people who roomed here. No doubt she would try to learn more about Cordelia's years in Boston. Juliet took a seat beside the fireplace with Mrs. Wetherall after her hostess had laid the tray on a table. She sipped the strong tea, grateful to have something warm in her stomach.

"I meant what I said," she told the landlady earnestly. "I'm glad Cordelia had a friend like you, especially at the end."

Mrs. Wetherall's eyes filled with tears, the lines at the edges creasing. She paused as if making a decision.

"Cordelia needed a friend," she said quietly. "I know she wrote you to say how well she'd done, but she wanted to spare your feelings. The truth is, she shared everything she had with a smooth-talking husband who was good only at gambling. He'd never had money before he came over from Ireland. He lost it all."

The revelation stunned and saddened Juliet. She'd assumed Cordelia's marriage had brought her joy. That was what Cordelia had led her to believe, she realized.

"I shouldn't be surprised," Juliet admitted, "given what I learned when we arrived. In some ways, maybe it's best that she's finally at peace, at rest with her husband."

The landlady studied her as if gauging her reaction. Juliet suspected the look did not bode well. She waited in uneasy silence, anticipating more bad news.

"You might as well know the truth," Mrs. Wetherall said after a moment. "Daniel didn't die as Cordelia said. He left her here with Marcus while he went west to seek his fortune in gold."

Juliet listened in disbelief, unable to process the newest revelation. "Surely, Daniel intended to bring his wife and son out west when—if—he struck it rich. Isn't that what most men do?"

"It's what their wives hope they'll do." Mrs. Wetherall spoke gently, as if she were slowly spooning Mum's birch-tree-sap tonic into Juliet's mouth in an effort to make the news more palatable. "He made it clear when he left he wanted nothing more to do with Cordelia and Marcus. They never heard from him again."

For a moment, Juliet was too stunned to speak. "That must have been about the time the War Between the States broke out. So, Daniel didn't even do his duty and fight as other men did."

"I'm afraid not. Out west all he did was accumulate gambling debts. The only people Cordelia ever heard from were men Daniel still owed money to after someone shot him dead in the street." She paused awkwardly. "I'm sorry, Juliet. But you deserve to know."

As she absorbed this new information, Juliet thought of her own brother, shot and killed in the war as a deserter. Her father had never spoken of Henry again, but Juliet's pain lingered. Papa's silence made it seem as if her brother had never existed.

"I don't understand why Cordelia didn't tell us," Juliet said in a small voice. "We would have helped her."

"She was afraid of your father. She felt she'd disappointed him once by marrying a man he didn't approve of. Shame is a terrible motivator." Mrs. Wetherall shook her head. "I want you to know how honorable Cordelia was right to the end. She paid off all Daniel's gambling debts, every last penny. She took his name, but she didn't want hers soiled because of him."

Juliet reflected on their youth, wondering how life had gone so wrong. She was ten and Cordelia eighteen when their mother died. She remembered her mother's thoughtful gestures—the ribbon Mum braided into her hair after she skinned her knee at hopscotch, the loving embraces, the patchwork doll she made while Juliet recovered from scarlet fever—and the tension after her death.

Juliet had turned to their housekeeper for affection. Clara had responded accordingly, her heart overflowing for her motherless charge. Cordelia had been expected to manage their home and help Papa deal with his grief when she could barely cope with her own. Papa withdrew to the university classes he taught, unable to speak of his pain, until Cordelia felt alone and neglected. So neglected, Juliet suspected, that she turned outside the family for comfort.

She had found it in Daniel Malloy, although she must have lost her faith quickly during the course of their marriage. Juliet tried to swallow the lump in her throat. To learn after Cordelia's death that her marriage had been a failure made her wish they'd stayed in closer contact. Instead, she had tended to Papa's needs at home and her own career as Stockton Village's schoolteacher.

Shifting in her chair with a sigh, Mrs. Wetherall observed the items laid out on the bed. "It's a blessing some of Cordelia's things were still at the shop. If only having them could bring her back."

"At least they'll help keep her memory alive." Juliet took a deep breath. "I have a favor to ask. Clara and I would like to visit Cordelia's grave. Would you be willing to take us?"

An indefinable shadow of doubt crossed Mrs. Wetherall's face. Her hesitation surprised Juliet. *Why would someone so devoted to Cordelia be reluctant to accompany her family to the cemetery?* The expression vanished as quickly as it had appeared.

"Naturally I'd be happy to take you, my dear," the landlady agreed, "although don't you think you might want to give it some time before you go? She was only buried a matter of weeks ago."

"But you said you gave her a decent burial." Alarm swept through Juliet. "She isn't buried in a pauper's grave, is she?"

"No, of course not. It's just that there's no headstone yet. Her earthly belongings weren't quite enough to cover the cost."

"I understand," Juliet said. "My father will take care of ar-

ranging that. We deeply appreciate all you've done for Cordelia and Marcus. I'm certain I'm ready to see the grave."

"Very well," Mrs. Wetherall agreed, her composure returning. "I'll take you as soon as you're ready."

"Thank you." No longer warm, the tea in the china cup
failed to soothe Juliet's raw nerves. "At the moment my nephew
is my concern. The fish market was closed earlier, but the
owner of the shop next door told me Marcus enjoyed going to
the waterfront. I called at some of the docks and plan to visit
others to talk with the captains. I have to believe the children
are still in town."

Her recollection of yesterday's confrontation with the Italian
shopkeeper rekindled her anger. Antonio Santilli might have
eyes that overflowed with warmth for his sister, but all Juliet
saw in their expressive depths was arrogance made more offensive by a lack of concern for Marcus.

"I don't appreciate Mr. Santilli's low opinion of Marcus. Nor
do I like the thought of returning to that market, with its fish
stench." She shuddered. "The neighborhood reeks of garlic."

"The smell is strong, but I do like the taste." The landlady's
eyes creased with amusement. "How ironic it is to see a modern
Juliet feuding with an Italian man. And with a sister named
Cordelia yet. Your parents must enjoy the theater."

"Our father is a retired professor of Shakespeare." Fate, Juliet reflected, could not have played a worse trick on her. Could
anyone be more misnamed? As it was, she considered herself
unlikely to find a suitable mate. That abominable owner of the
fish market was probably unfamiliar with the Bard, illiterate
even. Then she remembered how he'd compared Marcus to the
Artful Dodger. "Mr. Santilli accused my nephew of being a
thief. Marcus would only steal out of desperation. Let me show
you a picture."

Setting aside her biscuit and jam, Juliet rose from her chair
and moved to the nightstand. There she picked up a sepia-toned
daguerreotype in a velvet-lined leather case, the only photograph Cordelia had sent her. For a long moment she regarded

the rosy-cheeked boy in his Sunday dress suit. "Have you ever seen a more handsome boy? This is not the face of a thief."

Mrs. Wetherall frowned through her spectacles as she studied the picture. "My dear, Marcus is nine. This boy looks half that. Didn't you say it was four years ago that you last saw him?"

Juliet flushed, feeling as if she were about to be chastised for something that was not her fault. "Yes, but Marcus was raised in a respectable household. He knows right from wrong."

"Wait here," the landlady said. "I have something for you."

Mrs. Wetherall left the room, returning a moment later with a small tintype. She closed her fingers around Juliet's as she pressed the photograph into her palm. "This is a recent picture, one you can keep."

With a catch in her throat Juliet gazed into the face of a youth she hardly recognized. His expression was troubled, more serious than she remembered, with hardened eyes and a downturned mouth. In his face she saw naiveté mixed with a distrust that whispered of impending adulthood. This boy had aged too rapidly.

She could hardly breathe. Now she had all that was left of Cordelia. She hoped there was some naiveté left in Marcus.

She swallowed hard. "Even at nine, he is still an innocent."

"Of course he is. You know, I'd forgotten until just now something that might help," Mrs. Wetherall exclaimed. "Marcus likes juggling. When I found apples that were bruised or missing from my pantry, it was because Marcus had been trying to juggle. He spoke often of what it must be like to be a circus performer. I heard there was a traveling circus in town last week. I wonder if it's still here."

This was a substantial lead, the first Juliet had been given. Feeling jubilant, she stood the tintype on the nightstand, laying the picture of the younger Marcus facedown. No longer could she refuse to face reality. She turned and grasped the landlady's hands in her own.

"Thank you for the picture, Mrs. Wetherall. And thank you for that information. Now I know just where to start."

* * *

Salem Street rang with the chant of the hot-chestnut peddler and the clang of the cobbler's hammer when Antonio returned from bringing a pound of mussels to Mrs. Orsini on Unity Street. One of his first American customers, the old woman was homebound with gout. Seeing that as no excuse for her to miss out on her favorite dish, Antonio made a point to deliver it himself.

While his customers would expect the fish market to remain open as usual, his first obligation this morning was to find Maria. He'd expected her to come back last night, ready for a plate of sweet cakes or *scrippelle*, cold and tired of running, less feisty than when she left. When she didn't, doubt began to replace his conviction. She might come home yet, but he wasn't about to leave it to a whim. Chance had never been his friend.

Resentment filled him at the idea that Juliet Halliday's concerns might be valid. While he had notified the police of the children's disappearance, he doubted they would find the pair before he did, for he knew Marcus' habits better than anyone. As attractive and courageous as she appeared, the country woman knew little of her nephew's penchant for exploring little-known alleyways.

But Antonio hadn't found the children either. He'd walked the streets so much, he knew how policemen must feel. He would walk them again today, every lane and passage. His mood darkened as he recalled Marcus' desire to play outside rather than work indoors, balancing on the edge of the sidewalk as if he were walking a tightrope. By now, Marcus must have irritated some shopkeeper to the point where he would remember the redheaded boy if asked. The likelihood of that gave Antonio hope.

While he consulted with Giorgio and their uncle about the oysters he'd authorized them to purchase at the dock that morning, the grocer from next door came by.

"Any word about little Maria?" Rocco's face was anxious.

Antonio shook his head. "I called everywhere she might be, but no luck. I'm leaving Giorgio in charge while I go out again."

"I'll help if he needs it. God be with you in your search."

"*Grazie.* Marcus is gone too. His aunt's looking for him."

"That must be the red-haired signora who came asking for you this morning. I told her you were out searching for them."

Antonio stiffened at the idea that Juliet Halliday had gone in search of the children on her own. While she had their welfare at heart, her condescending manner branded her a blue blood. What did the upper classes know of the temptations city children faced? They had no idea what it was to be so poor, you were forced to leave your home to start over in a strange land.

Marcus' aunt had never had to learn a language to survive, Antonio told himself. He knew what was needed to survive in Boston. *She* was the foreigner here, not him.

Rocco shrugged. "She is trying to be a friend, no?"

"I can protect myself from my enemies. May God protect me from such a friend." Antonio sighed uneasily. "Where is she now?"

"Constitution Wharf. I told her how Marcus likes boats."

A new urgency coursed through Antonio. There was no telling what kind of trouble Juliet Halliday could get into at the docks. "I'm on my way."

He barely took the time to respond to greetings from fellow shopkeepers as he hurried toward Constitution Wharf. What sort of misfortune might she have encountered? Leave it to a visitor who knew nothing of the city to approach an area so rough, the hardiest of its well-heeled residents would not venture there alone. He had to admire her integrity, if not her common sense.

Even from a distance, Antonio could hear a commotion as he neared the waterfront. He had almost reached the wharf when he saw two men emerging from the enclosure, one with a bloodied face. The men stumbled, running from the covered shed where freight was being unloaded as if some fearsome entity were pursuing them. Antonio broke into a run, shouting for them to stop before they vanished into the crowd, making it impossible to locate them, much less chase them.

He had barely turned back toward the wharf when Juliet emerged from the shadows, clutching an umbrella like a weapon, her hair tumbling about her shoulders. The men must have accosted her. Alarm caught in Antonio's throat. Perhaps with so many dock workers moving about, her assailants felt no one would notice a robbery attempt. He rushed to her side.

"Miss Halliday, are you hurt?" He gripped her by the shoulders, examining her face for bruises but seeing no sign of any beneath the tousled red hair.

"I'm fine. You can unhand me now, thank you," she retorted. "It's fortunate it rained this morning, for I had my umbrella with me when I needed it. As you can see, I'm quite capable."

Nudging his hand from her shoulder, she straightened her deep gray dolman and adjusted her dark skirts, pinning up her hair as best she could. He doubted the effect was what she'd intended, for her mussed curls and unsteady gait revealed a childlike vulnerability he found appealing. He hadn't realized he was staring until she glared at him. He turned away quickly.

"I would remind you"—she surprised him by changing topics—"I took offense at your remark yesterday. My nephew is no thief."

Still she would not admit the truth, even to herself. Antonio noted the fire in her green eyes and the tightness of her lips before he made up his mind to speak, knowing he'd likely receive a rebuke.

"We have a saying in Italy. 'Steal a little, go to jail; steal a lot, make a career of it.' Let's hope Marcus doesn't go beyond the first stage." The defiance he saw in her eyes was about as effective against his conviction as the crooked cape she wore to protect her from the rain. "Seems you went looking for adventure just like your nephew did. Now we have to find him."

He let his gaze scan the harbor, taking in the Egyptian steamer unloading its cargo of sugar onto the wharf. His heart thudded as a more worrisome possibility occurred to him. He hoped Marcus hadn't decided to ship out to a foreign port. Would the boy have found a way to sneak Maria onto the ship with him? His companion did not appear to have noticed his new concern.

"I suppose your sister hasn't returned either," she continued.

"Not yet." As she turned, he saw that the lace neckline of her dress was torn. She opened her fingers slightly to reveal an oval-shaped cameo, ivory and caramel in color, gripping it so tightly her fingers were white. "Is that what those men wanted?"

"Papa gave one to each of us. I imagine Cordelia was forced to sell hers. I wasn't about to let thieves take mine," she said fiercely. "I have no children, but one day Marcus will marry and have a daughter. When he does, this will be hers." Her voice quavered as she choked back tears, a change so sudden, it startled him. "He'll get much more than this when I get hold of him."

Antonio remained respectfully silent as she fought to control her emotions, opening her reticule and dropping the pin inside. It reminded him of a brooch his mother had relinquished after they had arrived in America—one of many heirlooms she had sacrificed for their future. It was a sobering moment when it sold for a fraction of its worth, yet the promise of a better life in this new land was worth much more to the family.

"Come," he urged softly, taking her by the elbow. "You were wise to come to the waterfront. While we're here together, let's ask about the children. Marcus knew this area well. Being an adventurous lad, he might have tried to book passage somewhere."

Her eyes flooded with anxiety as she turned to gaze up at him. She was taller than most women, and the movement put her face in close proximity to his own. He could not help but notice the long lashes that framed her green eyes.

"If Marcus shipped out on a boat," she asked in a nervous tone, "couldn't he be anywhere in the world by now?"

Antonio shook his head, not wanting to worry her further with yet another concern. "The harbormaster knows Marcus. Now that the War Between the States is over, there's no shortage of men. The captains are less likely to hire a boy." Hearing the words aloud convinced him he might be right. It lifted his spirits to see the alarm in her eyes diminish. "I still want to ease my mind once and for all, and yours also."

"I know the children couldn't have gone far. I have another idea, but since I was near the docks, I came here first to rule out the possibility."

She sounded so relieved, Antonio did not want to disillusion her by sharing his doubts. Even if Marcus hadn't shipped out on a vessel bound for foreign ports, the neighborhood held countless temptations for a runaway. Food could be found more easily than ships. With its meat and cheese stalls, a resourceful youngster could hide in Quincy Market for weeks without being detected. The Tileston Street Market shipped food to Italian immigrants working on the western railroad. The child savers even found homes for orphaned or delinquent children with families in rural New England towns or in the Midwest.

Antonio doubted that Maria would ever have agreed to such an arrangement, but she was impressionable, and Marcus was unpredictable. If he had made their escapade sound like an intriguing adventure, who knew where Maria might have gone?

"You say you have another idea?" Antonio prompted.

"The woman who owns the boardinghouse where Marcus and his mother lived thought he might have run off to join the circus."

Here was an intriguing possibility, Antonio thought, and a very real one. He'd read in the *Evening Gazette* that a traveling circus had been set up on the Coliseum grounds for the past few days. He even remembered its name.

A stab of guilt mixed with regret stopped him in his tracks as he remembered how much Maria had wanted to go. He was reluctant to take time away from the market to bring her. Maybe Marcus had done the very thing Antonio had not bothered to do for her.

The circus was a much more tempting lure than boats that reeked of stale fish. It wasn't a smell Marcus liked even at the market. The sooner they found the boy, he was sure, the sooner he would get Maria back.

Feeling inspired, he took Juliet Halliday gently by the elbow and turned her toward Constitution Wharf.

"Let's have a talk with the harbormaster," he suggested. "Then we'll head across town to see if Mr. Tarry's Great American Extravaganza lives up to its name."

Chapter Three

What do we do now?" Juliet demanded, her steps slowing with exhaustion. "We seemed so close to finding them."

Discouraged by the day's failed efforts, she did not bother to open her umbrella against the steady drizzle that fell. Her hopes of locating the children at the circus had been dashed with the discovery that Mr. Tarry's Great American Extravaganza had left the Coliseum grounds three days ago. The police sergeant at the Hanover Street Station House remembered only that the circus was headed north.

Now, an hour later, she fought back tears of disappointment as she emerged with Antonio from the New England Home for Little Wanderers. They had called at the converted church on Baldwin Place on the chance that Marcus and Maria had been brought there. She had been relieved to learn the superintendent had not seen them, for it meant they hadn't left town on one of the orphan trains that delivered the city's wayward children to new homes in the country.

Yet they were no closer to finding Marcus and Maria. She tried to keep her voice steady as she spoke.

"We've visited the train station, police department, child-saving societies, and the waterfront," she resumed. "No child matching either description has left town. They must be here."

Antonio ambled beside her, maddeningly silent. When he finally spoke, the bitterness in his tone surprised her.

"Here among the immigrants and paupers, the police are so used to truancy, they expect children to come home on their own. We're the ones who are on our own now."

25

Juliet frowned. "I'm sure anyone who could help would do so," she objected. "We need a little luck, that's all."

"We'd have more luck if either child lived at a better address," Antonio said sarcastically. "Since they don't, the only way we'll find them is to visit the places they like. If you'd lived here as long as I have, you'd know that's how it is."

She winced to hear Marcus described as lower class. By her hometown standards, her family was considered well off. Marcus had been raised in a very different world. What angered her more was Antonio's implication that she was incapable of understanding because she wasn't used to city life.

"You speak as if people here aren't helpful," she retorted. "Yet I've seen many try to help. We can't be discouraged just because no one has seen them. They might come home on their own."

A sullen silence followed. Once the words had left her lips, she regretted them, but he'd angered her so that it forced her to release her frustration. The only place no one offered assistance was at the dock. It was only by chance, after she struck one assailant unintentionally with her umbrella, that she'd recognized its defensive uses. Antonio was so familiar with the city's dangers, he must think her a fool for going there alone.

"That's the most sensible thing you've said all day," he muttered. "Maybe Marcus and Maria came home while we were out. They have to tire of this game eventually."

Juliet decided to say no more. She'd offered her thoughts as to how the search should proceed, none of which Antonio took seriously. While she blamed him for Marcus' absence, she appreciated his efforts to look for her nephew. Despite the fact that he was often difficult and quick to anger, she found his presence comforting. Her manner was as authoritative as his, yet his tact had met with more success in approaching people than her efforts had. He must feel as discouraged as she did.

"Perhaps the best thing I can do at this point," he said over the bustle of Hanover Street, "is to see you safely home."

The silence between them amplified the creaking of wheels from a passing produce wagon. Juliet listened to the cries of the pushcart vendor hawking fresh clams and a boy no older than Marcus selling sweetmeats from a tray around his neck. She found it as hard to imagine her nephew working on the streets as it was to see him living in a boardinghouse.

"I was surprised Methodist Alley had no church," she admitted, "although there's barely room for the row houses."

"It used to have a church," he said. "We just passed the church that replaced the one in Methodist Alley."

Turning, Juliet studied the house of worship with its rooster weathervane. Antonio must be a man of faith to know its history, she decided. She saw that his brooding expression lingered. The assistance they'd received today had impressed her, but his experiences as an immigrant must have given him a different perspective. She reminded herself she should feel compassion for him, even if his assumptions made it difficult. He'd hired Marcus as a gesture of kindness to Cordelia, after all.

By the time they reached the boardinghouse, it was midafternoon. Over the course of their search, they had not taken time to eat. Juliet wondered if Antonio felt the same hunger she did gnawing at the pit of her stomach.

"You've been kind enough to see me home," she said as she turned the doorknob. "Would you like to come in from the damp?"

Mrs. Wetherall welcomed the pair with a boiling kettle of tea and plates of pot roast left over from last evening's meal. The sweet aroma of molasses and ginger that pervaded the dining room, she told Juliet, came from the baked beans and brown bread, two Boston favorites that sat in their customary place of honor on the sideboard. Juliet discovered the pot roast was still tender and succulent; she ate hungrily. Clara Crabtree joined them minutes later, disappointed but not surprised to learn they had not located Marcus and Maria.

"I was so sure Marcus would come home on his own," Mrs. Wetherall sympathized, sitting with them so she could tend to their culinary needs. "He always has before. Juliet, before I forget, a note was delivered for you."

The landlady retrieved a grimy slip of paper from the mantel and handed it to her. Wondering who would be writing, Juliet scanned the note tersely, reading each word twice. When she had finished, she crumpled it in her fist. She looked up to see suspense in the three pairs of eyes that met hers.

"It's from Marcus," she announced faintly. "He says he and Maria are going to his grandfather's house in the country because the city is no place for children. Since I'll be here for a while packing up his mother's things, he can travel by himself, he says, now that he's the man of the family." She flashed Antonio a scowl, feeling no triumph. "I told you he wasn't happy here."

Antonio's face whitened before his color returned along with his arrogance. "Where's home? Where does his grandfather live?"

"Stockton Village in Maine." A feeling of warmth filled Juliet at the memory of the white farmhouse, its garden crammed with flowers that had bloomed just before she left. "Marcus has never been there, but I'm sure he's heard so much about his grandfather from Cordelia that he can't wait to meet him."

She ignored Clara's look of disbelief and its accompanying warning glance, focusing instead on Antonio and Mrs. Wetherall. Since they hadn't met Papa, they had no idea how stern he could be. A grandson, she mused, was just what he needed to make him feel as inspired as he had been before Mum's death.

The Italian drummed contemplatively on the table with calloused fingertips, the rigidity in his frame making Juliet suspect he harbored misgivings. "If the children already left Boston, they probably went by steamship."

"It's the fastest way to reach the coast," Juliet concurred. "Not all railroads are direct."

"What's Stockton Village near?" he demanded.

"Bar Harbor and Bucksport are the nearest towns you might have heard of. Or Verona." She returned his dubious look with one of defiance. "Verona isn't only where Shakespeare's Juliet lived. There's a town named Verona close to where I live."

Antonio startled her by snatching the note from her fingers.

"It's certainly Marcus' scrawl. At least it's legible," he confirmed, adding with a glare, "although I'm certain you feel his penmanship would improve with schooling."

Ignoring his sarcasm, she applied her logic instead. "Marcus must have arranged to have the note delivered after they sailed. They shouldn't be traveling alone. I need to leave at once."

Antonio shook his head. "It would make more sense if I went."

She stared at him. "Why would I stay here without Marcus?"

His eyes sharp and assessing, he fixed her with a look that silenced any doubt she had as to his belief that he could find the children. She flushed under his scrutiny. It wouldn't do, she realized, to let him go to Maine alone, for Papa had always been suspicious of immigrants. Juliet had a different opinion and wondered how much of Papa's attitude stemmed from Cordelia's situation.

"In Italy," Antonio continued, "we have a saying: '*Bacco, tabacco e Venere riducono l'uomo in cenere*. Wine, women, and tobacco can ruin a man.' I can travel more quickly on my own."

"Taking the wine and tobacco instead of me, no doubt," she retorted.

"I wouldn't take either, because I don't use either. You, I know I can do without." The doubt returned to his face. "What makes you think this note isn't a trick? Marcus could have gone back with you if he wanted. And why take Maria?"

"It's an adventure." She spread her hands, exasperated. "Why can't you believe him? At least we needn't hire a detective."

"Wherever they are," Antonio muttered, "I'll find them and bring them home, I promise you."

"You might, but we need to find them quickly."

"You know, Juliet," Mrs. Wetherall interrupted politely, "Antonio has a good point. You'd do better not to travel alone."

"I have Clara." Juliet flashed Antonio a cool smile.

"It helps to have a man along," the landlady said. "Antonio is a man of his word. Once he makes a promise, he doesn't break it. You'll be safer traveling with him."

"Why would your nephew go to a grandfather he's never met? He barely obeyed his mother." Antonio shook his head as if Marcus were an incorrigible child even his aunt could not control. "More likely, they're chasing the circus and sent this note as a diversion."

"Now who isn't making sense? Marcus might be able to juggle apples from the pantry or—I don't know what from your market, fish heads maybe—but he doesn't have the skills to be a professional." Juliet's sympathy for him faded in light of his distrust. "Only you would suspect a child of trickery. If you don't believe him, you can stay here and hire another child to work for you while I make the trip, even though you don't think I can manage alone."

"The last time you tried, you were accosted by thugs on the docks." His condescending tone made her bristle. "Not the safest thing for a country blue blood, or the smartest. It's obvious you need help. I need to be there to find Maria and bring her home. Presumably, once we get to Maine, it's the last we'll see of you."

"I certainly hope not," Mrs. Wetherall interjected with a smile. "I've become used to Juliet's company. I would miss her."

Her indignation mounting, Juliet ignored the landlady's kind remark. She did not deserve the Italian-accented sarcasm that grated on her nerves. "You don't trust Marcus," she accused.

"Do you? The police told you he's run off before. Even they don't trust him." Antonio laughed bitterly. "I wish I hadn't. He's cost my business dearly."

His retort stung. Marcus didn't need to steal food to survive, for Mrs. Wetherall had cared for him since Cordelia's death. As hard as Juliet tried, it was difficult to deny the opinion of those who knew her nephew better than she did. That included Antonio Santilli. Averting her face, she blinked back tears, determined not to let him see her disillusionment.

When he spoke again, his tone was less argumentative. "We can make it to Bar Harbor in a day if we catch an early boat."

"You truly think Marcus would try to trick us?" she pressed.

His hesitation pained her more than his words. The look he

gave her pierced her vulnerability, his eyes so gentle and compelling, her doubts fled in their depths. "For all his dishonesty, he's intelligent. It would be just like him to send us one way while he goes the other. You see the best in him, and that's how it should be. But you don't know him like we do." He glanced at the landlady. "What do you think, Mrs. Wetherall?"

"Marcus has a good head on his shoulders, but he doesn't always use it." Their hostess frowned. "In that note, he says it will take time to pack. Yet he knew his mother had nothing."

Antonio picked up the note and read it again. "The city's no place for children, my eye. Marcus loves this city. Acts like he owns it. Who brought this note?"

"That boy Lawrence from the docks," said Mrs. Wetherall. "Marcus' young friend."

"I know the one. I'll try to find out where the circus is headed next." Pausing as if making a judgment, Antonio gave Juliet a tentative glance. She expected him to elaborate, but he surprised her. "So we travel by boat. Something we agree on for once. I know several captains who will take us."

"We're not traveling on a fishing boat," she said at once, dismayed by his idea. "We're going by steamship."

His nostrils flared. "Do you know anything about boats? I know the captain of nearly every ship that delivers to these docks. I talk with them every morning before you've lifted your pretty little head off the pillow. They'll get us there faster."

"I know enough to take a Boston Boat," she returned. "That's what we call them back home. They carry passengers and freight down the Penobscot, traveling the coast to Boston."

"I'd rather sail with a captain I know and trust."

"I'm traveling the way I know is best." Juliet raised her chin resolutely. "A first-class ticket for a private stateroom costs about three dollars. If money is an issue—"

Filled with acrimony, Antonio's eyes silenced her, warning that her tendency toward blunt speech had gotten her in trouble again.

"It's not. As I told you, I own the largest fish market in the North End."

"Yet you're so young," Mrs. Wetherall marveled, turning to him. "How did you manage such an impressive accomplishment?"

Before turning away he flashed Juliet a look of fury. Relief filled her when his reply put an end to the hostility.

"My mother's brother started the market before I brought our family here," he explained. "By the time we saved enough money to leave Italy, his health had failed, and I had to take over running the business. I put every penny, every minute I had into the market. Within a year, our customers doubled, and we needed a bigger shop. And Marcus became an employee." He reached out and covered the landlady's hand with his appreciatively. "You're a good customer and a fine woman, Mrs. Wetherall, for reminding me."

Juliet had been chastised, and rightly so. She had humiliated herself as well as Antonio by suggesting he could not afford the fare to travel by boat. She felt surprised and betrayed when Clara spoke up.

"I see the reason for your success," Clara gushed, something akin to affection in her voice. "Mrs. Wetherall served your salmon for dinner today, and it was as good as any I've had in Maine."

Juliet tried to keep from turning as red as the salmon as she tried to end the discussion of his fine selection of seafood.

"If we might return to the subject," she resumed, tempering her impatience, "I doubt we need to travel together."

Traveling with someone who felt he was always right, she reflected, would be excruciatingly difficult, even if he was correct much of the time. Antonio leaned against the cupboard, arms crossed over his chest, his eyes targeting hers.

"That's where you're mistaken. If we learn something along the way, we might need to combine our efforts in order to find the children." He challenged her with a hypnotic stare. *Mal comune, mezzo gaudio.* Trouble shared is trouble halved. Remember that."

"What more is there to learn?" Juliet asked, her frustration rising again. "We know they're on their way home."

"That's what Marcus wants you to believe," he said shrewdly. "Marcus is testing his wings."

"I suggest," Clara said, laying a discreet hand on Juliet's arm, "that before more time is lost you might consider packing."

"You're right, of course." New hope flowed through Juliet. "Thank you, Clara. I'll wire Papa and tell him to expect Marcus."

"I'll wire him while you pack," Mrs. Wetherall offered.

"I'd recommend you leave your frills behind when we leave," Antonio spoke up. "Bring practical clothing, if you have any."

Juliet held her tongue. How could she abide being on board a ship with such a difficult traveling companion? His practicality and physical strength might give her a feeling of safety, but his presence would make the journey seem long indeed.

The only thing that kept her from dreading the trip was knowing that when she reached Maine, she would find Marcus waiting. There they could proceed with their lives, and Marcus would attend school. Her school.

Before she reached her destination, however, she would have to contend with Antonio Santilli a while longer.

It did not take long to pack, for Juliet had not completely unpacked the few items of clothing and toiletries she'd brought from home. She secured all but the few essentials she would need. Since today's steamboat to Rockland had already sailed, they would be forced to spend one more night in Boston.

"This all seems so unbelievable." Juliet shook her head as she tucked Cordelia's few remaining articles in her luggage, glancing up at Clara. "Never in my twenty-four years did I expect to lose my sister so young. If I ever wed, I hope to have a marriage just like my parents', not like Cordelia's."

Laying a motherly arm about her shoulders, Clara startled her with her next words. "You could have had that if you'd encouraged Hans a little more," she reminded her gently. "I've never met a more patient man."

The opposite of Antonio Santilli, Juliet reflected with a touch of sarcasm, Hans was indeed patient. He had been so patient, she had never married him. He was probably still waiting for her.

"Hans wasn't the one for me. I don't really expect to find a marriage like my parents had." Juliet shrugged off her arm in embarrassment and continued arranging Cordelia's few treasures. "Anyway, what would my students do without me? I'm quite happy with my life as it is. And now I'll have Marcus. That might be enough of a complication without asking for more."

"I hope one day you'll change your mind." Clara's face was sympathetic as she studied Juliet, who turned away. "I wish things had turned out differently for Cordelia. You know I'd do anything to spare you this pain. I hope it wasn't a mistake coming here."

"It wasn't. I had to know the truth." She paused, holding a dress in mid-fold. "Clara, you trust Mrs. Wetherall, don't you?"

"She's given me no reason to doubt her," the housekeeper said without hesitation. "I believe she's completely sincere. I have a feeling she helped Cordelia in ways we can't imagine."

Juliet hesitated as she turned to the nightstand. Looking at the two pictures of Marcus, she packed the older one Cordelia had given her. She would wait until morning to pack the more recent one from Mrs. Wetherall. She would keep it close in her reticule.

From now on, Juliet vowed, her eyes would be open to reality. She would face whatever was coming head-on.

She felt a chill but decided to ignore it. She was heading home. Things would be better once she got there. Optimism flooded through her as she buckled her valise. "That makes me feel better. Right now, all I can think about is finding Marcus and Maria. That's my mission."

Yet she had one other mission to accomplish in Boston. Later that day, after the sun emerged at last and cast its gentle late-afternoon light on the cobblestone streets, Mrs. Wetherall set off with Juliet and Clara toward Copp's Hill Burying Ground, where Cordelia had been laid to rest.

Their walk took them through some of Boston's oldest streets. Juliet tried to focus on Mrs. Wetherall's belief that Marcus might be in the vicinity of his mother's grave or that he would return on his own as he had before. The possibility gave her hope, for the landlady knew his habits better than anyone. Yet, she found her thoughts returning to the visit she dreaded. Clara walked beside her, slowing her steps as she linked her arm through Juliet's.

"Are you sure you're up to this?" Clara asked.

"I'm sure," Juliet said in a low tone.

She looked up to see Mrs. Wetherall walking several paces ahead, close enough so they would not lose sight of her yet graciously allowing them space to grieve without intruding.

"This isn't how you'll want to remember her," Clara warned.

"I'm sure it isn't, yet there's no one else to represent the family," Juliet said. "Who knows if I'll ever return? Once Marcus is back where he belongs, I hope never to see this city again."

Boston might have been close to Cordelia's heart, but Juliet could not feel the same. The sights distracted her only momentarily. Stepping out of the shadow of the Old North Church where Paul Revere received the signal that British troops were marching on Lexington and Concord, she climbed Hull Street toward the cemetery with as much gravity as the troops must have felt. With the flowers they had brought resting in the crook of her arm, Clara gave the church a final admiring glance.

"Boston has such history," she marveled. "If your pupils were here, how excited they'd be. Billy Barton could pretend to be a patriot at the church where the fight for independence began."

Juliet's spirits lifted at the mention of her rambunctious charge. She had never imagined she would miss him so, but the city was so different from what she'd expected, it made her long for the familiar. Her heart beat faster as the cemetery loomed before them, its granite wall and wrought-iron fence separating the living from the dead. Mrs. Wetherall, now out of sight, had left the gate open for them.

Clara lifted her skirts away from the damp grass as they

entered the grounds in silence. Making her way along the dirt path, Juliet noted the markings on headstones that the British had used for target practice. Reading the names as she ascended the hill, she saw that Cordelia was buried among some of Boston's most eminent families. Tears sprang to her eyes. How much dignity was there in a lonely funeral with few to mourn one's passing?

She moved close to Clara as they walked, the wind whipping her hair from its arrangement. They had reached the highest point in the cemetery. Before them, the sunlight glistened on the harbor. They had crested the hill and begun their descent when they saw Mrs. Wetherall pause before a fence. The moment of farewell was at hand. The moment Juliet dreaded.

With slow steps and a heavy heart, she approached the patch of grass that was recently dug and replaced. She tried to check her emotions by taking in her surroundings, studying the tree beside the plot, the tall headstones on either side, a smaller one next to where Cordelia's marker would stand.

"It's a peaceful spot." Speaking in a hushed voice, Mrs. Wetherall wiped her eyes before she took Juliet's hand. "This is one of our oldest cemeteries. It's nearly full now. This plot belongs to Daniel's family, and it had room."

"Such lovely greenery," Clara murmured, reaching out to touch an overhanging maple branch. "It's the ideal spot, Juliet, don't you think? Cordelia would have liked this. The Malloys must have done well to be buried with some of our nation's heroes."

"Daniel was the exception, unfortunately," Mrs. Wetherall said in a subdued tone.

Juliet stepped forward as Mrs. Wetherall released her hand. She felt as close to Cordelia here as she had in years. How she wished she had taken time to get to know her sister better while she'd lived. As she knelt by the grave, Juliet made herself a silent promise to make up for the distance between them by caring for Cordelia's son, bringing him up as her sister would have wanted.

She looked away, glancing at the small headstone next to the spot where Cordelia was laid. The stone read simply, *Louisa*. Louisa, their mother's name. Judging from the proportions of the headstone, Juliet decided it must be a child's grave. Her heart quavered at the tangible reminder of the loss of one so little.

"I can't imagine losing a child at such a young age," she murmured, her pain lessening at the thought of those who had faced a harder loss. "Whose grave is this?"

"One of Daniel's nieces," said Mrs. Wetherall. "She was only a few days old. Makes me grateful for the many years I've had."

Juliet looked briefly for Daniel's grave before remembering he hadn't died here, as her sister had claimed, but had gone west instead, consigning his family to a life of poverty. When she learned of Cordelia's death, Juliet had pictured her buried with her husband. Too many things, she realized now, weren't as they should be.

Clara placed the floral arrangement they'd brought on Cordelia's grave and knelt to pray in silence. Juliet could no longer watch. She raised her eyes to the harbor beyond, the water sparkling as the sun dropped lower in the sky. Cordelia should have been buried with her face to the water off the coast of Maine, she thought fiercely, not here in Boston.

Why had she come here, leaving the town that had sheltered them in childhood? A gust of wind swept tendrils of hair across Juliet's face, obscuring her view. A sob caught in her throat.

She felt Clara take hold of her arm.

"Spend as long as you need," Clara whispered. "I shall be waiting on the path when you're ready to resume your mission."

By early evening the next day, Antonio stood at the rail of a steamboat that had sailed too many hours ago to know how long they'd been at sea. Gazing out over the still waters of the northern Atlantic, he wished he'd brought warmer clothes. He felt cold and too far from Boston. This far north, the frigid air made Boston feel like southern Italy.

He watched wisps of fog drift across the water before studying the thick clouds overhead. He glanced at Juliet leaning on the rail beside him and saw she was deep in concentration.

"Are the skies always this threatening?" he asked.

She rose to her full slender height, her profile reflecting her delicate beauty. "Not always. Sometimes days go by with no sun. It will probably be cloudy tomorrow when we reach Rockland."

Gloom descended on Antonio at the prospect. Life in northern New England was rugged, not nearly as compelling as in Boston, with its opportunities for prosperity and socializing. Whatever the situation, he would make the best of it as always, knowing it would make life more bearable. He wondered if Juliet enjoyed the solitude the north offered. Perhaps, he thought with surprise as she excused herself to head inside to her stateroom, she was hardier than he gave her credit for.

He tried to hide a smile as he pictured his mother's wagging finger and raised eyebrow. His insistence that he'd asked Juliet to stay in Boston fell on deaf ears.

"Do not let that redhead get the better of you. I don't like her looks," she warned. "Isabel is coming, and it won't be a day too soon. Once you marry a girl from your own country, your future will be set."

As if Mama had anything to worry about. Antonio had been betrothed to Isabel before he'd left Italy. They had endured many delays while exchanging letters. She would arrive in Boston soon enough. Through the suede pouch tucked safely in his pocket, he fingered the ruby ring intended for her finger— small and dainty, like Isabel herself.

He had no intention of becoming involved with a woman as outspoken as Marcus Malloy's aunt, as oddly attractive as she was, with her pale features, freckled face, and pixie charm.

But several factors made him uneasy about the journey. Whether Juliet recognized it or not, the dense fog rolling in spelled trouble. He hoped nothing would delay his finding Maria when they reached Stockton Village late tomorrow.

The dockhand, Lawrence, had seemed sincere enough when Antonio questioned him. He said he'd waved good-bye to Marcus and Maria as they set off from Foster's Wharf. Something about the boy seemed familiar. Antonio couldn't remember what, but the association was negative. The sensation only added to his apprehension.

He wasn't as convinced as Juliet that Marcus had been honest in his note. The likelihood that the children had run off with the circus was possible but slim. The idea might hold more excitement than cutting fish, but what type of entertainment did Marcus think they could provide? Much as the boy liked using a stick to balance, he was hardly a trapeze artist. He wasn't even a skilled juggler.

Still, it was more likely the boy would join the circus than visit a grandfather he'd never met. Antonio was relieved to learn in the previous day's *Boston Gazette* that Mr. Tarry's next destination had been Concord, New Hampshire. The newspaper account confirmed the policeman's recollection that the circus was headed north. If the circus spent a few days in each city, and Marcus and Maria had gone in pursuit, Antonio would arrive in Maine before them. He would give Juliet the satisfaction of going home to test Marcus' honesty.

He gazed into the impenetrable mists through which the ship threaded its way, knowing he sought an answer that lay beyond the range of his vision. Shepherding Juliet Halliday to Maine would be worth the trouble if it meant he would find Maria waiting at the end of the journey. He'd been a shepherd long ago in Italy. Now, it seemed, he must play the role again. He suspected that bringing Maria, Marcus, and Juliet together would prove more troublesome than guiding the sheep that wandered the hills without aim or direction.

His lingering doubts about agreeing to travel with Juliet had little to do with his mother's warnings. At the moment, his misgivings even tempered his amusement at her name. Although he did not have much in common with Mercutio, he suspected tomorrow would find him a grave man indeed for having permitted the redhead to accompany him on the trip.

Something did not feel right. Antonio knew it in his bones. He hoped he did not have to travel all the way to Maine before he found out what it was.

Chapter Four

Antonio was still at the railing half an hour later when the thickening clouds made him wonder if they would reach their destination before fog blanketed the steamship. He turned to Mrs. Crabtree, who had stepped outside with Juliet to watch the sky.

"Think we'll arrive on time?" he asked.

Clara's eyes turned upward. "There's a chance, but it's growing slimmer as these clouds grow darker."

A steamer might be faster than a fishing trawler, but Antonio found the New England weather even less predictable than he found his traveling companion. The clouds did not bode well. He glanced at Juliet. A rare smile played upon her lips, her features softened by sea mists.

"What's your opinion of this weather?" he asked impulsively.

"I'm not concerned about it." The enthusiasm in her voice surprised him. "I'm thinking how good it will be for Papa to have Marcus home. With Cordelia gone, it will give him new life."

If she pinned her hopes on a boy like Marcus, he thought, she was bound to be disappointed. He noticed Clara did not react. He'd be curious to know her opinion. Maybe a rural setting was what the boy needed. They wouldn't know until they reached Maine whether Marcus was telling the truth. The journey would be long either way, for their plans could be hindered not only by the weather but by this intriguing woman who seemed relentlessly determined to retain her ideals in the face of contradiction.

Antonio reminded himself to keep an open mind throughout the trip. He tried to remember she wasn't as well-traveled as he was. As Juliet turned to him, he couldn't help but notice this odd Maine light had made her green eyes clearer and more appealing.

"What are you thinking about?" she startled him by asking.

He spared her by not repeating his doubts. "About Italy. I worry that Maria won't know her homeland as I do. She was very young when we left. Nothing here matches the beauty of the countryside. She won't have the experiences I had growing up."

For once she listened without interrupting. "You might disagree once you see Maine's scenery," she countered when he had finished. "Don't you think she'll have a better life here?"

"Of that I have no doubt. But there are joys she will miss."

Antonio sensed her intention was to console him, but he preferred gentle comfort from a woman rather than blunt truth. Something about this journey reminded him of traveling to America. He wondered if his mind were playing tricks on him, if he would wake in the morning and think he was still in the Old Country.

"Maria will have other joys," Clara reminded him with a smile. "You made the best choice you could for your family."

"I cannot argue that." He returned the smile, grateful the chaperone had the wisdom and insight her traveling companion lacked. "It'll be dark soon. I think I'll retire to get an early start tomorrow."

"Count your blessings," Clara said, "and good night."

"Sleep well," Juliet rejoined. "I plan to enjoy the air a while longer."

That came as no surprise, Antonio reflected, for the air was as chilly as she was. As he headed to his stateroom, he looked back to see her gazing out to sea, no doubt thinking of her father and home. Her optimism made him smile. There were moments, he conceded, when that brisk air was refreshing.

* * *

He had no sooner departed than Clara turned to Juliet, the look on her round face more ominous than the sky.

"Juliet, you don't really believe Marcus' note, do you?"

"Why would he lie about going home?" While Juliet knew Clara wanted only the best for her family, indignation still crept into her voice. "Your skepticism makes me think you doubt Marcus."

"What I doubt is that Cordelia would have had much good to say about your father," Clara admitted, "despite what you told Mr. Santilli. I wouldn't think Marcus would want to go home after some of the things I can picture your sister telling him."

Juliet stared at her in confusion. "Cordelia loved Papa. She must have."

"I don't mean to upset you, dear. But there were hard feelings between your father and sister before she left home. Even if Marcus does go home, for lack of a better place, how do you think your father will feel having a child thrust upon him?"

"Papa seemed receptive to having him join us when I raised the idea. It will be good for him to get to know his grandson." New worries made Juliet uneasy. "I know he and Cordelia weren't on the best of terms, but I never understood why."

"This isn't the time to talk about the past," Clara said gently. "We'd do better to get some rest."

"I suppose that's best, with a new future ahead of us," she concurred. Her fingers encountered the stiff tintype in her reticule. Remembering the boy in the picture that Mrs. Wetherall had given her, and her pledge to face the truth, strengthened her resolve. "You'll see, Clara. This will all work out splendidly."

Juliet slept more soundly than she had any night while in Boston. The steamship's rhythmic motion rocked her into a gentle slumber, the salt air soothing her lungs after the odors of the city. With its factories, stables, and unfamiliar cuisine, Boston had more soot and manure than Stockton Village. In the comfort of her stateroom, she drifted off to sleep as if she were at home, happy that she soon would be.

Her rest came to a jarring end when she was jolted awake. As the steamship ground to a thudding stop, she was thrown from her bunk, landing in a pile of blankets on the hard floor. Fully awake and only slightly shaken, she called Clara's name and reached out to be sure her housekeeper was not injured.

"I barely had any sleep," Clara grumbled, grasping her hand.

Snatching up clothing, they dressed in the dark amid screams outside their door. With Clara beside her, Juliet found her way to the deck, prepared to calm passengers as she would her pupils at home. A distant fog bell clanged ineffectively as a hand gripped her arm. In the faint light she made out Antonio's silhouette.

"How did you find me so quickly?" she gasped.

"By your hair," he muttered.

In her haste, she had not bothered to bind her hair, its fullness interfering now with her vision. It hardly mattered, for the fog left little to see. Frightened cries on deck were hushed by reassuring voices, both masculine and maternal.

"What time is it?" Juliet asked.

"Around four, I think," Antonio said, gazing out to sea.

"We should have passed Portland Head Light by now. I think we're north of it." The fog made it difficult for Juliet to determine their location. "It's impossible to see without light."

"The captain drifted too close to shore," he said tersely.

"I'm sure the crew will land us safely." Anxious to get on with the journey, she hoped her words were accurate. "This coast is full of headlands. We probably ran off course in the fog."

"I think it's worse than that," Clara said quietly.

Antonio's affirmative reply made Juliet's heart sink.

"It is worse. We've hit ledge. Be quiet so we don't cause a panic, but I heard a deckhand say the steamer's taking on water."

After the chaos of the next hour, Juliet would remember more voices that sobbed and screamed than those that consoled and soothed. Experienced passengers who traveled regularly tried to calm the fears of those who didn't. Deckhands bailed out water as the steamship changed course. Setting her own fears aside, Juliet put herself among those who comforted others.

The fog lifted before the first light of dawn broke to reveal shoreline ahead. With the steamboat struggling toward land, it became clear they would land safely, and shouts of joy went up. Juliet watched passengers press toward the bow, relief mixing with anxiety in their voices. The rain that had begun during the night resumed, making the passengers' moods as unpleasant as their wet clothing.

"It's a good thing the captain managed to back the ship off the ledge and change course," Antonio said in an undertone. "We'll reach shore, even if we don't get as far as Rockland."

As a deckhand urged passengers to wait, Juliet focused on a woman who scrambled onto the railing before he could stop her. In shallow water at last, the ship lurched forward, causing the woman to lose her footing and tumble into the sea. Men laughed at her impatience, while children burst into frightened tears.

"She's fine," Antonio assured the youngsters quickly, with a kindness that impressed Juliet. "See, she's wading toward shore."

The prospect of submersion in Maine waters, icy even in spring, chilled Juliet. She waited while the steamer chugged its way toward shore and ground to a complete halt, prompting applause from passengers. They watched as the gangplank was lowered, many pushing forward in an attempt to leave.

Juliet stepped in line with Clara and Antonio, anticipation lifting her spirits. She wondered if Marcus and Maria had reached Stockton Village. She tried to see past the crowd as the exodus came to a sudden halt.

"What is the delay now?" she complained.

"What can you expect," Antonio retorted, "from a ship that has a saloon but no lifeboats? The owners should know rocks slow down a ship more than weight does."

Ignoring his objections, Juliet, hoping to learn the cause of the delay, edged her way toward the front through families that were huddled together. The disembarking resumed unexpectedly, the shoving after the long wait knocking her off balance. Before she could recover, struggling clumsily to regain her footing, she slipped and fell from the gangplank into shallow water. The last sound she heard was Clara's cry echoing above her.

The shock of the cold water took her breath away. Juliet leaped to her feet, the frigid current splashing her face, the water weighing down her skirts. Laughing, others followed her example, jumping into the sea in their haste to reach land.

Passengers, except for Antonio, sloshed past her. Instead, he waded into the sea to extend his hand, pulling her to shore.

"Dry land at last, but I'm soaked to the skin," she gasped, aware of the sight she must present as Clara reached out to her.

Antonio shrugged. "You made the wrong choice between warmth and patience. If you'd waited, you wouldn't be wet." He glanced around. "Looks like help has arrived. Too bad they're late."

Striving for grace as her heavy skirts clung to her ankles, Juliet swept her hair from her face, looking across the clam flats to where the steamer had grounded. "Who'd have thought this sandy beach would hide such treacherous rocks offshore?"

"Everyone would," Antonio said dryly. "These waters are full of unexpected rocks and shoals."

The less she said, Juliet decided, the better. How did he know more than she did about the geology of her home state? The foreigner might not appreciate the beauty of her native coastline, but she would not let his remarks detract from her relief at being close to home. She would rather be stranded on a clam flat in Maine than amid the squalor of Boston's poorer neighborhoods.

She watched fishermen gather on the shore, gawking at the beached steamship. A deckhand brought her a blanket that helped keep the chill at bay despite her uncomfortably soggy clothing. Clara had found a rock on which she made herself comfortable. Antonio followed her example, surveying the curious crowd.

"Now what?" he demanded above the wind. "The ship no doubt sustained too much damage to sail farther today."

"I heard one of the fishermen say we're near Bath," Clara said cautiously. "This is turning into a gale. We aren't likely to go anytime soon. We might not be able to travel today."

"We need to get home." Impatience flaring, Juliet fervently wished she could be home in time to ease her nephew's transition. As she assessed the damage to the steamship, relief replaced her frustration. She eased onto the rock beside Antonio. "At least we passed Fortune's Rocks and Cape Elizabeth. It's dangerous there."

"As if this trip hasn't been dangerous enough," Antonio retorted. "Fortune's Rocks. We've had nothing but misfortune. We don't even know Marcus and Maria came this way. If they are coming with the circus, we'll get home ahead of them."

In the early chill his skepticism was more than Juliet could endure. She tried to remain strong. "You're doubtful again."

"Do you see why you should have listened to me?" He glared at her. "I'd have chosen a more experienced captain, one I know, instead of someone too self-confident to send a distress signal."

"He made it to shore," she reminded him, their legs touching on the rock they shared. "What makes you think your captain would do better in these waters? No one has flawless vision in fog."

"Let's stop bickering," suggested Clara, reaching for her hand, "so we can concentrate on finding some breakfast, shall we?"

With those words, the housekeeper effectively silenced them. The dawn passed into a gray morning, with local authorities questioning the captain and attending to those suffering from shock and minor bruises. Another delay ensued as the crew allowed groups of passengers to take turns boarding the steamer to retrieve their belongings and change into dry clothes. As soon as the doctor pronounced passengers fit to travel, coaches were summoned to transport them to local facilities or other destinations.

By the time Juliet and her companions were seated at an inn in nearby Bath, the storm had increased in intensity. Antonio expressed his frustration over a belated but hearty breakfast of oatmeal, blueberries, and coffee.

"Even if the captain puts us on another ship, it doesn't look like we'll travel right away," he said. "I don't want to delay our departure longer than necessary. I'd like to get to Stockton Village as soon as possible, to see for myself that the children are there."

Finally out of her wet clothing, Juliet felt comfortable at last as she savored her first meal in Maine in days. She did not want her morning spoiled by skepticism, nor did she want to hear more doubts about her nephew's honesty.

"If Marcus said he'll be there, he will," she assured him.

"I'm uneasy about that dockhand in Boston." Antonio turned his brown eyes toward her. Her heart sank as she saw their amber flecks darken with suspicion. "I don't trust that boy. I can't recall where I've seen him, but I have a bad feeling about him."

"He delivered the note as Marcus asked and waved to them as they set off," she said wearily. "Lawrence has no reason to lie."

"He does if he was paid off," Antonio countered, focused on finishing his plate.

"I doubt Marcus has money to pay anyone." Juliet dismissed his fears by studying the Greek Revival and Federal homes beyond her window.

Antonio removed the linen napkin from his lap and laid it on the table, gazing out at the rain. "Seeing I'm finished, what would you say if I left you ladies here where it's dry while I check on the status of ships heading north?"

"We would thank you for your consideration," Clara replied.

Juliet was relieved not to have to face the storm beyond her window. Rain streamed down so rapidly, it blurred her view of the street and made the harbor beyond invisible. When Antonio returned fifteen minutes later, she was dismayed to see he was as wet as she had been after her accidental dip in the sea.

"The captain says there's no boat available until this afternoon," he reported grimly, "and he isn't sure he'll sail even then, with the seas this rough. It could be a long wait."

"You know, Juliet," Clara said with sudden inspiration, "I believe your father's cousin Muriel still lives in Bath. She's the one we visited several years ago."

A flicker of recognition returned to Juliet. "Yes, of course. Wasn't it Aunt Muriel who hosted the visit from Cordelia and Marcus? I always felt bad that Papa didn't come with us."

"Your father had his own reasons for declining. You were so taken with meeting your nephew and seeing Cordelia, you might not remember Muriel." Clara smiled. "I know she'd love to see you. Since we aren't leaving for a while, perhaps we could call on her."

Filled with anticipation, Juliet inquired at the inn's front desk about her aunt's address. Discovering Muriel Markham was well known in town, she arranged to have a messenger deliver a note to her. Within the half hour they received a reply from Aunt Muriel expressing delight at their unexpected visit to town and inviting them to call. Her private carriage, the note instructed, would soon await them outside the inn whenever they were ready.

The invitation filled Juliet with misgivings the moment she accepted her aunt's kind offer. As Antonio accompanied them to the carriage, discussing the weather with Clara, she wondered how she would explain his presence to her aunt. He must have read her mind, for he addressed the matter as soon as he was seated across from her.

"Something's troubling you," he observed politely, his eyes bright with curiosity. "You're more restless than usual."

Twisting her gloves in her sweating hands, Juliet hesitated. "I'd rather not go into detail as to why we're traveling this route in such haste," she admitted. "You don't mind, do you?"

"If the children are with the circus, we'll be home before them anyway, so we won't lose any time by visiting. I take it you don't want to discuss the circumstances." His dark eyes were filled with understanding as they met hers, fathoming her concern. "I imagine you want to preserve Marcus' reputation in your aunt's eyes."

The depth of his intuition both surprised and mollified her.

"I don't want to disillusion her," she said awkwardly. "Things were different when Aunt Muriel met Cordelia and Marcus. We were all under the impression that Cordelia had done well. She seemed happy, and Marcus was well dressed. We had no reason to think—"

"That she lived in poverty?" Antonio smiled when she hesitated. "One doesn't always negate the other. Marcus had a rather handsome outfit for church, as I recall. His mother seemed happy to me. Would it ease your mind to know we were fairly well acquainted? I thought enough of her to hire her son."

A hot flush spread across her cheeks. It had never occurred to her that Antonio knew Cordelia. She had so many questions about her sister, and here was someone who knew Cordelia better than she did. Antonio's family must have experienced similar hardships, she reflected, before his fish market turned a profit. Perhaps that was why he understood Cordelia's struggle more than Juliet did. He possessed insight she did not.

With the visit to Aunt Muriel's rapidly approaching, she did not want to engage him in a lengthy discussion about Cordelia. She would save that for another time. She took a deep breath.

"Thank you," she said simply. "It comforts me to know my sister's life wasn't as unhappy as I've imagined it was. You probably knew her better than I, especially the last few years of her life. I'd like to ask you more as we travel."

"I'd welcome the opportunity," he said, his tone earnest.

Minutes later, they braved the gusty rains once again before drying off by the fire in her widowed aunt's parlor. Muriel saw to their comfort, instructing her maid to serve tea and sweets as soon as they were comfortably seated. Her peacock-blue dress swirled about the floor as she sat, a profusion of silk collecting at her feet.

"I'm so glad you called, dear Clara." Reaching for Clara's hand, Aunt Muriel smiled at Juliet. "Clara's like a cousin to me. Her family has always worked for the Hallidays, so we practically grew up together. Tell me, how are things with my Cousin Albert?"

"The same as ever," Clara said. "He's well and keeps busy with his literary studies. One would hardly know he's retired."

"I suspected he'd be that way. I was shocked when he wrote me about Cordelia. Such a shame." Muriel's sober tone turned to one of disapproval. "I suppose he'll be the one to raise his grandson. Do you honestly expect him to welcome the boy?"

Juliet stole a glance at Antonio to see if Aunt Muriel's disparaging tone had made an impression. From his dark look, she decided it had. She looked away quickly to discourage further curiosity.

"It seems the best solution," Clara replied, dropping the subject into an awkward silence.

Aunt Muriel's gaze shifted to Juliet, taking in her dark gray clothing. "That's a rather casual mourning dress, isn't it?"

Juliet glanced ruefully at her dress. "My best dress got wet as I was disembarking after our ship ran aground."

"Oh, I'm not criticizing," her aunt said. "I've always felt mourning was a bit overdone. The lighter color flatters you."

"Thank you for including me in your invitation, Mrs. Markham." Antonio's voice, sudden and distinct, made Juliet jump. "It was very gracious of you. You have a lovely home."

"I do, don't I?" Aunt Muriel glanced about as if seeing it for the first time. "It isn't my doing, but rather my last husband's."

Juliet cringed, grateful that Antonio chose to ignore her frank speech and that her aunt hadn't mentioned it was her third husband. Antonio glanced at the carriages passing on the street.

"The house is well situated," he continued, "close to town yet rural. What did your husband do for work?"

"He owned one of the town's biggest shipyards. Juliet enjoyed the gardens on her last visit, but it didn't rain then." Muriel rested an imperative hand on Juliet's knee. "I'm glad your father has you to intervene on behalf of Marcus. I'm fond of him, but he's a bit hard on children, isn't he? You know firsthand."

Aware of Antonio's intense concentration without looking at him, Juliet nodded as she felt the color rise in her cheeks.

Muriel assessed him with a curious stare. "So this is the young man you're taking home to meet your father, is it?"

"Oh, no, nothing of the sort," Juliet said at once. Whatever would Antonio think? "Mr. Santilli is traveling home with us. He expects to find his sister waiting for him in Stockton Village."

Antonio gave Muriel a crooked smile. "Actually, I've a commitment to a young lady who will be joining me from Italy. We've been betrothed for several years."

"What a shame. You seem well suited to our Juliet." Muriel raised an eyebrow. "And what is this about your sister?"

Juliet's heart sank as she was forced to confront the very subject she'd wanted to avoid. She didn't want her aunt to know the truth. If Muriel could remember Cordelia as a good mother who had produced a respectable son, it would preserve the dignity of both. It was up to Juliet to protect the image that would be lost once her father recognized Marcus' wayward tendencies.

At the same time, Antonio's admission of an engagement had disrupted her concentration. Her body stiffened with inexplicable resistance at the idea. It shouldn't matter in the least, for his personal life meant nothing to her. What was more alarming was Aunt Muriel's suggestion that she was bringing an immigrant like Antonio home to Papa. With such terse stammering that she wondered what had become of her ability to articulate, she explained to her aunt how Marcus and Maria had disappeared from Boston after leaving a note. Muriel's face registered curiosity.

"It's not surprising, I suppose, what with the upbringing he's had. Still, I'm sure it will work out for him. He sounds like an industrious young man. As for you, my dear," she consoled Juliet, "I know you'll find the right man one of these days. In fact, I know of one who might be just right for you. One who would please both you and your father. Perhaps I'll suggest it to Albert in my next letter."

"Oh, I don't expect to marry," Juliet said hastily.

From the corner of her eye, she saw Antonio's head turn toward her and caught the humor in his eyes.

"Who says so?" he asked with mild amusement.

"Frankly, I've never seen myself with children," she admitted, blushing until her cheeks felt on fire. "With Papa and my schoolchildren to tend to, who would see to them if not me?"

"Now tell me, my dear," Aunt Muriel said severely, "is this your opinion or your father's? Never mind. I can guess."

Juliet felt Antonio staring at her, alert with interest.

"Your father seems to have a unique perspective," he said.

"That he does," Muriel said with a mysterious smile, "but you can decide for yourself when you meet him. He's marvelously intelligent but a bit dour. Much like his sister, rest her soul."

"Estelle was the aunt I grew up with." Juliet faced Antonio awkwardly. "After my mother died, Papa retired, and we sold our home and moved in with my aunt. She died a few years ago. If I do marry, of course, I hope to have a marriage like my parents had."

"Whatever suits you. You, my dear, seem capable of handling just about anything." Patting her hand encouragingly, Muriel turned to Clara, her face sad. "Cordelia never did find much joy in life, did she? I hope she was happier living in Boston with her son."

"I imagine she was," Clara murmured, her eyes downcast.

Juliet listened with uneasy fascination. Aunt Muriel painted Cordelia in such warm tones—surprising, since Papa always spoke of her with bitterness. Juliet found it uncomfortable to have her aunt speak so candidly of family matters in front of Antonio.

He mortified her by delving further into family matters.

"I was just telling Miss Halliday," he said, pronouncing each word with clear precision as he shot her an ominous glance, "how much her sister enjoyed Boston, Mrs. Markham. She visited my market frequently. It's their life in Maine I wonder about. Never having met Professor Halliday, I don't know what to expect."

To Juliet's relief, her aunt turned unexpectedly discreet, giving Antonio a tight smile. Whether the widow had indulged herself in memories she did not intend to share or realized the need to protect the family's interests, she quickly changed her tone.

"Well, now, Mr. Santilli," Aunt Muriel said easily, "you'll have an opportunity to get to know the professor when you arrive to claim your sister. He can be intimidating when one first meets him, but with his quick mind, I think you'll find him a stimulating conversationalist and a most interesting man."

Antonio gave her a tense reply as he fixed Juliet with an accusing stare. "I'm certain I will."

Chapter Five

Antonio had barely resumed his seat in Aunt Muriel's carriage, ready to return to the inn, before he startled Juliet by slamming the door behind him. The fury in his tone matched the fire in his eyes.

"I want you to tell me," he ordered in a low voice, "exactly what your Aunt Muriel meant by that."

Seated beside her, Clara laid a restraining hand on her arm.

"What do you mean, Mr. Santilli?" Clara stammered.

Juliet waited as he folded his arms on his chest. As if other forces controlled her, she couldn't help but notice the breadth of his shoulders and the intensity of his rich brown eyes, especially when he was determined. She wished he would fix his gaze somewhere other than on her. "I want to know why your aunt acted as if your father wouldn't want to see his own grandson."

"It must be your imagination again," Juliet said when she found her voice. "Apparently, you don't trust anyone in my family. Papa cannot wait to have Marcus home."

She kept her voice steady even though her conversation with Clara on the subject had left her as uneasy as Aunt Muriel's remarks had left Antonio. Revealing her uncertainty to him would only weaken her position and make the trip more unbearable.

She was dismayed to see her answer had not satisfied him.

"You seem very anxious to get home," he said suspiciously.

"Only because I want to know for certain that the children are safe."

He studied her, his eyes filled with a doubt so penetrating, she had to fight to keep from trembling. "Why did your aunt imply there was more?"

She had to pacify him somehow. Nothing but the truth would do. She decided on a partial truth. "Papa isn't used to having a child at home. He and Cordelia weren't on the best of terms."

His eyes burned into hers. "Are you telling me you aren't sure if Marcus will be warmly received by his own grandfather?"

"Cordelia married against his wishes. They hadn't spoken in years." Humiliation crept over Juliet at having to expose her family's private disgrace. "Does that satisfy you?"

"Finally, an honest answer." He glared at her. "I should have asked your aunt. She's the only one willing to tell the truth."

"Muriel uses too little discretion in giving her opinions." Clara sighed. "With Juliet's mother gone, she feels free to speak as she pleases. I'm sorry you had to hear that, Mr. Santilli."

"Tell me why Mrs. Markham feels her cousin Albert isn't suited to raising children," he requested, his tone softening.

"In his teaching days, Professor Halliday brought a touch of fire and brimstone to his classroom," Clara said in a manner Juliet found most diplomatic. "He approaches children the same way."

"That doesn't mean a man wouldn't feel affection for his own grandchild." Antonio glared at Juliet. "At first, I was reluctant to visit your aunt, because I was afraid it would delay us more. I'm glad we stopped. She prepared me for what's ahead."

"I'm as relieved as you to be heading home," Juliet agreed.

"I'll be relieved once we get there," he muttered. "The idea of two children being with your father makes me uneasy."

Juliet tensed, not about to allow any criticism of Papa even if he was sometimes belligerent. "If they joined the circus as you believe, we'll get home before them. You needn't worry."

Turning, she gazed at the raindrops that streaked the window, looking for relief in their random pattern. The children might already be home, for they had sailed in good weather. Although she couldn't forget Clara's concerns about Papa's reaction, she had no intention of sharing them with Antonio.

They rode in silence until Muriel's driver arrived at the waterfront. Antonio suggested the women stay dry inside the carriage while he went to find out when the next boat would sail. It was not long before Juliet saw him trudging back toward the carriage. Water dripped from the ends of his dark brown hair, plastering the curls against his neck. The expression on his face did not bode well. The news when Clara opened the door was what Juliet had feared as he leaned in to talk.

"Our steamer wasn't the first to run aground today," he said tersely. "A ship was wrecked not far from here. No one wants to risk going out in this gale. The seas are too rough."

"I can't blame them for that," Clara said. "We have to consider safety first."

"At this rate, we might spend another day here before we're able to continue," Antonio continued, concern in his tone.

Even Juliet had reached her limit, though she wouldn't admit it to Antonio. If they didn't leave Bath soon, they would lose another day. She made up her mind without consulting either companion.

"I, for one, do not intend to wait," she announced firmly. "I intend to hire a private carriage."

Antonio stared as if she had grown a second, less sensible head. "Where's the logic in that? That's the slowest way."

"You said if we wait much longer, we'll be here another day. You're the one who doesn't feel my father can handle children on his own." She purposely edged her voice with resentment. Her plan would relieve their worry by bringing them closer to home. "I can't think of a faster way. Why wait for the next ship? I say we hire a carriage and leave at once."

Troppi cuochi guastano la cucina, Antonio lamented. Too many cooks did spoil the broth. It had been the middle of the afternoon before they were able to procure a conveyance and set off. He wasn't sure why he'd let the blue blood talk him into traveling at all on such a day. But she'd managed to have her way once again, making him wish he'd set out alone.

His contribution would take a considerable portion of the funds he'd brought, leaving him with less than he expected. Even in the face of his misgivings, Juliet had been adamant. Why hadn't he insisted on a more sensible plan? Those green eyes with their long lashes had influenced his decision. For such a difficult woman, she possessed the most beautiful eyes he'd seen this side of Italy, as green as the hills where he grew up.

He gazed at the faded cushions of the seat she shared with Clara Crabtree across from him. The lumps and tears must make sitting uncomfortable, he thought from his corner seat, but what could they expect? The brougham they'd hired had to be at least a quarter of a century old. A fisherman had found them the only man in town so desperate for money that he would agree to drive in this gale.

Perhaps it was the late-day gloom or the driving rain that left Antonio feeling more pessimistic than usual. Restless, he shifted on his hard, too-small seat, wishing Isabel would arrive from Italy. The marriage was arranged before he sailed to America. It was time he settled down.

For three years, Isabel had been delayed by her father's illnesses. Antonio wished they were settled comfortably in the warm, dry apartment above the fish market. Maria would be in his lap, safe and sound, with Mama scolding her for stealing the last of the *mostaccioli,* laden with chocolate and almonds.

Instead, he rode in this dreary brougham, shivering as he pursued Maria and Marcus through the wilds of Maine. Across from him sat a woman who apparently had no commitments to any man, no ties at all other than to a father who impressed him as overbearing and manipulative. If she weren't such a disagreeable, headstrong sort, she might have made some man a handsome wife. Her presence did little to ease the pain of Isabel's absence. Such an opinionated woman could hardly compare to Isabel, no matter how spellbinding her eyes were.

To pass the time, Antonio looked out the window across pastures that occasionally appeared between groves of trees.

He kept an eye out for sheep, surprised at how few he saw. In Italy, the sheep wandered the hills in all weather. He remembered a fellow passenger on the journey from Italy who had planned a life as a farmer in northern New England. Wondering where that man was now, Antonio said a silent prayer, grateful that God had shepherded his family to America and placed them in fortunate circumstances.

"You seem very intent, Mr. Santilli." Clara interrupted his reverie in the gathering dusk. "Do you see anything of interest?"

"Meadow after meadow, Mrs. Crabtree. Nothing more." He leaned back and smiled. "The view reminds me a bit of Italy."

"The landscape can get tiresome. And it's *Clara*. You must miss the activity of Boston. Did you own a fish market in Italy?"

"No, I was a shepherd and later a fisherman."

"That must have prepared you well for your market in Boston. Does all your family work there?"

"All except our father. He was a cook for a wealthy family before he went to war. What I know about food I learned from him. He died in Italy. My family has been happy here in America. How could they not be?" Hesitant to reflect too far into the past, Antonio paused before relaxing into the conversation if not the physical surroundings. Looking toward the future held more promise. "What I miss is the chance to cook a good meal. I don't plan to own a fish market forever. One day I want to own a restaurant. One of Boston's finest, like the Parker House."

"It won't surprise me if you do. I remember that salmon you prepared," Clara reminded him. "I know what a good cook you are."

"Thank you. I hope you mean that sincerely."

"I do mean it. You have a wonderful future ahead of you."

The future, Antonio reflected with frustration, held more uncertainty than he liked. *Maria could be outside in this downpour.* Wherever she was, he prayed she'd found shelter. For a brief but fervent moment he hoped Juliet was correct in assuming the children had gone to her father's and that Maria was welcome there. While the chances were slim, Maria would be somewhere safe. At least, he hoped she would be.

His thoughts swirled about the visit with Muriel Markham. Her implication that Professor Halliday would not provide a suitable upbringing for a child left him uneasy. The last thing he needed was reason to distrust Juliet's father.

As his attention turned indoors, he wished he could see Juliet in the growing darkness, visualizing the determination in her face that proclaimed her intent to do things her way. He wondered what was going through her mind and why she remained silent. Was she asleep? Understanding Juliet as he had begun to, he wouldn't be surprised if she pretended to sleep. Not knowing was unsettling, with an opportunity to ask about her father right before him. He returned the conversation to Clara and their destination.

"I look forward to meeting Professor Halliday," he admitted casually. "I'm fairly well read in literature. I expect we could have some fascinating conversations on the topic."

"I'm sure you could," she agreed.

Her noncommittal reply reminded Antonio he would have to be subtle if he expected Clara to open up. Juliet's Aunt Muriel said Clara's family had always worked for the Hallidays. He respected her loyalty and discretion, knowing she would protect her employer before she would say anything unflattering. He must tread carefully to win her trust.

"I imagine when Professor Halliday was my age, he felt a similar ambition," he pressed. "It must have been frustrating for him, raising children while having so many opportunities."

"Especially after their mother died." Clara raised an eyebrow. "That's a perceptive observation you made."

Antonio grimaced. Straightforward honesty would have to do. "Mrs. Markham's words about his reaction to his grandson's arrival concerned me. If Maria chose to go home with Marcus, I want to be certain she will be safe and welcome in his grandfather's house. You said Mrs. Markham speaks the truth freely. You also said Miss Halliday's father had a fire-and-brimstone approach to raising children."

"I only meant he was strict with his daughters." Clara blushed an alarming shade of scarlet, no doubt embarrassed at hearing her words repeated. "He was trying to protect the girls and keep them safe while raising them on his own. It's the same way you feel about your sister. With your father gone, and Maria so young, you must have a large hand in raising her."

"I do. I understand those concerns." As true as that was, Antonio suspected Clara had not been entirely forthcoming. He would try a new approach through a discussion of the red-haired woman who dozed on the seat opposite him. He nodded toward Juliet. "Does she always sleep so soundly while she travels?"

"She rarely travels." Clara sounded surprised. "When she does, she's usually alert, sometimes more than is good for her. Poor thing, she needs to rest. This trip's been hard on her."

"Being raised by an overprotective father takes its toll," Antonio resumed. "Several times I've heard her express the belief that she doesn't plan to marry. That surprises me."

"Why is that?" Clara demanded with unusual bluntness.

Antonio shrugged, feeling defensive suddenly. His gaze slid to Juliet's face, taking in her elegant beauty. "She's so graceful and attractive, I'd expect her to have many suitors."

"That's her protective father again. He tends to discourage suitors, often without meaning to. There was one young man, but he gave up after some resistance from her father." Clara chuckled, more at ease now. "I think he frightens them off. That was certainly the case with Hans. Juliet seemed smitten with him before her father put a stop to it."

So there *had* been admirers. Clara's words gave Antonio a start, but for another reason. A picture had begun to form in his mind, ugly and offensive. He hoped he was mistaken, yet he'd seen discrimination too often to mistake it for any other attitude. He'd worried about how Maria would be received by the professor, though her accent was so slight after seven years in America that one could hardly tell she'd been born abroad. His mood blackening at the thought, he fought to keep his resentment in check.

"I imagine it was difficult for Professor Halliday," he said tightly, "seeing one daughter unhappily married to an immigrant while a second was being courted by another foreigner."

"It was," Clara said carelessly, "although Hans was born here—" She caught herself, her face turning redder than before as she averted her head. "As a father raising his daughters alone, he felt a great need to protect them."

Fearing she'd said too much, Clara leaned back against the cushions, turned her head toward the window, and closed her eyes. Antonio let the conversation drop. As the housekeeper dozed off, he retreated within himself, satisfied with what he'd learned. Clara's candid words confirmed his suspicions. Juliet's father was prejudiced, like many old-time New England aristocrats.

Their conversation had revealed as much about Juliet Halliday as about her father. Antonio wasn't surprised she'd had serious suitors. Men would have to be blind not to be drawn to her delicate beauty and regal bearing. He was forced to grin as he realized her fierce determination was part of that appeal. It wasn't long afterward that the housekeeper joined her in slumber. Clara's abrupt snoring left no doubt as to her exhausted state.

They rode in silence as twilight brought raindrops clattering at the windowpanes. Juliet finally stirred, perhaps awakened by the snoring beside her. Her red curls loosened from their bun as she shifted against the cushions. Antonio sensed her eyes on him in the dark, confident now that she was awake. He seized the chance to explore his concerns about her father with her directly.

"Finally, some company," he said with a smile.

She snapped to attention at the sound of his voice. "How far have we traveled?" she asked quickly.

"You've been asleep for some time, but we still have a ways to go, according to your housekeeper. We had a pleasant talk about your father." He paused, allowing time for his words to sink in. "Mrs. Crabtree told me how enjoyable he found teaching, despite having the responsibilities of raising a family alone."

Juliet was silent for a moment. "She did?"

"Yes, right after we spoke of the many opportunities America offers, even to immigrants. Especially to them." The words made him clench his teeth. Remembering her affection for her father, he tempered his anger. "I imagine your family experienced the same satisfaction as mine, living such a prosperous existence."

When she spoke, he heard doubt in her tone. "I suppose it was prosperous. As children, we didn't think much about it."

"It's clear your father enjoyed his academic work. Was your mother content also?"

His question met with a brief silence before she spoke.

"Since I was ten when she died, I can't say for certain, but I imagine she was. We didn't often talk about her, for fear we'd upset Papa. He missed her so." Juliet leaned forward, the light from the clouds highlighting her features, revealing a look of curiosity. "What an odd question, Mr. Santilli. Why do you ask?"

"It seems to me your sister wasn't entirely happy."

For a moment Juliet was silent again. "Why did you tell me she was?" she asked in an accusing tone.

"She seemed happy enough in Boston. I knew nothing of her earlier life. She never spoke of your father." Intrigued by their home life, Antonio decided to challenge her. "I wouldn't think she could be happy being on bad terms with your father."

She seemed flustered by the question and glanced downward. "He felt Cordelia married beneath her. What of it?"

Antonio shrugged. "Wasn't it her choice to marry?"

"Of course, but as you saw firsthand, it didn't turn out well. Papa was right in thinking Daniel couldn't be trusted."

"I didn't know Daniel. But given your sister's experience and your father's domineering nature," he ventured, watching her reaction, "it doesn't surprise me that he hopes you won't marry."

When she spoke, her tone was defensive. "I'm sure he'd prefer I find someone suitable first. What are you implying?"

Antonio couldn't help but smile. It was no wonder she hadn't made an appropriate match. Perhaps she believed she'd found her mate in the young man, Hans, that Clara had spoken of. Finding the right suitor for such a headstrong daughter would be a challenge for any father, especially one whose older daughter had married a scoundrel. And one with a distaste for immigrants, especially now that the country overflowed with daily arrivals from foreign ports.

"I'm concerned about your father's controlling nature," Antonio confessed, his tone deliberately casual. "Your Aunt Muriel's doubts about his desire to raise his grandson worry me. I want to know Maria will be safe if she goes home with Marcus. Even Mrs. Crabtree admitted your father took a hard approach to raising children."

"Clara exaggerated," Juliet returned, her tone defiant. "Papa is a loving and responsible parent who will treat his grandson as his own. He'll do the same for Maria if Marcus brings her home. I hope you believe that. Otherwise you'll worry for nothing."

Antonio accepted her words at face value, suspecting she would lie to protect her father. Even in adulthood, she chose to preserve her vision of her father. While Antonio didn't blame her, her reassurances didn't relieve his concerns for Maria. He would have to accept her assessment or argue the point. He chose not to argue. Pushing the matter would get him nowhere.

"I believe you," he conceded. "I didn't mean to offend you when I suggested your father would prefer you not marry. I meant he must have found it difficult to separate from the daughter named for Shakespeare's most loyal child. I imagine he'll be reluctant to see you leave too. He'll be alone once you marry."

"Not entirely." She shrugged, irritation edging her tone. "I doubt I'll ever leave Maine. I have students to consider. At two dollars a week, our village couldn't find a steady teacher, so I assumed the position. I'm deeply committed to my work."

"Haven't you ever cared deeply enough to commit yourself to another?" he countered. He knew she would be even more protective of her father and his eccentricities than Clara had been, yet he couldn't resist probing further.

She stared at him, the light from a roadside lantern spreading across her delicate features. "No, I haven't," she said in a tone that left no room for discussion. "There hasn't been anyone I've cared about as much as my schoolchildren."

Warming to her topic, she spoke of her students and the traveling library she'd established for those whose farm chores kept them from attending school. While Juliet Halliday might not be the best judge of character, she'd accomplished a great deal professionally. The pride in her tone revealed a dedicated woman deeply attached to her young charges. Clearly, she didn't want to discuss the beau whom Clara had mentioned. Her feelings must be quite deep. Falling silent, she looked out the window.

"I wish the rain would let up," she said anxiously.

Knowing she wanted to avoid discussing her family, he closed the subject out of respect for her. She'd earned her privacy with her devotion to such a difficult father, even if Antonio despised his prejudicial nature. He followed her gaze out the window. The downpour had left the smaller roads rutted and slippery, making the ride uncomfortable and probably unsafe.

He'd begun to wonder if it was worth continuing the journey when he heard the sickening sound of splintering wood beneath the vehicle.

The carriage stopped abruptly, jolting Juliet forward. He reached out to catch her shoulders firmly in his hands before she could be thrown from her seat while Clara snapped to attention from her slumber, reaching for the door handle. Antonio ensured neither was hurt before he opened the door.

He stepped down from the carriage in time to see the driver, who must be soaked to the skin, lower himself to the ground to survey the damage. Antonio bent to look beneath the carriage. A back wheel had come off its axle, and a spoke had splintered, signaling the end of their ride.

"Looks like we won't be going anywhere tonight," the driver announced.

Antonio stared in disbelief as the elderly man shook his head.

"Old wheel," he explained. "Not much I can do about it now. I have no pole to lash under the axle. Nearest blacksmith's three miles away. I wouldn't get far before I'd float away in the water collecting along the road."

Antonio looked around, his visibility not more than inches. "There must be trees down along here. Isn't there one that's long and sturdy enough to use so we can continue?"

"I have no rope," the driver shouted, his hand sheltering his eyes from the rain. "You can try it if you've a mind to, but you'll be as wet as I am."

Antonio knelt to look under the carriage, his knees soaking wet. Having mended his share of wagons since his boyhood, he hoped to offer a suggestion. After studying the broken wheel, he had to agree with the driver. They would get no farther tonight.

As he tried to think of another idea, Juliet emerged from the carriage interior, shielding her face from the rain with her hood. It took her only a moment to realize the news was not good.

"This cannot be," she said in a rebellious tone.

She leaped down from the carriage and stooped to examine the wheel. Antonio couldn't think why, for her expertise could hardly extend to travel. He turned back to the driver.

"Where can we find shelter?" he shouted over the wind.

The driver squinted at him. "Ever been to Maine before?"

"No."

"No use talking then," the man said bluntly, "for what you want ain't here. There's no shelter in these parts."

"There must be shelter somewhere," Antonio argued. "How are we supposed to proceed?"

"We don't. We bed down for the night, right here in this carriage." The driver opened the door to protect himself from the rain. "We won't find help at this hour. You getting back in?"

Antonio saw Juliet's head turn sharply at the suggestion. He sensed her indignation even in the dark.

"I've no intention of spending the night in the carriage," she declared. "Surely there's an inn within walking distance. We're close to Rockland, aren't we?"

"Not close enough to walk in this," the driver retorted.

Her headstrong attitude annoyed Antonio even while he

admired it. While he wished she had more patience, he marveled at her sense of direction in this lonely territory at night. She glanced in both directions.

"Are you certain this is the coach road?" she questioned the driver. "I think you've taken a wrong turn."

"It's the road I always take," the coachman insisted. "Looks different in the dark."

"I'm going in search of a place to spend the night," she announced. "Will you hand me my suitcase, please?"

"Juliet," Clara gasped, stepping into the doorway of the carriage, "where do you think you're going?"

"I'm going home," she retorted. "It might take longer than expected, but at least we'll get there."

Antonio was amused to see Clara fumble with her umbrella. She knew Juliet well enough to know she was serious.

"Suit yourself," the driver muttered over the howling wind.

Stepping up to retrieve her luggage, he deposited her case on the ground before ensconcing himself firmly in the doorway. Antonio knew the coachman was ready to seek protection if they did not change their minds soon.

"Come along, Clara," Juliet said, picking up her bag. "We'll find a cottage along the road. Until then, we have our umbrellas. Will you join us, Mr. Santilli? The rain's letting up."

A glance at the driver's soaked and muddy clothing convinced Antonio it would be foolhardy to remain in the carriage. If the wheels were old and poorly tended, the roof probably was as well.

As he turned to Juliet, he saw strength and determination in her eyes where the light from the clouds touched them. Her raw beauty rendered him unable to reply. *She walks in beauty, like the night,* he reflected, feeling like Lord Byron. The thought left him giddy.

"Will you join us?" Juliet tried again, unaware of his fascination. "Or are you too exhausted for a woodland hike?"

Antonio snapped to his senses. He laughed abruptly. "First our steamboat captain is too inexperienced to want to stop, and now our carriage driver is too experienced to want to proceed.

I can hardly allow two ladies to travel on their own in this. Looking for an inn might be our best chance."

Leaning inside the carriage, he told the astounded driver of his decision to leave, and then he removed his luggage and Clara's.

"Allow me," Antonio offered, ignoring Clara's protests as he carried her bag. "This is why God gave me two strong hands."

As Clara thanked him profusely, he watched Juliet set off by herself with as much fortitude as if she were leading her own army. Antonio seized the chance to address Clara privately.

"I'm glad we have a willing leader. She's impulsive but not well traveled, as you pointed out. Does she know her way?"

Clara looked up the road after Juliet. "As the crow flies perhaps. I'd put my trust in the stars, if there were any."

Antonio glanced heavenward as the wind scattered the clouds. The moon revealed a sliver of itself before it flirted with the next cloud bank and slipped behind it. *Inconstant and unreliable,* he thought with annoyance. He would have to rely on his judgment.

"If it clears, we might see stars yet," he told Clara. "Can you read the stars?"

"A little," she said with less optimism.

He smiled at her effort to copy Juliet's fortitude while recognizing her own shortcomings. "I can."

Clara grinned with relief. "Then we're safe."

Chapter Six

As they walked, Antonio watched the rain let up, just as Juliet had predicted. They might indeed see stars before long. They hastened their pace, catching up with their leader after some difficulty. Her pace was quick. He followed her in the dark, wondering how she could still feel optimistic despite the challenges of this trip. And how, under such wretched conditions, did she manage to maintain such beauty?

"Do you know of any cottage that would welcome us this time of night?" he asked.

Juliet slowed her steps and looked about. The dim moonlight revealed only the sheen of wet bushes on either side of the road.

"I don't see any lights ahead, so I can't be sure where we are," she confessed. "I've ridden this road many times, but I don't recognize this stretch. Maine can't have changed that much in the time we've been gone, can it, Clara?"

Her wry remark made Antonio smile as he bent to strap his suitcase over his back. "Not unless you're Rip Van Winkle. Here, give me your suitcase. You'll need two hands to hold your umbrella in this wind."

Juliet paused in her tracks as he hoisted her bag with his free hand. "God also gave you a strong back, I see."

"I don't plan to test its strength by wasting time." Antonio wasn't surprised her bag was the heaviest of the three. He had expected it might weigh more than it did. "Let's keep walking."

The dense shrubbery along the roadside offered no clue as

to location. Antonio had begun to suspect the area to the west would be more populated when a narrow break appeared in the hedges.

"Finally, a sign," Juliet said in relief. "If this path runs inland, I think we'll find something. Shall we try it?"

Antonio allowed Juliet and Clara to step through before he went after them. Walking in silence, he followed Juliet's lead, comfortable with the terrain and her refusal to hesitate. He preferred courage to fear, even if it was misplaced, surprised at the admiration he felt for her. The path seemed promising even when it turned to patches of underbrush.

As they continued, Antonio began to question their direction. Unable to tell from the sky if they were still heading north, he suspected after several turns that they were walking parallel to the road again. His frustration grew, along with concern for their safety. As soggy vines clutched at him, he struggled to push aside overhanging branches, allowing a thin stream of moonlight to reach them from the clearing sky.

"I don't want to discourage anyone," he announced, unable to remain silent any longer, "but I think we've gone the wrong way."

"I'm not sure this is leading anywhere," Clara agreed, sounding alarmingly out of breath.

"It will come out somewhere," Juliet insisted. "And the rain has probably stopped for good. Even if it were raining, I certainly wasn't going to spend the night in a broken—"

She got no farther. Clara gave a shriek as Juliet dropped from view before their eyes, tumbling into a hole in the wet earth. Antonio set down the suitcases, flung his own case from his back, and reached into the shadow's depths, hearing groans from below.

"Miss Halliday! Are you—"

"Fine," came the muffled response. "But my ankle isn't."

Antonio pushed aside the reeds tangling about his legs and knelt in the darkness, feeling the wet against his knees. He was unable to see clearly either the ground beneath him or the pit into which Juliet had fallen. As he bent lower, he saw the outline of her head and shoulders in the watery light. "Can you stand?"

"I can try," came her voice from below.

Feeling awkward, he moved a hand down her arm tentatively before easing it toward her back. Her waist felt slender and fragile as he slipped his fingers beneath the impractical sacque coat she had donned after changing out of her drenched cloak. He discovered her midsection was firm enough to grasp.

As he did so, she gripped him around the neck, threatening to choke him as he lifted her to her feet and raised her from the hole. Clara fussed over her to make sure she wasn't badly hurt as he set her down, making sure her feet were on solid ground this time. While she'd held him securely enough to cut off his breathing, the blue blood was as light as an angel in his arms.

"Oh, Juliet," Clara cried in a muffled voice, embracing her. "I was terrified we'd lost you. Are you all right?"

"You've found me," Juliet said, her voice equally muffled in her housekeeper's solid shoulder, "and I'm no worse for wear. Well, perhaps a little. I feel as if I've aged a decade falling into that hole."

"Take a step," Antonio encouraged. "How does the ankle feel?"

As Juliet attempted a wobbly step, she clutched his elbow so tightly, he thought the bone would snap. Surprised such a delicate woman could possess such strength, he tightened his hold around her waist, which was slippery with mud. When she spoke at last, her tone was light, but he felt her body tremble and heard her teeth chatter.

"I don't think walking is advisable," she admitted, "but it's too chilly to stay here. Watch that hole; it's the size of a small ocean."

Her ability to laugh in the face of pain made Antonio smile even while he gritted his teeth at her foolhardiness in charging ahead. He berated himself for not stopping her. Judging from the steps she took gingerly, she must be in excruciating agony but too proud to admit it. At least she recognized the need for diplomacy under trying circumstances. She had more depth than he'd given her credit for.

He considered their situation. They'd gone a distance without having seen as much as a candle in a window. They hadn't even seen a window, he realized. He had no idea how far they'd have to go before finding shelter. Nor did Juliet. Clara appeared too tired or frightened to be able to orient herself. They were so far from the road, he worried they might find nothing for the rest of the night.

Now Juliet could not walk. He could not carry her and the luggage. It might be easier, preferable even, to abandon her rather than the suitcase, but he had no choice. He remembered thinking she would be more a hindrance than a help, though a most attractive hindrance. So far, he'd been correct.

He turned to his traveling companion. Juliet's back was to the moon, leaving her face in darkness and her thoughts impenetrable. He guessed she had enough fortitude not to resort to tears.

"It seems my only choice is to carry you," he announced.

Juliet turned to stare at him, the movement throwing enough light to make out the suspicion on her pinched pixie face. The look was so typical, he couldn't help but smile despite their plight.

"Surely you don't expect to carry me through all these brambles," she challenged.

"You can walk if you prefer," he rejoined, "but I think you'd find being carried more comfortable in your present state."

"My state." Her lips tightened with indignation. "I've walked farther than this in worse states, I can tell you. When you live in the country, you get used to walking. Up here we haven't the conveniences you're accustomed to in the city."

With that she turned and took a clumsy step forward, moving so quickly, she nearly twisted the other ankle. Fortunately for her, Antonio's quick reflexes saved her from a more serious fall.

"Let me help," he offered again, more gently this time, his

fingers still attached to her upper arm. "Your walk reminds me of my grandmother's."

She gave him a sharp glance. "I've only twisted my ankle. I'm not crippled, after all."

"Neither is my grandmother," Antonio replied lightly, "but her walk is still steadier than yours. You're the one who said you felt as if you'd aged a decade with that tumble you took."

"I'll consent to being carried," she conceded reluctantly, releasing a sigh of frustration. "It's hardly necessary, however, to compare me to your grandmother. What about my luggage?" she added feelingly.

"Let's leave it." Clara's voice was filled with relief. "The idea of moving on is more appealing."

"I'm afraid you'll have to go without the niceties for one night." Amused, Antonio could only imagine in the dark the chagrin on Juliet's face. "Are we ready, Clara?"

She answered in the affirmative. And with that Antonio slipped a firm hand under Juliet Halliday's knees and swept her up in his arms despite her protests, as enchanted by the emotional strength that could not hide her physical frailty as he was by her resistance.

It was fully another mile before a dim light fought its feeble way through the darkness. Juliet's spirits soared at the sight. She hoped she hadn't imagined the faint glow visible through branches sagging with raindrops. As the traveling trio followed the light, she saw that it came from a lantern hung on a cottage across a field. She was so relieved at the idea of a warm night's rest that she laughed through the tears she'd struggled to hide.

"It's been worth it," she gasped, cringing as pain spread about her ankle, "even if I don't have any nightclothes with me."

"You're lucky you have any clothes left at all." Antonio set her down gently beside a tree where she could balance. "Your other dress is still wet from this morning's dip in the ocean.

And we're nearly out of money, so let's hope there are friends ahead. Wait here while I knock at the door."

Juliet leaned against the oak as she waited with Clara, watching Antonio make his way across the yard. It had to be near midnight. The thought of him waking the residents worried her, for she did not want to put anyone out on a night like this.

Instead, she turned to Clara, who had apparently conversed openly with Antonio during their ride when she wasn't snoring. Knowing her housekeeper as she did, Juliet guessed she had attempted to pacify Antonio and smooth over the troubled waters in which Juliet had managed to immerse herself.

"What was all that talk in the carriage?" she demanded.

"What talk?" Clara asked.

The exhaustion in Clara's voice reminded Juliet that her top priority was to find her a bed. While they waited, she might as well address the topic she'd raised. "That talk about Papa. Mr. Santilli claimed you said Papa found it difficult to raise children. What else did you tell him?"

"Nothing more than what I said when we left Muriel's," Clara said in surprise. "We talked while you were sleeping, but he was just making conversation. He's a pleasant young man."

"If a bit curious. I'm uncomfortable having attention turned on me. My life isn't that interesting."

Clara gave her a glance filled with meaning. "Maybe he thinks it is. You're the daughter of a retired professor. And you're a teacher, a young woman uncommitted to anyone."

Juliet looked away, unwilling to consider the implication. "That has nothing to do with Antonio Santilli. He's betrothed. He and his Isabel will be married as soon as she comes from Italy."

She fell silent, embarrassed by the slight sarcasm she heard in her own voice. Feeling vulnerable, she was reluctant to explore feelings she hadn't even recognized until now. As the night air settled over her, she realized only his arms had protected her from the chill. The feeling had been anything but unpleasant. She'd felt safe in his strong and supportive hold.

She watched Antonio knock on the distant door, waiting until a woman opened it. In the lantern light she saw the resident gesture for him to enter. Juliet was relieved she didn't seem perturbed. She turned to Clara, her voice unsteady as she spoke.

"His questions make me think he doesn't like Papa," she said with trepidation. "I certainly hope he's civil to him when they meet."

"Who do you think wouldn't be civil?" Clara paused, smiling. "Antonio's main concern is Maria. He needs to know she'll be safe if she gets there before he does. But I don't think Maria is his only concern. He's concerned for you also. He understands the losses you've endured, between Cordelia's death and Marcus' disappearance. I hope you're aware of that."

For a long moment, Juliet could find no response. Afraid to put her emotions into words, she couldn't keep her voice from shaking. "But there's Isabel."

"She's across the ocean in Italy, while you're here in the flesh. Don't discount the strength of your influence, my dear. How could Mr. Santilli help but notice you? You're a lovely, charming girl." Humor filled Clara's voice. "And to think he hasn't even seen you at your best."

Juliet was unable to ignore Clara's words. Her heart leaped with a giddiness she couldn't explain as she watched Antonio emerge from the cottage and hurry back toward them.

"I believe he's bringing good news," Clara predicted.

Antonio was out of breath by the time he reached them, but his relief was evident in his ruggedly handsome features. His face shone with triumph despite being lined with a weariness that pained Juliet.

"Mrs. Rose Ryan and her family live in that house," he said with a broad smile. "She says we're welcome to spend the night."

"Bless her," Juliet said gratefully, feeling her aches melt away at the news.

"I don't know where she'll put us all in that little cottage," Clara said, "but I'm so tired, I could sleep standing up."

"Let's go in, shall we?" He gave Juliet an awkward smile. "I don't expect you to walk through this field. You've walked enough tonight. I'll carry you." A note of humor filled his voice. "That way, you can't take a wrong turn."

"And just how do I know Maria didn't inherit her wanderlust from you?" Juliet teased as he drew her body toward his.

He lifted her in his arms as if the wet clothing weighing her down was as light as goose feathers. For once, she felt safe and protected. As they walked in silence across a meadow that seemed to stretch endlessly before them, she relaxed in his strong arms, enjoying the warmth of his closeness, her foot temporarily relieved of pain.

She hoped she was not a great burden. He had already carried her over unpaved roads, through briar patches, and now among dark fields with treacherous hollows. Despite the uneven ground, his step remained steady, giving her a feeling of security despite the uncertainties they'd endured on the trip.

She gazed up at his profile in the thin moonlight that broke between the clouds, aware of the confidence with which he carried not only himself, but her. She noted the determination in his eyes, the set of his jaw, the strength she felt throughout his frame. More than mere brawn, his was a strength that permeated his entire being. His expression of concentration surprised her. He seemed more distracted than burdened.

"Aren't you pleased we've found shelter?" she asked.

"I'm relieved," he said, stumbling over a clump of grass.

"If it's money you're concerned about," she offered, hoping to ease his worry without offending him, "I'm sure we'll be home before we run out."

"It's not money." He shifted her closer to his chest as he picked his way through the field. "I was hoping it hasn't been raining like this back in Boston. I wonder how my mother is doing running the store without me."

Until now Juliet had thought only of what lay ahead for the three of them. She hadn't considered the family Antonio had left back in Boston. The image of his mother waiting desperately for news of her young daughter filled her with sudden remorse and guilt as she reflected on how selfish she had been, thinking only of her own worries. The realization made it hurt to breathe.

Antonio carried her up the cottage steps onto the porch. As they entered the parlor, a woman who must be Mrs. Ryan greeted them. A slight woman with wiry brown hair peppered with gray, she settled Juliet in a rocking chair by the hearth without delay.

"There, there, my dear," she crooned, "how does that feel?"

"I've never felt anything better in my life," Juliet said through chattering teeth. "After the chill of that rain—"

" 'Ere, don't say a word," Rose Ryan consoled her in a heavy Irish brogue. "When yer husband knocked at the door, I was sure it was me own. Paddy works at the sawmill, but tonight he's out on the town again, if ye catch me meanin'." She rolled her eyes. "I don't expect him back till late."

"Husband?" Alarm rose within Juliet as if a train she could not avoid was speeding toward her. "Oh, no, it's—"

Arranging a worn but cozy afghan over Juliet's shoulders, the Irishwoman went on heedlessly.

"It's fortunate ye're married," she said with a wink, "since we've only beds for two. But we'll make do. Ye aren't the first guests I've had come by this time o' night."

Horror coursed through Juliet as Antonio's eyes met hers across the room, warning her to remain silent. She was in no position to tell the truth. This remote cottage might be the only dwelling for miles. On such a stormy night, hampered by a badly sprained ankle, she had little choice but to cooperate.

"We can make do," Clara said hastily. "We're so grateful for your kindness. I'm Mrs. Crabtree—Juliet's aunt. The floor is fine for me. I'm sure Mr. and Mrs. Santilli feel the same."

Now Clara was lying as well. The idea mortified Juliet. Her housekeeper shot her a glance that silenced any protest she might have made. Juliet tried to adjust to the idea of pretending to be Mrs. Antonio Santilli, wondering if she should attempt an Italian accent.

It was too late. She'd already opened her mouth. A feeling of dismay settled in as her pretend husband spoke up.

"We are most grateful for your hospitality," Antonio said, bowing respectfully to Rose Ryan. "I admit I feel a bit like Odysseus. I hope I needn't travel twenty years like he did in order to reach home."

"I'd no idea I'd have such an educated guest tonight." Mrs. Ryan beamed, giving Juliet a confidential glance. "What a treat it must be for women like us to have such a well-read husband. Where were ye headed?"

Juliet had to suppress a grin in spite of herself. They were already so deep in deceit, another lie could hardly hurt.

"To Stockton Village," Antonio explained, giving Juliet a smile reflecting slyness and amusement. "I didn't grow up in this area like my wife and her aunt did. I've no idea where we are."

Mrs. Ryan registered surprise. "Why, ye're in Hope," she exclaimed. "'Tisn't much more than a stone's throw from Belfast. Ye could practically walk home."

"Given the sad state of my wife's ankle," Antonio said more glibly than Juliet would have liked, "I don't think we'll try."

The throbbing in her ankle made Juliet grimace. "Home is still too many miles away, unfortunately."

"You rest, dear," Antonio said, laying a reassuring hand on her shoulder that startled her, as comforting as it was irritating. "You'll feel better tomorrow."

I doubt it, she thought with clenched teeth. What choice did she have? Here she sat, covered in mud, ankle swollen, dress soaked from the rain. She had brought only two other dresses, expecting her trip to Boston would be brief. And those were in the woods in a suitcase she'd probably never see again. She sat up at Antonio's next gesture as Mrs. Ryan talked with Clara on the far side of the comfortable parlor.

"I know you've been through a great deal," he murmured with surprising tenderness, kneeling beside her chair, "but that ankle will heal in time. And tonight you'll have a soft place to lay your head. For a time, I was beginning to worry."

With that, he leaned down and lightly kissed her forehead. Her exhaustion disappeared as his lips caressed her, gentle as butterfly wings. The gesture caught her off guard. In her drowsy state, she found herself enjoying his touch. With his sincere manner and eyes full of kindness, she believed he had her dignity in mind for once.

He had found them a place to stay. Rose Ryan had given her the chance to rest her ankle and kindly offered them a room for the night. A room they would have to share. In her desperation, Juliet was certain she could lie convincingly to her hostess.

But she was less certain she could spend the night comfortably in the same room with Antonio Santilli.

Chapter Seven

Her ankle throbbing, Juliet rocked gently in her chair as the others made overnight preparations without consulting her. It was so long after midnight, she was sure, that no one was moving quickly. Instead they worked steadily and methodically, discussing the comforts necessary for a good night's sleep.

Trying to keep from nodding off, Juliet watched as the hearth fire threw shadows across the wooden floor beyond the rocker to the braided rug. In such a cozy setting, she began to feel at ease with the proposed arrangements. That was fortunate, she mused, since she was powerless to object. Clara explained to Mrs. Ryan how their carriage had broken down on the road while their hostess prepared tea.

"There, dear, now drink up," Rose Ryan urged Juliet, placing a cup on a table beside her. "This hot brew'll bring ye right round. You, too, Mr. Santilli." She eyed Antonio's mud-covered trousers and jacket. "I'm sure ye've a mind to wash yerselves, but it's so late, ye might want to wait till morning."

"That's wise," Clara agreed, seated on a stool near Juliet.

"Thank you for your kindness, Mrs. Ryan. But we didn't mean to put you out of your bed." Finishing his tea, Antonio gestured toward the door. "My wife and her aunt are exhausted. I'm sure they'd be more comfortable indoors. The barn's fine for me."

The cautious, steady look he gave Juliet made her blush. Was he truly thinking only of her honor in speaking to Mrs. Ryan, or had he spent enough time with her tonight and felt he needed some distance? With slight alarm, she hoped that wasn't the case.

"I wouldn't dream of it," Mrs. Ryan said. "And it's Rose, me dear. We'll have no formality here. If me girls weren't asleep, I'd give you their bed. The boys could sleep by the fire, but the trundle's not fit for guests. Why doesn't Mrs. Crabtree use this cot? You can both sleep in my bed. I'll room with the girls."

The tea had lulled Juliet into a placid state from which she was once again jarred at the idea of sharing a bed with Antonio. She had almost been spared the indignity, only to be cast back into the possibility. She jumped to attention as Rose readied extra blankets.

"Please, Rose," Juliet tried again, "I can't ask you to leave your bed, especially at this late hour."

"I don't sleep till Paddy's home," Rose insisted. "This'll teach him to stay out late. It's not often we have guests, like in those fancy places in Bar Harbor. I'll just tidy the room a bit."

As Clara helped Rose carry blankets into the small bedroom, so small the room could be seen in its entirety from the doorway, Juliet turned to Antonio in panic. She lowered her voice so their hostess wouldn't hear the urgency in her tone.

"What are we to do?" she whispered, hoping the thudding of her heart didn't sound as loud to him as it did to her.

He bent so close, she couldn't help but notice the golden flecks in his brown eyes and feel his breath against her skin. *"A mali estremi, estremi ridemi,"* he said softly. "Desperate times call for desperate measures. I've spoken of Italy enough that you can pretend to know a little about it. Remember, you're my wife."

Juliet trembled as he lowered his face until it was just inches from her own. The closeness left her breathless, the amusement in his eyes reflecting anticipation at the role he was about to play. She'd never seen such warmth and enthusiasm radiate from him. His sudden intensity left her without a shred of sense. For a moment, she was unable to respond.

"We're lucky to be here at all," he reminded her gently, his teasing tone turning practical. "We'll do what we must."

They resumed their roles as Clara and Rose Ryan returned to the parlor. Juliet felt her skin tingle as Antonio rubbed her back rhythmically, his fingers moving in slow, comforting circles over the dampness of her dress. Their hostess turned to them, a congenial smile on her face as trepidation swept through Juliet.

"The bedroom's all set," Rose said. "Make yerselves just as comfortable as if ye were at home."

And how was she to do that, Juliet wondered? The lantern lit their way as she and Clara returned from the outhouse together, having relieved themselves for the night. Clara assisted her as she hobbled along on the ankle that still pained her.

"Don't give tonight another thought," Clara urged. "Just relax and rest your ankle. Tonight will give us a chance to collect our strength for the rest of our journey. Before you know it, we'll be home again with your papa, Marcus, and Maria. It might even happen as soon as tomorrow. Won't that be wonderful?"

"Yes, it will be," Juliet agreed, wishing she were home already, tucking Marcus in instead of worrying about sharing a room with Antonio. "But first I have to get through tonight."

Clara regarded her kindly. "I know it's difficult, my dear. I'm sure you never expected to spend a night with any man other than Hans Eichmann. Try to put him out of your mind. You'll have plenty of opportunities with men. By tomorrow this charade will be over, and we can continue on our way."

Filled with exasperation, Juliet wasn't sure whether she wanted to laugh or cry. Hans Eichmann was the furthest thing from her mind at the moment. How could Clara possibly know Antonio posed far more of a danger to her heart than Hans ever had?

They spoke of Rose Ryan's kindness and other topics of little consequence until they returned indoors. Once Clara settled herself on the cot in the parlor and said good night, Juliet had no choice but to go to bed. The flannel nightgown

Mrs. Ryan had loaned her was three sizes too big, but it kept her decent and warmed her in the chilly darkness.

She made her way to the bedroom slowly, afraid to face Antonio. What was he thinking? Would he consider her immodest for sharing his room? And what of her reputation? Her father lived only about thirty miles away, well within gossiping distance.

It wasn't as if she had a choice in the matter, she reminded herself, stranded in the wilds of rural Maine as they were. She realized she hesitated because of Isabel. Having angered Antonio on more than one occasion, she didn't want to do anything to incur Isabel's wrath. Sleeping in the same room with him would certainly do that if Isabel were ever to find out. The realization stung with an intensity Juliet hadn't expected.

She'd thought of arranging a pile of blankets in the bed between them for modesty's sake, but watching Antonio head into the bedroom as she went outside with Clara only gave her more time to worry. As she entered the room, she was startled to see he had made himself a bed on the floor. She had worried for nothing. She felt relieved—and oddly disappointed.

At her entrance, Antonio rolled over and sat up. "I thought you'd be more comfortable if I slept down here," he said with a grin. "I'd be fine anywhere after that adventure."

"I feel the same." Juliet couldn't help but smile with relief at being rescued. The pain in her ankle returning, she sat tentatively on the edge of the bed, ready to broach the subject closest to her heart. "You offered to tell me more about Cordelia's life. I'd like to take you up on that now."

Antonio sat up and leaned against the wall, eyeing her curiously. "What would you like to know?"

"You said you thought enough of her to hire her son."

"That's right. She often did the shopping for Lillian—Mrs. Wetherall—and she brought Marcus with her from the time he was little. As he got older and money was hard to come by, she asked if I could use some help in the market. I took him in without hesitation. I knew he'd been raised in a good household."

"Then they weren't always suffering." Juliet repeated the words as if to confirm them for herself, almost afraid to breathe, her voice faltering.

"Quite the contrary. She and Marcus had many good times. There were picnics in the Public Garden, evenings of singing at the boardinghouse. I brought food once or twice. Your sister had a beautiful voice. A happy, carefree voice." Antonio's gentle smile when she felt her face brighten made her blush. "Her life wasn't nearly as unhappy as you seem to think it was."

Juliet warmed to the subject. Relief flowed through her, knowing Cordelia had found joy with her son even in reduced circumstances. She listened as Antonio described amusements on Boston Common, balloon ascensions and military displays, his stories revealing a side of Cordelia Juliet didn't know existed.

"You don't know what it is to be a younger child," she pointed out. "Sometimes I feel I've always lived in Cordelia's shadow." The topic made her wistful. "I suppose that's why I'm as protective of Papa as I am. I want him to see how much I care, how much I depend on him for his wisdom and advice."

"You needn't apologize for your devotion to your father. It's an admirable quality, one not everyone possesses. At this point in time," he reflected, the tenderness in his voice lingering as his reminiscences came to a close, "I think I know your nephew better than you do. That will change when you get home. You have a lifetime to get to know each other. You'll see what a fine boy he is at heart."

The time had come for Juliet to acknowledge what Antonio had known all along.

"I know Marcus is a wayward boy," she admitted. "He hasn't had the privileges I had growing up, and it shows in his actions. I worry about what will happen when he comes home. It has as much to do with his behavior as it does with Papa's acceptance of him. Do you think he could ever come to love me?"

She spoke tremulously, wondering at the fear in her voice. Marcus had known only the love of his mother before this.

Would he accept her now as his caregiver, an aunt she scarcely knew? He had run away from her, choosing to travel alone. Such an admission of worry had burst out of her deepest fears. She'd never expressed such emotions before, not even to Papa or Clara.

"It won't be the same without his mother, but I've no doubt he'll come to love you. How could it be otherwise?" Antonio's eyes locked with hers in a moment of complete trust. A moment that stopped her heart from beating. "Who could not love you? If I had to judge by Cordelia and Marcus, I would know you'd been raised in a loving home as well."

"Thank you for this," she said after a moment, a huge breath escaping her. "It's given me insight I didn't have before."

The power of her emotions fell without awkwardness into the void between them, a void created by physical and emotional weariness. It was late in the night as they prepared at last to extinguish the lamp. Juliet felt her deepest burden lift from her soul, as if Antonio had taken a key and unlocked it, releasing fears she'd kept hidden away for too long. For once, she did not belabor the discussion, content instead to go to bed with hope in her heart. Hope of returning to Papa, of getting to know Marcus, of traveling home with her new protector all filled her thoughts.

"Sleep well," Antonio said lightly.

His inquisitive brown eyes searched Juliet's face, making her blush. While his logic made sense, she didn't want to disillusion Rose by giving her the chance to guess the truth. As long as they were pretending to be a married couple, they ought to play the part.

They could be, after all, she mused. He was surprisingly well read, enough so he knew Cordelia's reputation from Shakespeare and the story of *The Odyssey*. It was natural that Rose had such a high opinion of him. Rose suspected Antonio was more literate than herself, the professor's own daughter.

A pang of humiliation swept through her for having underestimated him. She remembered with shame suggesting Antonio might not be able to afford the fare of traveling by ship. Yet, he was a tremendous success at running the family business. It could not have been an easy accomplishment for an immigrant. It would not have been easy for even the wealthiest of Boston's citizens.

She forced her thoughts back to the present and the problem at hand. There remained the impropriety of sharing a room with a man to whom she was not married, a man betrothed to another. Yet she did not want to risk further deception and possible exposure of the truth.

After bidding Antonio good night, she turned on her side and lay still, her face to the wall. As she pondered her future, her fears of disgrace dissipated like dew at the dawn. Within a short time a husky snoring from the floor stilled the worries in her active mind. The sound allowed her to relax into a smooth stillness, like water at low tide along Stockton Village's coast.

Juliet smiled in her weariness. Having already drifted off to sleep, the man beside her had her interests at heart. Before she descended into slumber, she took a moment to remember the protected feeling of being carried in his arms, enjoying the sensation once more. Since her ordeal began, she had not felt so cared for, so safe.

She closed her eyes at last, comfortable for the first time since leaving the steamship. Within seconds she was asleep.

"Isn't it just the dearest thing?" Rose Ryan gushed the next morning as she doled out eggs with glistening yolks, hearty crusts of bread, and slices of grilled tomato to her guests. By the time the accompanying slabs of bacon appeared, Juliet was almost too full to enjoy them. "Our very own Juliet and her husband under my roof. I've never heard of anything so romantic."

"Or unlikely," Antonio quipped.

He gave Juliet a smile, his arm brushing hers as they sat in close proximity not only to each other, but to Clara and the other members of the Ryan family. It was not only unlikely, Juliet told herself, but impossible. She smiled into her lap, almost unable to look at Antonio in the presence of Rose and her children.

A more star-crossed journey she couldn't imagine. His courage had impressed her throughout. Between his attempt to repair the carriage and his chivalry in carrying her through the wet woodland, he'd brought her many miles closer to home.

But over the reality of the breakfast table, she could think of little other than Isabel's promise to travel from Italy to join Antonio in Boston. While Juliet had shared a room with him the previous night, she knew it meant nothing over the course of time. Worst of all, she had enjoyed the experience. She picked at her breakfast, her appetite vanishing with her joy at the memory.

At least she had the chance to meet Paddy Ryan before he went off to work at the sawmill. Rose had made such derogatory comments that Juliet was surprised when she watched him across the table entertain his youngest children with magic tricks that made them squeal with delight. Rose's words last night had made her wonder if their relationship was star-crossed as well. Juliet saw no sign of that this morning, with the bright sun streaming in the kitchen window and the crowded kitchen filled with laughter.

She had watched Antonio and Patrick Ryan talking before the Irishman began entertaining the children. The men chuckled about common issues they dealt with daily, concerns about which Juliet was embarrassed to realize she knew nothing. Their similarities surprised her. While Paddy was coarse and outspoken, Antonio was refined and careful in his speech. Their desire for an American life and their hard work gave them a bond that excluded her. She felt a little thrill of pride seeing how comfortably Antonio fit in.

Paddy Ryan's tricks worked their magic not only on the children but also on the guests. Juliet could not shake the giddiness that crept into her own mixed emotions. Even Antonio seemed caught up in the gaiety. He surprised her by standing up.

"I've a trick as well," he said mysteriously, eyes widening as he glanced from the face of one child to the next. "You might not know it, but the lovely lady sitting beside me became my wife a matter of days ago in Boston. This is a wedding trip of sorts for us, and you have been kind enough to be our hosts."

Juliet nearly choked on her bacon, unable to imagine what on earth he would say next.

"Your mother reminded me last night," he continued to the children, "that a couple ought to show the world how happy they are once they're joined in matrimony. My trick on our wedding trip is to make a smile magically appear on my wife's face."

Fearful she would strangle from their lies, Juliet forced the bacon down her dry throat, cringing as Antonio turned to her. How far would he carry this charade? Reaching for her hand, he lifted her trembling fingers in his own.

"With all the traveling we've done, I haven't had a chance to present my bride properly with her wedding ring," he announced. His steady gaze never left her face as he drew her to her feet with the compelling grip of his hand.

Juliet could scarcely breathe, unable to draw her eyes away from his. She failed to steady either her hand or her nerves. She sensed no one else in the room was able to breathe either, including Clara, who had to be as startled as she was.

"Now that you've married me, my dear," Antonio continued, a glint of amusement in his eyes that only Juliet could see, "let me give you the ring that was destined for you."

He uncurled the fingers of his other hand, the act exposing a small suede pouch. From it he removed a delicate ring. Gold filigree, slightly tarnished with age, held within its prongs an oval ruby, small yet fine, its glint as bright as the gleam that lit Antonio's eyes.

Juliet couldn't believe what she was seeing. As if in a trance, she was unable to control her reaction as he slipped the ring onto the third finger of her left hand.

"This was my mother's," he said quietly. "She gave it to me after my father died, intending it to go to the bride of my choosing. That would be you."

"It's lovely," Juliet murmured. Stunned as she was into a

stupor, her voice sounded like a croak. She dropped into her chair, senseless.

"Oh, dearie me," Rose said breathlessly, "I've never witnessed anything so lovely in me life. Remember, Paddy, how we felt the same many years ago? It's hard to imagine now, but that was us when we courted. And where is your ring, Mr. Santilli?"

"How could I have forgotten?" From the pouch Antonio withdrew a second ring, a wider band that he started to slip on his own finger before he reconsidered. He glanced down at Juliet. "Would you do the honors, dearest?"

Feeling inadequate and unprepared for such a moment, Juliet rose mechanically, taking his left hand in her shaking fingers and slipping the ring onto his third finger.

"Now it's official, my love," she heard him say softly, her own eyes lowered, afraid to meet his.

As Rose wiped sentimental tears from her eyes, she bustled about, removing bowls from the table, squeezing Juliet's shoulders as she did so. Clara rose to assist her as the two chatted about the joys of witnessing matrimony in its earliest stages. The children clapped and returned to their chatter while Paddy Ryan announced awkwardly it was time to go to work.

Taking her seat, Juliet remained there amid the commotion, content to sit in the Ryans' kitchen as long as she could. She studied the ruby, too embarrassed to look at Antonio, so overcome with emotion, she couldn't speak. She was aware of him rising to help clean up, as if he understood she needed time to recover from the gesture. If she'd had any concerns about how authentic her marriage appeared, he had settled them with this act. She saw him exchange a look of amusement with Clara in passing.

Juliet felt more than humor as she twisted the narrow band about her finger. It fit perfectly, as if it were meant for her. She could hardly breathe as she stared at the deep red stone. Her birthstone. There was no way Antonio could know, caught up as he was in this giddy moment, that her birthday was in July.

The ring was hers, meant for her. If only for today, she reminded herself. The ring he'd placed on her finger, her birthstone, symbolized their special union—a union that would end when Isabel arrived.

Chapter Eight

Now I know you'll be wantin' a bath, Mrs. Santilli," Rose announced a half hour later, interrupting her thoughts. "Why don't we set up the tub in the kitchen? Kathleen can bring you anything you need."

Caught up in the morning's joy, Juliet found the prospect of a bath irresistible. Kathleen, the eldest daughter, began preparations so Juliet might bathe in private. After Rose sent the children outside to do chores and the kitchen had cleared of people, Juliet lowered herself into the metal basin. She felt her limbs relax, the soothing water caressing her skin and removing the layers of mud that had caked on when she'd fallen in the woods. Despite the cool rainwater, the bath felt comforting.

She could barely take her eyes from her left hand, the ruby gleaming as if she really were a new bride. Rose had placed the tub by the window, where the morning sunshine fell on Juliet, catching the glint of the stone, calming her spirits while it eased her aches. The ring was not hers to keep, yet somehow the excitement of having it on her finger filled her with a child-like hope she'd never known. She chided herself back to reality, realizing she was too old to play pretend.

The game would last only until she, Clara, and Antonio left the Ryans' home. Then they would return to reality. Juliet was surprised by the depth of her disappointment at the realization of how quickly their time together would come to an end. Kathleen stuck her head inside the door partway through her bath.

"I don't mean to disturb you, Mrs. Santilli," she said respect-fully. "There's homemade soap—oh, good, you found it."

"Thank you. That was thoughtful of you." Juliet smiled.

Kathleen frowned, seeing Juliet struggle to reach her back. "Do you need help? That mud must feel awful. What an ad-venture you've had. As if marriage isn't adventure enough."

Kathleen didn't know the half of it, Juliet thought, trying to hide an indulgent smile. She hadn't given a thought as to how she must look. She felt so stiff, she welcomed the attention. Rose insisted rainwater created better suds, and she was right. The sun on Juliet's flesh, the rhythmic motion of the sponge along her spine as Kathleen gently rubbed, and the water massaging her skin combined to lull her into a near stupor.

She almost forgot where she was until Rose's voice outside forced her out of her haze and back to reality. Juliet heard Rose in her Irish accent asking Antonio to retrieve something from the kitchen. She couldn't make out the words, but she recog-nized the reluctance in his subdued tone. Before she could pre-pare herself, the kitchen door was opened, and Antonio stepped inside. He froze in place, his eyes locking with hers.

How dare he stand there without moving? As her embarrass-ment rose, he turned away quickly, sparing her dignity. Juliet had never felt more vulnerable, although Antonio had behaved as a gentleman. Since he remained in the kitchen, she did the only thing she could think of to protect her modesty, leaning forward until only her shoulders and knees were exposed. The soapy water provided cover as Kathleen scrubbed her back. She dared not move too quickly, for fear the girl would suspect their secret.

Juliet raised her head slowly, her eyes meeting Antonio's as he glanced toward her. His silent apology was clear in his breathless, stunned reaction before he pulled his gaze away.

"Excuse me," he stammered, "Rose needs a big bowl—this must be it. I—I'm sorry."

Antonio waited, as if collecting his thoughts. Why, Juliet fretted, did he not leave? Knowing she was hidden by the wash-tub's high front end, she lowered herself farther into the sudsy water, shivering despite the heat of the tub. She had wanted to avoid this deception from the start.

The movement, though discreet, was not lost on Kathleen. "You're cold still? 'Ere, let me give you more water."

Before Juliet could protest, Kathleen scooped hot water from a bucket beside the washtub and poured it in. The bath became so intensely hot, Juliet was tempted to step out, but Antonio still remained. It was no less than she deserved, she thought, for her deception.

"Sorry to disturb you, dear," he murmured. "I'd best go back out."

At least he had the grace to keep his eyes averted. *Always the gentleman,* she thought with a grimace, *even under the most trying of circumstances.* Once he was safely outside, Juliet sat up slightly, her skin prickling with the burning sensation of the water. Kathleen burst into giggles.

"Oh, Mrs. Santilli," she said dreamily, "I hope if I ever marry, my husband adores me that much."

With only Kathleen in the kitchen, Juliet found her breath again, removed somewhat from the heat of the water and the heat of the moment. Her senses returning, she managed a shaky smile.

"Finding the right man isn't easy. Men can sometimes pretend to be something they aren't." Juliet chose her words carefully, thinking of the number of men who fit that description, from Cordelia's husband to her own pretend husband. She hoped the younger girl would not take her too literally. "I have no doubt you'll find the man meant for you when the time is right."

Perhaps I will as well, she told herself. The idea filled her with a pang of unexpected grief. It would not be this man, who already waited for Isabel.

Timing was everything, and hers had been the worst. She cringed at the thought of Isabel's reaction if she were ever to discover Juliet had slept in the same room as her betrothed.

And enjoyed the sensation more than she ever imagined.

In the ensuing silence, Kathleen readied towels while Juliet reflected on Antonio's curious entrance. No harm had been done. The soapsuds and her quick reaction had protected her privacy and saved her dignity. When she faced him again, she would act as if nothing had happened. Nothing had, she reminded herself.

She blushed furiously at the memory of the encounter, her indignation and embarrassment returning in force as the bubbles melted away. At least he'd had the decency to leave, however much he had seen. Though her appreciation mixed with irritation, she was grateful for his discretion. He'd played his role as husband admirably. Obviously, he knew more about drama than she thought.

At the same time, she felt oddly flattered that it had taken him more than a moment to look away. The thought warmed her cheeks faster than the heat of the water had.

By lunchtime, Juliet found the feeling of being physically refreshed slipping away, only to be replaced by frustration. She could not reveal to her hostess her desperation to find her nephew and his friend safe at home, but Rose Ryan insisted they could not leave until the doctor examined her ankle.

"Ye look like ye're ready for some air. 'Ere, take me shillelagh," she offered, handing Juliet a sturdy oaken walking stick that appeared to be carved by hand. "This'll give ye support. Don't go too far, now. Dr. Clark will be here soon."

With the aid of the shillelagh Juliet hobbled outdoors to sit in the rocking chair on the porch. As she struggled into her seat, she watched Antonio, his attention focused on Kathleen Ryan, helping her clean up after he'd assisted in preparing the hearty lunch Rose wanted them to have before they set off for home.

Juliet was surprised and ashamed to find herself resenting him for being so helpful, though she couldn't fathom why. She sat and pondered her own bad mood, glad when Clara interrupted her.

"What a good cook he is," Clara said as she joined Juliet on the porch. "Those clams were delicious, yet so simply prepared. I can still taste the lemon and pepper. And the garlic. The perfect accompaniment to potatoes and cabbage. Antonio says it's the way seafood is prepared in the south of Italy."

Why wouldn't he help with the cooking? Juliet asked herself in reckless silence. He owned a fish market and hoped to own a restaurant one day. She wouldn't expect to find him anywhere but in the kitchen. He had a warm, loving family at home that he provided for and missed as much as she missed her own. Rose's family seemed happy and content, probably much like Antonio's.

"What do I know about Italian food?" she brooded aloud.

Clara stared at her. "Don't tell me you don't recognize fine food when you see it. You tasted it, didn't you?"

"Yes, but I'm sure my opinion was influenced by Kathleen."

Clara's eyebrows furrowed. "What are you talking about?"

"She complimented his cuisine as if she'd never had anything like it. That must be why he paid her so much attention."

"She probably *hasn't* had anything like it. I don't imagine there's much Italian food around here. Antonio was simply being nice to his hostess' daughter. She thinks he's married to you, remember," Clara added.

"No doubt he feels right at home. Rose Ryan has a big family, just like he does. It couldn't be more different from mine." Feeling the color flame in her cheeks, Juliet gave the rocking chair a violent push with one foot. Before she could stop herself, her feelings poured out. "Why does Papa paint Cordelia as being so awful? Everyone who knew her liked her more than I expected. Mrs. Wetherall, Aunt Muriel, even Antonio. They feel bad for her, as if she's deserving of sympathy, rather than being the cause of Papa's grief."

"You felt that way in Boston when you saw how she lived. She had a hard marriage and a hard life. You know your father can be difficult. Even you hoped he wouldn't die of apoplexy if the children got home first." Clara smiled gently, squeezing Juliet's hand. "You have only your father's perspective. You've always seen her through his eyes and heard his version of what happened. Cordelia might have told the story quite differently."

A brief calm stilled Juliet's emotions and stopped the

churning inside. Somehow, she could not let go of her disapproval of Antonio's criticism. Papa had cared for his children after Mum died. Juliet's family had much more than Antonio's in a material sense, yet his seemed happier and more attached to one another. Unable to fathom the uneven distribution of joy, she resented him and hated herself for feeling as she did.

"I wish Antonio wouldn't question Papa's motives," she said stubbornly. "It's as if he's made up his mind not to like him without having met him. Does he think his own family is better?"

Juliet was taken aback by the unexpected rebuke that followed from Clara.

"He certainly does not. It's taken him a long time to reach the degree of success he has. You might not know this," Clara returned, leaning back in her chair, "but his father was a national hero in Italy. He fought in the revolution that claimed his life. Since Antonio has also lost a parent, you have more in common than you think. Give him credit, Juliet. Did you know early this morning, before you were awake, he traced our steps back through the woods to retrieve our belongings? I call that a man who cares for your welfare. A man who cares for you."

Clara fell silent, leaving Juliet riddled with guilt as her pride slipped away in one swallow. She felt crestfallen at the realization of how she had unintentionally belittled him. For a long time, she had seen him as little more than an immigrant, a former shepherd, a fisherman even.

How little she knew of the immigrant experience. What did she know of war, for that matter? All she understood of the War Between the States was secondhand from reading newspaper accounts and hearing her father's reaction. Her own brother had run when the fighting at Antietam became too intense. He had never been the hero Antonio's father must have been.

Her gaze fell on the ruby that graced her hand, a hand scraped by brambles from her fall, marred by calluses from correcting papers. How perfectly the birthstone fit. The ring gave her beauty, a loveliness borrowed until it was returned to its rightful owner.

A ring not meant for her. A ring intended for a woman who had the courage to leave her homeland to start life anew in another country, in a different language.

Not intended, Juliet forced herself to admit, for a woman too cowardly to face her fears of commitment, of defying her father, of caring for a wayward nephew who might not love her. She did not want to think she came from a family of cowards. Shame rushed through her at the recognition of her own conceit. Clara's hand covering her own startled her to attention.

"It isn't my intention to hurt you, child," Juliet heard Clara say softly, Juliet's eyes too filled with tears to see the woman who had been a substitute mother to her. "I just want you to see what's before you. You can't split love in half. Marriage doesn't stretch that far. Don't resent Antonio because of the demands your papa makes on you. Don't you think I've seen the way you look at him? He feels the same, Juliet."

"He has Isabel," Juliet said, shocked at the fierceness in her tone, at the intensity of her own jealousy.

"She hasn't come yet. Do you ever wonder why? Antonio's been here seven years." Juliet looked up, surprised to see the worry in Clara's face. "I want you to be happy, dear. I know you care for him, and I believe he feels as you do. It's your papa's reaction that worries me. I don't think he's ready for this."

Clara placed the emphasis on the last word, Juliet noticed, where it belonged. An even bigger question was whether Juliet herself was ready for what was to come.

She had endured significant changes on this trip. She was no longer the contented, obedient daughter who'd left Papa less than a week ago. A restlessness she'd never experienced stirred within her, making a whirlwind of her once settled existence.

Yet, for her, nothing had changed ultimately. She hadn't planned to wed when she set out, and now she never would. The difference was that she would know there was someone meant for her, someone who was engaged to another. It didn't matter that he had flaws: that he was quick to anger, that he rightfully resented being a victim of discrimination, that his quick tongue offended her at those times he underestimated her.

Somehow Juliet saw past those. Antonio's insight, patience, and determination to support his family diminished his flaws and raised him in her esteem. Yet, he was not likely to see her as anything more than a loving daughter trying to compensate for her sister's failures in their father's eyes. Even if he saw her in a more flattering light, Papa would never permit an immigrant to court her. Similar circumstances had ruined Cordelia's life.

"Who could not love you?" Antonio had said to her. He could not, for he had Isabel. Juliet resented a woman she'd never met, a woman who had never set foot on American soil. A woman who had fewer material things than she did.

She had one thing Juliet could never have. She had Antonio.

Clara had reason to be worried. Papa had sent her all the way to Boston with her companion to retrieve her nephew and bring him home to Maine where he belonged.

No part of the trip had gone as planned. Papa would be severely disappointed when he learned the truth. Not only had she lost Marcus, she'd managed to lose her heart in the process—and to an immigrant yet.

Antonio helped the Ryan daughters wring water from the pile of wet laundry heaped on the washboard after lunch. He'd been pleased with the hearty fare he helped Rose prepare in honor of their leavetaking. While not elaborate, the meal had been almost filling enough to sustain them for the rest of their journey.

Despite his conversation with the children, he couldn't keep his mind off the woman who sat so quietly across the table from him. Juliet hadn't looked at him directly since he'd unexpectedly caught her in the bath that morning. He'd seen her vulnerable expression, pale throat, and thin shoulders above the water, the fear in her eyes when he'd invaded her privacy. He fully expected she would want him to continue the pretense of being husband and wife in front of the oldest Ryan girl. He was surprised by her embarrassed reaction and his own disappointment over it. He'd rather have seen joy upon his arrival than suspicion.

Lunch was no better. He'd hoped that if he paid attention to Kathleen, his traveling companion might feel less intimidated by his presence. The plan didn't go as he'd hoped. He hadn't found a moment to explain to his pretend wife his hesitation to honor Rose's request to fetch a bowl from the kitchen. Rose believed they were married. He wasn't about to raise her suspicions now, after the kindness she'd shown them.

He couldn't keep his thoughts from reverting back to last night's conversation at bedtime. The trust Juliet placed in him made his heart soar. More than anything, he'd wanted to illuminate parts of her sister's past that would otherwise have remained in shadow, leaving Juliet in doubt forever. He was one of very few who could enlighten her.

Yet, she'd avoided the subject of her father. He went along with her silence, hoping it might encourage her to speak freely. Instead she had kept her distance ever since.

He wondered if it was Hans who filled Juliet's thoughts. Until Clara had told him, Antonio had had no idea there was anyone special in Juliet's life. Juliet said little about Hans when Antonio raised the subject of her father's attitude toward a suitor. If she were waiting until she and Hans could find the right moment to present the idea of a betrothal to her father, she might fear that Antonio's presence in the kitchen had compromised her virtue.

Shamefaced, he lowered his gaze. He would never intentionally cause her a moment's grief. At the same time, a stab of envy pierced his usually serene spirit. Could it be that Hans held a special place in her heart, but her father's desire to protect her had kept her silent? The young man must be special indeed, if the subject had been too painful for Juliet to address.

From across the yard, he watched Juliet assist Rose at the clothesline, hobbling about with the aid of a walking stick. Clad in Kathleen's lavender homespun dress for lack of anything dry, its ruffled collar exposing her neck and framing her throat in a most flattering way, Juliet looked feminine and sweet. He had seen her insecurities emerge and her obstinacy disappear in the last few days. This woman was far more appealing than the stiff aristocrat he'd known in Boston.

Antonio glanced briefly at the gold band on his left hand. Unaccustomed to its weight on his finger, he wondered if he could live up to its promise. The ring represented about as much truth on his hand as his mother's ruby did on Juliet, for Hans might replace it with his own one day. Antonio's resentment stung. Her suitor was a lucky man to have the affection of a woman like Juliet. Dismay filled Antonio as he realized she'd return the ring at some point, and he'd be forced to repeat the gesture with Isabel. The idea of doing it a second time seemed hollow now.

Kathleen drew his attention from the rings as she ran into the backyard to announce the arrival of Dr. Clark at the front door. Over Juliet's protests, Rose led her inside, insisting the visit was necessary as she called to Antonio to follow. By the time he reached the parlor, Juliet waited anxiously on the couch for the doctor to examine her ankle and give his permission for her to travel.

"Hold your wife's ankle, Mr. Santilli, while I wrap it," Dr. Clark instructed. "This bandage should give her enough support so she can walk without putting undue pressure on it. It's a bad sprain, but it isn't as bad as I first thought."

Antonio didn't dare look at Juliet's face as he lifted her skirts tenderly above her knee. Holding her calf steady as the doctor wound the bandage snugly about her ankle, he felt the delicacy of her skin. The tenderness in her ankle must have left her in great pain, for he felt her leg tense as she gritted her teeth between tightly closed lips. Her knuckles turned white as she clutched the arm of the sofa.

It cost her dearly, Antonio knew, to pretend she had the emotional strength to endure it. Relieved the injury wasn't more severe, he was grateful he'd been the lucky one to rescue her. The sensation of carrying her in his arms, holding her close against his chest, was a memory that lingered like the wild orchids in the hills around his home in Italy, sweet yet strong.

"That's better," Dr. Clark said when he'd finished. "I see no reason you can't continue your journey with the aid of a walking stick. You can rest once you're home." He smiled at Antonio. "You'll have to do the chores for a few days, I'm afraid, while your wife heals. I'm headed for the coast if you need a ride. I can take you as far as Camden."

"Doing chores isn't a problem," Antonio promised. He allowed himself a glance at Juliet, the brightness in her face at the prospect of home lifting his spirits. "What do you think, my dear? Shall we take Dr. Clark up on his offer of a ride?"

"That would be wonderful," she said, relief in her tone. "It's so kind of you, Doctor. Will we all fit in your carriage?"

"We'll make room. There's space in the back where I put my medical supplies. It will be faster than waiting for the coach."

As easily as that, Antonio realized, their short visit with the Ryans was about to end. What would happen to his time with Juliet once they were at her home? Would the end of their journey also put an end to their association?

With that jolt of reality facing him, he no longer felt as enthusiastic about reaching their destination.

Chapter Nine

It wasn't long before they were ready to leave. Antonio had barely unpacked his belongings and had few items to replace in his knapsack. He was glad he had retrieved their luggage from the woods as promptly as he had, for there would be no chance now. In the time it took Juliet and Clara to pack, he helped Rose Ryan plant tomatoes. The weather was promising, he observed as he gazed at the blue sky, ideal for a ride through the countryside.

How ironic their pretend marriage was about to come to an end now that they'd reached a truce of sorts, seeing each other with mutual respect as they pursued the children. Having Juliet as his pretend wife was perfect practice for the day he would be wed.

Wed to Isabel, he reminded himself with a start. With a sense of guilt he realized how little he'd thought about Isabel during the past few days. His mother would be pleased that he genuinely looked forward to marriage when the time was right.

Except Antonio wasn't sure the woman was right.

Even if she were, when would the time be right? When Isabel was ready to leave Italy? By then, Juliet might be wed to her beau, even though she had convinced herself she'd never marry. Maybe caring for Marcus would challenge her enough to keep her fulfilled.

The thought made Antonio smile. Not only was he relieved, he was happy that Isabel hadn't come yet. He wished she never would.

For if she did, he reflected with a sense of impending dread, he would be marrying the wrong woman.

The smile left his face just as quickly. He certainly could not entertain the prospect of courting Juliet. How could someone so refined and sophisticated feel any attraction to someone as inadequate as he must seem to her? Juliet Halliday had been raised with poetry and eloquence, the daughter of a noted professor who taught Shakespeare. Merely being in his presence would make Antonio feel like a fraud. With her father's suspicious attitude toward immigrants, he didn't stand a chance. Hans was an easier obstacle.

Antonio was learned now and proud of it. It had not always been so. He had been illiterate until a few short years before he came to America. He spent hours aboard ship reading and studying, preparing for a better life on the other side of the Atlantic. It was on the journey that he discovered Lord Byron, when he'd read "She Walks in Beauty." At the time, it had reminded him of Isabel. Shakespeare had come next. And then, of course, Juliet.

Antonio had respect for himself, knowing he had earned it. Yet, would his hard-won literacy be enough to satisfy Juliet's father? The idea of meeting Professor Halliday intimidated him.

The professor's intolerance toward immigrants smacked of a discrimination to which Antonio was accustomed. He had lived long enough among Boston's wealthy aristocrats to know most turned their backs on the impoverished immigrants who set foot on their docks from European ports daily. To upper-class Bostonians, the Irish were invisible, and the Italians were little better. To defeat such prejudice was a victory Antonio might never see in his lifetime.

Juliet's emergence from the cottage brought him back to the present. While she couldn't walk as gracefully as usual, she still walked in beauty. When she was finally ready, taking what seemed an unnecessarily long time—just as the women in his own family tended to do—Antonio assisted her into the front seat of Dr. Clark's open conveyance, planning to ride alongside Clara in back. He handed up her walking stick before lifting their suitcases into the back of the wagon. Juliet turned to watch, her eyes filled with earnestness mixed with what looked like melancholy.

"You've been so kind, Antonio," she said. "I appreciate all you've done for us more than you will ever know."

Glancing into her face, he saw sincerity in her soft green eyes. The blue blood had been replaced in recent days by the real Juliet, a sensitive and gentle woman who was confident enough to reveal her emotions. He felt his giddiness return, powerless to stop it as he moved to stand beside her, gazing up at her on the front seat of the wagon.

"Since I can't contact any of my acquaintances out here," he said, "let's take that local boat of yours up the Penobscot—the Boston Boat. It should ease your mind to know we're almost home."

"It does." With a brief, uncertain smile she turned away.

As the sunshine softened her pale cheek, he realized how deeply the past few days had touched him. Studying her profile, he was surprised that her expression wasn't entirely happy. He noticed her fingering her reticule again, no doubt reminded of the photograph of Marcus within. A boy she didn't yet know.

"Aren't you relieved we're going home?" he asked, concerned.

"I'm glad," she assured him. "And Clara just learned from Mrs. Ryan that the circus has been in Portland. That confirms what you suspected. Mr. Tarry is heading north, just as we are."

"I'm glad to hear it." Antonio felt his worries about Maria ease a bit but was surprised to hear the doubt in Juliet's voice. "What about your feeling that Marcus' note was sincere, that he was headed home? Don't you believe it still?"

Her eyes clouded. "I don't know what to believe," she admitted. "I have misgivings about the future. All parts of it."

"But we're so close." He laughed, covering her hand with his. "You should feel happy and relieved, not worried."

"I don't know what we'll find. I don't know how I'll raise Marcus by myself. From what you've described, I'll have a very difficult boy to cope with." She shook her head, bewilderment crossing her face. "I once told you, I've never really pictured myself with children. I meant it."

"But you're a teacher," he reminded her. "You'll be fine."

"It's different having your own." She seemed embarrassed to raise the subject. "Papa's of the opinion I will never marry, and I always felt the same. I don't know what kind of reception Marcus will face without me there. I almost hope he's joined the circus so we get home before he does."

Antonio was startled to see tears spring to her eyes.

"My father isn't noble like yours," she admitted. "He isn't any kind of hero, much less one who fought for his country. He's more likely to fight for his principles. Even my brother was a deserter during the war. What if Papa doesn't accept Marcus?"

"He will," he said automatically, his grip tightening on her hands as he squeezed them in his own. He knew as he spoke he felt no such confidence. Juliet's father might well reject both children, viewing them as guttersnipes fit only for the likes of Boston, especially after his differences with Cordelia. Antonio pulled his worries under control. No father could be so harsh.

"I'm frightened," Juliet whispered, her eyes boring into his from her perch in the wagon.

"Everything will work out for the best," he assured her, gazing into her eyes. "You'll see. We haven't long to wait now."

She looked away, her attention caught by a distant movement. "Dr. Clark is coming. I suppose we must leave the Ryans' sooner or later. Now that the time has come, I confess I don't quite feel ready." She gave him a nervous smile. "I have money in my suitcase to pay him. I must do that before we go."

"I've taken care of it," Antonio said carelessly, turning away, aware of her gaze on him. "Where's your dress? I mean—"

Juliet blushed a becoming shade of rose at his mistake, her olive eyes amused beneath their long lashes. "I know what you mean. I traded dresses with Kathleen. Mine still wasn't dry, so I left it with her as thanks for the family's help." She gazed at the trees, her tone deliberately casual. "I appreciate your discretion this morning. One might consider it almost chivalrous."

"Almost?" He smiled, happy to see her addressing the issue. "Speaking of discretion, I see the whole Ryan clan has gathered at the window to see us off. Here they come now, with Dr. Clark and Clara."

Juliet turned toward the house, smiling as the family approached across the yard. "They're very curious about us."

"Can you blame them? They don't get many visitors. We've played our part well. I wouldn't want to disappoint them now."

She turned her face to Antonio's, their eyes meeting. Impulsively he went to the driver's side and climbed into the wagon to sit beside her. It was only natural to celebrate his wife's recovery, after all. Juliet watched him with an inquisitive but inviting expression. When he saw no discomfort in her eyes, he lifted her hand in his, raised it to his lips, and kissed it.

"A touch of affection," he explained. "Within the context of our marriage, of course."

Her eye caught the tender humor in his. She responded in kind. "Of course."

Then, cradling her face between his hands, Antonio stroked her cheeks with his fingers, his heart soaring as he felt the softness of her skin. The shock he'd seen in her eyes during their unexpected morning encounter was gone. In its place he saw curiosity, encouragement even. Slowly he lowered his face, his lips covering hers, experiencing their moist fullness. He enjoyed the experience with an intensity he hadn't expected.

Juliet did not pull away but instead relaxed into the kiss. At the doctor's approach she pulled herself upright, moving away slightly. Antonio jumped down, his feet hitting the ground but feeling as light as if he'd landed on the cottage rooftop.

"I expect the ankle to heal nicely," Dr. Clark told Juliet as he stepped up beside the wagon. "Take my advice, young lady, and stay off it once you get home. Your husband will need to change the bandage until you're completely recuperated."

Glancing toward Antonio, Juliet managed a smile that made his heart skip a beat. "Thank you, Doctor. I don't think my husband will mind. He's a very helpful sort."

Antonio did not hesitate to add his thoughts. "I'm probably better able to care for her than anyone."

It was all he could do to tear himself away from Juliet, who seemed so content, she beamed as brightly as the sun. He took Clara's hand as she approached and assisted her into the back of the wagon, settling her comfortably on the hay before hoisting himself up and sitting on his travel bag.

With his fellow travelers Antonio waved a bittersweet goodbye to the Ryan family standing beside the cottage gate. Rose and Kathleen waved vociferously, calling their fond farewells when the party set off. Dr. Clark chatted with Juliet as they turned into the road, the noise of carriage wheels on gravel drowning out their voices.

Antonio wondered if she could feel his eyes on her. He found it hard to remove his gaze from her worn black bonnet with its tattered ribbon. She appeared to have recovered from the shock of her interrupted bath. He turned to Clara, prepared to take advantage of the privacy the noise offered. She spoke first.

"Are you looking forward to getting on with our journey?" she asked with a smile. "These two days have been a fascinating interlude, especially that wedding."

"It has been pleasant. But we need to focus on the future. I look forward to finding Maria safe." Antonio stretched out his legs in the hay before him. He was glad to have another chance to speak privately with Clara before meeting Juliet's father. "I have concerns about the next stop on our journey."

"That's only natural," Clara agreed, assuming a formal tone, "since you haven't met Professor Halliday."

He wasn't surprised to see that she understood without explanation. He glanced forward to make sure Dr. Clark still had Juliet engaged in conversation.

"I'm concerned not only about Marcus and Maria, but about what her father's attitude has done to her," he said quietly, nodding toward Juliet. "She contradicts herself, saying she can't see herself with children, yet she's a teacher about to assume care of her nephew. She doesn't expect to marry, but I think her father has convinced her of it. She's bound for disappointment because of his expectations." He shook his head, angered by what he saw as manipulation on her father's part. "He must be a selfish old man."

"Don't let her know you feel that way," Clara advised. "She adores her father, selfish or not. She thinks he walks on water."

Antonio shook his head. "There's only One who does that. I'd like to know more about the professor."

Clara gave him a warning look that revealed her reluctance to say anything that might betray her employer. He reassured her before continuing.

"I worry that he dominates her," he explained. "You once mentioned a suitor from her past. A man named Hans."

"Hans Eichmann." A troubled expression crossed Clara's face before it vanished into her vault of discretion. "Perhaps I shouldn't have mentioned him. Juliet seemed very much in love with him at one time. I was certain he was the one."

He joined his hands behind his head. "Obviously, he wasn't."

"How can you be sure?" Doubt in her voice, Clara stared at him. "There's still Isabel to consider."

Antonio resisted the thought but knew he had to address it sooner or later. "Yes, there's Isabel. But there is also Juliet. And there's more at stake now. Has no one else offered for her?"

Clara shook her head. "She hasn't encouraged anyone. Her students keep her too busy to consider the possibility of marriage. Frankly, I think no man has had the courage."

Antonio grinned in spite of his worries. "To approach her father, or her?"

"Maybe both."

Antonio studied Juliet's profile up ahead while he still could. So that's how it was, he reflected. She'd rather shield her fears behind a confidence she didn't possess than defy her father. He suspected that if he probed deeper, he'd find enough insecurity to keep men at bay the rest of her life.

His eyes dropped to the heavy gold ring on his left hand. The ring had to remind Juliet of their bond as much as it did him. Surely, her devotion to her father wasn't stronger than her desire to live the life she wanted. She hadn't met the right man.

But that, he suspected, had already changed. Somehow he had to find a way to open her eyes.

The miles to Camden passed too quickly for Antonio. While his mind was squarely in the present, his heart remained focused on his recent change of heart. Shortly after they arrived in town, they learned a Boston Boat would head north within the hour, saving them more time.

Clara excused herself soon after to visit a tearoom, a discreet gesture for which Antonio was grateful. The housekeeper had provided an opportunity for him to have a private moment with Juliet before meeting her father at last.

Antonio refrained from offering Juliet his arm as they approached the docks to wait for the boat that would take them home. From her silence, he sensed she was preparing for their return, trying to decide what to do if they found Marcus and Maria at home—and what to do if they didn't. She probably worried more about the reunion with her father than he did. Hoping to ease her tension, he asked her about the architecture and flora of the region as they strolled along.

When they had exhausted the topic, Antonio searched for the words to apologize for criticizing her father when Juliet began fingering the ruby. Abruptly, she pulled the ring from her finger and turned to him, her lovely eyes brimming with misery.

"I cannot keep what isn't mine," she murmured, her voice trembling, "so I'm returning this to you. May Isabel wear it in good health."

His heart sank as Juliet thrust the ruby at him. Reluctantly he removed the gray pouch from his pocket and slipped the ring inside.

"I was surprised how perfectly it fit you," he admitted, returning the pouch to his pocket. "As if it were made for you."

"I wasn't surprised. The ruby is my birthstone." A smile spread across her dainty features abruptly, brightening her face as if the sun had emerged from behind the clouds. She raised her eyes to his. "I'll always be grateful for all you've done, Antonio. For carrying me even while I felt like an old woman. And for what you did for the Ryan family. You made them feel like they were part of the adventure. They were, of course."

"It was my pleasure. And though you use the past tense, it isn't over yet." He spoke softly, his eyes never leaving hers. "I'm sorry to see our days together come to an end."

"Was the ring really your mother's?" With the ruby out of her hands she managed to pull her emotions under control.

"Yes. After we came to America, she didn't wear it anymore. She felt she'd left her husband behind in Italy. I think she left part of her heart as well."

Juliet guessed at the sentiment he'd hoped not to express.

"So she gave it to you for your future bride. And what about this ring?" She touched her finger gently to the band he wore, pulling it away quickly when the tip brushed his flesh. "Was it your father's?"

"Originally, yes. I suppose I ought to put it away."

Antonio hesitated longer than necessary. Once the ring was out of sight, the pretend marriage was gone as well. He slipped it into the pouch, trying to ignore the gesture's significance.

"More recently it was worn by my older brother," he said.

He saw surprise in her eyes. "I thought you were the oldest in your family."

Antonio shook his head. "Carlo drowned in a boating accident before we came to America. I always felt I had to live up to his accomplishments. I considered myself inferior somehow, second best in my mother's eyes. Strange, after Carlo was gone, I had even more to prove than when he was alive."

Juliet watched him with knowing eyes, listening to his feelings on a subject he knew was familiar to her.

"I always felt inadequate next to Cordelia," she admitted softly. "Papa loved her so. He was shattered when she left. Sometimes I've felt as if I were living in her shadow."

"You once said I didn't know what it was to be a younger child. You see? We have more in common than you thought."

Antonio gazed at the sky as the sun split the clouds, relieved to see blue before they sailed instead of gray. "I suppose comparing our travels to *The Odyssey* isn't all that far-fetched. Odysseus was a shepherd once, like I was."

"Odysseus was a warrior," she reminded him, "and you're a warrior of sorts, too, battling the stigma of prejudice." She reddened at having raised a subject too close to home. *Her own home,* he thought. She continued in a tone less fierce. "Different from your father's, but a battle nonetheless. Here's our boat."

Juliet fell silent, undoubtedly worrying about the same thing he was—that the worst battle lay ahead. As Antonio watched her, hearing the horn of the Boston Boat approaching the dock, he knew there was only one person to whom he had to prove himself.

She stood before him now.

Though it extended the time he was able to spend with Juliet, Antonio found the passage to Stockton Village agonizingly slow. The ride was marred by Juliet's unexpected seasickness.

"It's just nerves," he comforted her, rubbing her back as she stood by the railing.

"I thought I'd calmed them," she murmured, even her voice queasy. "At least the salt air makes me feel a little better."

"It isn't that unusual," he reassured her. "When I sailed from Italy, I found even calm seas can upset the stomach."

"But I've sailed all my life," Juliet protested. "I don't know why this trip is different."

It was the impending return, he knew, that had upset her. This trip was harder, because so much was at stake. No one knew what lay ahead once they dropped anchor. All Antonio knew was that reaching her hometown represented the end of their life together.

He was convinced her self-doubt revolved around her family. No doubt Professor Halliday had lost his older daughter through what he saw as betrayal. Consequently, he'd tried to turn Juliet into the loyal daughter, just like Cordelia's namesake. Juliet, he suspected, was more like her own namesake.

Antonio would not make her life more difficult by arguing with her father about his opinion of immigrants. He already regretted the derogatory remarks he'd made, realizing the comments had only widened the barrier between himself and Juliet. It was far more urgent that they find the children and tend to their needs.

Yet, he remembered thinking early on in their trip that at some point he would feel like a grave man for agreeing to travel with Juliet. He had more in common with Mercutio than he'd previously believed.

It wasn't a sword, but Cupid's arrow, that had pierced him, he knew now. And the chances were good that he would fall as swiftly as Mercutio had.

Chapter Ten

Juliet did not relax until the big white farmhouse came into view and she had limped across the front porch to Papa's waiting arms. Night had fallen by the time they reached home, but her feeling of relief was greater than at any time she could remember. His embrace was more comforting than it had felt in years. The strength of his hug made her feel like a child again.

"You can't imagine how wonderful it is to see you, Papa." With a final squeeze, she held him at arm's length. Shock crept over her. She didn't remember him looking this frail.

Releasing her father, she stepped inside the house, taking care not to twist her ankle further. She looked about the parlor, its cozy furnishings in the same places they had been as long as she'd lived there. While the sight comforted her, she was surprised how shabby it appeared. It was as if the whole room needed a change, refreshing and long overdue, to perk it up.

"What's happened to your ankle?" Papa demanded behind her.

"It's a long story," Juliet said, looking around for Marcus as Clara came indoors, Antonio lagging behind her, "but I'll be fine. Papa, this is Antonio Santilli, Maria's brother. He helped bring me home safely. Without his help and Clara's, I'm not sure I would have made it."

Antonio bowed with respect. "It's an honor to meet you, Professor Halliday."

"Oh, Papa, it's so good to see you again." Untying her bonnet and tossing it on a chair, Juliet turned to her father eagerly. "Are the children upstairs? I'd like to see them."

Her father frowned at her, his white mustache twitching in a signal that meant something was wrong. "So would I," he replied in his raspy voice. "Marcus is not here."

For a moment Juliet thought she had misunderstood.

"But I wired you," she said faintly.

"I received your message," he said, exasperation in his voice, "but if Marcus is coming, it's by a mule that's even slower than the one you must have taken. He hasn't arrived yet."

Juliet felt her throat constrict. "What do you mean, he hasn't arrived? He left Boston before we did."

"I'm afraid you're mistaken, my dear. He isn't here, nor is his little friend."

Terror flooded through her. If Marcus and Maria had headed directly home, as she believed they would, they should be here by now. Had they followed the circus? Not knowing what to think, she looked to Antonio for confirmation. His expression was numb, unreadable.

"You haven't heard from them, sir?" Antonio asked her father.

"That's what I said," Papa snapped. "I assumed there was a change in plans. Since no one takes the time to keep me informed, I've no way of knowing what's going on."

Juliet did not want to alarm her father, but the absence of Marcus and Maria here at home, where they were expected, was a bitter disappointment. Could it be that she and Antonio had come all this way for nothing? She could barely conceal her worry. Clara walked up beside her, laying a hand on her arm to reassure her.

"I'm sure everything is all right, Professor." Clara spoke up quickly, glancing at Juliet. "I wonder if they followed the circus after all."

"What's this about a circus?" her father demanded.

"Papa, you haven't heard of any circus in the area, have you?" Juliet asked, her anxiety building.

"I know nothing about a circus. At any rate, I know my grandson doesn't belong in one," her father scoffed. "Could he have remained in Boston?"

"We looked everywhere we could think of before we left the city," Antonio answered after an awkward pause. "We felt sure they would be here. We spent all our money getting home. I didn't think we'd use so much, but with our misadventures—"

"You mean you don't know where the children are? They're obviously somewhere you didn't think of." Her father looked from one to the other, raising an eyebrow as he fixed his gaze on Antonio. "If you'd searched carefully enough, it seems to me, you would have found them. I don't care what it costs, young man. My grandson's life is at stake."

Juliet saw Antonio give her father a dark look. She was glad Papa turned away before their eyes met. She fought her light-headedness as she addressed Antonio.

"Where could they be?" she asked in a near whisper. "Could we have missed them along the way? Do you really think they followed the circus after all, as Clara suggested?"

"We didn't miss them," he said slowly. "Marcus tricked us, like I said he did."

Juliet heard a sharp thud as her father's cane struck the floor behind them. "Whatever is going on, Juliet? Why is there no sign of the boy? I demand to know where my grandson is."

"I'd like to know where my sister is," Antonio snapped. He turned away abruptly, his tone edged with reflective bitterness. "If only Marcus' mother hadn't died so young. The boy's had a hard life. What else can you expect from someone like that?"

Both he and Juliet jumped in alarm as her father slammed his cane down, letting it clatter to the floor. Papa's eyebrows drew together, giving him a fearsome appearance, hands on his hips.

"What do you mean, 'someone like that'? My grandson is a fine boy."

"I intended no insult, Professor," Antonio said, his courteous tone filling Juliet with relief. If only it would pacify her father.

"I'm sure whatever behavior you take exception to is nothing that can't be mended once he's home with his family," Papa said emphatically. "If he has any objectionable qualities, it's because he has had to work for a living instead of going to school. His boss probably didn't pay enough to make the work worthwhile."

The truce was short-lived. Juliet tensed as she saw Antonio draw himself up.

"Excuse me, sir," he began respectfully. "I was his boss. He was paid as much as is customary for a child in the city. No more but no less. He was given a reasonable wage."

Juliet's heart sank as her father frowned at Antonio. "You fail to understand, young man. Perhaps it is because you are a foreigner, but it's my opinion that you are more responsible for his disappearance than anyone else. We might all be better off if children remained in the classroom where they belonged. If you hadn't come here, Marcus might still be safe and sound, and we would know where he was."

"And what of my sister?" Antonio shot back. "Your grandson left town with an eight-year-old child. It's her I worry about."

The men faced each other across the room. Juliet remained rooted where she stood, too shocked to defend Antonio. Jaw firm, eyes filled with an emotion she couldn't fathom, he stared at her father. Relief filled her as Papa turned his glare upon her, for it would deflect his anger from Antonio.

"I don't know what possessed you to bring this ruffian into my home, Juliet, but I'll expect him to be gone by morning. The hour is late. The children are supposedly headed here. Since there's nothing more we can do this evening, I'm going to retire. We shall continue this tomorrow."

With his familiar, perpetual scowl, her father snuffed out his pipe, ignoring Antonio. As he stooped to pick up the cane he'd thrown to the floor, Juliet rushed to his aid, nearly colliding with Antonio as she did so. Antonio reached it first, offering the cane solemnly to her father. She watched Papa accept it slowly, his eyes never leaving Antonio's face, as if he feared this unwelcome visitor would strike him if he weren't vigilant.

"Instead of taking advantage of my hospitality and making derogatory remarks about my grandson," her father said slowly, "you might help by searching for him instead. Once we find him, I have no intention of returning him to your service so you can put him to work doing slave labor again. Good night, Juliet."

Her father turned unsteadily and hobbled toward the stairs, waving his hand dismissively as she moved to assist him, a sharp pain stabbing at her ankle. Juliet dropped her arms to her sides helplessly. She could not imagine a worse introduction for the two men she cared about most deeply. Her father's behavior should not surprise her. Yankee to the core, he was an educated country gentleman well respected by his peers in his teaching days and by his neighbors.

Yet he had little idea of the pressures of living in a city like Boston. Having dismissed his elder daughter from his life, he could not know how it had worn her down, taunting and tainting Marcus with its temptations. At the same time, she reflected, those pressures had toughened Antonio, prompting him to rise to the challenge of becoming the best at what he did amid the city's hardships.

Trying to adjust her shattered expectations, she watched her father mount the stairs slowly. Not only had she assumed she would find Marcus and Maria waiting, she'd hoped her father would approve of Antonio. If Papa had any idea of the ordeal she'd endured, he would thank Antonio for coming to her aid. The absence of either left her in a state of stunned disappointment.

Juliet waited until he had turned the corner toward his bedroom and she heard the door close before she turned back to Antonio. She was almost too embarrassed by Papa's behavior to speak. Clara saved her the trouble, addressing them sympathetically.

"Why don't you both wait here while I go upstairs and prepare a room for Antonio? It will only take a few minutes," she offered. After giving it more thought, she appeared to change her mind, glancing from Juliet to Antonio. "Take as long as you need. Whenever you decide to come upstairs, the room will be ready."

"Please excuse my father," Juliet begged after Clara left. "He's so worried about Marcus, he can't think clearly."

"You needn't apologize." The tension left Antonio's face as he grinned. "We're awfully close to Verona, after all."

She had to laugh at his words. "He's treating you like a Montague. I'm sorry, Antonio." She felt the heat rise in her face as she grew serious again. "I never expected this. I worried he'd be filled with alarm, wanting us to work together to find the children."

Antonio shrugged, shaking his head. "How like my mother he sounds. I can hear her saying the same. 'If you hadn't come here, Maria would be safe and sound.' They forget nationality means nothing when a child's welfare is at stake. But we're home, the rain's over, and you can finally rest," he reminded her, adding cautiously, "Even if you don't think you can, you must try. Why don't we go out on the porch? Be careful of that ankle."

He held the porch door open as she stepped into the night, closing it quietly behind them. The warm night air enveloped her, welcome after the rain, as the sound of crickets reminded her she was home again. Uncertain that her legs would support her after witnessing such behavior from her father, Juliet appreciated the gesture. She looked up into the sky, enjoying the countless stars. She hadn't been able to see them in the city's haze.

"With Cordelia gone, Papa can't bear the thought of losing Marcus. I appreciate you trying to make light of it." She tried to quell her anxiety, but her sense of urgency refused to subside. "I worry about the children. There has to be an explanation. Maybe they didn't come by steamship after all."

As her emotions built, she was overcome with humility at his efforts to comfort her. She leaned against a post wearily.

"Antonio, it isn't just Papa's behavior I have to apologize for. It's my own. I said some harsh things. Please forgive me. Marcus obviously led Maria astray." She dropped into the rocking chair, her legs shaky. "You're probably right. What if he tricked us and went elsewhere? We might never find them. Maybe photographs are all I have left of him."

"Hush," he murmured, laying a strong, supportive hand on her shoulder. "We'll find them. We reached our goal by coming here."

"Only because I believed him," she said darkly. "Trusting him was my mistake. Maybe they went after the circus."

She felt Antonio reach for her hand in the darkness. She gave it willingly. In the silence, she heard a sigh escape him softly and his quiet breathing afterward. He was the only man who could calm her fears about the children's welfare. When he spoke, she knew he chose his words deliberately.

"I think they'd rather join the circus than visit a relative Marcus has never met. I could be wrong. For your sake, I hope I am." Kneeling beside her, he gave her a tender smile in the moonlight. "Wherever they are, I'm sure Maria is safe. Marcus wouldn't go off without a plan and a way to take care of them. He's a responsible boy. Very much like his aunt."

Despite his kindness, an acute sense of helplessness crept over her. "But they could be anywhere. Before, I only had to worry about the city. Boston seems so small now. How are we ever to find them in a country as big as ours?"

He gave her a look of surprise, running his fingers through her hair. "It's the first time I've heard you describe the country as ours. I'm glad you decided to share it with me."

He rested his hand on the small of her back as she leaned forward. His touch made her feel safe in the face of the unknown. She couldn't see his face in the shadows, but she could hear his smile in his voice. She wished she could share his confidence.

"If the children aren't here, where on earth could they be?"

Juliet stood up restlessly, taking a step forward as he followed her. Leaning back against his shoulder, she gazed beyond the trees toward the endless stars above their heads.

"The country's too big," she murmured. "As big as the heavens with its inconstant moon and stars. I can't fathom any of this."

"Just because they aren't here doesn't mean we won't find them," he said gently. "They're on an adventure, a journey of their own. It's frustrating for us but fun for them. They'll return when they're ready."

Juliet couldn't keep her lip from quivering. "You don't think they've come to harm?"

"Your nephew's too clever for that. As you say, they might be coming here by some other means." Taking her by the shoulders, Antonio turned her about so they were face-to-face. "I finally remembered where I'd seen Lawrence, the boy from Foster's Wharf."

"Where do you know him from?"

"He stole produce from a stall in my neighborhood. Don't worry. We'll go into town first thing tomorrow and ask around. Even if they didn't come home, maybe they passed through."

As she studied his face so close to hers in the moon's soft glow, she wondered if he were tempted to kiss her. She hoped he would. The moon might have been inconstant for Shakespeare's Juliet, but for her it had never been more steady.

He gave her no chance to reflect further on his assessment of Marcus' friend from the docks. As if reading her mind, he lowered his face to hers, brushing their lips together lightly.

Feeling as if she were in a trance, she wished he would repeat the act, but he pulled away. A little laugh escaped him. She felt acute disappointment as he removed his hand from her waist and took hold of her hands.

"I don't dare linger," he announced softly. "I wouldn't want Professor Halliday to accuse a guest in his home of keeping his daughter out past curfew. It's late. You're more tired than you know. Sleep is the best thing right now."

"Don't leave," she said in desperation, "no matter what my father says. Please be here in the morning."

Raising her fingers to his lips, he kissed them tenderly.

"Did you think I would leave you to search for the children on your own? We'll find them," he promised softly. "Wherever they are, they're together. I'm sure of it. And they might not be as far away as you think."

Juliet was surprised to find a note from Clara on the kitchen table the next morning saying she and Antonio had gone for a walk. Not surprising, she thought. Antonio would probably keep as much distance from her father as possible.

At least he hadn't left in the night. For that she was grateful. Even if he was betrothed to Isabel, she wanted to enjoy his company as long as possible. Having him here kept alive the impossible dream of love that she harbored in her heart.

After dressing and eating quickly, she sought out her father. She found him at his desk in the study, his mood so reasonable, she wondered if his mental status had become impaired during the night. Either that, she worried, or Antonio had left with no plan to return, and Clara had covered for him.

"Papa, I'm going into the village with Mr. Santilli this morning," she announced. When no reaction came, she continued. "Maybe we'll find some clue that Marcus passed through town but didn't come home, though I don't know why he wouldn't."

"An excellent plan, my dear," he said casually, his gaze on the papers before him. "We must find him. It's what your mother would have wanted. I'm making a list of relatives to whom Marcus might have turned, both in and out of state. Should I expect you and Mr. Santilli back by lunchtime?"

Juliet was astonished her father would entertain the idea of Antonio staying after his remarks the night before. She considered broaching her disappointment but thought better of it. She needed to focus on finding the children.

Reluctant to disturb the present peace, she answered in the affirmative before kissing Papa good-bye and setting off to wait for Antonio. A morning of searching lay ahead of them.

Antonio let Juliet take the reins as they made the short drive to town in her father's phaeton. Riding kept her from aggravating her ankle, and driving took her mind off the pain. Seeing her optimistic state helped him relax and focus. He wasn't as convinced as she was that Marcus and Maria were in the area.

"People would notice and remember two children they'd never seen before," Juliet said with conviction. "Marcus and Maria are strangers here. We don't know they didn't pass through."

"Except they never went home," he reminded her.

"Maybe Marcus was afraid. You've seen how formidable Papa can be." She sighed in frustration. "No one knows him better than I. Cordelia must have seen a side of him I know nothing about."

"It's possible the children came here but never went home. They might be hiding in town." Antonio doubted that was the case. While he was no more certain about them joining the circus, it was still more likely than calling on a hostile grandfather who probably gave Marcus nightmares if his mother ever talked about him. "Since he's never met his grandfather, maybe he was afraid he wouldn't be welcome."

"I wouldn't have recognized him if Mrs. Wetherall hadn't shown me that recent picture," Juliet said quietly.

In silence, they drove by merchants' homes, past the tinware shop, the barrel factory, and Stockton Shoe Factory, to the harbor where barks and schooners were moored. Juliet pointed out the site of the Fort Point Hotel, scheduled to open next year. There was pride in her voice as she described the bowling alley and dance pavilions that were to be built inside a hotel designed to attract Boston's elite. As they continued along the waterfront, Antonio watched dockhands ready lumber, granite, and potatoes for transport while vessels from Cuba and the South Seas unloaded their cargo.

"Sounds like the new hotel will be a lot fancier than Mrs. Wetherall's boardinghouse." He laughed. "Let's try some of these shops. Maybe they've seen the children."

They stopped the cart to inquire in the confectioner's shop and at the notions purveyor's store, places Juliet thought the children might be likely to visit. No one claimed to have seen Marcus or Maria. Suspecting she was struggling to remain optimistic, Antonio bought her a sweet before suggesting she drive past the schoolhouse where she taught.

"Mrs. Owens filled in for me until school ended," Juliet said, growing subdued as they passed the small school. "There's the smithy. We could have used his services during our travels."

Antonio was riveted by scenes of everyday life in her village, curious about the place Juliet called home. Far from being the rural site he'd expected, Stockton Village bustled with activity but in a less hurried way than Boston. He seized the opportunity to raise an issue that had been plaguing him.

"You moved here after your father retired?" he clarified.

"Yes, from Waterville College. I grew up in Farmington, west of here, but I think of this as home. We traveled abroad when I was young. Papa slowed down the last few years because of his health. My mother always suffered from wanderlust." She smiled nervously. "Maybe that's where Marcus gets the tendency."

"Could be." Curious, he thought, that her father had gone abroad yet resented the immigration movement. It was almost hypocritical. "This must have been a big change for your father."

Juliet shrugged. "Not really. We came here to live with his sister. She was widowed by then, so it was just the three of us."

He suspected she might grow defensive if he pursued his line of questioning, yet his fondness for her compelled him to speak. Before he could go on, she addressed the issue directly, drawing the horse to a stop in the light mist that had begun to fall.

"I admit Papa can be difficult," she conceded, "especially with strangers he sees as a threat, but why did you ask?"

At the risk of upsetting her he plunged in wholeheartedly. "Is it because he fears losing you? You say you want a marriage like your parents had, yet you don't plan to marry. It sounds like a contradiction."

She took a moment to compose her thoughts. "It has less to do with Papa than with having so much in my life, between caring for him and our home. And teaching matters to me. Not only that," she rushed on, cheeks reddening, "but sometimes I wonder who'd be interested in a spinster like myself, alone so long."

"I don't know why you'd worry about such a thing," he said frankly as she colored further. "You're a lovely young woman."

"Thank you for saying so," she returned, "but my hair is too brilliant a shade for someone used to the dark hair most Italian women have. I doubt I could hold a candle to your Isabel."

She gazed at him, her green eyes offering a challenge as she placed the emphasis squarely on the name of his betrothed. Her words gave him hope. He had feared that once she was home, she'd forget the intensity of their moments together. Perhaps she hadn't.

"You could hold a candle to any woman," he told her, his tone steady. "You would make any man proud to call you his own."

She turned away quickly and fell silent, but only for a moment. "What does this have to do with my father?"

"You are direct, aren't you? No doubt, more so than most men can handle. Maybe even more than Hans can handle." He studied the beautiful oval of her face, amused by her forthright manner. "Before Aunt Muriel can step in and recommend some inappropriate young man, I feel I must speak. I fear your father is trying to keep you to himself and is lowering your opinion of yourself to do it."

"I don't believe you know me well enough to—"

As Juliet's glance fell on a shop window behind the carriage, she froze in mid-sentence, her rigid pose bringing Antonio to his senses. Following her gaze, he was too startled to speak until he realized he was looking at a daguerreotype in a studio, visible even through the drizzle.

The photograph featured a young girl who was all too familiar and precious. There was no mistaking Maria, with her curly black hair and enormous eyes in a sweet, round face. Juliet's nephew was beside her in the picture, the pair dressed as a bride and groom.

"It's them," Juliet quavered.

Chapter Eleven

Faced with their first real lead at last, Antonio grabbed Juliet's arm and pulled her from the carriage inside the photographer's shop. A man in a dark apron looked up from a desk where he had been reviewing pictures, startled by their arrival.

"May I help you?" he asked politely.

"These children," Antonio demanded, knocking over another photograph in the window as he snatched up the daguerreotype. "This picture. Did you take this?"

The photographer drew back in alarm, studying it through round spectacles. "I did."

"When?" Juliet was breathless with suspense. "Where did you see these children? They've run away. We're trying to find them."

The shopkeeper blinked, looking at the faces of the children. "I took that portrait last week, when the circus was in Concord. I happened to be in New Hampshire visiting relatives."

Recognition dawned on Antonio as Juliet uttered a cry of joy.

"Just as you thought," she said in a hushed voice.

"I remember them," the photographer said thoughtfully. "Those children were the bride and groom in a Tom Thumb wedding."

"With Mr. Tarry's Great American Extravaganza," Antonio prompted.

"That's right. It wasn't hard to get them to take a serious portrait. They didn't smile much."

It figured, thought Antonio, that Marcus' photograph made

125

it home before he did. It sounded as if the boy had little reason to smile in his new job. He looked quickly at Juliet.

"Didn't the Ryan family say the circus was going to Portland?" he asked tensely.

"It was in Concord for a few days," the photographer reflected. "I think it was headed for Portland next."

"Where was it going after that? Please try to remember," Juliet urged.

"Heading west." He frowned, deep in thought. "Skowhegan is its last New England stop."

"Did the children appear to be well fed?" Antonio asked cautiously. "They weren't mistreated that you know of?"

"They didn't seem to be," the shopkeeper said in surprise. "They were typical youngsters. They seemed more tired than unhappy when I took their picture. They had moved around a lot."

"Thank you for your help," Antonio exulted, shaking his hand. "You might just have saved the lives of those two."

They left the studio and hurried back to the phaeton. Antonio reached for Juliet's hand, unable to keep from smiling.

"This is great news," he announced. "Not only do we know they're safe, but we know where to find them."

"I've never been so relieved in my life," Juliet exclaimed, hardly able to contain her jubilation as he assisted her into her seat. "I wonder if Marcus left Boston to become a juggler."

"Of course he did. That's what got him into trouble in the first place." Humor tempered his impatience as he took a deep breath. "We've learned much today, but we have a big task ahead of us. How quickly can we leave?"

"If we pack right away, we can take the train from Belfast this afternoon and be in Burnham Junction by tonight," she replied. "From there we can take a carriage to Skowhegan."

He'd be lucky, he thought, if he had the money to pay the fare at this point. "It's a relief to know they're safe and in the care of adults. We might see them by tonight."

"And then we'll bring them home, where they belong." Juliet shivered with rising enthusiasm. "If the children aren't actually here, I suppose the photograph is the next best thing. You see? Marcus probably did plan to come see his grandfather, after the circus finished performing locally."

Antonio stole a sideways glance at her. It didn't surprise him that she still thought the best of the boy. He was glad. Marcus needed someone to defend him. More than anyone Antonio knew, Juliet had the conviction and the heart to do it. "How do you figure that?"

"He was coming to the area of the state where Papa lives."

"The circus wasn't. Not really." How like Juliet to want to believe the best. Enchanted by her sweetness, he gave her a grin. "You can stop worrying. Within a day or two they'll be home."

"I'm afraid I'll believe it only when I see it." Juliet shook her head vehemently, her tone serious. "I've learned a thing or two about my nephew. I wouldn't put anything past him. I want to catch him before we lose him forever."

Juliet gazed absently at the towering pine forests beyond the train window that afternoon, with Clara dozing beside her. How could anyone sleep, Juliet wondered, with their destination so close? At least Clara wasn't snoring. Across from them, Antonio silently counted the money he had left, no doubt hoping he had enough to get himself and Maria back to Boston.

Watching him, Juliet wondered what would happen once they reached Skowhegan. Would she claim her nephew and head east while Antonio took Maria and went south? Their parting might leave no chance to see each other again. Mrs. Wetherall had said Antonio was a man of his word. He would marry Isabel once she arrived.

Dear Mrs. Wetherall. Would Juliet ever see her again? She doubted it. The landlady had said she'd be safe with Antonio. She had been, all but her heart. Juliet listened to the train tracks rattling beneath them, realizing with a sense of anguish the resolution ahead might not be the one she'd been hoping for.

She shifted in her seat, settling in for the ride to Burnham Junction, thinking about the question that had puzzled her since she'd bid Papa a hasty good-bye earlier that day. He and Antonio had parted on surprisingly civil terms. Rather than ask why, she'd simply been grateful. She would do better to think about Marcus.

"Do you still think we did the right thing by not sending a telegram to Mr. Tarry?" she asked Antonio.

"I'm certain," he assured her. "We know the children are safe. They're also tired, which means they aren't likely to have the energy to run. We already know Marcus knows how to elude the police. Better to take them by surprise, don't you think?"

She had to agree. The steadiness of the ride lulled them into a restful state. Just as well, she thought, since they were powerless to do more until they reached their destination. While she appreciated Antonio's attempt at light conversation, she knew he must wonder what they would find.

She felt herself blushing as red as her hair when he tucked a stray lock behind her ear and let his fingers caress her cheek. Turning over, Clara discreetly pretended not to notice. For that Juliet gave silent thanks.

Settling back in her seat as Antonio gazed thoughtfully out the window, Juliet wondered if he was thinking about returning to Boston. Did he genuinely care for her? She wished she knew. Despite the sophistication she felt when she was home in her own village, she'd come to view herself differently during her journey with Antonio. Until now, she had always considered Papa, with his education and refinement, her hero. Antonio was not educated, nor would she describe him as refined.

Yet Papa had never been so practical. Moving the family on a whim, he agreed to travel and enjoyed it whenever Mum had suggested it. In retrospect, she realized, it was more than a young father with two daughters should have undertaken.

Antonio Santilli, on the other hand, was both romantic and practical, adventurous in a way Papa wasn't. As the owner of a market, the largest in Boston's North End, he was easily able to provide for a wife and family. She remembered how he comforted the children on board the steamer when the woman tumbled overboard. She could not remember Papa ever being so kind.

A stab of regret rushed through her as she realized Papa wouldn't be likely to accept an immigrant as a potential suitor for her. Certainly not this *ruffian,* as he had referred to Antonio.

Juliet let her mind wander, imagining life if Antonio would agree to come north. She pictured the seafood market he would run, the best the town had ever seen. But would he consent to leave his mother, uncle, and younger brothers and sisters behind, along with everything he'd established in Boston?

She doubted it very much. His moving to Maine was as likely as her moving to Italy. Her heart sank at the thought.

If only he'd come home with her, she thought wistfully. If only he could attain his goal of opening a restaurant like Boston's Parker House in Stockton Village. Maybe he could get his start as a chef at the new Fort Point Hotel. Her hopes were about as realistic as the chance she could survive happily in Boston. Still, she couldn't deny herself the dream.

She should be satisfied to have Marcus home safely. She sighed as she closed her eyes to shut out the truth. Even if nothing more could come of it, she was glad she hadn't missed the chance to make Antonio's acquaintance.

Opening her eyes briefly, she saw he'd nodded off. The soft snoring so familiar to her from their night in Rose Ryan's cottage comforted her now. Her troubled thoughts were finally overcome by restless dreams. She nodded off to the rhythmic chugging of the rails beneath her.

She remained that way until the crashing thud of a train coming to an abrupt stop threw her to the floor.

As soon as he looked out the window, Antonio was able to judge the situation accurately. Through the dust that was settling over the landscape, he could make out the grotesque angle of the engine. With its front end in the air and its back plunged in a watery ravine, it would have looked like a toy were it not for the urgency of their plight. Pieces of track appeared to have let go beneath the train, reduced now to useless metal fragments.

It was more than an hour later that he stood outside in the rain. Juliet and Clara huddled beneath a shared umbrella.

"We were so close." Juliet's tone was tinged with despair.

"The brook must have been washed out by the rain, and the track collapsed under the weight of the train. You can see where they're preparing to lay new track. It could be a while before the train will run again." Seeing her worried face, Antonio tried to lighten the mood. "These delays are becoming far too common."

"Just like the uncommonly bad weather," Clara muttered.

"It's fortunate no one was seriously hurt," murmured Juliet. "Between the rain and this dim light, I can't tell what color my bruises are. Clara's right. I've had enough of the weather."

"Good thing you had your cloak over you. It provided padding and kept you from being more severely injured." Pushing up his sleeve, he surveyed his black-and-blue arm. "Neither the rain nor our bruises will keep us from traveling. The question is how."

An hour later they were seated in a private carriage once again, this time with a driver more experienced than the driver they'd had when they'd left Bath. This time, Antonio didn't argue with Juliet's suggestion. Now that they knew the location of the circus, it was imperative they reach the children quickly.

"Every year, Skowhegan holds the state's biggest agricultural fair," Juliet said as they set off. "The circus is most likely set up at the fairgrounds."

"It was kind of your father to lend us the money to travel," Antonio said quietly.

"I'm afraid that was the only kindness he showed." Juliet sighed. "If nothing else, going home gave us the means to continue our search. This time," she added with a smile, "maybe we'll finally be able to bring Marcus and Maria home."

"Let's just hope we can keep them there," Clara added with a weary smile.

* * *

The sun had dipped lower in the sky by the time they finally reached Skowhegan. Antonio hoped the circus hadn't closed for the day or, worse, completed the end of its run. His hopes soared once they crossed what Juliet said was the Kennebec River and he glimpsed tents and flags between the treetops.

"The Great American Extravaganza is still at the fairgrounds." Antonio was almost too impatient to remain in his seat. "Now let's hope the children are still with the circus."

As the driver brought the carriage to a complete stop at the gate, Antonio quickly surveyed what he could of the circus' layout within the fairgrounds. From the window, he glimpsed the boxcars lined up at the back of the activity near the woodland, wondering if that was where he would find the children. He hastily withdrew money from his pocket, giving the driver a handsome fare as Juliet jumped awkwardly from the vehicle, heedless of her graceless appearance.

Squeezing each other's hands for luck, he and Juliet set off into the circus grounds, with Clara in close pursuit. They picked their way through the crowd, looking carefully among the acrobats and the wire walkers for any sign of the children.

"I suppose there's no point in looking for the jugglers," Antonio said dryly. "From what the photographer said, we should be searching for a wedding in progress. A miniature wedding."

Along their path, painted wooden cages held an ostrich and llama while a camel performed tricks in a ring. As they hurried past the knife thrower, Juliet inched closer to Antonio. He drew her to him, hoping the familiar gesture comforted her in their unfamiliar surroundings. They waited as an elephant, its head and back brightly costumed, was paraded leisurely through the crowd.

"It's a wonder children can cope with the circus lifestyle," Juliet said in an undertone. "All this traveling over the last week has just about done me in—"

Suddenly he saw them. As two groups of visitors moved in opposite directions, a vision in white appeared before them. A tiny chapel had been set up beside a colorful bed of flowers for participants of the Tom Thumb wedding. Posed in front of the door, having acted out their part for yet another day, Marcus and Maria appeared too tired to act happy any longer. His face sober, Marcus sat down on a log in the church's garden setting.

A more star-crossed pair Antonio had never seen.

His heart skipped a beat. There was Maria, dragging her bouquet wearily as she dropped down beside Marcus, the wreath that held her veil in place crooked in her mussed curls. Despite her exhausted appearance, her innocent face hinted at what his mother had looked like, not only as a child, but also on her wedding day—an odd juxtaposition that tugged at his heart.

He gripped Juliet by the shoulders and turned her about.

"Look," he whispered huskily.

Chapter Twelve

Antonio released his grip on Juliet's shoulders, feeling her stiffen upon seeing the children across the circus grounds. He held his breath as he waited for her reaction. She cried out, startling a group of passersby, the ecstasy in her voice painful and joyous at the same time. A group of bridesmaids in pink and ushers in black and white gaped in amazement as Juliet rushed toward them, closing the short distance in a few steps.

"Marcus!" she shouted, catching the pair in a hug. "Maria!"

Antonio was beside her in a moment, gathering Juliet up in the embrace. Maria wiggled free, leaping into his arms.

"Antonio!" she burst out tremulously. Tears streaming down her cheeks, she buried her face in his shoulder, her tiny fingers clutching his neck. He closed his eyes and held her tight. "I knew you'd come. I just knew it."

"Do you remember me, Marcus?" Juliet asked breathlessly, staring as she held him at arm's length. "I'm your Aunt Juliet."

"Aunt Juliet," said Marcus quietly. "I'm glad to see you."

Antonio had expected the boy to be defiant, but Marcus' voice was sincere and resigned. Antonio could see the relief in his face at their arrival. Marcus had had enough of freedom.

"I was sure I'd find you juggling your way across the country," Antonio said, tousling the boy's red hair.

Marcus' face fell. "I wanted to show how well I can juggle, but Mr. Tarry says I'm not good enough. He put us here instead."

His tone was so crestfallen that Antonio couldn't help but want to shower the boy with kindness, his anger forgotten amid his joy at finding him. He saw in Marcus' eyes the piercing disappointment the boy felt at being deemed not good enough to perform the skill he considered himself best at. Antonio was pleased that Juliet took notice, her eyes grateful as they met his over her nephew's head.

"You're good enough for Boston," Antonio consoled him. "Back home people applaud when you perform. They miss you."

The reminder brought a proud smile to Marcus' face, though Antonio detected a hint of dismay on Juliet's that he couldn't explain. She should be happy, given the fact they'd located the children. She turned her attention to Marcus.

"Not that we're encouraging you to go back to working on street corners," Juliet told him quickly. "In fact, young man, you deserve a severe reprimand—"

"But we'll deal with that later," Antonio finished, giving her a tactful grin. Clinging to his leg, Maria stared at Juliet, no doubt curious since she'd never seen her before. Antonio laid a hand on the head of each child, glancing from one to the other. "How did you two manage all this time?"

"It was easy to get out of Boston," Marcus admitted. "After that, it got harder. But I've been taking good care of Maria, like a man should," he hastened to add.

"Just as I've done for your aunt." Antonio smiled, turning to Juliet just in time to see her lovely eyes widen.

"You taught me how to take care of a family, Mr. Santilli," Marcus went on. "I watched you with your own. I've proven I can do a man's job."

"I'm sure you proved it over and over on this journey, *fanciullo mio,* and I'm proud of you," said Antonio. "But a boy your age shouldn't have to."

Marcus glanced up at him with a look of puzzled dismay.

"I know you don't expect kindness from me," Antonio said with regret. "I've been hard on you. But that's going to change."

"I can work," Marcus protested. He turned tired eyes to his aunt beseechingly. "I want to go home. Please can you take us? I'm tired of the circus. I promise I'll work hard at the market."

"Me too, Antonio," Maria piped up. "Take me home."

Maria's curls fell across her face as she leaned her head against her brother's leg. Laughing, he reached down, lifting the veil from her head and laying a gentle hand on Marcus' shoulder.

"No more working for you, *giovinetto.* Time for you to get back to school." Antonio tossed the veil in the air, catching it playfully and flashing Juliet a smile. "If only I could juggle as well as Marcus. Too bad we have to give this back to Mr. Tarry."

Carefully he placed the flowers on Juliet's head and arranged the netting about her hair. She looked at him as if he had lost his mind. Her expression touched his heart.

"Marcus and Maria," he said abruptly, waiting until both children ran to his side, "you've probably had enough adventure for a while. Once you've settled down, however, maybe one more trip would be in order. How would you like to see Italy?"

He knelt between them, placing an arm around their shoulders as he glanced from one to the other. The children looked at each other, their eyes huge with excitement. As they shouted with joy, he noted that Juliet stood by silently. She and the children watched in wonder as Antonio took the filmy veil, bouquet, and top hat and laid them at the door of the little church.

"You won't need these props anymore," he said carelessly. "I think it's time we all went home."

Listening to Antonio's unexpected speech, Juliet felt giddy. She could not remember ever being as happy as she was now, although she couldn't have been more confused. Antonio gave the children time to run on ahead in Clara's care before turning his full attention to Juliet.

"We need to wire your father and my mother with the news," he announced. "They'll be relieved to hear the children are safe, if somewhat weary and wiser."

"It's the best news we could give them. I'm not surprised the children took such good care of each other. They were so far from home." All she and Antonio had done during most of their journey was argue like children. She decided the time had come to broach the subject that troubled her most. She raised the topic gingerly, keeping her tone light. "What does that mean, going home? You take the train to Boston while Marcus and I go home to Papa?"

Antonio shrugged. "I think the children have other ideas. They seem to have become as close as brother and sister during their adventure. I'd hate to separate them now. That invitation I made extends to you as well. In fact, we might even go on ahead."

She looked into his face, waiting as she tried to imagine what he was leading up to.

"Italy is a wonderful place to honeymoon," he continued. "It worked for my parents."

Juliet's heart skipped a beat. As they approached a bridge that led to a small island, he signaled to Clara to turn. With the children scurrying ahead, he and Juliet crossed the bridge hand in hand. "I noticed a beautiful church—a real one, not like Mr. Tarry's—across this bridge as we came through town. It's a shame to come all this way and not make use of it, don't you think?"

Juliet stopped, staring into his warm eyes. "Even when you're not speaking Italian, you still manage to confuse me. Are you saying what I think you are?"

"I think we're speaking the same language." His eyes twinkled, teasing her as they studied her reaction. "That is, if our pretend marriage wasn't preparing you for a life with Hans. It wasn't, was it?"

"What on earth are you talking about? I have no intention of marrying Hans. I was never serious about him."

"Then you never cared for him." Antonio froze, motionless. Finally a smile spread slowly across his face. "I hope Clara won't be too disappointed when you break the news to her."

"I cared for him in the beginning. Was rather headstrong about it, in fact. That must be what Clara remembers." Confused, Juliet thought back on conversations they had during their journey. "I was young. I soon realized he wasn't the man I wanted to marry, but there was no graceful way out of it. I was relieved when Papa came between us and ended it."

Antonio grinned. "I'm relieved to hear it."

"But Hans isn't the problem." Frowning, Juliet watched his face carefully. "What about Isabel?"

"I don't think I can go through with it," he confessed. "I came to know you on our journey. I saw you at your worst but also at your best. Over time, you turned my irritation to admiration. And then to love. Look at all we've been through. We survived a grounded steamboat, a carriage accident, a sprained ankle, and a train wreck." As naturally as if they'd been married for years, he slipped her hand through the crook of his arm. "I was hoping you'd consent to give me your hand in marriage."

Juliet stopped in her tracks, gazing up into his handsome face, his warm eyes meeting hers. She was afraid to believe what she'd just heard. She had to remind herself to breathe.

"I-I'd be honored, but I don't know how we would ever work it out," she faltered. "Would your mother approve of a woman who teaches school for a living?"

"How do you think she survived when she came to this country?" He smiled gently. "She worked for a living. She had to. She understands America is different from Italy."

Juliet sighed with relief. "How will we ever convince Papa?"

"I think he can be persuaded." He teased the tip of her nose with his forefinger. "He isn't as intimidating as you think."

His carefree tone disturbed her. Marriage was hardly a matter for overconfidence, especially in the case of her father.

"We've come this far," she ventured. "I think we should go back and talk to Papa before we take the next step."

"My dear, it's already settled. You see," he admitted, amusement in his tone, "I discussed matters with your papa before you and I left Stockton Village."

Her heart nearly stopped. Most people were too afraid to approach her father with any subject that might antagonize him. The future of his only remaining daughter topped the list.

"I've already asked your father for your hand in marriage."

Antonio looked pleased with himself as he waited for her reaction. "So you see, our trip to your home wasn't wasted."

"But—how—?" she gasped, remembering her father's anger toward Antonio the first night. "He actually said yes?"

"Not quite. That night at your home I stayed up after you retired. I was still in the parlor when your father returned. I apologized for my comments about Marcus. I told him of our travels—" He colored slightly. "Before I knew it, I'd admitted my feelings for you and asked for your hand. At first he refused, but I was sure I could change his mind. He finally agreed." His eyes twinkled. "On one condition."

Juliet blanched with alarm. Papa must have made him promise something unimaginable, something impossible to provide. "What condition? One you can never hope to meet, I'm sure."

"I had another reason for wanting to find Marcus. Your papa promised me your hand in marriage—if you agreed, of course—provided I return his grandson to him." Antonio gave her a smile that combined shyness with hope, the most enchanting combination she'd ever seen on his beloved face. "We shook hands on it. There's nothing to stop us now."

Juliet felt as if every care had been lifted from her soul. Until she remembered their differences.

"But where will we live?" she asked with apprehension.

"I thought about that," he said, a hint of intrigue in his voice. "It's a big question. One of us would have to move."

"I would never expect you to give up your fish market."

"I didn't think you would. Living in Boston has advantages, even for children. How would you feel about it?"

"I've thought about it too," she admitted, giving him an awkward but playful smile.

Antonio squeezed her hand gently as they walked. Juliet gazed up at the steeple of the church before them.

"Wouldn't it be wonderful if we could be married here?" he said.

She looked at him in disbelief. "Here? Now? Won't your family object to a wedding if they aren't present? They haven't even met me."

"It would be hard to find a place that would satisfy both families," he agreed. "My mother would rather not visit the wilds of Maine, as she calls it. And I doubt your father would enjoy the bustle of Boston. Wouldn't Skowhegan be appropriate for a wedding? We could make it a beginning rather than an end."

"There are other practicalities," she argued, "such as a license—"

"Which can be taken care of easily enough." He patted her hand. "It's too bad the children are too young to stand up for us as witnesses. If they weren't, I'd insist we have the ceremony performed right now."

As they reached the path that led to the door of the island church, he turned to her, love shining in his eyes. She laid her head on his shoulder. She'd never felt so blessed, so contented. She wished she could enlarge the bridal outfits the children wore and change places with them.

Here everything was so perfect, so idyllic. So simple. She wished it could stay this way forever.

The circus world behind them, they left the fairgrounds in a state of weary happiness. As they headed toward the center of town, Juliet suspected the children were more exhausted than she was despite the energy they displayed. They ran on ahead toward a sparkling lake as their guardians walked slowly behind.

As much as Juliet wanted to remember the bliss and ignore the feeling creeping into its place, a warning voice inside reminded her that others, from her side as well as Antonio's, hadn't had their say in the matter.

And when they did, she knew, the voices and emotions would sound very different.

Antonio wasn't surprised that Marcus and Maria received a far warmer reception from Juliet's father than he had. He was happy to see it, for all was finally as it should be. After listening to his grandson talk about his circus experiences for twenty minutes, Professor Albert Halliday appeared to take an instant liking to the arrogant youngster.

"The boy is wise," Juliet's father said, sounding startled and impressed as they lingered at the supper table. "Thinking of ways to earn a living already. You'll go far, boy, mark my words. With a little guidance, who knows what he might accomplish?"

He continued to warm to the new arrival during the evening, surprising Antonio as he extended some compliments to Maria while Juliet updated him on their trip. The professor shook his head as she described the damage the train had suffered and their subsequent carriage ride. Despite the exciting story his daughter told, Antonio observed, his attention always returned to his grandson.

"Just you wait, my boy," he said, patting Marcus' shoulder. "Life here will be better than what you've known. Take my word."

"Now that he's with such a loving family, how could it be otherwise?" Clara agreed as she pulled dessert from the oven.

"He'll settle in beautifully, especially in the care of his Aunt Clara," Juliet assured her, ruffling Maria's hair affectionately. "Your mother will be so happy to see you, Maria. I'd be surprised if she ever lets you out of her arms again."

"In all the excitement, I nearly forgot," Juliet's father said suddenly, turning to Antonio. "A telegram came for you."

Antonio frowned. "Here? Who could have sent it?"

The professor reached toward the sideboard, handing him an envelope with a raised eyebrow. "Someone who knew of your plans."

His brow furrowing, Antonio saw it had come from Boston addressed to *Mr. Santilli, care of Halliday.* He tore the envelope open, hoping it didn't contain bad news. It was from Lillian Wetherall. Surprised, he rushed past the date to scan its contents. They were succinct and factual.

"Your mother wants you to know Isabel DiLorenzo has arrived. Hope all is well."

He folded the letter in a state of shock. All had been well, he realized, until this moment.

"Antonio, you're pale." The unexpected alarm in Juliet's voice returned him to the present. "Is everything all right?"

He gave her father a furtive glance, relieved to see the professor engaging his grandson in conversation. This was neither the time nor the place to discuss the contents of the telegram. He tucked it in his pocket and managed a stiff smile.

He had to make this work with Juliet. Somehow he would find a way.

"Everyone at home is checking to make sure things are fine." He put his arm about her shoulders. "And they are."

Juliet's face turned so white when he read her the telegram late that evening, he was afraid she might faint. It was the last thing she wanted or expected, judging from her reaction.

Antonio led her outdoors to the rocking chair on the porch, where he made sure she was comfortably seated. While Clara had retired early, it had taken Marcus a long time to retire, and her father even longer. He and Juliet had to make the most of their time alone.

"What does it mean?" she asked in a small voice. "It changes our plans."

"It does not change mine," he assured her fiercely. "I knew when I asked your father for your hand that it is you I love, not Isabel. We were young when we were engaged, the arrangement mutually agreed upon by our parents. Now that I'm older, I can judge for myself." Reaching gently for her shoulders, he turned her face toward his in the moonlight. "It's clear to me, as clear as the moon above, that you are meant for me. No other."

The inconstant moon, he thought with an uneasy heart.

"I feel the same. How could it be otherwise?" Juliet took a deep breath that stirred him with its sincerity. "But what are we to do now that things have changed?"

"Nothing has changed. We'll marry as planned. My family will understand. Those plans were made too long ago for any of us to know how things would turn out." Antonio paused, reflecting. "I didn't think Isabel would come to America. It's been so long, I began to wonder if she'd changed her mind."

"Antonio," Juliet asked, her voice tight, "does Papa know?"

"I'm not foolish enough to tell your father I was engaged to another while asking for your hand." A tense sigh escaped him. "I intended to disentangle myself from Isabel in private before asking your father. But here at your home, when I was already out of his good graces, I had to tell him how I felt. I took a risk, but I believed you felt the same."

"I do." She jumped to her feet, the chair rocking violently behind her. "I always have."

She took a step toward him, her arms outstretched, seeking comfort. He enfolded her in his embrace, his cheek feeling the softness of her hair. He rocked her silently for a long moment, the chirp of crickets keeping time with their breathing.

"Here's what we'll do," he said after a minute. "We'll spend some time here helping the children adjust before we head home. I can write my mother and tell her of our plans."

"That isn't the way I want to be introduced to your mother," she said anxiously. "As the woman who destroyed Isabel's hopes, maybe even her life, after she came all the way from Italy."

Juliet pulled away from his arms, shivering. He would not let Isabel's arrival disrupt the life they had planned. It felt so right, bringing Marcus and Maria back to Boston together.

"We can think about this over the next few days," Antonio told her, pressing his lips to the top of her head. "Trust me, it will all seem easier in the morning light."

Yet, even as he spoke, he wondered what tomorrow would hold. Patience was in order, for the decisions they faced would change lives. Uneasiness crept over him as he debated his next step. There were barriers to be overcome, formidable ones, none of them as easy as leaving Italy had been despite its hardships.

Not the least of those was Juliet's father.

Chapter Thirteen

The days that followed were filled with an awkward, ominous quiet. Juliet felt a storm brewing despite the sunshine that seemed finally to want to stay for a while.

"It will break my heart if Marcus and Maria have to part," she said as she watched the children from the kitchen window. Tossing pails of water at each other for relief from the heat, they seemed unaware of the tension she and Antonio faced.

"Why do they have to?" Clara asked in surprise. "Haven't you told the children about your plans to go to Boston?"

"Not yet," Juliet admitted. "I don't know if we still can. I don't want to disappoint them."

Clara crossed her arms on her chest. "You will if you back out. It's time to follow your heart, Juliet, like Antonio does."

To avoid the subject, Juliet looked out at the youngsters. The sight filled her with a contentment nothing else could.

"It's uplifting to see how well Papa's adjusted to his grandson. Marcus responds to you too. I think you remind him of Mrs. Wetherall. I'm glad he has such good influences." Juliet smiled with satisfaction, thinking of the rapport she'd established with students in her school and wishing she could do the same with her nephew. "Even if I don't appear to be one of them. How to make Marcus happy as his caregiver seems to be eluding me."

"The boy misses his mother," Clara reminded her gently. "She was hardly in the ground before he left town. What you're going through is hard, but think of all that boy's endured. He's been through a lot for his young years, poor child."

143

"I don't know how to reach him." Juliet was relieved to have her nephew home, yet she couldn't keep exasperation from creeping into her voice. "He seems so distant. He likes Antonio, he's fond of you, and he adores Papa. It's me he doesn't seem to care for."

"Your father and I are brand-new to him," Clara pointed out. "You had the hardest task. You're the aunt who was chasing him to take him away from the life he knew. He'll come around in time."

"I haven't seen any sign of it," Juliet said bitterly.

"I know it's frustrating. All he knows is his mother left him like his father did. In time that will change. You won't take her place, but you'll fill the shoes left empty with her death."

Juliet gazed at her in alarm. "I don't know if I can do it."

"You love him, don't you?"

"Of course. More than just about anyone."

"Everything has a way of falling into place. You'll see." Clara squeezed the back of her neck the way her mother had in childhood. "Antonio's made up his mind how he wants this to work out. You have too. You just aren't ready to admit it."

In her heart, Juliet knew that Clara was right. Antonio's drive, emotional strength, and uncommon wisdom had convinced her he was a man worth loving. Yet, she felt pressured by the one person from whom she least expected it.

"You're the one I love," he reassured her one twilight after Papa had retired early and Clara had taken the children for an evening walk. He repeated the words he told her regularly. "Not Isabel."

"I believe you. I just hope your family isn't disappointed in your choice." Despite the time she'd had to think over the prospect of moving to Boston, she dreaded his family's reaction. "I don't want to be a source of discord among your relatives."

"My family will respect my decision. They will love you." He gave her an affectionate embrace, removing his arms when she didn't respond. "What else is there? Now that you're home, you seem reluctant."

"I'm afraid of your family's reaction. And something else might stand in our way." Juliet hesitated to express her concern. "I have a feeling Papa won't agree to let go of Marcus."

"He promised I could have your hand if I returned his grandson. Don't you think he'll keep his part of the bargain?"

"I think Papa's changed his mind. I don't think he wants us to go," Juliet admitted. "And Marcus needs his grandfather, but he also needs both of us."

"Yes, he does. But why should he have to choose?"

She felt a lump in her throat. "That's the dilemma I face."

"It's time for you to start life anew." Speaking softly, Antonio cradled her face in his hands. "Your mother and Cordelia are gone, but we could start our own family. That way your family would grow. What do you think?"

Juliet blushed at the idea. It appealed to every part of her heart, yet she did not see how it was possible.

"Papa needs me here," she said plaintively. "He expects me to take care of him. There's no one else to do it."

"Clara could, but you'll want her in Boston with us." Antonio smiled. "Is there any reason we can't take your father with us?"

"Your apartment is already too small."

"There is always room for more. We can find a larger place."

"Papa won't want to go," she argued. "There are too many memories of Cordelia in Boston."

"You and Marcus will be there. And maybe new grandchildren." As he drew her into his arms again, her heart fluttered at the prospect of children. "What grandfather could resist?"

"But his happiest memories are here." Knowing her father as she did, Juliet shook her head doubtfully. "It isn't only that. I don't think I can leave my schoolchildren behind."

Antonio laid his hands on her shoulders, tender as an angel's touch. "You care so much for youngsters. Don't you see what a wonderful mother you'd be? It isn't only your father who needs to change his thinking," he teased, "it's his daughter. One thing you haven't learned yet is that families are created, not just bred. I know you want a marriage like your parents had."

"That's how it's supposed to be," Juliet countered.

"True, but I don't think it's the case here."

She froze in bewilderment, stopping his hand from caressing her face. "What are you talking about?"

"It's the teacher who needs the lesson," he said, amusement in his voice. "I know you want to believe your parents' marriage was perfect. How could it have been? Cordelia left home early and married unhappily. Whose example did she follow?"

"What's your point?" She took a step back from him, putting a distance between them. "Are you worried I'll do the same?"

"Only if you marry someone besides me." He spread his hands. "I want you to be happier than Cordelia was. That's my point."

Antonio squeezed her shoulders with such gentleness, she closed her eyes, almost unable to bear it. No words could express her fears. Her silence did not stop him from continuing.

"I'm afraid you're having second thoughts based on your father's doubts," he chided her tenderly, "not your own. There's only one mind you have to make up, Juliet, and that's yours."

Papa stared at Juliet as if she'd lost her senses when she broached Antonio's plan in private that evening.

"I won't let him go. How could I get along without Marcus?" he protested. "Now that I've come to know my grandson, I want to be here to watch him grow up. He's a fine boy. He has potential."

"Of course he does." Juliet took a deep breath, wondering how to get him to reconsider. "That's why he should grow up in a place like Boston. He'll have opportunities I never had."

Papa spoke as if he hadn't heard the proposition. That was possible, she thought. He probably closed his ears at the first mention of leaving Maine.

"You wouldn't lose your grandson, Papa," she continued. "You'll never lose Marcus. You would come to Boston with us."

Her father harrumphed at the idea, muttering objections under his breath as he paced across his study so many times, she feared he would wear out the floorboards.

"Think of the academic opportunities," she tried again. "The universities, the museums, all within walking distance. You could introduce Marcus to all of it. You once said being retired isn't as stimulating as teaching was."

Papa's pacing slowed before he resumed his seat behind his desk. "I don't want to leave, Juliet," he said, the quavering in his voice startling her. "This is all I know, all I've ever known. The countryside, the walks in the lane, the garden. It's where I've spent my life. The place where your mother lived."

There was no arguing with that. He seemed so heartbroken at the idea of Marcus leaving that she dropped the subject. She understood his reluctance. The boy finally had a man's guidance and leadership, the direction his own father had never provided.

To her surprise, Papa had been remarkably affectionate toward Marcus, almost more than she had been. But Papa and Marcus weren't the only ones who needed affection.

She and Antonio did also. What would happen to them?

Juliet was not surprised when Antonio continued to beg her for a decision. He wanted an answer sooner than she had one.

He broached the subject again while Clara harvested strawberries with the children in the back garden. Juliet found it difficult to make him understand Papa's position.

"Returning to Boston is the best thing for Marcus. You know that, don't you?" he persisted. "If your father refuses to come with us, we might have to go by ourselves."

"I can't take Marcus away from him. Please don't ask me to," she pleaded. "Having a grandson was just what he needed. They've formed a wonderful bond. It's rewarding to watch them together."

"Marcus believes we're going back to Boston," Antonio reminded her. "We mentioned that to the children in Skowhegan, remember? Maria wants to know when she can go home to her mother, and my mother is desperate to see her. What am I to tell them? I can't postpone my leave much longer."

Juliet felt guilty thinking of the torment the girl and her mother must be going through. She had no solution. To hasten the decision, she beseeched her father to reconsider.

"Papa, you aren't being fair," she told him one afternoon, struggling to maintain her composure. "You promised Antonio my hand. He kept his part of the bargain. You need to do the same."

"When I made that promise to Mr. Santilli," her father said in a tight, logical voice, "I had not yet met my grandson."

Juliet saw with crystal clarity the effect Marcus had had on Papa's emotions, how the boy had turned his grandfather's heart. If only, she thought with sudden resentment, Cordelia had made up with Papa before her death. How happy they might all have been together instead of struggling as they were now.

Was she to be denied the opportunity for the same kind of happiness her sister had sought, in the city where her sister had lived and died? She feared the answer was not the one she wanted.

"I'm sorry, Juliet," her father said, interrupting her thoughts, "but I've changed my mind about my agreement."

"But, Papa, I love him," she said faintly, "and he loves me."

"I love you also," her father replied. "And I love my grandson. I plan to raise him here in Maine, where he belongs."

Her father returned to his reading and his pipe. With his usual method of avoidance he had dismissed Juliet once again. Quietly she slipped into the hall, closing the door behind her.

She leaned against the wall and took a deep breath. Put in the position of having to choose between the two men she loved, she was forced to end the conversation. Her only option was to stand up either to her father or to Antonio. Both would be upset by whatever decision she made, perhaps even angry with her.

Either decision would alter the lives of both men forever. Wishing one of the two would compromise, she walked downstairs slowly, wondering what had happened to the headstrong attitude that had disappeared when she needed it most.

Burdened by the decision she still had not made the next morning, Juliet chose not to accompany Antonio and the children on a ride to town, deciding instead to take a solitary walk close to home where her slow gait would not keep anyone waiting.

She had kept enough people waiting. Walking would give her a chance to consider her future once again. She knew Antonio would drive the children along the route he had taken with her.

He might even point out to Marcus and Maria the village schoolhouse where she taught. Would she ever return to teaching? Soon she would have to decide whether to have Mrs. Owens continue in her place when school resumed.

She was no closer to a solution as she opened the garden gate and entered her front yard, surprised to see Clara on the front porch. *Something must have happened,* Juliet thought with alarm. The housekeeper held the screen door open, a look of urgency on her face.

"There's been an accident," Clara said quickly. "Your father is fine, but he took an awful fall from the porch steps about a half hour ago. He's resting upstairs."

"Is he badly hurt?" Juliet felt herself tremble with fear. "Has the doctor been notified?"

"He doesn't appear to be seriously hurt. It's his back. The doctor is with him now."

Juliet found Dr. Simmons upstairs sitting by her father's bedside, chatting with his patient.

"If you're discussing the upcoming church picnic, it can't be too serious." Juliet studied her father with a feeling of relief. "First my injury, and now yours. Papa, how did this happen?"

The look on his face told her he was annoyed with himself. "I was trying out a new toy for Marcus, tossing his whirligig into the air to see how long it would stay aloft, when I missed the top step. My own clumsiness. Now I'll be laid up until Dr. Simmons says I don't have to stay in bed any longer."

"The best thing I can prescribe at this point is rest," the doctor cautioned. "That's a nasty sprain. You took a bad fall."

Juliet remained in the room long enough to convince herself her father wasn't more seriously injured than he'd admitted. Then she reviewed directions with the doctor on how to care for him properly. Walking him downstairs when he'd finished his visit, she was glad to be able to talk with Dr. Simmons in private.

"I understand there's some question of your father being invited to go to Boston with you," the doctor said in surprise.

Juliet hadn't expected Papa to speak of the matter to him. She decided to avoid mentioning Antonio until plans were set.

"My sister is buried in Boston," she explained, "and it's where Marcus has spent his life. He'd have opportunities there he wouldn't have here. We've had difficulty convincing Papa to consider moving. I suppose this sprain will put an end to that."

Dr. Simmons shook his head. "It isn't so much the back that prevents him from traveling as that weak heart of his. Your father is stubborn, Juliet. Making him leave if he's already reluctant would put more strain on him. I can't recommend it."

"I understand completely," she said soberly. "I would never ask Papa to do anything against his will, especially leave home."

"You tell him I don't want him taking any chances."

In parting, she accompanied Dr. Simmons outside, realizing she had nothing left to decide. The decision had been made for her. How would Antonio react? Would he choose to remain in Stockton Village? She returned to her father's room with a heavy heart.

"I saw you walking Dr. Simmons to the gate. What did he have to say?" her father demanded as soon as she returned. "Did he tell you anything that he isn't telling me?"

His words made her smile. "Don't be so suspicious, Papa. He told me the same thing he told you. You'll have to stay here until you're feeling better. You mustn't take any chances."

"That much I knew. What does he expect?" Papa said, his tone indignant. "I can't very well go to Boston like this, can I?"

Juliet grumbled aloud to herself as she poured water from the pitcher she'd moved closer to his bedside.

"Naturally not," she muttered. "If I didn't know better, I'd think you did it on purpose."

His hearing certainly hadn't been affected. "What was that, Juliet?" he said sharply. "It wasn't as if I did this intentionally. I hope that isn't what you're implying."

"Of course not, Papa." She tucked in the blankets at his feet, averting her face. "I understand how you feel, believe me."

Juliet could only imagine how Antonio felt as she gave him the details of Papa's accident on his return from town, her heart filled with trepidation. He displayed no hint of emotion but instead listened patiently. Was he angry? Did he think her foolish? Expecting the worst, she wouldn't blame him for either.

"I suppose this will force us to make a decision," he said after he appeared to think it over.

"I'm sorry," she blurted. "I know it isn't what we planned."

"No, but you have to abide by your father's wishes," Antonio said. "Right now, he needs you more than I do."

Juliet started to speak but held her tongue.

"I want you to remember this. Through it all," he told her, "I loved you for yourself. Not because you were your father's daughter. You've been trying to compensate for your sister's failure in your father's eyes, but you needn't have. Your father loves you for who you are." He was silent for a long moment, ominously silent. Finally he released a tight sigh. "Then it's decided."

"What do you mean? What's decided?" Juliet's heart thudded.

"Life isn't a game of chess, Juliet," he said, shaking his head, "even though it might feel like it right now. It's more complicated than that. Someone needs to make a move. Since we can't resolve our differences, I'll be the one to take that step."

Panic swept over her. "What move? Why must you take any step?"

"I can't stay here any longer. It isn't fair to make my mother wait. I'm taking Maria home. Where she belongs."

He spoke the last with a touch of sarcasm that chilled her. It reminded her of her father's feelings toward Marcus.

"But we haven't decided anything yet," she said awkwardly.

Antonio shrugged with a helplessness that left her fearful. "By choosing not to decide, you've made your decision. It's too late to change it."

Juliet started to object, but he raised his hand to silence her.

"It isn't your fault. The battle lines were drawn before we came here. Your father put you in a position where you had to choose, and now you can't leave. It seemed to me you made your choice even before his fall." He gave her a brief, sad smile. "Only one adult needs to leave this house, and that's me."

Chapter Fourteen

The steamy late-summer days gave way to autumn almost imperceptibly. The leaves in Maine began to turn before Juliet realized how much time had elapsed in Antonio's absence. She'd always loved the autumn colors, but this year she barely noticed the gold, russet, and crimson covering her yard. Her thoughts were far from the landscape, turned inward, where her heart languished in lonely isolation.

Since Antonio had left, she'd received one letter. He described how relieved and joyous his mother had been to be reunited with Maria, how well Mrs. Wetherall was doing, and how the fish market continued to thrive. It contained no mention of Isabel.

Busy with Papa and Marcus, and unsure what Antonio expected, Juliet debated how to respond while the days slipped away. Before she knew it, another month had passed in silence. After that, she saw no reason to write. By now, he had probably married Isabel.

He was a man of his word, Mrs. Wetherall had said. *Once he makes a promise, he doesn't break it.* And he had promised to marry Isabel, long before he ever met Juliet, before she had ever gone to Boston.

With her busy schedule, it wasn't hard to keep Antonio from her thoughts. Between the schoolchildren to whom she'd returned to teach and her situation at home, her life was full. Yet, she often found herself remembering Antonio's suggestion that her family life was somehow flawed.

True, she was the daughter of an overbearing father who

expected her not to marry. But she'd never expected to, nor did she want to, not even Hans. If she was more submissive than Cordelia, what did it matter? Until now, she'd always been happy.

Was she still? The question wasn't as easy to answer anymore. Papa seemed happy enough. Juliet was puzzled, yet fascinated, by the change in him. He continued to display his affection for Marcus openly. One day, they watched the frogs in the creek behind the house together for over an hour. Frogs delighted Marcus, as did the kite Papa had made him. Marcus appeared to thrive under the influence of his doting grandfather.

Yet, in quiet moments, Juliet detected a restlessness in her nephew. It was a wistfulness that was palpable, as if something were missing from his otherwise happy, bucolic life. As he sat gazing out the kitchen window, he appeared to be looking for something, but whatever it was never came. He sat in the same spot each afternoon before supper when the house was quiet. One day Juliet laid aside the cookbook to sit with her nephew.

"What would you like to eat tonight?" she asked.

"Whatever there is." Marcus shrugged. "It don't matter."

"Doesn't," she corrected him. Whatever it was he didn't want to talk about mattered greatly. Gently, she laid her hand over his, almost afraid to allow herself the emotional closeness. "You must miss your mother very much. I know I do."

Marcus turned to her, a dubious look on his face. "Sure, I do, but that's not what I'm thinking about."

"What's on your mind?" she asked, welcoming the chance to talk in depth.

"I'm bored," he complained. "I miss working. Mr. Santilli has probably given my job to somebody else by now."

So this was the cause of his unhappiness. The mood had begun shortly after Antonio left. Perhaps Marcus did belong in Boston, even if Antonio had married another. Brushing the thought from her mind, she tried to convince herself Marcus was better off where he was. The adjustment was simply taking longer than she'd hoped.

As the days wore on, his mood only seemed to worsen. Admitting his feelings about losing his job at the market had evidently opened a deep wound, one he had not recovered from. Juliet raised the matter with Papa one evening after Marcus was in bed.

"Perhaps we could find him a job," she suggested. "Something small. There must be some task he can do. Farmwork maybe."

"The boy doesn't need a job," her father retorted. "He has a good life now, between school with you and time with me."

She rephrased the idea. "Maybe he needs to get outdoors more, to do physical work. He was used to stocking shelves in Boston."

"I won't have my grandson stocking shelves. That's in the past. If he wants work, he can reorganize bookshelves for me."

And does Cordelia belong in the past as well? she was tempted to ask. Papa's irritation surprised her. She didn't want Marcus exposed to his occasional melancholy after the boy had lost his mother. Papa grew cranky or elusive whenever she raised the topic of Cordelia. With Marcus home safe and sound, she'd expected Papa to be less critical. He had no reason to be angry anymore.

It wasn't prejudice, Juliet was certain. Antonio would have been a positive role model. She realized one day that despite Papa's criticism of Cordelia, he probably never knew what her life in Boston was like. He might be less disapproving if he understood all she had endured after recognizing her mistake in selecting a husband.

One rainy evening, Juliet felt it was time to share the story of her sister's bleak existence after Daniel Malloy had left to pan for gold in California. At her words, her father slammed the book he'd been reading onto a side table. The gesture made her jump.

"Your sister made her choice," he said, his tone so cold, she could hardly believe he was speaking of his own daughter. "She had to live with the consequences of her decision. We all do."

Juliet absorbed her father's hostility like a blow. While he'd lost a daughter upon Cordelia's death, she had lost a sister and Marcus a mother. She and Papa had been devastated to learn of Cordelia's death five months before. He'd had differences with Cordelia, but Juliet vividly remembered the trembling lip, the moist eyes, and the disbelief on his face as he read Mrs. Wetherall's telegram. How could he have recovered from the pain so quickly?

"Papa," she said in a low voice, trembling with anger, "that isn't fair. You can't speak that way around Marcus. Cordelia was his mother. Why weren't you able to forgive her for what she did? She died without your forgiveness." She softened her tone. "I don't know why you're still angry, but it doesn't matter. All that matters is that you think of Marcus' feelings before your own. If you don't, you'll lose your grandson the same way you lost his mother."

Unable to comprehend her own fury that had led to such an outburst, and ashamed of the wrathful tone she'd used with her father in his weakened state, Juliet rose and made her way upstairs. With no clue how to begin to understand his anger, she had no idea how to deal with it. All she knew was that, with a child under their roof, her approach was no longer adequate.

Papa was a good influence academically on his grandson, but his negative attitude toward Marcus' mother made her wonder if her nephew really would be better off in Boston. Nothing seemed to alter Papa's opinion of Cordelia and the decisions she'd made in her youth. Despite her love for her father, it became increasingly difficult for even Juliet to tolerate his moods.

The following morning, as if Mrs. Wetherall had heard her thoughts, Juliet was surprised to receive a letter from Boston. Her emotions dulled by pain, she read of the new boarders with whom the landlady shared her home. There were also changes in the neighborhood that were likely to improve residents' lives. It was the end of the note that twisted her heart.

While I have no doubt you and Marcus are happy in Maine, Mrs. Wetherall wrote, *I wish you would reconsider your decision. If there is any chance we might look forward to a visit from you both, I would encourage you to make it soon. Take it from one who has lived seven decades. Build your own family. Live your own life. Remember that love is not something you control. Live life as if tomorrow will not wait, for often it won't.*

In closing, Mrs. Wetherall expressed her affection and asked Juliet to keep in touch. Tears filled Juliet's eyes as she scanned the note a second time before refolding it. She hesitated to read between the lines, fearing her imagination was playing tricks on her. The letter moved her as nothing else had since her return home.

Mrs. Wetherall had not spoken of Antonio, yet the blank spaces on the page whispered his name across the miles. The letter tempted her to book passage on the next boat to Boston.

Then she remembered Papa, considered his physical limitations, and changed her mind.

The sidewalk in Boston outside the North End's largest fish market was crowded with customers. So crowded it made Antonio wonder if a schooner had delivered a cargo of customers in addition to the morning's catch.

"It's the quality of the fish, Mr. Santilli," Mrs. O'Hara exclaimed, who hugged her two bags after she refused his offer to carry them home for her. "It's the freshest anywhere. It's as good as I ever had even back home in Ireland, bless me soul."

Mrs. O'Hara reminded him of Rose Ryan, who had so kindly opened her home to him in Maine. He tried not to think of the similarities. Better to put those memories from his mind, happy as they were. With Irish and Jewish customers coming to his market on a regular basis now, he reflected, it might be time to expand his offerings. He stepped into his tiny office to reconcile his accounts.

"Mrs. Cummings' son just brought this order," his brother Giorgio announced, sticking his head in the door with a broad smile. "It's even longer than her list from last week. We must be doing something right, eh?"

"Did you hear that, Maria?" Antonio asked as his sister wandered into the room, putting her chin on her arms as she leaned on the desk. Since it was not a school day, Maria had spent her afternoon in the market, scurrying about and getting underfoot while being instructed to keep out of the way as she watched her family at work. "We're doing better than we ever imagined. Isn't that wonderful?"

"I guess." She shrugged.

"It should make you happy." Antonio gathered her into his lap in a sweeping hug that made her smile. The look didn't last, however. "One day you'll grow up and have opportunities I never had when I was your age."

"But I have no one to share it with, now that Marcus isn't here." Maria pouted. "It's no fun anymore."

"But you have friends," Antonio reminded her, at a momentary loss, "both at school and in the neighborhood."

"But it's boring," she complained, intertwining her fingers in her lap. "None of them know how to juggle like Marcus did. Marcus was fun. He was my best friend." She looked up with pleading eyes. "I miss him, Antonio. Can't you bring him back?"

"I miss him too."

Antonio was troubled by the change he had seen in his sister in the last few months. She'd experienced happy moments too, often related to her accomplishments at school. Yet a profound disappointment had lingered since her return from Maine. He did not know how to repair the emotional damage Marcus' absence had caused. Nothing he offered seemed to ease her sorrow.

When Lillian Wetherall came by later in the day to buy clams, she admitted she was just as mystified by Maria's subdued mood.

"I think it's Marcus she misses, I'm sorry to say. I miss him too, along with his aunt. There's not much we can do about it, I'm afraid." She smiled briefly in parting. "I suppose it won't be long before we'll see Isabel working in the shop."

He heard Mrs. Wetherall exchange pleasantries with someone as she was leaving. Antonio looked up to see a welcome face as Isabel's cousin, his closest friend, approached him. Their families had sailed from Italy together, and Raphael had done as well in Boston as Antonio had from the time he'd opened his cheese shop. He greeted Antonio with his customary Italian salutation, but his expression did not hold the cheer it usually did.

"You look as if the roof just collapsed on your head," Antonio said with concern. "Anything wrong?"

"You know me well, my friend." Raphael studied him, his eyes affectionate but grave. "I'm afraid I've called with sad news."

Chapter Fifteen

For over a month, Juliet watched patiently as her father struggled to recover from his injury. Sometimes she felt he should have made more progress than he had. She had no reason to believe he was pretending to be more seriously ill than he was. With Marcus at home, he had every reason to want to recover as quickly as possible.

"In the beginning," she admitted to Clara one afternoon, "I hoped if Papa recovered quickly enough, I might be able to go to Boston to see if a relationship was still possible with Antonio." She sighed. "I'm afraid all chances of that are gone."

Clara paused in putting out the plates. "You won't know unless you try," she countered.

Unable to fight off her burden of responsibility, Juliet shrugged. "The problem hasn't gone away. Marcus is still my first responsibility, and Papa wants me here. I just wish he wouldn't express his anger toward Cordelia in front of Marcus. Such strong resentment doesn't come out of nowhere. Papa must have loved her deeply to have been so hurt by her actions."

"Try to be tolerant of your father. He does have his weaknesses when it comes to dealing with children." There was sympathy, if not conviction, in Clara's tone. "Your father went through some difficult times. He loved Cordelia very deeply. She was the light of his life."

"I wish his emotions were easier to fathom," Juliet murmured. "Sometimes I think he'd rather have Cordelia here than me."

"Hush, don't say such things," Clara admonished. "Sometimes we have only ourselves to blame for how things turn out."

Juliet stared after her as Clara went outdoors to pick the last of the marigolds for the supper table. Who was Clara faulting for their actions? Cordelia, Papa, or both? Juliet herself might be at fault for not making a different decision about her future. She believed she'd made the best decision possible for Marcus. Yet, as she watched the autumn unfold, she'd begun to doubt herself.

She watched Clara through the kitchen window, melancholy stealing over her. She was convinced of only one thing. She was certain the life they knew now wasn't what anyone here wanted.

Not even Papa.

It was later that day when Juliet realized she had noticed subtle changes in Papa in the past week. A weakness had come over him that wasn't there before. He was often confused as to the day and sometimes even whom he was addressing. When a persistent cough started up, Juliet felt it was time to summon Dr. Simmons.

"Pneumonia," the doctor said grimly when he emerged from her father's room. "I'd like to hospitalize him, but he refuses."

The diagnosis alarmed Juliet but didn't surprise her. Nor did her father's attitude. "Hospitalization meant the end for my mother," she reflected. "Perhaps it's just as well he remains here. Clara and I can care for him where he'll be comfortable."

"You mustn't blame yourself for what's happening," Dr. Simmons warned her. "I advised him to sit up as much as possible these last few weeks. I know he's been outside, but he's still spent more time in bed than I'd like. He's grown steadily weaker the last two years. It's to be expected, at his age, with his heart and lung issues. It's stubbornness that's kept him going."

A deeper concern filled Juliet when she saw no change in her father over the next few days as he fought fever and chills intermittently. As his lucid moments became fewer, she and Clara took turns sitting by his bedside.

"The only conversations he has these days are with himself," she told Clara worriedly. "I'm afraid he won't come out of this."

When his mind wandered, he spoke often of Juliet's mother and Cordelia, addressing them as if they were still there. When he addressed Juliet at all, he startled her by speaking to her as if she were still a child.

Juliet went looking for Clara one morning while her father slept more soundly than he had in days. She checked upstairs and down, reluctant to call too loudly for fear of disturbing him, until she remembered that Clara had gone into the village with Marcus for some lettuce.

Juliet was reluctant to go through Papa's things on her own. Yet, she had to face the possibility that her father, now in his seventies, might not recover. To help keep her worries at bay, she decided to look for the addresses of relatives who would need to be notified should Papa not survive.

She was surprised to find no family information in his study. If she was expected to provide for him in his old age, she had to know where he kept important papers and household accounts. She wished she had asked him sooner instead of waiting until now, when he was unresponsive much of the time and the burden of running the household fell solely on her.

After a half hour of searching through desk drawers and pigeonholes, she realized that the office must be dedicated only to academic studies. Perhaps he kept personal papers in his bedroom. Fortunately, she and Clara had moved Papa into the sitting room earlier that morning, settling him beside a window so he would at least have a view of the ocean to calm him while he was awake.

Trudging upstairs, she made her way quietly past the sitting room, relieved when no sound greeted her from behind the closed door. Sleep would do him as much good as anything now. She tiptoed into his bedroom, closing the door behind her softly.

The desk beside the window gleamed as the morning light fell across its cherry surface. Here she found all that was missing from downstairs. Household accounts, bank statements, papers, and family letters were still in their envelopes. Here, she thought, she would find addresses of relatives who lived out of state.

Idly she perused the envelopes, recognizing the names of distant cousins she hadn't seen in years. Returning the stack to its slot, she decided she might as well acquaint herself as much as possible with household affairs. She opened the desk's single drawer to make sure she hadn't missed anything of importance.

There she found more business papers, neatly folded, most from a decade ago or more. Among the items was Papa's will. With a catch in her throat she set it aside. At least she had located it in case it was needed. As she ran her hand toward the back of the drawer, her fingers encountered the corner of an envelope that she pulled forward.

The return address made her pause. Addressed to her father, the letter was from Boston. She assumed it was from Cordelia until she realized the familiar writing was not in her sister's hand. The letter had come to their old address in Farmington. Her heart stopped briefly as she saw the name in the corner: *L. Halliday.* Louisa Halliday. She'd read enough of her mother's recipe cards to recognize the penmanship.

With trembling fingers she turned over the flap and withdrew the letter from the envelope. She felt guilty opening it, knowing what it meant to Papa. He must have kept this letter because of his deep love for her. But when had Mum ever been in Boston?

Pausing, she decided this was not the time to worry about respecting her parents' privacy. Anything that would bring Papa solace would help. In the event he didn't pull through, she thought with a heavy heart, seeing this note might comfort him.

The words she read made no sense at first. In the note, Mum apologized to Papa for leaving Maine and going to Boston with

a man whose name Juliet did not recognize. She wasn't prepared for the shock that flooded through her. She remembered
how her mother disappeared from the house one day and Papa
telling her Mum had fallen ill and been taken to the hospital. It
was a week later that Papa told her Mum had died.

The letter told a different story. Her hands shaking, Juliet
felt her knees weaken to the point where she could no longer
remain on her feet. She needed to sit on Papa's bed before
she fell, her legs barely reaching the floor. This was not the
mother she knew. She felt like a child again as she continued
reading.

> *There might be times you will need to contact me. Pad-*
> *raic and I do not plan to return to Ireland as we dis-*
> *cussed, even though we felt we might do better to return*
> *to his homeland. Instead, I will spend my life in Boston.*
> *If you need to reach me, you will find me there.*
>
> *I'm so sorry, Albert. I know you can never understand*
> *or forgive me for what I've done. I don't expect it, leav-*
> *ing you and the children as I did, so Padraic and I could*
> *be together. I did so knowing you'll provide the best home*
> *possible for our children.*
>
> *I understand I have no legal right to the children,*
> *but they will soon be grown-up. I know you will give*
> *Henry adequate guidance, but the girls' needs will*
> *change. Cordelia is nearly grown, but she needs your*
> *love and protection now more than ever, as does Juliet.*
> *They will continue to need you. Lavish them with the*
> *affection you showed me early in our marriage. Treat*
> *them well, Albert, especially Juliet. I might have given*
> *you no reason to believe me, but one day I will make it*
> *up to her.*

But she never had. Shock and anger surged through every
fiber of Juliet's being. Her mother had not kept her word. She
might as well be dead to Juliet, for she had never been in
touch. Her mother had not died, as her father led her to be-

lieve, but instead had run off with an immigrant. A man named Padraic.

So much for having a marriage like her parents'. Juliet's ideal shattered like the looking glass over her father's shaving stand. Their marriage had been false, staged for the children's benefit. A lie. The reality left her crushed, disillusioned. How would she ever see her mother the same way again? How could she feel the same?

She thought of Henry, having disappeared so completely from their lives, keeping in touch long distance through letters until word of his desertion and subsequent death had reached them. Papa had never spoken of him again.

Henry must have felt abandoned by their mother. Had her leaving home prompted his own leavetaking? Perhaps Papa, as emotionally devastated as he was, hadn't been able to give Henry the guidance he needed to save him from his fate.

Juliet read the letter again, noting her mother's words about her father's aloofness. Had Henry left because Papa made life intolerable for him as well? Emotions butted against each other as her resentment collided with understanding. The revelations made her head spin. She'd always assumed her mother was dead.

In reality she had left of her own free will. Mum's closing line, requesting Papa to "tell Juliet the truth after I'm dead," held no joy for her. She could not begin to fathom its meaning.

One fact was clear. Her mother had not died, as Juliet had believed for the past fourteen years. She sat bolt upright. Could it mean her mother was still alive somewhere? The possibility filled her with hope and apprehension at the same time.

Her reflections came to a halt with the crashing of the screen door downstairs. The sound returned Juliet to her senses. Perhaps now she would get some answers.

"I want the truth," Juliet demanded. "After all I've been through, Clara, you know I can handle it. What happened between Papa and Cordelia? Where is my mother? I need to know. Please."

They were in the backyard, far from Marcus and the maids indoors, where she could talk and shed her emotions in private.

"All in good time, child, all in good time," Clara said gently. "Your mama always intended for you to know the truth. I believe now is the time."

Clara moved her chair closer to Juliet's, the October leaves falling around them as she did so.

"We'll leave the others in charge of your father. Don't worry," Clara directed, placing a firm hand on Juliet's arm. "I've instructed Lucille to let us know at once if anything happens. We left him resting, and I expect him to remain that way. So." She studied Juliet with a look of regret. "You read that letter from your mama."

Juliet released a deep breath of frustration. "There's so much I don't understand. I always thought Mum died. But she ran off with another man." She shook her head in bewilderment. "It's unthinkable. Why did Papa pretend all these years?"

"Out of love for you, child. Why else?" Clara paused with a smile, studying the landscape before she turned back to Juliet. "I know it must look as if your mother is all to blame and your father did no wrong. That isn't entirely how it was. My family worked for the Hallidays before I was born. I knew your papa long before I went to work for him."

Feeling vulnerable, Juliet left her chair and settled herself instead in the grass at Clara's feet, making herself comfortable with the closest person she had to a mother. Her head shot up at the words, Clara's gaze a sharp reprimand.

"Don't get me wrong," Clara said. "Your father always had my loyalty, if not my sympathy. When he met your mother, life changed for us all. Your papa was all work, same as he is now. Your mama was more fun loving. She enjoyed people and liked dancing. They were very much in love. This might surprise you, but your papa was quite dashing when he was young. Your mama thought so. He knew poetry and quoted Shakespeare. Your mama was so pretty. He was enchanted with her. But there isn't as much merriment in Maine in wintertime as there was in Baltimore, where she grew up. She wasn't happy without the parties and the excitement. She tried her hardest, but she couldn't make it work."

"So she found someone else." Juliet's tone was accusing. "Someone she cared about more than her own children."

"It isn't that simple, Juliet. She was different from your father. She was headstrong and impulsive, like your sister." She put a comforting arm around Juliet. "Now you, you're just like your papa. Responsible, helpful, headstrong in your own right. But always with other people's welfare at heart. You adjust your needs to suit others. That's what your papa did."

Clara stroked Juliet's hair with gentle fingers. "Your mother had a gentleman companion. She knew they could never marry. Divorce would have scandalized you and Cordelia. Your father made life hard for your mother. You know how he is. He cares deeply, but he doesn't show it. Once Cordelia was grown, your mother couldn't take it anymore. She relied on Cordelia and me to take care of you after she left. She had no way of knowing Cordelia would also leave."

"Papa told me she died," Juliet blurted. "He'd rather have me believe she was dead than tell me the truth."

"He was protecting you, child. He wanted only what was best for you. He didn't tell you right away after your mama left. He waited, hoping against hope, assuming she'd change her mind and return, realizing she made a mistake. That never happened."

"Tell me about Cordelia's leaving," Juliet said quietly. "What came between Cordelia and Papa? He's always resented her so, and now it seems to me he was being unfair."

"Odd how history repeats itself." Clara smiled sadly. "Your mother went off to Boston with an Irishman, and Cordelia did the same. Followed in her footsteps and ended up in an unhappy marriage. It was the final blow for your papa, losing the daughter who was always so aptly named. I'll admit she was his favorite when you were younger. He's capable of enduring a great deal, but he doesn't show his emotions. Cordelia struggled with his aloofness after your mother left. She looked outside the family for acceptance, and she found love with an Irishman, like your mother did."

Juliet had stopped listening, her thoughts focused on Papa. Clara's explanation had given her a new understanding of his wary nature. She felt her respect grow for the father she once considered emotionally distant and hypocritical. She saw him now as a parent who sheltered his children, protecting them against hurt and social disgrace. He had even chosen to preserve Juliet's vision of her absent mother to save her pain.

It was the loss of his wife that had made him bitter. All this time, she had thought it was because he missed her mother. She had never guessed it was because he blamed himself and felt he couldn't make up the loss to Juliet.

And all while she thought he was being selfish. Juliet felt humiliated and remorseful for her unkindness.

"Every time Papa hears my name," she said, anguish filling her heart, "he must feel resentful. The daughter he loves is gone, and I'm the one he has left."

"He loves you more than you know. I hope you can see that."

Grief stabbed at her as she remembered Antonio telling her that her father loved her for who she was. The urgency in Clara's tone convinced her it must be true. The only thing she was beginning to see clearly was something she remembered from Boston.

She hadn't thought much about it at the time. A small gravestone beside Cordelia's cemetery plot. A stone that read simply, *Louisa*. Louisa, their mother's name.

She remembered thinking how devastated the parents must have been to lose a child so young. Mrs. Wetherall claimed the gravestone was that of Daniel's niece, who died at only a few days old. The size of the headstone had led Juliet to assume it was a child's grave. But Mrs. Wetherall had lied to spare her feelings.

She saw it clearly now. Cordelia was buried with their mother. Her grave was what had kept Cordelia in the city. The longing to see their mother might have been what led her to Boston in the first place. Daniel Malloy wasn't the only one with family there. It explained Mrs. Wetherall's reluctance to show Juliet the grave. She must have known at least part of the story.

The stone had no last name and no date, but Juliet was sure it was their mother's. The plot had belonged not to the Malloy family, but to her mother's companion. They were buried together, although they'd never married. Papa hadn't granted her a divorce for fear of bringing disgrace upon his children.

Clara, she realized, must have known as well. No wonder Clara had wanted to turn back as they approached the boardinghouse for the first time.

"I'd like to believe Cordelia kept in contact with someone from home all those years," Juliet said. "She confided in you."

Clara sighed. "Since I brought the mail in, I was able to keep her letters from you and your father. Cordelia didn't want anyone to know how she lived. I didn't know how bad her situation was until you and I went to Boston."

In a flash, Juliet understood why Cordelia hadn't turned to Papa for help. She hadn't died alone, after all. She'd chosen to be buried with the only family she felt she still had, the family she knew best.

Juliet realized that part of Papa's anger was that Cordelia, the child he'd named, the daughter who was supposed to be as loyal as the one in Shakespeare's play, was loyal to her mother. Cordelia must have known their mother was living in Boston with the man she loved. Now Juliet understood why Papa had never gone to Boston to see his grandson. It wasn't because of Cordelia.

It was because of their mother.

Juliet put her face in Clara's lap and wept.

"You were so young when it happened," Clara said soothingly as if reading her mind. "You were eight years younger than Cordelia. Once she left home, it was easy to hide the truth."

Juliet was too upset to reply. Her world had been turned upside down. At some point, she had been disillusioned with all of them—Cordelia, her brother who had turned cowardly during the war, Marcus, Papa, now her mother. Even Clara, for concealing the truth from her.

"Why didn't Papa tell me she ran off?" Juliet demanded.

"He was protecting your mother's memory for you," she said.

"You should have told me."

"You and I still had time together," Clara said. "I had to be loyal to the memory of your mother and to Cordelia."

Someone had to be, Juliet thought recklessly. It certainly couldn't fall to Papa to do it. He had often claimed immigration was ruining the country. What Juliet had seen as prejudice on his part was bitterness. Her heart ached as she realized the pain he must have felt to see Cordelia act as their mother had.

She thought of her father's willingness to travel when they were younger, all to satisfy her mother's wanderlust. No wonder he hated immigrants so, even Antonio. Especially Antonio, Juliet realized with a start. She was the only female in the family who hadn't deserted her father because of an immigrant.

"How incredibly sad," she said slowly. "Cordelia's marriage was much like Papa's, wasn't it? Neither one worked out."

"Your papa wanted to spare you that. And even though you can't see it now, your mother loved you. With Cordelia being so much older, your mother could talk with her and explain why she had to leave. Cordelia was devastated, but she understood why your mother felt as she did. Cordelia herself was a young woman ready for marriage." Clara brushed Juliet's hair to one side, smoothing the strands that had loosened in the afternoon breeze. "But it was you your mother worried about. That's why she left you a letter."

"For me?" Juliet sat up. "After all these years?"

"That's right. Your mother gave me a letter to give to you when you were old enough." Juliet was startled to see Clara wipe a tear from the corner of her eye. Her hands shook as she removed an envelope from her pocket. "I've kept this in a safe place in the house for years. I guess that time is now. You're old enough."

"So this is how my mother wanted it," Juliet said in a small voice, almost too fearful to accept the letter Clara offered her. She took it with trembling fingers.

"This way, she could put her feelings for you into words," Clara explained. "Her own words. She knew you were in good hands. You were deeply loved. What do you think kept me here all these years?" Squeezing her shoulder affectionately, Clara rose discreetly, leaving Juliet to read her letter. "I'm going to check on your father. I'll let you know if anything changes."

Somehow, Juliet could not bring herself to open the letter here, in her backyard, when one of the servants might come out. She needed a private place, one with meaning. She remembered the apple orchard where she used to swing in her youth.

Slowly, she made her way toward the back of the property. The trees were bare of fruit now, the apples either already eaten or stored for the winter. After looking for a moment, she found her swing, the ropes and wooden seat still intact, though the bolts were rusty. She was happy to see they held as she tested it.

Unable to wait another moment, she tore the letter from its envelope. There had been too many revelations today, all unhappy ones. She hoped this letter, one that reached across the years, would give her some closure as well as a beginning. Holding her breath, she unfolded the note.

The opening paragraphs recounted the changes that had led her mother to the decision she'd made. They included reassurances of her love and affection for her children and explained, as Clara had, the reasons she felt she needed to leave. Her spirit had been stifled by Papa, she said. But never by her children, she assured Juliet, whom she loved with her entire soul.

You must know, my darling, that regardless of what else you hear, I loved your father. He was a good man, and we were wildly in love once. But we were not well suited.

I hope and pray your life will be different from mine. When you find a man you can give your heart to, by all means do it, no matter what your father says or who he might choose for you. Love is yours to give. It is not a decision to be made lightly, nor is it one to have thrust upon you.

Tears streamed down Juliet's face as she folded the page, replacing it carefully in the envelope that had waited fourteen years to be opened. She thought about Papa, lying unconscious upstairs, his life perhaps closing in on its end. She thought about the mother who'd loved her, the mother Juliet so recently believed had died long before she had.

Papa must have feared being abandoned by all three women in his life. Juliet knew now she had done the right thing by staying. She felt surrounded by love, even while she felt alone with Antonio so far away. An overwhelming, satisfying sense of finality filled her, despite her tears.

And without another thought, another moment wasted, she jumped from the swing and ran back toward the house. She'd uttered words she'd regretted, words she couldn't take back now, but they could be softened with words from the heart. Words that had to be said, that could not wait.

Words that were a matter of life and death.

Upon returning to the house, Juliet was told her father had been moved back to his bedroom. The news alarmed her, for she feared he'd had a setback. To her great surprise, Papa was awake and propped up on the pillows when she entered his bedroom.

She pulled a chair alongside his bed and reached for his hand, squeezing it gently, lovingly. "Aren't you looking well today?" she said softly.

"I'm feeling well," Papa said, sounding surprised. He looked more elderly and frail than she'd ever thought possible. How rapidly his health had failed. "You know, I've been thinking. My grandson really does deserve the best. I believe what he needs," Papa added with a thoughtful frown, "is to return to Boston."

He stared at Juliet, waiting for a reply she was too overwhelmed to give. All she could do was stare.

"Don't you think I see how unhappy the boy is?" he prompted. "He needs to be back among memories of his mother. I can see firsthand he won't be happy in the country. He has too much energy. He needs people and activity around him. Juliet?"

"Yes, Papa," she gulped, shocked and happy at the change in his attitude. "What about your memories of Cordelia?"

"Memories belong to the past. 'What's in a name?'" An affection her father rarely displayed creased the corners of his watery eyes. "In Shakespeare's world, Cordelia might be the loyal child. In mine, it is my Juliet."

She held her breath, trying to stifle the sob that caught in her throat as he squeezed her hand. His grip was so feeble as to be almost useless. She returned the gentle pressure, the fiercest of loyalties tugging at her.

"It's time I release you as well," he continued. Amusement filled his eyes at the confusion he saw in hers. "'Renounce thy father and deny thy name.' Take another name. How does Juliet Santilli sound to you?" The brightness in his eyes faded suddenly, as if a cloud had crossed the sun. "I could not go, my dear, before releasing you."

"I need no release, Papa," she said faintly. "It was my choice to stay."

"And it was admirable of you to do so. But it is no longer in *my* power to choose. It appears I will follow Cordelia, and in the same year. Antonio awaits you in Boston. Do you think I have not seen the loneliness in your face, the longing to be elsewhere? Marcus is more outspoken with his desires, but I see it in you as well, no matter how you try to hide it. It would be better for both of you to be there."

His words touched and bewildered her. She struggled to find a reason to refute them. "I stay not only for you, Papa. I have students here. It was good of Mrs. Owens to replace me during your illness, but when you're well again, I'll return to teaching."

"Don't you think it would be easier for the town to replace its schoolmistress than for Antonio to find another bride?"

Papa's eyes were keen as he stared into hers. The look was so intense, it took her breath away.

"He does not want an Italian girl, my dear. He wants you. It's as simple as that. Love, when it is true, is quite simple." He spoke with such earnestness, she allowed her gaze to meet his again. "He will find that out, if he hasn't already. Don't you know how hard it will be for him to break the news to his mother? There are children everywhere who need a good teacher. Do not limit yourself to remaining close to home, child, as I limited Cordelia. As I limited myself and your mother."

Juliet struggled to find her voice, to find the right words.

"Very well, Papa," she said meekly. "If Antonio feels the same, perhaps Marcus and I will go to Boston. But we could not go without you."

Even as she spoke the words, she knew in her heart it was unlikely he would survive the journey. Papa gave an easy shrug, his eyes brightening but never leaving her face.

"Then it's settled," he announced. "I shall have to come with you. I'll finally have a chance to pay my respects properly at Cordelia's grave."

He leaned back in the pillows, his energy spent, although his smile remained. He took her hand in both of his.

"I give you my blessing, child," he murmured, his voice raspy, "and ask your forgiveness."

"There is nothing to forgive, Papa." Her own voice was barely a whisper. "You have given me the best life possible. It is all anyone could ever wish for."

"Then I can sleep in peace now," he said with a smile and a yawn. "Since that is what I need most, I must ask you to let me rest for the day."

And with that he turned his face away, drifted off to sleep again, and released Juliet's hand.

Her heart was filled with joy and hope as she went to Papa's room the next morning. They'd parted in such good spirits the day before, with her father's slight strength suggesting a possible recuperation, that she hoped he would feel the same optimism she did toward the future. She went to his room early, going to the windows to part the drapes and allow the sun to fill the room.

"Good morning, Professor," she said easily as she gazed out, enjoying the sight of the rippling blue water beyond the window. "Time to rise and shine and give the orders for breakfast. What shall we bring you today?"

With the drapes open, she glanced back toward the bed. Papa's face bore a peaceful expression she hadn't seen in years. It made him appear younger. The slight smile on his withered lips brought a wider one to Juliet's features. She crossed the patches of light on the floor to his bed, sunlight warming her skirt.

As she approached, she recognized a stillness in his face not typical of her father. Calling his name softly, she took his hand in hers, surprised by its coldness.

Minutes later Clara confirmed what she feared.

"He must have gone to his reward during the night. It was a peaceful death. We should all go so quickly." Clara slipped her arm around Juliet. "My shoulder is here, child, if you need it."

Juliet was too stunned to cry. While death had appeared imminent from the severity of his pneumonia, Papa had seemed so alert less than twenty-four hours ago. It was hard to reconcile the man she saw today with the father who'd been so agreeable yesterday. It was also hard to believe the father she saw the day before was the same one she'd grown up with. Now she had neither.

"I hope I wasn't wrong to shelter you," Clara said. "Maybe I should have shown you Cordelia's letters. She worried about you, just like your mother did. Cordelia considered herself a second mother to you. But relations here made it hard for her to remain, and when love called for the first time in her life, well . . ."

Her voice trailed off. Juliet finished the thought.

"She couldn't say no. I don't fault her for leaving."

Free of her father's influence, Juliet felt charitable toward Cordelia for the first time. She wondered why she hadn't been able to make the same decision. Doubt nagged at her, an almost welcome relief from the prospect of planning his funeral.

"You must forgive me," Clara said, her voice breaking.

Juliet turned to embrace her, releasing her after a long moment in which they both shed pent-up tears.

"You did it out of love," Juliet said gently. "How could I hold that against you?"

Shaking her head to clear her mind, Juliet stepped to the window, gazing out at the water without seeing.

"I'm glad I have you, Clara," she said in a small voice. "I'm so sorry for the times I was annoyed with you. I never understood until now. I didn't realize Cordelia had reason to be angry at Papa. I thought it was the other way around." She shook her head, finding it hard to absorb the sudden changes. "You're all I have now. What would I do without you? It's as if all the people I've revered for so long have feet of clay."

"Like fallen idols." Stepping up behind her, Clara laid a hand on her shoulder. "Put your faith where it belongs, Juliet."

Juliet thought how much Papa had sacrificed for her. She reflected on what Antonio had said—that she was living her life for her father, fulfilling his wishes rather than her own.

"How can I," Juliet faltered, "when all the lessons I've been taught are false? It's as Antonio said. I finally understand Papa, but it's at such a cost. I've never felt so disillusioned."

"That will pass. You have a mind of your own to make up," Clara reminded her. "Your life is yours now to do as you will."

There was no time to reflect on her words, Juliet realized. There would only be time to grieve. She remembered telling Mrs. Wetherall how private Cordelia had been. She'd used the word *secretive*. No wonder the landlady had found it difficult to track down the family to notify them of Cordelia's death.

Yet, she must have known the family's address if Clara wrote to Cordelia regularly. The fact that she hadn't contacted them sooner told Juliet that Cordelia wanted her burial to be private. Could she really have assumed her family wouldn't come?

Then she remembered. The realization made her smile even as she fought back tears. Cordelia had not been alone.

She'd had their mother with her.

Chapter Sixteen

A shower of golden leaves rained down on Marcus. He twirled as they fell around him, settling in haphazard piles at his feet. Juliet looked up from her raking to see her nephew silhouetted in the afternoon sunlight; her heart was warmed by the sight even while she watched her labors wasted.

From beside the porch, where she bent down to pick some lingering marigolds that she had missed, Clara anticipated Juliet's reprimand. "Don't you have some arithmetic waiting to be done?" she reminded him.

"I did most of it. What if I count to a hundred instead?" Marcus challenged. "I'll count all the yellow leaves I can find."

"What if I take you inside," Clara suggested, "so we can see if that pumpkin pie I put in the oven is ready?"

The brightness of the sun and the exertion of raking had taken its toll on Juliet. Wiping her brow with her sleeve as Clara ushered Marcus indoors, she dropped down on the porch steps, finished with her day's efforts. The leaves would never remain under control with her exuberant nephew waiting to fling them skyward.

She gazed at the sun as it dropped in the heavens, wishing she might find peace in the slanting rays that spread over the late-afternoon landscape. It was time to put her disillusionment behind her. Before that could happen, she knew, she had to overcome her own self-doubt.

She had made her decision. She would stay here, where she'd lived with Papa. She had not heard from Antonio again and did not expect to. She would content herself with the small family

178

she still had, made up now of Marcus and Clara. Work would occupy her mind. Teaching held the joy it always had for her. She'd stay on as schoolmistress as long as Stockton Village needed her, probably until she met the same fate as her parents and sister.

Sometimes, though, her days felt empty. It must be Papa's absence in his study, at the head of the dinner table, here in the garden. Although she treasured her relationship with Marcus, her life somehow consisted of less than it had before. Her chance for a relationship with Antonio was gone, sacrificed to other ideals. The woman he had waited so long for had come.

Juliet had to believe he was happy. She would end her life here alone, never having known what marriage was like. She tried to convince herself that her life had turned out the way it was meant to.

She stood up, ready to go inside and check on supper. As she did, a slight movement at the end of the lane caught her eye. Her heart dulled when she realized it wasn't who she thought it was. The man she saw among the trees was merely a traveler burdened by a trio of suitcases. How could Antonio be here after all, with such a large fish market to run back in Boston and most certainly married to Isabel by now? It wasn't possible.

But her words didn't match the vision that grew clearer as the figure rounded the bend. It did not take her long to recognize the determined step, the strong shoulders, the waves of dark hair.

Even from a distance, she knew it was him.

Unable to restrain herself, she ran down the porch steps to the man, who dropped his luggage and opened his arms to her. He looked as strong and calm as always, greeting her with a gentle laugh as he folded her in an embrace. She held him, with no regard for the neighbors in their windows who gaped in astonishment at how forward their village schoolmistress had become.

"Antonio," she gasped, clutching his jacket.

In his arms, she felt as if life were being breathed back into her. After a moment, she released him, her sense of propriety returning. She smoothed her hair and took a step back, holding him at arm's length, unable to take her eyes from his beloved face.

"Why did you come back? I'm surprised you were able to get away. Who's running the market? How is Maria? And— and what about Isabel?"

Antonio smiled tenderly, taking her hands in his. He gazed into her eyes as if searching for something. As she ran her fingers over his, she realized there was no thick gold band where she had expected one.

She looked at his hand in disbelief. Her senses had not betrayed her. She raised her eyes to his in a question.

He shrugged, his eyes locking with hers. "You're looking for a ring I wore only once, at the Ryans' home. For a long time, it didn't mean what it should to me. It represented only Carlo's success. For years I tried to make it up to my family for the loss of Carlo, even though his death had nothing to do with me. But I was the next child in line, as you are." He raised his fingers to her cheek, stroking it gently, his eyes searching hers. "I see the same in you. You've fulfilled your duty, as I have. Surely you see that now."

"Now I do." Her statement barely above a whisper, Juliet's voice broke despite her smile. "But the ring."

With a sigh Antonio dropped his hands, sliding them into his pockets. "A while back a friend brought me some news. Isabel did come to America. But while we were apart, she decided to marry someone else, someone who also wanted to come to America. They did come. Together."

Shock flooded through her. *How could any sane woman refuse marriage to such a man?*

"I'm so sorry," she murmured mechanically, her heart pounding.

"Are you? Apparently she reached the same conclusion I did." Taking Juliet's hand, he lifted it to his lips and kissed it, his eyes never leaving her face. "We were each destined to marry another."

Her heart refused to stop pounding.

His expression sobered. "Clara sent me a telegram telling me of your loss. I wanted to give you time to grieve in private, but I had to express my sympathy in person. I'm sorry, Juliet. Your father was an admirable man with strong ideals."

His eyes probed her heart and soul. There was no hiding from him. She did not try. Instead, she buried her head in his shoulder and wept openly, noisily, releasing her deepest pain in the comfort of his closeness. When she finally lifted her gaze, she felt the pain ease from her being, as if she could let go at last without guilt or remorse.

"Now as for Maria," Antonio resumed, placing his arm about Juliet's shoulders, "she hasn't been very happy, I'm afraid."

Juliet stiffened with alarm. "Is she all right?"

"She's fine physically. But she misses her best friend. She has no one to juggle with."

"It sounds as if she isn't any happier than Marcus." Juliet sobered. "He's just beginning to show some spirit again. I think it's the change in seasons rather than any change in him."

"I'm not surprised. Why don't we keep walking?"

He reached for the three pieces of luggage. Juliet watched, fascinated, as he tried to adjust them to fit the way they had before, just as he had on the night they left the broken carriage in the storm.

"It looks as if you've come to stay, but why three? Did you bring Maria?" Looking around, she extended her hand to help, picking up a valise. "This one is so light."

"Maria's at home. Two of these are empty." He grinned at her puzzled expression. "One is for your things, the other for Marcus'. I've come to take you back with me."

Juliet stood still, too stupefied to move, the empty case hanging from her hand.

"It's time for those rings to mean what they should. They signify a deep love and an important promise. I asked you once," he teased, "but I didn't receive the answer I wanted. Perhaps I should ask again."

Bowing on one knee, he reached out to her, forcing her to drop the suitcase as she placed her hands in his.

"Juliet Halliday, will you marry me?"

Wondering if the two rings were still in a pouch in his pocket, she was not about to waste any more time by waiting for him to find them. Her breath refused to come, yet the words burst from her without hesitation this time.

"Yes. Oh, yes, I'll marry you, Antonio."

Laughing, she collapsed into his waiting arms. He planted a longing kiss on her forehead.

" 'Grow old along with me,' " he whispered, resting his forehead against hers. " 'The best is yet to be.' "

"You even know Browning. Papa would be so proud." Juliet sighed deeply, closing her eyes. "You were right. It was the teacher who needed the lesson. I've learned so much since you've been gone."

As they drew apart from each other, she took his sleeve and started toward home, pulling him along after he'd rearranged the suitcases.

"And to think I wasn't here to help," Antonio said with mock disappointment. "Tell me all you've learned, my love."

"Well," she said thoughtfully as they walked, "I've come to realize families are created as much as they are bred, like you said. I've learned that life is more than just a position, even if I am committed to my work. I've discovered Marcus needs to grow up in Boston."

Her heart fluttered at the look of joy that spread across Antonio's face as she announced her decision.

"That's the most sensible thing you've said all day." He smiled, mocking the statement he'd made in their early days in Boston. "He'll get a good education there."

"Perhaps he might go to work as well," Juliet added. If Antonio was willing to reverse his position, she would do the same. "Is there any reason he can't do both?"

"He's smart enough. Work is an education, after all."

Juliet considered the possibilities. "He might be able to work in the market after school."

"Or on weekends. If his aunt will allow it, that is."

Once again Juliet was impressed with Antonio's insight. Marcus would benefit from both.

"Not that Boston could do a better job than you have." He gave her a teasing glance. "He's had the best schoolmistress in town since he's attended the Stockton Village school. But in Boston, he can go to school with Maria."

Juliet could not remember a time her plans had looked more promising. "Juggling makes him feel so good about himself that I don't think it matters when he works, as long as he has the chance to perform and go to school."

"All that matters is that this Juliet will share eternity with her true love." Antonio paused as they reached her gate. "That's as it should be, don't you agree?"

Her heart filled with a warmth she'd never known as she smiled up at her husband-to-be.

"For once, Mr. Santilli, I do."

Chapter Seventeen

As soon as she heard the cry of the newsboy amid the growing late-day bustle outside the market, Juliet knew it must be time for supper. Just as the thought crossed her mind, she saw her nephew's wavy red hair appear in the doorway over the piles of paper she'd spread across her husband's desk.

"Supper's almost ready, Aunt Juliet," Marcus called. "We have company tonight, remember? Mrs. Wetherall is here."

"Oh, excellent. I didn't even hear her come in."

To her surprise, instead of running off as he always did, he took his time, approaching her slowly where she sat behind Antonio's desk. There, he gave her a quick, unexpected hug before releasing her. Filled with love at the gesture, Juliet didn't try to hide the broad smile that spread across her face.

"What was that for?" she asked.

"For bringing me back here," Marcus said in a sincere voice. "For letting me do what I love most. Maybe someday I'll have my own circus."

It wouldn't surprise her in the least, she realized. Enjoying the visible signs of his happiness too much to return to her paperwork, she watched as he ran back out. In the month he'd been attending school in Boston, he'd proven himself to be among the brightest pupils in the class.

As Marcus reached the door of the office, he nearly bumped into Antonio's mother, who appeared from around the corner. He steadied himself with her apron as she caught him by the shoulders. Juliet was about to remind him of his manners when he apologized for his haste.

"I'm sorry, Grandma." Marcus' voice was so meek and polite, Juliet was glad she'd remained silent.

"There's a good boy." Ruffling his hair before he hurried away, Theresa Santilli turned to Juliet. "I see he told you Lillian is here. If only I could get Maria to be so polite. Always in a rush, that girl."

"I can't blame her for being in a rush to catch up to him." Juliet smiled. "If only Papa were alive to see him."

"He watches from a better place. A good man, your papa was. He and I, we would have been friends." Theresa nodded sagely, giving her daughter-in-law a loving smile. "My son chose well when he chose you. I hope the others choose as well when their time comes."

Juliet thanked her and promised to finish her work quickly as Theresa left to return to the apartment. Once again she was late for supper, Juliet realized with a shred of guilt. At least it was only a shred. She was grateful that Theresa and Clara shared the cooking duties. It allowed her time to work on lesson plans for her evening classes. She felt fortunate to have a husband as understanding as Antonio.

It had been a long day, and she looked forward to sharing this particular evening with friends. She knew Mrs. Wetherall would understand and forgive her tardiness. This afternoon, the headstone had been erected on Papa's grave, reuniting him finally with Cordelia in Boston. He was with the family as he'd wished. Marcus would never forget his grandfather, surrounded as he was by reminders of his ancestry.

Collecting her papers into a pile, Juliet looked up, smiling as her husband entered the office. He shook his head, closing the door behind him.

"It's nice to have a wife my mother approves of," Antonio announced. "She tells me so every day. Not all girls could meet her standards."

"That's what she tells me every day," Juliet said. "I'm lucky she approves of my work."

"I told you she would. Getting ready for the night school again," Antonio observed, eyeing the piles on his desk with interest. "No man ever had a more hardworking wife, I'll say that. Working at home or at the market all day, then teaching school to working children in the evening."

"No woman ever had a more rewarding life." Juliet moved to the front of the desk to envelop his hands in hers. "The children who have to work for a living need a night school so they can continue their education while helping their families. At least they'll have a more promising future."

"The children of Boston need dedicated teachers." Antonio laid his hand tenderly on her cheek. "They've found the best in you."

"I know your mother doesn't mind if I work, but are you sure you don't?" she worried.

"How could I object? You spend most days in my store. You should be allowed to follow your heart at night. As long as you leave some time for me, that is." Pulling her into an embrace, he kissed her forehead lightly. "Do you think their future is as promising as ours?"

She couldn't answer that question. All she knew for certain was that her namesake in Verona had never been as happy as this Juliet was now.

The

Miniature
Schnauzer

An Owner's Guide To

A HAPPY HEALTHY PET

Howell Book House

Hungry Minds, Inc.
Best-Selling Books • Digital Downloads • e-Books • Answer Networks
e-Newsletters • Branded Web Sites • e-Learning
New York, NY • Cleveland, OH • Indianapolis, IN

Howell Book House
Hungry Minds, Inc.
909 Third Avenue
New York, NY 10022
www.hungryminds.com

For general information on Hungry Minds books in the U.S., please call our Consumer
Customer Service department at 800-762-2974. In Canada, please call (800) 667-1115.
For reseller information, including discounts and premium sales, please call our
Reseller Customer Service department at 800-434-3422.

Library of Congress Cataloging-in-Publication Data
Stark, Jeannette.
The Miniature schnauzer: an owner's guide to happy, healthy pet/Jeannette Stark.
p.cm.
Includes bibliographical references
ISBN 0-87605-397-5
1. Miniature Schnauzer. I. Title.
SF429.M58P35   1996, 2001   95-54101
636.7'55—dc20   CIP

Manufactured in the United States of America

15 14 13 12

Series Director: Kira Sexton
Book Design: Michele Laseau
Cover Design: Michael Freeland
Photography Editor: Richard Fox
Illustration: Jeff Yesh
Photography:
   Front and back cover photos by Jeannie Harrison/Close Encounters of the Furry Kind
   Joan Balzarini: 96
   Mary Bloom: 96, 136, 145
   Paulette Braun/Pets by Paulette: 2–3, 7, 8, 9, 14, 23, 28, 30, 34, 41, 43, 54, 55, 96
   Buckinghamhill American Cocker Spaniels: 148
   Courtesy of the AKC: 17, 19, 20
   Sian Cox: 5, 12, 32–33, 37, 49, 52, 66, 134
   Dr. Ian Dunbar: 98, 101, 103, 111, 116–117, 122, 123, 127
   Dan Lyons: 96
   Cathy Merrithew: 129
   Sue Norris: 56, 58, 60
   Liz Palika: 133
   Susan Rezy: 96–97
   Jeannette Stark: 59
   Judith Strom: 10, 26, 27, 36, 38, 40, 44, 96, 107, 110, 128, 130, 135, 137, 139, 140,
   144, 149, 150
   Kerrin Winter/Dale Churchill: 21, 24, 72, 74, 80
Page creation by: Hungry Minds Indianapolis Production Department

Contents

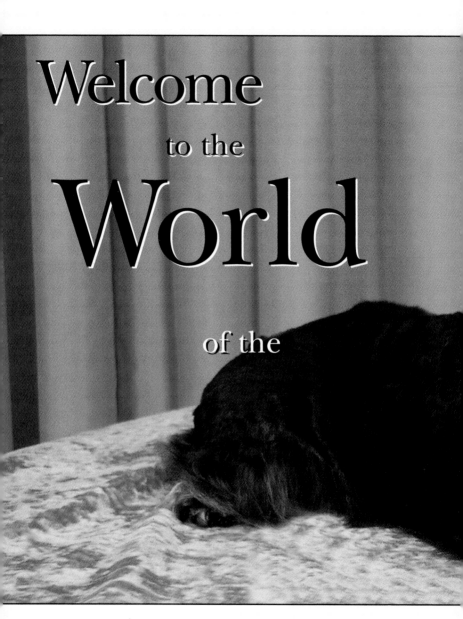

Welcome
to the
World
of the

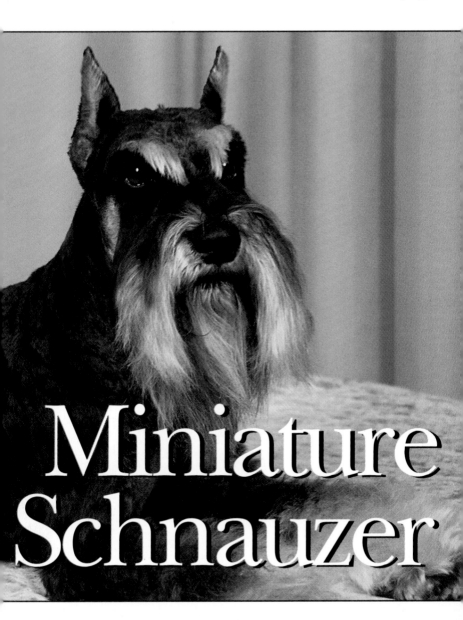

part one

Miniature Schnauzer

External Features of the Miniature Schnauzer

Muzzle

Cheek

Stop

Skull

Shoulder

Forearm

Wrist

Crest

Neck

Withers

Elbow

Pastern

Dewclaw

Back

Stifle or Knee

Loin

Croup

Hock

Toes

chapter 1

What
Is a
Miniature
Schnauzer?

"Discerning" is the word that most accurately describes a Miniature Schnauzer owner, whose search for a dog with distinctive qualities led him or her to this breed.

"Distinctive" is the word that most accurately describes the Miniature Schnauzer, for he is very affectionate without being overbearingly gushy; highly intelligent with some degree of independence; extremely curious but not destructive; elegant in appearance without being froufrou; highly protective yet underwhelming in size; and equipped with the bonus of all bonuses, a nonshedding coat with no trace of a doggy odor.

The Miniature Schnauzer is equally comfortable in a small city apartment, a manored estate or a country farm, and thrives as easily in a house overflowing with children as in one with a single owner. She is

5

delighted to be the love of your life, but will also enjoy sharing your affection with a cat or another dog. Simply put, she's a fits-all pet for the discerning.

The Dog's Quality

The breed standard describes the ideal or perfect specimen of a breed and is written by each breed's parent club and approved by the AKC (American Kennel Club). If your Miniature Schnauzer falls short of the standard written by the AMSC (American Miniature Schnauzer Club), don't despair. The perfect dog (of any breed) has neither been nor ever will be bred. Judges are guided by the ideal illustrated in the standard, awarding each win to the dog that most closely resembles this standard.

Breeders are guided by the standard in an attempt to breed that elusive perfect dog. The first dog show ever held grew from a dispute among hunters, each claiming ownership of the perfect dog. It is quite understandable if you argue that your dog is perfect. There's only one problem: *I* own the perfect dog!

There are two types of dogs available to the buyer: pet quality and show quality. A Miniature Schnauzer of pet quality is deemed so because he either has a disqualification or a fault as described by the standard. He may have a coat too soft in texture or an improper bite, be too large or too small or lack any quality required—but in no way is he less desirable as a companion.

Pet-quality dogs are usually available for a lower price than show quality, but it sometimes happens that a breeder is left with an unsold show-quality prospect he cannot keep. Its gender may not be what the breeder wanted; another litter may be on the way, creating a

WHAT IS A BREED STANDARD?

A breed standard—a detailed description of an individual breed—is meant to portray the *ideal* specimen of that breed. This includes ideal structure, temperament, gait, type—all aspects of the dog. Because the standard describes an ideal specimen, it isn't based on any particular dog. It is a concept against which judges compare actual dogs and breeders strive to produce dogs. At a dog show, the dog that wins is the one that comes closest, in the judge's opinion, to the standard for its breed. Breed standards are written by the breed parent clubs, the national organizations formed to oversee the well-being of the breed. They are voted on and approved by the members of the parent clubs.

time or space problem for the breeder; the puppy's fault (remember, he's not perfect) may be one the breeder must avoid. For whatever reason, the breeder may sell a show-quality prospect at a pet price.

Here a black Miniature Schnauzer is framed by two salt-and-pepper dogs.

To Show or Not to Show

If your sudden and unexpected ownership of a show-quality prospect triggers your interest in exhibiting her, many things must be considered. Grooming a Miniature Schnauzer show coat is an extensive and intricate procedure, requiring a lot of time, talent and effort. Your ability as a handler, if you're inexperienced, must be acquired and finely honed. Exhibiting a dog in the conformation ring can be costly, time consuming, physically exhausting and, more often than not, heartbreaking to a newcomer. On the other hand, it's a fascinating sport, and nothing beats the high of a big win. If nothing else, it's proof of your dog's relationship to perfection.

If you are determined to have a fling in the ring with your show-quality dog, by all means, have at it! Learn all you can from the dog's breeder, who will anxiously offer encouraging help. Seek advice and help from an expert groomer of the breed, an experienced handler of the breed and dog-involved friends. Attend conformation classes with your dog and, most of all, have fun in the effort.

Your first step is to study the breed standard thoroughly and be honestly convinced that you and your dog belong in the conformation ring.

For the dog of either show or pet quality, obedience training is fun and will bind you and your dog like no other activity. Exhibition in the obedience ring is another satisfying and enjoyable option, especially since Miniature Schnauzers are quick to learn and enjoy the sport.

The Miniature Schnauzer is a robust and handsome fellow.

Understanding the Breed Standard

The following is a discussion of the elements of the breed standard for the Miniature Schnauzer. To get a copy of the official breed standard, write to the American Kennel Club at 51 Madison Avenue, New York, NY 10010. Ask specifically for the Miniature Schnauzer Standard.

GENERAL APPEARANCE AND TEMPERAMENT

The standard's description of the Miniature Schnauzer's general appearance depicts no fluffy, cutesy little dog. Rather, he is a handsome fellow and she a classy lady. A puppy easily falls into the little fluff-of-a-dog slot, but those sturdy bones and squarish body, even at a young age, predict the robust and proportionately impressive adult who somehow replaces the fluff.

His appearance and attitude, clearly identifying him as a terrier, are purely deceptive He has little, if any, terrier in his background; he simply looks and acts like one. Those eyebrows, that beard and his alert and active disposition have placed him in the AKC Terrier Group, but most registries throughout the world will argue the point. However, a look at him in the Terrier Group at any AKC show offers a strong and convincing argument that he seems to belong there.

The standard's ideal temperament (describing an alert, spirited, obedient, friendly, intelligent dog with a willingness to please) is abundantly evident in the typical Miniature Schnauzer. A vicious Miniature Schnauzer would be an extreme rarity, such behavior resulting only from neglect, abuse, or terribly poor judgment in its handling. Shyness is equally rare; a wise buyer avoids the puppy (of any breed) that sits endlessly in the corner while her littermates boisterously romp and play. She is not necessarily displaying sweetness: more likely, it is shyness. If a Miniature Schnauzer puppy sits in a corner, it should only be because she is resting between rounds with her littermates.

Thick whiskers accentuate the rectangular shape of the Miniature Schnauzer's head.

HEAD

A good Miniature Schnauzer head is a beauty to behold, and balance is the key, particularly if the head is in balance with the rest of the dog. The unwrinkled forehead enhances the flat and fairly long topskull (the area behind the eyes) ending at a slight stop (the indentation between the eyes where the nasal bone and skull meet).

The foreface (the area in front of the eyes) is strong and at least as long as the topskull. Both parts (foreface and muzzle) are parallel to each other, separated by the stop. Thick whiskers accentuate the rectangular shape of the head. A head that is coarse (lacking refinement) and cheeky (prominently rounded, thick, protruding) is a no-no. A scissors bite (fully defined in the standard) is required.

This Miniature Schnauzer has natural, uncropped ears.

The keen expression of the small, dark brown, deeply set, oval-shaped eyes almost resembles a frown, which perhaps conceals the dog's studied contemplation of his next move.

EARS

If the ears are cropped (if a portion of the ears have been surgically removed), they must be identical in shape and length with pointed tips, in balance with the head, set high on the skull, carried perpendicularly at the inner edge and they must stand erect. Uncropped (natural) ears must be small, must be V-shaped and fold close to the skull.

About Cropping

The very mention of cropped ears in the standard indicates the approval of ear cropping in the United States. In those countries where the procedure is illegal, their standards make no reference to cropped ears of any breed, and the exhibition of any dog with cropped ears is prohibited. In the United States, however, an uncropped Miniature Schnauzer is at a disadvantage in the conformation ring, since the procedure admittedly enhances the dog's keen expression.

The problem with ear cropping is that it is performed during the most crucial period in a dog's young life, when any physical or emotional trauma should be avoided. Many breeders with unsold puppies automatically have their ears cropped at the optimum cropping age, in the event they might display show quality.

If an uncropped puppy is bought as a pet, however, the new owner might consider the puppy's welfare and avoid the traumatic and expensive procedure. True, those wider V-shaped ears (or one of them) might stand up awkwardly, giving the dog a comical appearance, but there is always the chance that the uncropped ears may behave properly. In any event, the puppy will not have been subjected to a painful and unnecessary surgical procedure at a particularly stressful time, merely for cosmetic reasons.

If the thought of a comical Miniature Schnauzer is a bothersome concern, there are products that weigh down folded ears, so not to worry. Discuss product information and its proper application with a breeder or handler of a breed (such as the Shetland Sheepdog) that requires natural folded ears.

BODY

The Miniature Schnauzer's body should be very square. The length from the chest (the front of the dog beneath the head and neck) to the stern (tail) bone should be equal to the height, measured from the floor (or wherever he is stood) to his withers (the highest point on the shoulders, immediately behind the neck). Ribs are well sprung and deep (the opposite of a slender, flat-sided dog). The brisket (the foreport of the body below the chest, between the forelegs, closest to the ribs) should extend at least to the elbows. While robustness is desirable, too much is as bad as too little.

THE AMERICAN KENNEL CLUB

Familiarly referred to as "the AKC," the American Kennel Club is a nonprofit organization devoted to the advancement of purebred dogs. The AKC maintains a registry of recognized breeds and adopts and enforces rules for dog events including shows, obedience trials, field trials, hunting tests, lure coursing, herding, earthdog trials, agility and the Canine Good Citizen program. It is a club of clubs, established in 1884 and composed, today, of over 500 autonomous dog clubs throughout the United States. Each club is represented by a delegate; the delegates make up the legislative body of the AKC, voting on rules and electing directors. The American Kennel Club maintains the Stud Book, the record of every dog ever registered with the AKC, and publishes a variety of materials on purebred dogs, including a monthly magazine, books and numerous educational pamphlets. For more information, contact the AKC at the address listed in Chapter 13, "Resources," and look for the names of their publications in Chapter 12, "Recommended Reading."

The topline (the topmost outline of the dog from just behind the withers to the tail set) should be straight, declining at a slight angle as it travels from the neck to the tail. A topline is faulted if it is swayback (a concave or hollow curvature of the area behind the withers and somewhat forward of the tail set), or if it is a roach back (convex or bulging curvature over the rear area of the topline).

The forelegs (front legs) are straight up and down. The hindquarters (rear assembly) have strong-muscled, slanting thighs (the upper thick part of the leg connected to the hip). They bend at the stifles (the "knee" joint between the thigh and the second thigh) and are straight from the hocks (the collection of bones forming the joint between the second thigh and the heel) to the heels (at the rear of the lowest part of the hind leg just above the foot). Hindquarters that are bowed (hocks turning away from each other) or cowhocked (hocks turning toward each other) are undesirable.

If you decide to show a Miniature Schnauzer in conformation or obedience, study the standard, talk to others and have fun!

GAIT

When moving at a trot, the Miniature Schnauzer's forelegs move straight forward. The hind legs move straight, traveling in the same planes as the forelegs. The feet point straight ahead. Faulted movements are single tracking (all footprints falling on a single line of travel), sidegaiting (dog moving forward with body at an angle), paddling in front (so named for its similarity to the swing and dip of a canoeist's paddle, the front legs swinging forward on a stiff outward arc), or high hackney knee action (the high lifting of the front feet resembling the gait of a hackney horse).

COAT

The show coat can make or break a dog's show career. It is double with a hard, wiry outer coat and short undercoat. The head, neck and body coat must be plucked. When the stripped coat grows, it must be long enough for the judge to determine texture, while the coat length of neck, ears and skull is decidedly shorter. The furnishings (beard, eyebrows, legs and underbody hair) are fairly thick but not silky. The standard does not describe a clipped coat, because it is a disqualification in the ring, but it is highly attractive, practical and easily maintained. It is the most popular and logical style for a Miniature Schnauzer pet.

SIZE

If a Miniature Schnauzer is under 12 inches or over 14 inches in height, the dog is disqualified. There is no need to disqualify, excuse or dismiss an over- or undersized pet Miniature Schnauzer from your home.

COLOR

There are three recognized colors, each being spectacularly beautiful: salt and pepper, black and silver and solid black. The colors and their patterns are described in the standard and are easily understood.

Enjoyment of Your Dog

No matter how closely or distantly the breed standard describes your Miniature Schnauzer, you'll clearly enjoy him. He'll adapt to whatever lifestyle you provide, at home or on vacation. He's a great camper, sailor or hiker, yet will lie contentedly at your feet on a cozy evening. He considers the guardianship of your home his mission in life and will demand the responsibility. His insistent barking, however, is a coverup for a soft heart: Don't be shocked if he leads an intruder to the family safe.

But don't forget—the perfect dog does not exist. Except mine. Maybe yours.

chapter 2

The
Miniature
Schnauzer's
Ancestry

Like most breeds, the Miniature Schnauzer's precise development has been theorized by researchers, relying on artwork, descriptive references and records that survived the rigors of time. What is known is its membership in the three-sized Schnauzer family: the Giant Schnauzer (25.5 to 27.5 inches for males, 23.5 to 25.5 inches for females); the Standard Schnauzer (18.5 to 19.5 inches for males, 17.5 to 18.5 inches for females); and the Miniature Schnauzer (12 to 14 inches for both sexes).

Each of the three sizes is a distinct and separate breed. The Schnauzer family's origin in the cattle lands of Germany is undisputed. Translated into English from the German language, *Schnauze* (pronounced *SHNOW-tsa*) means snout, muzzle, spout or nose; and the breed's Germanic name, Schnauzer (pronounced *SHNOW-tser)*, describes a rough-haired terrier.

A Drover's Dog

All authorities recognize the Standard Schnauzer as the original size and prototype of the three breeds. The common link connecting all theories of Schnauzer ancestry concludes that stocky drovers' dogs formed the foundation from which the Rottweiler, Doberman Pinscher and Standard Schnauzer descended in the fifteenth century.

The crosses that produced the Standard Schnauzer are thought to be the black German Poodle and gray wolf Spitz upon wirehaired Pinscher stock. Bred for sagacity and fearlessness, he was an impressive rat catcher, yard dog and guard. In 1905 the first Standard Schnauzer was imported by a breeder in the United States.

While German drovers admired the Standard Schnauzer's appearance, soundness and power, they needed a larger specimen for cattle, so they generated the Giant Schnauzer—probably from early crosses with smooth-coated droving and dairymen's dogs. They then crossed the dogs with rough-haired sheep dogs and, eventually, with the black Great Dane and possibly with the Bouvier des Flandres.

Development of the Miniature Schnauzer

Many authorities agree (and disagree) about how the breed or breeds crossed with the Standard Schnauzer to develop the Miniature, giving credit to the toy gray Spitz, Pomeranian, Poodle, Wire-haired Fox Terrier, Miniature Pinscher and Affenpinscher. The most widely accepted theory is that the Affenpinscher and Poodle were crossed with small Standard Schnauzers to produce the Miniature Schnauzer. Whatever the crosses, aren't we fortunate that those founding German breeders admired the Standard Schnauzer but preferred it in a smaller package?

The Miniature, developed as a stable or farm dog, was used as a ratter and guard dog, though not a fighter. Because of her small size, she was invited to join the family as a companion, performing with great success. It was an unplanned function, highly appreciated and valued.

All breeds of dogs were developed with specific capacities to serve their owners. Breeds whose function was to work had to work: they were not expected to be pets. Because of her happy nature the Miniature who became a pet continued to perform her intended duties.

If your Miniature Schnauzer displays heightened pleasure chasing rabbits or squirrels, or adamantly stands her ground against an intrusion

---

WHERE DID DOGS COME FROM?

It can be argued that dogs were right there at man's side from the beginning of time. As soon as human beings began to document their existence, the dog was among their drawings and inscriptions. Dogs were not just friends, they served a purpose: There were dogs to hunt birds, pull sleds, herd sheep, burrow after rats—even sit in laps! What your dog was originally bred to do influences the way it behaves. The American Kennel Club recognizes over 140 breeds, and there are hundreds more distinct breeds around the world. To make sense of the breeds, they are grouped according to their size or function. The AKC has seven groups:

1) Sporting, 2) Working,
3) Herding, 4) Hounds,
5) Terriers, 6) Toys,
7) Nonsporting

Can you name a breed from each group? Here's some help: (1) Golden Retriever; (2) Doberman Pinscher; (3) Collie; (4) Beagle; (5) Scottish Terrier; (6) Maltese; and (7) Dalmatian. All modern domestic dogs (*Canis familiaris*) are related, however different they look, and are all descended from *Canis lupus*, the gray wolf.

with a biteless bark, she is not being nonsensical; rather, she is yielding to her natural instincts as a ratter and guardian.

Her primary function today is family pet, a mutually agreeable arrangement between owner and dog. While many Standards and Giants perform their usefully intended functions today, most have been liberated from their tasks, enjoying life as companions in the comfort of their owners' homes; some enjoy both roles simultaneously.

Establishment of the Breed

The Miniature Schnauzer is reported to have been established as long ago as 1859, and in 1889 Miniature Schnauzers were introduced as an exhibited breed at German shows. The earliest specimens bore little resemblance to the breed's appearance today.

From left to right, Ch. Handsome of Marienhof, Ch. TMG of Marienhof and CH. Kubla Khan of Marienhof.

Beyond its then stocky structure, terrierlike head, wiry coat and cropped ears, the prettification was absent. A ratter or guard didn't need stylized grooming, a richly colored coat, a profuse beard, eyebrows or leg furnishings. The early colors ranged from black, yellow and cream to black and tan. The occasional salt-and-pepper coat emerged later.

The Affenpinscher influence seems apparent in the breed's earliest picture, sketched in 1907. It depicts an eight-year-old dog, Jocco-Fulda Lilliput, who lived to be sixteen and is the first Miniature Schnauzer registered in the Pinscher-Zuchtbuch (the German studbook, commonly referred to as the PZ). That registry, first published by the Pinscher-Klub in 1902, was enjoined by the Bayerischer Schnauzer-Klub, forming a joint registry in 1918. Even in the midst of a World War, dog-involved people remained dog involved.

German breeders have developed an incredible number of breeds, and are admired for their patience and unfaltering efforts to fix type, for their documentation of breeding records and for their perseverance in tracing breed ancestries. Their expertise in developing the three sizes of Schnauzers from various sources of crosses, producing each amazingly comparable to the others, is an extraordinary accomplishment. Among the ravages of World War II was the loss of early breeding records during the bombing of Germany. That is why there is an enormous void in the recorded history of breeds developed there.

The Early Imports

In 1923 two Miniature Schnauzers from the kennels of Rudolph Krappatch in Germany were imported by W. D. Goff of Massachusetts. Misfortune struck those imports. The male died, leaving no descendants, and the female's two litters were unproductive.

The following year, three females and one male from Krappatch's kennel were imported by Marie Slattery, whose kennel name was Marienhof. Three years later, Slattery imported a three-year-old male. This dog, Cuno, is credited as having been more effectively influential on the breed's development in the U.S. than any other imported sire. Not a particularly outstanding specimen in every respect, Cuno nevertheless earned his American championship and passed on the few outstanding qualities he did display (and other qualities not evident) to his get (puppies), siring fourteen American champions who produced the same fine qualities for many generations.

Intrigued by Slattery's early Miniature imports, other Americans imported 108 dogs and bitches during the following ten years, but extinction of most of those lines became common: additional imports became unregistered pets or died without being registered.

Amsel, one of Slattery's original imported bitches, made an astonishing contribution to the breed. She was the first Miniature to be exhibited in the U.S., the dam of the first American-born litter (whelped in 1925) and the double granddam of Ch. Moses Taylor, the first American-bred champion. (Moses Taylor actually tied with Don V. Dornbush as the first American champions, because they earned their titles on the same day at different shows.)

But Amsel's place in history lies in the frequency of her name in the pedigree of probably every American-bred Miniature Schnauzer. Amsel's recurring name is an indication that her genetic propensity for producing offspring of superior quality must have been overwhelming. Otherwise, her progeny would have been dismissed as unlikely improvers of the breed

American and Canadian Ch. Jonaire Pocono Rough Rider, UDT, in 1959.

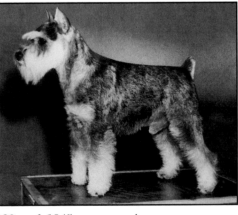

and the appearance of her name in pedigrees would have disappeared in her lifetime.

Changed Appearance

From time to time a breed's standard is changed. The Miniature Schnauzer's original maximum size was limited to 12 inches, and between 1930 and 1945 ear cropping was forbidden. Personal preferences to stylize the breed's appearance led to the breeding of luscious furnishings and darkening the pepper coloration to create a sharper contrast in the salt-and-pepper coats. Those gains, however, softened the ideally hard texture of the coat, and a sleeker, terrier-type style of Miniature emerged in the late 1940s.

A Great Dog's Influence

Any reference to the Miniature Schnauzer must include mention of a great dog, Ch. Dorem Display, a strongly line-bred male, whelped on April 5, 1945, by Dorothy Williams at her Dorem Kennels. He was a terrier type, and even today would be a more than worthy contender in the ring.

His outstanding show record was beginning to soar as his record as a producer was being established, siring a total of forty-two champions. While Display's record as a champion producer is enviable, perhaps even more outstanding are the extended generations of his creation, whose own records as champion producers and huge winners were great.

A legend in the breed, Ch. Dorem Display.

Clearly, this dog had an unprecedented effect on the breed. As you doubtless have guessed, Display's ancestry, thoughtfully and meaningfully line-bred for almost two decades, goes back to a litter sired by Cuno out of Amsel.

If you wonder how an unequaled special dog like Display is bred, the answer is simple. All you need are great dogs, a thorough knowledge of genetics and a ton of luck!

The Breed's Popularity

Through the dedication of the pioneers who established the breed in its early years in America, the Miniature Schnauzer survived the difficulties of becoming rooted long before it flourished. Some of the issues were gaining AKC recognition as a breed apart from the Standard Schnauzer, gaining the privilege of exhibition apart from the Standard at shows and establishing the American Miniature Schnauzer Club as the breed's parent club (in 1933, again apart from the Standard). The problems didn't grow from any animosity between the two breed factions; each simply wanted status as an individual breed. When the difficulties were solved and the Miniature and Standard Schnauzers were afforded separate status, gaining public recognition then became a slow process.

Gaining Admirers

Interest in obedience greatly increased in 1946, introducing the breed to the general public. As the breed improved, Group placements and Best in Show wins increased, exposing the breed to show-minded individuals. Those exposures caused a proliferation of owners and breeders, and the popularity of Miniature Schnauzers rose in the 1960s.

Although the salt-and-pepper coat became and continues to be the most popular color, blacks and black and silvers began to gain favor as the breed's popularity in general

The Miniature Schnauzer owes his popularity to his charm and versatility.

was soaring. Today, the quality of those formerly rare color-coated specimens is equal to the quality of the salt-and-pepper Miniatures, thanks to the breed's newer crop of pioneers, who appreciated and dedicated themselves to the rarity.

The breed's popularity is such that it is common to see at least one Miniature Schnauzer in most of the obedience classes in America. The breed is also popular with the viewing public: Miniature Schnauzers were a favorite breed in stage-performing dog acts in Germany, and Florence Bradburn's four Elfland Miniature Schnauzers took part in the 1955 filming of *The Bar Sinister.*

The breed is also consistently pictured on boxes and bags of various dog foods and other canine-related products, and it is not uncommon to see a Miniature Schnauzer in non-dog television commercials and newspaper and magazine advertisements. The Miniature (usually clipped) appears as the starring family's or its neighbor's pet in movies or TV shows. There is little chance that such roles for these dogs will disappear, because let's face it: in a show coat, their appearance is outstanding; in a clipped coat, they're outstandingly cute.

How the Miniature Schnauzer Ranks Among Breeds

A conscientious breeder becomes nervous when his breed nears the number one spot in popularity, fearing the breed's downfall in the hands of less-than-knowledgeable opportunists anxious to breed quantity rather than quality of any popular breed. The Miniature Schnauzer's climb from obscurity was slow, but in the 1970s reached the top ten most popular breed status based on American Kennel Club registrations. It remained in the top ten for a number of years, just recently dipping lower.

In 1994 the Miniature Schnauzer had 33,344 individual registrations, ranking it the fourteenth most popular breed registered by the AKC. It is highly unlikely that the breed will ever be in danger of becoming unpopular: it is too appealing in appearance, temperament and intelligence. Add to that a vast network of dedicated, devoted and principled breeders who, as members of the parent club, are determined to protect the breed, and you have a breed loved by many and harmed by few.

chapter 3

The **World**

According to the

Miniature Schnauzer

Which dog do you want? One that will do anything and everything you tell him to do because he is so naturally dutiful? Sounds good. Or one that, although well trained to obey, might ignore an order? Sounds bad.

Well, let's test these two dogs. Let's order them to go into the street to play. The first dog will go into the street, not because he is dutiful but, more likely, because he doesn't know what to do unless he's told what to do! Not an independent thinker. The second dog will move toward the street immediately, but if traffic is whizzing by, he will refuse to go out there to play. He is too intelligent to obey a command that places him in danger.

Admittedly, the speculative example is somewhat ludicrous, but it demonstrates that a well-trained, obedient dog may choose not to obey every command. When not? When he feels endangered; when he doesn't understand the order; or (surprise) when he's not in the mood! This second dog is the Miniature Schnauzer.

Is He All That Perfect?

The Miniature Schnauzer will obey you when he must, but is an independent thinker.

With no disrespect to the breed's developers intended, you've probably heard the expression "stubborn Dutchman." The Miniature Schnauzer, obedient as she is, does not escape the significance of that expression. Most assuredly she can be stubborn at times, but be grateful that her independent nature precludes her need for constant guidance. She knows what to do, when to do it and how to do it.

The Miniature Schnauzer enjoys life because he can find his own amusement. He's smart and he knows it. He's tough enough and he knows it (though we know he's not as tough as he thinks). He knows he's a knockout traffic stopper, and he takes pleasure in cleverly outsmarting you. He recognizes your mood and knows when outsmarting you will make you laugh and when it'll get him into trouble.

In essence, your Miniature Schnauzer knows he can get by with just about anything because he's amusing, smart, tough, eye-catching, clever and knows how to handle you. He is convinced he's the best thing that ever happened to you and knows you're the best thing that ever happened to him. He is, after all, a Miniature Schnauzer. And you are, after all, his best friend, housekeeper, chef, caretaker and landlord. How lucky can you be? In return, he loves you and responds to your every wish—when he's in the mood. A fair exchange, he figures.

Understanding Natural Instincts

Any individual dog of any breed becomes what she becomes through the molding of her development. A Miniature Schnauzer's instincts as a vocal guard dog create not a mere barker, but an extremely insistent barker.

It is illogical to expect her to be a half-hearted alarmer of trouble or a soft-spoken dog at play. With your understanding attitude and effective training, she can become an acceptable alarmer of anything she considers suspicious, learn to greet the mail carrier with a wagging tail, and be playful without deafening the neighbors with her persistent racket. Your disagreement with her noisy disturbance must be evident from the moment of her first yip. Certainly, she's allowed to bark, but the volume and objective must be nonirritating.

An extremely effective tool (for any misbehavior) is an empty soda can into which you've placed a few nuts and bolts, with the lid resecured. When your dog misbehaves, shake the can to startle him, which will stop whatever he's doing. To halt his unnecessary barking, shake the can and say, "Quiet." When he stops barking, praise him. If he barks again, correct him. With your

A DOG'S SENSES

Sight: With their eyes located farther apart than ours, dogs can detect movement at a greater distance than we can, but they can't see as well up close. They can also see better in less light, but can't distinguish many colors.

Sound: Dogs can hear about four times better than we can, and they can hear high-pitched sounds especially well. Their ancestors, the wolves, howled to let other wolves know where they were; our dogs do the same, but they have a wider range of vocalizations, including barks, whimpers, moans and whines.

Smell: A dog's nose is his greatest sensory organ. His sense of smell is so great he can follow a trail that's weeks old, detect odors diluted to one-millionth the concentration we'd need to notice them, even sniff out a person under water!

Taste: Dogs have fewer taste buds than we do, so they're likelier to try anything—and usually do, which is why it's especially important for their owners to monitor their food intake. Dogs are omnivores, which means they eat meat as well as vegetable matter like grasses and weeds.

Touch: Dogs are social animals and love to be petted, groomed and played with.

consistent reaction to his outbursts, eventually, he'll recognize the meaning of "Quiet" without the shaker can.

Excellent Alarms

To his credit, he considers salesmen, delivery services and unknown visitors as intruders—a view that should be respected. It makes no sense to end his value as an alarmer. What does make sense is for him to learn that his alarming barks should cease at your, not his, discretion; you're only training him when to stop an alarm or warning bark, not to eliminate it or its value.

When you've reached the final phase of training to time the dog's dutiful alarm barking and minimize the decibel factor of her normal day-to-day barking, you'll think you have it made. Wrong! There is one concession you must make to overcome a typical Miniature Schnauzer's intrinsic need to vocalize and exhibit stubbornness. She will have the last word. Her life depends on it. Without it, she won't get through the next five minutes. In spite of your dedicated training, in spite of her dedication to you, she will have one last grunt.

The Miniature Schnauzer is curious by nature.

A Serious Sniffer

His instinct as a ratter makes him a natural for serious sniffing. His curious nature is credible, but a sniffing habit becomes an annoyance during a simple walk down the street, and devastating if he is to be exhibited in the conformation or obedience ring. Any unacceptable habit is cured by subjecting him to the habit's source and correcting his expected misbehavior.

While out of his sight, distribute sniffable morsels on the ground. Bits of a hotdog or fat removed from a chop or steak, particularly if they're sizzling hot, are as enticing as it gets. With your dog on a training collar and leash, walk him into and through the delicacies, with verbal and physical corrections the instant he lowers his head or moves toward the enticement. "Leave it" or "No" are good commands, and an upward, effective pop on the lead is the physical correction, always followed by praise. Consistent and frequent (if necessary) sessions will allow him to satisfy his natural curiosity about life, investigating where he must, but will discourage his tendency to sniff for no good reason.

Your Miniature Schnauzer will tend to be very playful, although not hyperactive.

Reinforce the training indoors at home by tossing a treat on the floor with the verbal stop command, a pop on the leash (if necessary), then pick up the food and offer it from your hand with praise. Eventually, the dog should react without leash corrections. To reach this point, and turn the exercise into a trick, toss the treat, pop the leash (when necessary), pause several seconds, give a verbal "OK" (or any consistently used word), and allow her to eat it. Gradually stretch your paused time. Eventually, she won't need the leash and will enjoy performing her new trick. You haven't abandoned your training against sniffing by allowing the treat, since she reaches it by sight, not by scent.

Other than those trick-related treats and the food in his bowl, never allow your Miniature Schnauzer to eat food from the floor, whether it is intentionally or accidentally dropped (and do "accidentally" drop food from time to time, preparing yourself to correct any sneak attack).

A Day in the Life of a Miniature Schnauzer

With his barking and sniffing instincts narrowed to an acceptable measure, the Miniature Schnauzer becomes a dog of considerable versatility. He enjoys a soft lap with the same quiet satisfaction as does any toy breed (all of whom are bred for lap-sitting duty).

Most Miniature Schnauzers will enjoy dress-up time, as they're decked out in fake antlers at Christmas, a frilly Easter bonnet, Halloween ghost garb, or in a tuxedo, tutu, or clown suit. Those who do consider the costuming a demeaning frivolity manage to endure the embarrassment without much glee but with small objection.

Miniature Schnauzers don't object to "dress-up" play—even if they take on the role of baby in a basket.

As a nonshedding breed, many are allowed (if not welcomed) to enjoy the comfort of chairs, sofas and beds. She'll happily cuddle next to you if you're napping or bedded down for the night. If you awaken to a more distantly positioned dog, she didn't tire of your companionship; she moved to cooler comfort.

If your preference is to strictly forbid all comfort from chair, sofa and bed, expect obedience from the dog in your presence, but don't bet on her compliance in your absence. Good odds are that she'll leap to the floor from the no-no at the sound of your return. That move to comfort isn't misbehavior, it's a sign of intelligence, as is her hiding the evidence.

Playtime!

With his costumes, lap-sitting, cuddling, naps and meals out of the way, it's playtime, a Miniature Schnauzer–required activity. Armed with a toy, he'll amuse himself endlessly. If he's toy-less, he'll manufacture a game. A moving shadow on the floor (as tree limbs sway outside on a breezy day) offers paw-pouncing challenges; a housefly elicits a superb degree of eye-darting and air-chomping; the click of temperature-changing appliances (the refrigerator, furnace or air-conditioner) requires his attentive watchfulness for the next click—he dares it to fail. Very few natural or man-made noises, movements or objects are incapable of his play-creation efforts.

CHARACTERISTICS OF THE MINIATURE SCHNAUZER

Smart

Likes to bark

Stubborn at times

Doesn't shed

Curious

Fun-loving

Agreeable

It is a wonder, with her innate curiosity and busy attitude, that the Miniature Schnauzer is not hyperactive. She has managed to be intensely curious, busy, playful and fun-loving, with a nicely balanced acceptance and need for quiet times and activities. She reaches an extremely agreeable happy medium. Children must learn not to tax that happy medium by overtiring her.

The Non-Terrier Terrier

This is one terrier that is not particularly anxious to run away. Given the opportunity of an open gate, he may leave the yard to satisfy his curiosity and do a bit of exploring, but it isn't likely that he'll stay away permanently. He's a homebody at heart. Because of that satisfaction with his home environment and his small size, he's not a fence jumper (and, thank goodness, with your training he's no longer a fence barker). Even with his nonroaming tendencies, however, never, never, never give him the opportunity to do so.

An Eager Learner

This is a dog that really likes to learn. After one class session (whether it's puppy, obedience, conformation, agility, etc.), she'll look forward to the next, if only

because she's such a quick learner. While being trained to execute any part of an exercise that typically elicits an aggressive response from many terrier breeds, any objection the Miniature Schnauzer may have won't be physical; it'll merely be a refusal, but she will eventually get around to the exercise. The Miniature Schnauzer is very trainable. Expect a snag or regression—

The Miniature Schnauzer is very trainable.

every dog experiences the phenomenon—but our perky little learner will bounce back, recovering nicely.

The "TTT" (Typical Terrible Terrier) syndrome doesn't apply to our Miniature Schnauzer. He's untypically agreeable. The one exception may be a male used at stud to sire litters. Any scrappy behavior on his part is a warning to any other male that "any female in sight is mine, so back off." He's being very macho, and while we understand his attitude, we control that fellow on a short lead to avoid physical confrontation.

More Information on Miniature Schnauzers

NATIONAL BREED CLUB

American Miniature Schnauzer Club, Inc.
Mrs. Carma Ewer, Secretary
8882 South Easthills Drive
Sandy, UT 84093-1813
AMSCsec@aol.com

The club can send you information on all aspects of the breed, including the names and addresses of organizations in your area. Inquire about membership.

WEB SITES

The Miniature Schnauzer Web Ring
www.mtnhighminis.com/webring.html

Visit this Web site for a casual survey of the Miniature Schnauzer's world. Information is broken up into small categories, and covers topics such as housetraining, puppyhood, socializing, crate training and obedience.

Simply Schnauzer: Health & Nutrition
http://members.aol.com/smplyschnz/health/
healthmenu.html

This extensive Web site allows you to click on your preference—nutrition or health—before proceeding further. Whichever topic you choose first, be prepared for in-depth and thorough information.

Miniature Schnauzer CUR (Canine Underground Railroad) Information
http://home.earthlink.net/~msfriends/
rescueboard/volunteer.html

To find a Miniature Schnauzer rescue organization in your area, logon to this Web site. The Schnauzer Rescue Contact list is elaborate—you're sure to find a big-hearted rescue organization near you.

Living

with a

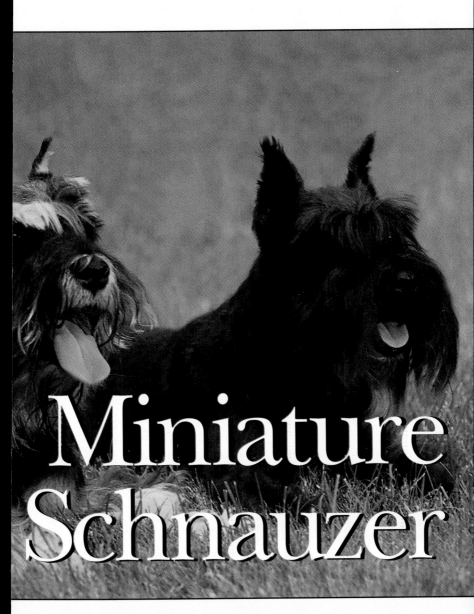

Miniature
Schnauzer

Bringing Your
Miniature
Schnauzer
Home

What an exciting time! A puppy is entering your life, and even more exciting—it's a Miniature Schnauzer, who'll grab your heart as you grab her. Aware of the responsibility that accompanies her, you're prepared, long before her arrival, with all of her needs. Since her first two weeks in your home will be highly stressful for her (and you), your preparedness will minimize your anxiety and heighten your eager and joyful anticipation.

Before your puppy's arrival, your selection of a veterinarian to whose care you'll entrust your puppy may necessarily rely on the recommendations of dog-owning friends and neighbors, or other knowledgeable sources. After your puppy's arrival (preferably within forty-eight hours), your veterinarian should give her a checkup and vaccination schedule, and answer any questions you may have.

Collars and Leashes

Her first collar may be a simple fabric puppy collar with a nonslip buckle. As she matures, continually check its size to determine when it will need to be replaced with a larger and more durable collar. When she's fully grown, you may prefer a metal or fabric slip collar, commonly but improperly called a "choke" collar, but properly designated as a training collar. If that is your choice, it's fine, but a training collar should be worn only in your presence when you are training her. If one of the metal rings becomes caught on a doorstop or any other object, the collar will, indeed, become a "choke" collar as your dog frantically attempts to pull herself free.

The leash you get for the puppy may be six feet long, wide enough to accommodate the size of your hand, made of leather or fabric. If a leather leash is preferred, you'll spend more money but it will last forever (unless chewed).

Doggy I.D.

If your puppy becomes separated from you, he'll be more easily rescuable wearing a collar with an attached ID tag imprinted with your telephone number. Two options of a more permanent nature are available, each utilizing a central system to identify any dog in its program. Tattooing (usually on your dog's inner thigh) of your personally selected number is a method that has been in use for many years and is relatively inexpensive. A more recent identification process involves the surgical implantation of a microchip below the skin near the withers; it is a more expensive method performed by your veterinarian. Tampering of the bar code, which must be read by a scanner, is impossible, whereas a tattoo number could be altered.

Safety on the Road

Driving with a dog in your vehicle jeopardizes her safety unless she's confined in a crate, or protected by a product specifically designed for pets—a canine car

PUPPY ESSENTIALS

Your new puppy will need:

food bowl

water bowl

collar

leash

I.D. tag

bed

crate

toys

grooming supplies

seat or seat belt. To avoid the possibility of a head or eye injury, she should never be allowed to travel with her head poking out of an open window. On a hot, sunny day, your dog must never be left unattended in a vehicle, even for a brief period and even with the windows lowered a bit. In minutes, the vehicle's interior will become an oven, and the dog will suffer a heat stroke leading to her death.

Providing for Your Puppy's Comfort

Luxurious comforts for the puppy may satisfy your needs, but he'll have no objection to simplicity. His bed should be small and cuddly; washable; well ventilated; nonchewable; and free from drafts in a warm, quiet spot somewhat near (but not in the midst of) the family's center of activities. As the puppy grows, a larger bed will be needed. The soft surface on which he'll sleep may be a washable blanket or pad, or a pillow with a removable cover for laundering.

Young puppies chowing down!

Using a Crate

Rather than providing him with a bed, a crate is preferable, since it serves every described requirement, is portable and multipurposed. As a den animal, the dog considers a crate a natural environment, and your choices of its soft sleeping surface are the same as those described for a bed. Since his bed "must grow as he grows," a puppy-sized crate must be replaced to accommodate that growth. If the initial crate is adult-sized, its interior area may be partitioned with a piece of plywood that may be moved as the dog's size increases.

Introduce the puppy to her crate following a period of playfulness, when she is sleepy. If necessary, gently coax her acceptance with a treat, soothing praise and quiet petting. A puppy's consistent daily routine is sleeping, eating and playing. At times, while hard at play, she'll flop into a nap. With naps so high on her list of priorities, you'll have many opportunities to acquaint her with her crate. Eventually, she'll need no urging. By leaving the door open, she'll seek comfort in her crate whenever she isn't eating or playing. Even as an adult and throughout her life, she'll take frequent and long daily naps. It's a dog's life—if only we could be so lucky!

Missing Mommy

If your puppy cries or whimpers because of the separation from his mother and littermates, a hot water bottle (containing warm water) beneath his bedding may comfort him. His withdrawal from his mother's heartbeat may be eased by the pulsation of a ticking clock wrapped in a towel, placed in his bed. His distress should dissipate in three or four nights.

You may wish to purchase a bed that will be large enough for your dog when she becomes an adult.

If, during those few stressful nights, you're of the inclination to take him to bed with you (and the writer admittedly shares that inclination), please don't roll over on him!

The puppy's food and water bowls should be untippable, made of stainless steel and washed daily. To protect her beard from becoming drenched, you might prefer a pet water bottle with a spout from which she'll drink.

Houseproofing

Chewing is inevitable. He's not being naughty; he's teething—a painful process. His curiosity is inevitable; he's a puppy. There are preventive measures you can take that will avoid potential danger.

With patience, you can easily train your puppy to relieve herself outside, when and where you want her to.

Unplug, remove or cover electric cords, and place childproof guards over unused electrical outlets.

Do not allow your puppy access to any potentially hazardous household, garden and maintenance products, such as bleach, cleaning fluids, detergent, disinfectant, drugs, mothballs, fertilizer, insecticides, antifreeze and any product that might be harmful if ingested, smelled or spilled on him.

He must not have access to aluminum can tabs, nails, pins, plastic bags or anything hazardous or small enough for him to swallow.

You should also be very wary of all house plants, most of which are poisonous to your dog.

Housetraining

You cannot tackle housetraining halfheartedly. Your dedicated time and attention are necessary for a successfully housetrained dog, and Miniature Schnauzers are extremely cooperative. The time to start is the day your puppy arrives. She'll indicate the need to relieve herself by circling (she's searching for the "right" spot), then squatting. If you play your role perfectly during the training process, which may require only a few weeks, you'll be relieved to know that she won't be relieving herself in the house.

The value of that multipurpose crate becomes apparent as a tool for housetraining. The puppy will show his respect for this very private place of his own by keeping it clean. Except for playtime and mealtime, he'll be in his crate with the door closed.

The first thing in the morning, and after each nap and each meal, and once each hour (except through his night's sleep), he must be allowed to relieve himself. Carry him outside to an area you prefer him to use, identifying each trip by saying "Outside," or whatever word you'll be using with consistency. As he circles, searching for that perfect spot, happily and continually encourage him with any trigger word you prefer.

When he is about to relieve himself, immediately stop talking and remain absolutely silent. After he has completed his function, lavishly praise him with your excited appreciation—"Good puppy!" "Fantastic!" "Wow!" "What a good boy!" Play with him a bit before carrying him into the house for a play period.

> ## HOUSEHOLD DANGERS
>
> Curious puppies and inquisitive dogs get into trouble not because they are bad, but simply because they want to investigate the world around them. It's our job to protect our dogs from harmful substances, like the following:
>
> ### IN THE HOUSE
>
> cleaners, especially pine oil
>
> perfumes, colognes, aftershaves
>
> medications, vitamins
>
> office and craft supplies
>
> electric cords
>
> chicken or turkey bones
>
> chocolate
>
> some house and garden plants, like ivy, oleander and poinsettia
>
> ### IN THE GARAGE
>
> antifreeze
>
> garden supplies, like snail and slug bait, pesticides, fertilizers, mouse and rat poisons

If you exercise absolute consistency in your trigger words, timing and praise (after the puppy is reliably housetrained), eventually she'll learn to relieve herself on command! On those hourly occasions when she's brought outside but doesn't relieve herself, bring her inside and watch her carefully, in case she decides she really does need to relieve herself. Of course, she won't relieve herself every time you take her outside; you're merely offering her the opportunity so that she can be praised when she does. Her connection with your praise when she performs outside and your displeasure when she performs inside will teach her which choice affords her the better deal.

Paper training is an alternate method. Cover most of the floor with layers of newspaper. Change the soiled paper, leaving only a "reminder" of urine or smeared stool to encourage your puppy's understanding. Gradually reduce the covered area until a few layers of a single page are left in the area you wish to be used.

When your puppy has had all of her vaccinations, it is time for her to romp outside.

Your admonition when the puppy has an in-house accident should not include yelling, slapping, or rubbing his nose in the deposited offense. Any "accident" does not indicate that he's a bad puppy or is dumb; he simply doesn't understand the procedure yet. Be patient; he'll learn. Startle him with the shaker can and a firm "No" to stop his behavior. Show him his mess with another "No" and clangy can, and take him outside immediately (you're not angry) to allow him to finish relieving himself. Only when he never, never, never has an in-house accident is he completely house-trained. Until then, patiently continue the procedure.

Providing Pleasure

Your puppy will get her early exercise while playing in the house. When all of her puppy innoculations have been given, she can be taken outdoors to play, gradually increasing the length of time. When she's about three months of age or even earlier, she may be taken for regular walks once or twice a day after a meal. Hopefully, she'll meet strangers on these outings, which will help her become socialized. She'll get exercise playing with outdoor yard toys; a clean old tire will intrigue her; two or three heaped haphazardly will delight her. Anything she can climb safely will build muscles. Jogging is debatable. To please you, she'll jog as long as it takes; when she tears around the yard, she'll stop when she's tired. The yard has resilient grass; sidewalks are for jogging. Yes, she started as a drover, but when's the last time sheep grazed on a concrete pasture?

Although your puppy will play for hours, he will relish time to rest.

Types of Toys

Toys are not only a source of amusement, but are also necessary for a puppy's development. An enormous variety of toys will tempt you, but one extremely popular chew treat that dogs adore should be avoided; anything made of animal hide (available in sticks, chips and knotted bone-shaped strips) is potentially dangerous. When a bit of its originally tough consistency becomes softened from being chewed and breaks off, it can lodge in the puppy's trachea or cause internal problems. Your puppy's toys should be his own balls, chewable items and stretchy dog toys—whatever eases the stress of his painful teething period.

41

As his teething progresses, he'll enjoy cotton rope tug toys and toys made of harder rubber.

Another toy your puppy will thoroughly enjoy is one of the thick fleece toys enclosing a squeaker. She'll love it for chewing, flipping into the air and chasing, but mostly for its squeaker, which she hears but can't reach to swallow. Other toys containing squeakers may offer her amusement, but when ripped in play, reveal the dangerously swallowable squeaker. Balls of all sizes with a variety of coverings are also fun.

As the puppy grows, his toys should accommodate his ability to retrieve, pull, flip, bounce and zigzag. When he shows a definite preference for a particular toy, rush to the store to buy a duplicate; he'll need it after destroying the original. If he shows little interest in a new toy, be patient; he'll probably enjoy it later. Your interaction with his toy-playing will teach him whatever pleasure the toy offers, and he'll decide which toy is more fun with or without your company. When you find yourself chuckling at your puppy's playful antics with a toy while your favorite televised movie (which you've waited for all week) fades into "The End," you won't even care that you missed it.

chapter 5

Feeding
Your
Miniature
Schnauzer

If you don't want your puppy to become a finicky eater, don't feed him steak, twice-baked potatoes and cherries jubilee. Feed him dog food that is nutritionally complete and balanced.

Commercial dog food manufacturers spend millions of dollars researching dogs' nutritional needs so that their products are nutritionally complete and balanced. Their ongoing research ensures consumers that their products meet the requirements of a public that has become extremely health-conscious, even where their pets are concerned.

Your Miniature Schnauzer's food is doing its job if your dog is healthy, in good weight and his stools are well formed (not loose or rock hard) and generally consistent with his size (not too big, not too

small). An occasional digression should cause no concern, since his system may be affected by stress, a sudden temperature change, a severe thunderstorm, or a
crisis in the family's daily routine, among other causes.

A healthy adult dog will have one or two bowel movements a day. Because of the frequency of a puppy's
daily meals, he will have several each day. A healthy
dog's urine will be yellow and clear.

Nutritional Needs

Dogs, like people, have certain nutritional needs.
But those of a dog are different from those of people,
so don't think you can
feed your Miniature
Schnauzer what you
eat and expect him
to thrive. Let's look
at a dog's nutritional
needs.

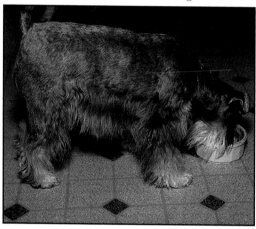

*Feed your dog a
high-quality
commercial dog
food.*

Dogs need proteins,
carbohydrates, miner-
als, fats, vitamins and
water.

Proteins Proteins
are the foundations
for building muscle and connective tissue. They also
assist in enzyme and hormone functioning. Proteins
are obtained mostly from animal-based ingredients.

There are high-quality proteins and low-quality proteins. High-quality proteins are those that are used better by the body, and include beef, poultry and lamb.
Poorer-quality proteins are those from vegetable
sources or meat by-products. Though higher is better,
more is not; excess protein is filtered through the kidneys and excreted, and too much protein makes the
kidneys work overtime.

Puppy foods should contain about 25 percent protein.
You'll see this stated on the bag of food you buy. Adult
dogs need less, but consult with your veterinarian,

because the amount may be determined by the growth
and activity level of your individual dog.

Carbohydrates   These are the starches, sugars and
fiber that provide energy, and are found in foods like
bread, pasta, potatoes, vegetables, grains and sweets. In
dog food, these are the grains and vegetable products.
Bodies need carbohydrates to help digest proteins,
too, but again more is not better. Excess carbohydrates
are stored as fat.

Minerals   Sodium, calcium, iron,
zinc, potassium—all are essential
minerals. Minerals build bone and
teeth and are needed for cell functions. Minerals come from a variety
of sources, from fish to fruit.

Fats   Fats have a bad rap. They're
blamed for obesity, heart conditions and some cancers. But eliminating fats is not the answer; in fact,
fats are as necessary as other nutrients. It's the amount and type
of fats that matter. Fats help with
vitamin absorption, cell functions,
hormones and healthy coat and skin.
They also make foods taste good.

Vitamins   Vitamins are responsible for numerous functions in the
body. But they need to balance.
Commercial pet food manufacturers have come closest to providing
that balance for our pet dogs, and
most veterinarians advise against
supplementing a quality food. If
you're not sure, ask your vet or
breeder.

HOW MANY MEALS A DAY?

Individual dogs vary in how much
they should eat to maintain a
desired body weight—not too fat,
but not too thin. Puppies need several meals a day, while older dogs
may need only one. Determine
how much food keeps your adult
dog looking and feeling her best.
Then decide how many meals you
want to feed with that amount. Like
us, most dogs love to eat, and
offering two meals a day is more
enjoyable for them. If you're worried about overfeeding, make sure
you measure correctly and abstain
from adding tidbits to the meals.

Whether you feed one or two
meals, only leave your dog's food
out for the amount of time it takes
her to eat it—10 minutes, for
example. Freefeeding (when
food is available any time) and
leisurely meals encourage picky
eating. Don't worry if your dog
doesn't finish all her dinner in the
allotted time. She'll learn she
should.

Water   Water is the single most important nutrient,
because without it life ceases to exist. Dogs drink more
water than people; therefore, it's important for your
dog to have access to fresh water at all times. (The only

exception to this is during early puppyhood, when you should take your puppy's water away after his last nighttime walk before bed. That way he won't need to go in the middle of the night.)

How Much to Feed a Puppy

During her period of intense growth and development, a puppy requires almost twice the amount of most nutrients per pound of body weight compared to an adult dog's needs. At six to eight weeks of age, a puppy requires at least three times the adult dog's caloric requirements per pound of body weight. Because of these nutritional needs, you should feed your puppy three or four times a day. Ask your veterinarian or breeder how much per meal; you don't want your puppy to eat too much, but you certainly don't want to underfeed her.

This caloric requirement gradually decreases to twice the adult dog's needs until the puppy is sixteen weeks old and continues to gradually decrease, reaching an adult dog's caloric requirement at about one year of age. The number of meals you feed will decrease, too, until your puppy is eating one or two meals a day.

Manufacturers of the best brands of puppy food have taken all of these requirements into consideration, and since the amounts fed to your puppy gradually decrease over her growth and development period, the decreased caloric ingestion is automatic. During that first intensive year, a nutritional and balanced diet will develop strong bones and teeth, clear eyes and a healthy coat and will promote healthy body functions.

Your Puppy's Feeding Routine

Your puppy's food bowl and water container should be placed where they are clearly visible to you, but out of the path of foot traffic. Both containers should be scrubbed frequently to avoid bacterial contamination. Fresh, clean water should be available to your puppy and throughout his life at all times.

You have two choices of feeding routines: scheduled feedings (allowing you to determine her mealtimes) or self-feeding (allowing her to determine her mealtimes). Scheduled feedings are preferable. They make for easier housetraining (keeping in mind the rule that what goes in must come out fairly soon afterward) and, in the long run, a healthier dog. Self-fed dogs tend to be fussier, so you may not recognize a loss of appetite as a health problem until it's serious, whereas if your normally eager-to-eat Miniature Schnauzer won't eat, you'll know there's a problem right away.

Discourage Fussy Eating

So your dog doesn't develop a fussiness problem, the best thing to do is keep to a feeding schedule, put his bowl down and leave it down for ten to fifteen minutes at the most. If he's not finished eating in that time, remove the extra food. Do not let it sit out so he can eat it at his leisure. When mealtime comes around again, feed the normal amount and use the same rules. He'll learn that if he wants all his dinner, he'd better eat it right away. And you'll learn when he's not feeling well by how much he's eating.

While a roly-poly puppy is cute and healthy, don't allow her to become an obese adult by overfeeding or through lack of exercise. If she does become overweight, decrease the amount of food she's offered until she's in

---

HOW TO READ THE DOG FOOD LABEL

With so many choices on the market, how can you be sure you are feeding the right food for your dog? The information is all there on the label—if you know what you're looking for.

Look for the nutritional claim right up top. Is the food "100% nutritionally complete"? If so, it's for nearly all life stages; "growth and maintenance," on the other hand, is for early development; puppy foods are marked as such, as are foods for senior dogs.

Ingredients are listed in descending order by weight. The first three or four ingredients will tell you the bulk of what the food contains. Look for the highest-quality ingredients, like meats and grains, to be among them.

The Guaranteed Analysis tells you what levels of protein, fat, fiber and moisture are in the food, in that order. While these numbers are meaningful, they won't tell you much about the quality of the food. Nutritional value is in the dry matter, not the moisture content.

In many ways, seeing is believing. If your dog has bright eyes, a shiny coat, a good appetite and a good energy level, chances are his diet's fine. Your dog's breeder and your veterinarian are good sources of advice if you're still confused.

proper weight, then maintain the proper amount, and make sure she gets plenty of exercise.

Types of Food

Commercial dog foods come in three basic forms: dry, canned and semimoist. Which should you feed your Miniature Schnauzer?

Dry food, commonly called kibble, is an easy and economical choice for the owner and a sound nutritional choice for the dog. It doesn't spoil easily, it's not smelly and it's crunchy so it offers him the opportunity to chew. If he prefers his food moistened, and puppies usually do, add room-temperature water to the bowl, wait until the food is just a bit mushy, then feed him. The rule is, "Let the food moisten in the bowl, not in his tummy."

If you wish to change your puppy's moistened meals to dry food, gradually reduce the amount of water until she is eating dry meals. Any time you change brands, do so gradually by adding small amounts of the new food to her current food until the new brand has replaced her former food. If the brand you are feeding contains all of her essential nutritional needs, there is no need to supplement her diet (as discussed in the section on nutritional needs).

TO SUPPLEMENT OR NOT TO SUPPLEMENT?

If you're feeding your dog a diet that's correct for her developmental stage and she's alert, healthy-looking and neither over- nor underweight, you don't need to add supplements. These include table scraps as well as vitamins and minerals. In fact, a growing puppy is in danger of developing musculoskeletal disorders by oversupplementation. If you have any concerns about the nutritional quality of the food you're feeding, discuss them with your veterinarian.

Canned food is a sound nutritional choice, but it's more expensive to feed on its own, and it doesn't give your Miniature Schnauzer the opportunity to chew. It also stains a Mini's beard, requiring more after-dinner attention to cleanliness. However, some owners feel guilt-ridden if they don't add at least some tasty canned food to the dry food. If that describes you, your dog won't object, and veterinarians have found that people and dogs are happiest feeding a 75 percent dry/25 percent canned meal.

Semimoist foods are convenient and easy to use. Many come in prewrapped servings so all you have to do is open and serve. To retain their texture and taste, however, semimoist foods contain dyes and preservatives that aren't needed in canned or dry foods—or in your dog.

Offering table scraps will diminish your dog's appetite for his regular diet. An occasional bit of leftover lean beef or skinless chicken as a special treat (apart from your or his mealtime) will do no harm.

Good and Bad Foods

Although premium commercial dog foods are a staple of your Miniature Schnauzer's diet, let's face it—your puppy is also going to get food from your table occasionally. Below you'll read about why it's very important that the food from your table not be given to her during your meals, which encourages begging and other bad manners. But you can add extras to your dog's regular meals, or use human foods as treats.

Regardless of the feeding routine you choose, you should make sure that fresh, clean water is always available to your dog.

Dogs can eat many of the same foods we eat. They love meats—hot dogs, chicken, beef—cheese, pasta, bread and snack food like popcorn or chips. The obvious. But dogs also love vegetables—steamed or raw carrots, broccoli, cooked spinach or peas—and fruits like melon, apples, even grapes.

Some foods should be forever off-limits for your Miniature Schnauzer. These include poultry bones or any sharp or splintering bones. Spicy foods may upset your dog's stomach, and chocolate can kill your Miniature Schnauzer: *Do not give him chocolate in any form!*

Avoid Bad Table Manners

If you're annoyed by the interruption of recorded tele-phone sales pitches at dinner time, you'll be more annoyed by your dog pestering you during your meals.

To avoid her pesky behavior, you mustn't allow it. The first time she places her paws on your lap, your immediate reaction must be a stern "Off" as you push her away. You're not angry; your attitude is quite matter-of-fact as you continue to eat. She'll probably try again, plac-ing her paws on your lap. As many times as are necessary, continue to push her away with a stern "Off," exhibiting your unchanged atti-tude until she simply gives up. She may try again during that meal or the next or the next, but will only be subjected to your consistent reaction.

When you're convinced, after months of your puppy's proper behavior and no bothersome paws on your lap, that he's reliable, sneak a piece of meat on the table edge and hope he attempts to swipe it. If he does, you know what you must do. Sometime later, try to trap him again, and if he ignores the bait, praise him, but under no circumstances should he be rewarded (at least at that moment) by giving him the meat treat.

Persistent whining or barking during your mealtime may be cor-rected with your "No" and a shake of the noisy can (see Chapter 4 for more details). Keep that can handy, particularly during your puppy's early training period. He must learn what

TYPES OF FOODS/TREATS

There are three types of commer-cially available dog food—dry, canned and semimoist—and a huge assortment of treats (lucky dogs!) to feed your dog. Which should you choose?

Dry and canned foods contain similar ingredients. The primary difference between them is their moisture content. The moisture is not just water. It's blood and broth, too, the very things that dogs adore. So while canned food is more palatable, dry food is more economical, convenient and effective in controlling tartar buildup. Most owners feed a 25% canned/75% dry diet to give their dogs the benefit of both. Just be sure your dog is getting the nutri-tion he needs (you and your vet-erinarian can determine this).

Semimoist foods have the flavor dogs love and the convenience owners want. However, they tend to contain excessive amounts of artificial colors and preservatives.

Dog treats come in every size, shape and flavor imaginable, from organic cookies shaped like post-men to beefy chew sticks. Dogs seem to love them all, so enjoy the variety. Just be sure not to overindulge your dog. Factor treats into her regular meal sizes.

behaviors are and are not acceptable, and you must always be alert and ready for corrections with the can's use. The cooperation of every family member must be made clear. If you've managed to teach him not to pester you while others are sneaking table scraps to him, the poor puppy will be utterly confused, wondering why you're so mean to him.

Children, especially, must learn not to "accidentally" drop bits of food on the floor. They'll feel quite satisfied if they're encouraged to wait until a later time after each meal when they may offer a treat to the puppy. Let them join in the puppy's training, but under your supervision.

Feeding the Older Dog

As dogs grow, their nutritional needs change. For that reason, a third period follows the rich formula for puppies and the maintenance formula for adults, and that is the senior formula. The canine senior citizen is less active and his digestive system has changed, so his nutritional requirements are different as well. Commercial dog food manufacturers have addressed these changes and provided senior diets for senior dogs. Consult with your veterinarian about which is most appropriate for your pet.

chapter 6

Grooming
Your
Miniature
Schnauzer

Possibly considering your friends to be "stuck" with their shedding, smelly breeds, you'd better withhold your temptation to gloat. Your Miniature Schnauzer's ideal nonshedding, nonsmelling coat doesn't just sit there looking beautiful without attention given to it. Your time and trouble, however, are worth the effort; consider the result. Gloat, if you must!

Grooming Equipment

Even though you may have your Miniature Schnauzer groomed at a commercial establishment, you'll need to maintain her appearance between visits. A grooming table, whether homemade or purchased, is ideal for the procedure if it's fitted with an adjustable post, but a rubber bathmat or any nonslip surface placed on a table may be substituted. Proper lighting is essential. A smooth-surfaced doctor's jacket, nurse's uniform or grooming smock is ideal clothing for you, certainly better than the hair-grabbing sweatshirts and T-shirts worn by many professional groomers. Grooming tools you'll need are a slicker brush, coarse-toothed comb, hemostat, nail clippers and a canine nail file, all of which you must regularly disinfect.

If you clip your dog yourself, scissors and electric clipper blades should be sharpened by a reputable shop specializing in the maintenance of grooming tools. Treat your tools with respect; dropping them on the floor will force them out of alignment. The ideal bathing facility will be an appropriately sized tub with a spray hose; less ideal, one tub for shampooing and another for rinsing with a plastic cup or dipper. The dog should be bathed with a quality shampoo especially formulated for dogs, and the nail clippers should be suitable for a medium-size dog. Equipment to strip a show coat should be discussed with the person who will help you with the procedure.

Preparing Your Puppy for Grooming

Since grooming will become a regular and daily part of your Miniature Schnauzer's life, teach him to stand for very short periods by holding him up under his tummy while you stroke and softly praise him, saying, "Stand." If he wiggles (and he will), patiently continue the procedure for a moment, then stop. He's learning, and you don't want to push him to the limit. If he tries to sit (and he will), gently lift him under his tummy and remind him to "Stand."

When the puppy is comfortably and agreeably content to remain standing for a while, gradually extend the time, but it isn't necessary for him to remain standing for hours. Even an older dog occasionally needs to change his position momentarily. If your puppy tries to nip you, lightly tap his nose with a serious "No bite." He should also be taught to lie on his side to have his

**GROOMING
TOOLS**

pin brush

slicker brush

flea comb

towel

mat rake

grooming
glove

scissors

nail
clippers

teeth-
cleaning
equipment

shampoo

conditioner

clippers

legs and underside groomed. Introduce him to the clicking noise and "feel" of the metal nail clippers as they're merely tapped against his nails. Lift each foot, letting it rest on your hand, until he allows you to hold it gently. Before any grooming session, permit your puppy (or adult) to relieve himself. Until he learns to stand on a table, he may be placed on your lap for his grooming sessions.

Eye, Toenail and Ear Care

Every day, check your Miniature Schnauzer's eyes because many dogs accumulate a bit of mucus in the corner of each one. Use a tissue or cotton ball to remove any matter, or wipe the area with a product

specifically made for eye tearing; you can also use a dampened cloth containing a tiny amount of shampoo, then rinse with clear water.

Your dog's toenails must be trimmed or they'll curl into a discomforting length that will not permit her to walk properly on the pads of her feet. If clicking is heard as she walks, her nails are too long.

It is essential that you accustom your puppy to the grooming process when she is still young.

Any scissors may be used for a very young puppy, but commercial nail clippers are necessary when the nails grow thicker. Two types are available: the plier and the guillotine. The latter is recommended since it's designed to enable you to see how much you're cutting, and the most popular brand has a replaceable blade. Always have a blood coagulant ready in the event you cut the quick (the vein that runs through the center of each nail). Pet shops carry a styptic powder product that quickly stops the bleeding when the nail is dipped into it, or you may use a silver nitrate stick. You'll be cutting a lot of nails throughout the dog's life, and it's inevitable that you'll cut a quick. Apply the coagulant, and stop feeling guilty.

Nail-Clipping Tips

You'll also need a nail file specially designed for dogs' nails. Lift a foot and allow it to rest on your hand with your thumb stroking the top. Do not tightly grip the foot or pull the leg; you'll only cause resentment, resistance and refusal to cooperate.

If you introduce the procedure slowly, patiently and gently, the puppy will be more cooperative. If the hair on his foot covers his nails, making it difficult for you to see them, wet your thumb and push the hair back to expose the nail (or poke the nails through an old nylon stocking).

Snip off a tiny bit at first. If your puppy allows you to continue, proceed until she tires. It's a successful first session if you've clipped even just a few of his nails. Cut any remaining nails in several sessions, if necessary. If clipped every two weeks, your dog's nails will be comfortably and properly short.

Your Miniature Schnauzer's ears will need regular attention.

When using the nail clippers, hold them according to the packaging directions. At a point just below the bend of the nail, cut each nail at a slight upward angle toward the dog. Round off each nail with the nail file. If the nails ever grow too long, clip them as short as possible just beyond the quick, then file the tips every other day (which will force the quick to recede) until the nails are the correct length.

Tending the Ears

Since the Miniature Schnauzer is a breed whose coat continually grows, the ears require constant watchfulness. The hair inside the ears, if not removed, will grow downward into the ear canal. Canine products specifically manufactured for the care of ears include powders, liquid cleansing solutions and odor reducers.

If your dog is groomed professionally, be sure that the groomer completes the procedure on each visit. If you groom your dog yourself, you'll be responsible for its

A daily brushing will keep the coat healthy looking.

undertaking. Sprinkle some powder into the ear and fluff it around by gently tapping the ear's surface with your forefinger. Your dog will be manageable if you hold her head gently against your body with your free hand.

The powder's purpose is to allow your thumb and forefinger to grasp and pull out the easily visible hairs inside the ear near the surface. Be sure to remove only a few hairs at a time or you'll cause pain. Continue to withdraw the hair until that part of the ear has been cleared of hair. Spreading the ear will enable you to see the hair growing deeper inside the ear. If necessary, add more powder.

Using a hemostat (an invaluable tool), grasp a few strands of hair and withdraw them. Be careful with the hemostat; avoid poking the skin or grasping a bit of flesh with it. After the ear is cleared of hair, the powder must be removed or it will accumulate bacteria. Using a cotton ball or a cotton swab dipped into baby lotion (but not dripping with it), gently wipe the inside of the ear. Any time hair accumulates, it must be removed.

Whether your dog is groomed professionally or by you, regularly check the ears for any wax or dirt that has accumulated—a normal expectancy. Place three or four drops of a commercial canine ear cleansing solution into the ear and massage the ear at the base for three minutes to distribute the solution. With a series of cotton swabs, gently cleanse the ear, removing all of the accumulated debris. Then use a cotton ball to remove all of the liquid solution.

Coat Care

Your Miniature Schnauzer should be brushed daily; minimally two or three times a week. When her puppy coat is long enough to groom, gently brush it with a slicker brush, which has wire bristles that bend. With your fingers, remove any burs or foreign matter from her coat. Mats, which are knotted hairs, should be separated by your fingers and the end teeth of a coarse comb into smaller and smaller sections until a comb may be drawn through them.

While being careful to avoid digging the bristles into the skin, the coat must be brushed thoroughly from the skin outward, not merely the coat's surface. The coat first is brushed in the direction in which it grows, then in the opposite direction, and finally again in the direction in which it grows. This procedure will remove dirt and loose skin particles, stimulate circulation and secretion of the natural skin oils and ensure a healthy coat.

The furnishings of each leg are brushed in a downward direction, starting at the feet, then moving upward to the next layer and the next layer, until the entire leg is brushed. It is rebrushed in an upward direction, and again downward.

The beard and moustache are brushed starting at the outer edge, moving to the next layer, etc., until you've reached the skin. You will then "proof" your brushing by combing everything with a coarse-toothed comb. An adult Miniature Schnauzer with a clipped coat needs so little maintenance that he can have a spiffy appearance every day of his life. A daily brushing of four legs, two eyebrows, a beard and a mustache is a small investment of time for such a great return.

The Bath

Any bath must be preceded by a thorough brushing and combing of your dog's coat. Thoroughly soak her with warm (not hot) water. If she shakes herself (and she will), quickly place your hand on the top of her head—which doesn't guarantee your not being drenched, but may help. Be ready to go into preventive action whenever necessary—at least once during the bath, and several times after the bath. It's a natural doggy thing. To prevent water from entering her ears (which could lead to serious problems), place a small bit of absorbent cotton in each ear. Avoid getting soapy water into her eyes; you might consider using tearless shampoo or placing a few drops of mineral oil in each eye before bathing.

If your Miniature Schnauzer frequents the outdoors, an occasional bath is necessary.

When your Miniature Schnauzer is thoroughly wet, work up a lather on her back with shampoo and briskly rub her coat. Shampoo her head, legs, chest, tummy and rear. Remove the cotton from her ears, then, without using shampoo, wash them inside and out with a clean, dampened and wrung-out washcloth, and place fresh cotton in each ear. Again avoiding water in her eyes and ears, thoroughly rinse her with warm, not hot, water until no trace of shampoo remains in her coat. Then rinse again! If it is necessary, bathe and rinse her again.

Quickly squeeze the excess water from the puppy's coat and place her in a towel to absorb as much moisture as possible. Towel dry her with another towel (or blow-dry her with an electric hair dryer) until she is barely damp. With a clean brush and comb, groom her coat to make sure that it is free from mats.

The Clipped Coat

If your dog is to sport a clipped coat styled at a commercial establishment, be sure the groomer understands the breed and is familiar with the attractive pattern. Many groomers allow the underside coat between the forelegs and rear legs to be so long, and start so high on the dog's side, that it resembles a lace curtain. Display to the groomer a picture of a Miniature Schnauzer in a show coat; indicate that you prefer the unexaggerated length of coat beneath the chest to taper as it reaches back to the tummy and rear legs.

If you decide to clip your dog, study the procedure; learn from an experienced friend, breeder or other helpful soul, then enjoy a permanently (and less expensively) maintained Miniature Schnauzer. The clipped coat pattern is relatively easy to learn and simple to perform.

A well-groomed Miniature Schnauzer will make you both proud.

The Show Coat

Maintaining your Miniature Schnauzer in a stripped coat is not easy, and it is not likely that a commercial groomer will know the procedure or be willing to accept the challenge. You will have to learn from an exhibitor, breeder, or professional handler. Perhaps one will allow you to watch the procedure and teach you the technique. Not only is it intricate and time consuming, it must be done in several stages and be precisely timed for each show season.

The stripped show coat displays the Miniature Schnauzer in his most typically attractive appearance, but the periods between a "blown" show coat and her next new show coat are lengthy and create an almost unattractive appearance. Your lifestyle, time, energy and needs must determine which appearance is the more suitable for you.

chapter 7

Keeping Your
Miniature
Schnauzer
Healthy

The first thing you should do after you get your puppy is schedule a visit with a veterinarian. It is important to establish a good rapport with your veterinarian; after all, this is the person to whom you are going to entrust the health of your dog for possibly many years to come.

If you don't have a trusted veterinarian already, ask your breeder or other Miniature Schnauzer owners in the area for recommendations. Call veterinarians in your area and ask if they've treated Miniature Schnauzers before. Also ask what their policies are on visits, emergency care and anything else you're concerned with.

Once at the veterinarian's, pay attention to how the staff and the vet handle your dog. Is the waiting room clean and comfortable for the animals? Do you have to wait a long time with no explanation why? Is the veterinarian interested in answering your questions and does he or she handle your dog well? If you don't get a good feeling about the people or the place, keep looking.

It's your responsibility to be a good patient, too. Train your Miniature Schnauzer to accept handling by the veterinarian. Get her used to the vet's office by taking her in every once in a while even if she doesn't have an appointment.

Many dogs get anxious in a vet's office between the smells and strange animals. They associate the place with bad things, and no wonder! It's your job to make your veterinarian's job easier by paying attention to your dog's condition and training her to be polite. These are easy things to do with a Miniature Schnauzer, a lovable dog who needs regular grooming.

> ## YOUR PUPPY'S VACCINES
>
> Vaccines are given to prevent your dog from getting an infectious disease like canine distemper or rabies. Vaccines are the ultimate preventive medicine: they're given before your dog ever gets the disease so as to protect him from the disease. That's why it is necessary for your dog to be vaccinated routinely. Puppy vaccines start at eight weeks of age for the five-in-one DHLPP vaccine and are given every three to four weeks until the puppy is sixteen months old. Your veterinarian will put your puppy on a proper schedule and will remind you when to bring in your dog for shots.

Vaccines and the Diseases They Prevent

During the first few weeks of your puppy's life, he received protection against all of the infectious diseases to which his mother was immune while nursing. Protection from the diseases was being passed through his mother's milk. After weaning, it became necessary for him to be innoculated against those diseases, since the protection was no longer being supplied by the mother's milk.

Your responsibility is to have him examined annually by your veterinarian, who will administer the annual "booster" innoculations to prevent the diseases which are common to all breeds of dogs. Those diseases are discussed below.

DISTEMPER

This is caused by an airborne virus and is a potentially fatal disease. Symptoms include loss of appetite and weight; thick, yellow discharge from the nose and eyes; and a dry cough. There may be vomiting and/or diarrhea. Distemper used to be quite common, but today's vaccines have made it easy to combat.

HEPATITIS

This virus is transmitted through contact with an infected animal's urine, stool or saliva. It affects the liver and cells lining the blood vessels. Symptoms include high fever; thirst; loss of appetite; red eyes; discharge from the eyes, mouth and nose. Recovery or death are possible.

LEPTOSPIROSIS

This is a highly contagious bacterial disease that's acquired through contact with an infected animal's nasal secretions, urine or saliva. It causes damage to the digestive tract, liver and kidneys. Symptoms include weakness, signs of depression, reluctance to move, frequent drinking and urination, bloody diarrhea, red or jaundiced eyes. Can be transmitted to humans.

PARVOVIRUS

A deadly virus that comes in two forms. Parvovirus attacks bone marrow, lymph nodes and the lining of the gastrointestinal tract. Enteric (or diarrhea form) causes depression, appetite loss, vomiting, bloody diarrhea, fever and death. Myocardial (or cardiac form) rapidly attacks puppies' hearts, leading to sudden death.

A highly infectious virus that attacks the respiratory system. Symptoms include an intermittent dry, hacking cough, possible nasal discharge. The disease is caused by several viruses and a bacteria known as *Bordatella bronchiseptica.* While not fatal, the disease spreads rapidly.

CORONAVIRUS

A highly contagious viral infection of the gastrointestinal tract. Symptoms include vomiting, diarrhea, fever and dehydration. Your veterinarian may not recommend immunization, since individual pet dogs are less susceptible to its spread than are kennel dogs.

RABIES

A fatal infection of the central nervous system affecting all mammals. Dogs may be initially vaccinated at three months of age. Depending on state laws, an annual or three-year vaccination should be administered. Almost every state requires vaccination against the disease, which is transmittable to humans.

When to Call the Veterinarian

In spite of the excellent care and protection against disease a dog is given, illness will strike occasionally. The dog cannot communicate verbally that something is wrong, but she will exhibit symptoms to indicate a problem. Her body language, any deviation from her normal behavior, and her apearance may offer clues. If any changes are obvious,

---

WHEN TO CALL THE VET

In any emergency situation, you should call your veterinarian immediately. You can make the difference in your dog's life by staying as calm as possible when you call and by giving the doctor or the assistant as much information as possible before you leave for the clinic. That way, the vet will be able to take immediate, specific action to remedy your dog's situation.

Emergencies include acute abdominal pain, suspected poisoning, snakebite, burns, frostbite, shock, dehydration, abnormal vomiting or bleeding, and deep wounds. You are the best judge of your dog's health, as you live with and observe him every day. Don't hesitate to call your veterinarian if you suspect trouble.

or if one or more of the following symptoms are noted, they should be brought to the attention of your veterinarian:

- constipation or diarrhea
- shivering
- fever
- watery eyes
- runny nose
- coughing
- loss of appetite (or ravenous appetite without weight gain)
- vomiting
- increased urination
- restlessness
- straining to urinate
- labored breathing
- weight loss
- increased water intake
- lameness
- paralysis
- obvious pain
- nervous symptoms

Internal Parasites

Webster's defines a parasite as "a person who lives at the expense of another or others without making any useful contribution or return." The internal parasites that affect your Miniature Schnauzer are not people, they are worms. They make no useful contribution, and, undetected, they can rob your dog of blood, food, energy and, possibly, life. If your puppy or dog is acting listless, won't eat, coughs a lot without coughing anything up, seems to have a bloated belly, or if you notice white slivers in her stools, she may have a type of worm. There are several described here.

HOOKWORMS

These have hooklike mouth parts by which they attach themselves to the intestinal lining. They commonly occur in puppies, but adults also may be infested. They are contracted when the dog swallows the parasite's larvae, or when the larvae penetrates the dog's skin. They are visible only under a microscope. A mildly infected dog has diarrhea, loses weight and has a poor coat. A heavily infested dog becomes weak and anemic from blood loss. The condition is treatable, but infection is avoidable by keeping the dog's environment sanitary. Remove feces frequently, keep the lawn short and relatively dry and wash down paved areas with disinfectants.

ROUNDWORMS

These are very common in puppies, and adults acquire them by licking contaminated ground or eating smaller animals carrying roundworm larvae. Affected puppies are weak and thin with potbellies; have dull, dry coats; are diarrhetic; and cough and vomit.

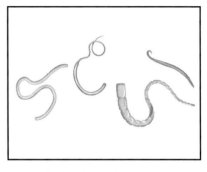

Roundworms look like white, firm, rounded strips of thin spaghetti about one to three inches long, and often coil like springs. Adult dogs who become infested may show no signs of infection. The condition is treatable, and the sanitary program described for prevention of hookworms is recommended. Roundworms can be passed to children, in whom serious diseases can result.

Common internal parasites (l-r): roundworm, whipworm, tapeworm and hookworm.

TAPEWORMS

Rare in puppies, tapeworms more frequently infest mature dogs, who have eaten an infected host—a piece of meat, an animal, or an insect (a flea or louse). The head of the worm attaches to the intestinal lining and produces egg-filled body segments, which eventually break off and are excreted.

The detached segments may be seen in the hair around the dog's anus, in her bedding, or in the stool. When alive, the segments are off-white and flat and wave back and forth; when dried out, they may become

65

yellow, translucent and look like grains of rice. Symptoms may be weight loss and diarrhea. The veterinarian's medication is necessary for treatment.

WHIPWORMS

These are thin, white, shaped like a whip, less than an inch in length and difficult to see. They inhabit the dog's lower intestinal tract. Some infected dogs exhibit no symptoms, while others will have intermittent watery diarrhea, anemia, weight loss, weakness and a generally poor appearance. Medication is necessary for treatment. Because dogs become infested by licking or sniffing contaminated ground, a dry and sanitary environment, as mentioned, should be maintained.

Whenever your dog has been outside, make sure to check him for ticks when he comes in to keep him and your house tick free.

HEARTWORMS

Heartworms enter your dog's bloodstream following the bite of an infected mosquito. They mature in your dog's heart, reaching a length of five to twelve

inches, and present a very serious, life-threatening problem. An infected dog will tire easily, have a chronic cough and lose weight. While an infected dog may be treated with drugs to destroy the adult worms, it is far simpler and safer to treat your dog with preventive medicine.

Every year, before being put on the preventive (Ivermectin), your veterinarian will take a blood test for the presence of heartworm in your Mini Schnauzer's blood. The test must be negative before the preventive is started. The preventive comes in two forms: a pill given every day, or a pill given once a month.

GIARDIA

Although this is not a worm like the other internal parasites we've discussed, giardia is an internal parasite nonetheless. It is a protozoan, and it infects animals through water. Giardia is a common parasite of wild animals, so any water source from which wild animals drink can be infected, and if your Mini Schnauzer also drinks that water, he can get infected from it. That's why it's a good idea to bring water from home if you go on a trip with your dog, especially an outdoors-oriented trip. Diarrhea is a symptom of a giardial infection, so if your dog develops diarrhea shortly after you've been camping, for example, you can suspect he's been infected. Make sure to tell your veterinarian you suspect giardia for this reason.

External Parasites

FLEAS

A dog infested with fleas has a very serious problem. She will suffer a loss of blood, have intensely itchy skin and can contract a serious parasite—tapeworms.

If you see your dog scratching and biting to relieve irritating itching, he may have fleas. Examine his skin by pulling back the hairs. Any small black and white specks are probably flea feces or eggs. If you crush

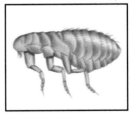

The flea is a die-hard pest.

some of the black specks between your fingers and they leave red spots, they're definitely flea feces—digested blood. You may even see the fleas moving quickly through the hair.

If your Miniature Schnauzer has fleas, the only way to get rid of them completely is to treat both your dog and the environment. That means the house and the yard, the car—any area with which your dog has come into contact. This is everything from carpets to furniture to your bed to the dog's spot outside. It will be necessary to rid every area of not only the fleas, but also the flea eggs, which hatch into a new crop in eight to ten days. Fumigation with a commercial insecticide (a flea fogger) or the services of a professional exterminator may be necessary.

If fleas are a serious problem in your area, discuss a preventive program with your veterinarian or experts at a specialty pet supply shop. Your veterinarian may want to prescribe a new medication that your dog takes once a month and that kills the fleas that bite your dog. It works by sterilizing the fleas when they bite your dog, therefore, flea eggs won't hatch.

Treat your dog at the same time you treat the house, car and yard to avoid reinfestation. Your Miniature Schnauzer will need to be combed with a flea comb to get most of the fleas off him. Next, bathe him with a flea-killing shampoo. There are lots of them out there, so ask your veterinarian or a breeder for a recommendation. If your dog must be dipped in a flea or tick solution, sprayed or powdered with a flea preventative product, he should not also wear a flea collar during the shampoo's, spray's or powder's extended effective period. Young puppies should not be subjected to insecticides, collars, sprays, etc.

Ask for a recommendation where insecticides and indoor foggers are concerned, too. And whatever products you use, be sure to follow the instructions on the label and read the precautions before you begin using.

FIGHTING FLEAS

Remember, the fleas you see on your dog are only part of the problem—the smallest part! To rid your dog and home of fleas, you need to treat your dog *and* your home. Here's how:

• Identify where your pet(s) sleep. These are "hot spots."

• Clean your pets' bedding regularly by vacuuming and washing.

• Spray "hot spots" with a non-toxic, long-lasting flea larvicide.

• Treat outdoor "hot spots" with insecticide.

• Kill eggs on pets with a product containing insect growth regulators (IGRs).

• Kill fleas on pets per your veterinarian's recommendation.

TICKS

Ticks are small, wingless insects that come in many sizes depending on which part of the country you live in. They live in places of dense undergrowth, such as woods, fields and grassy dunes. And they carry disease, most notably Rocky Mountain spotted fever and Lyme disease.

If you live in a rural area or an area with a heavy deer population, you should check your Miniature Schnauzer's entire body for ticks every day.

To remove a tick, wet a cotton ball with a tick-killing spray or shampoo, or with rubbing alcohol, and apply the cotton ball to the insect. This will stun it. Then grasp the tick with a pair of tweezers and firmly but

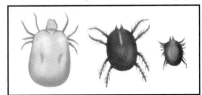

Three types of ticks (l-r): the wood tick, brown dog tick and deer tick.

gently pull it straight out. If the head is not removed, don't worry—it will not grow a new body! Place the removed tick in a sealable container of alcohol or burn it with a match; ticks are hearty creatures and can survive being flushed down the toilet or drain.

Lyme Disease Since its discovery in Lyme, Connecticut, in the 1970s, Lyme disease has spread to almost the entire United States. It is a virus spread by deer ticks, whose hosts are deer and mice.

When an infected deer tick bites another animal, it passes the disease through its saliva into the blood. On people, the site of an infected deer tick bite will usually develop a red circle around it. On dogs, this circle could be difficult if not impossible to see.

The best prevention is intervention: Check your outdoor-loving dog every day for these pests. Symptoms of Lyme include joint stiffness and pain, and lethargy. Your veterinarian can perform a blood test to detect for Lyme disease, but if it comes back negative, don't rule Lyme out. Have your dog retested.

If caught soon enough, treatment with antibiotics clears up the conditions almost immediately. Lyme is a serious disease, and you should keep a close eye on your Schnauzer if you know she's been exposed.

MITES

Mites are microscopic organisms that affect different areas of the dog's body, and generally cause a condition known as mange. Ear mites live and feed in the dog's ear canals, causing her to vigorously shake her head and scratch her ears, visibly demonstrating her extreme discomfort. Your veterinarian can teach you how to clean and treat the problem with medication formulated to eliminate ear mites.

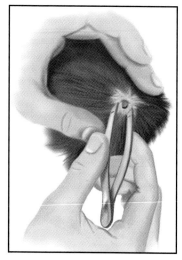

Use tweezers to remove ticks from your dog.

SCABIES

This is a condition that spreads rapidly between dogs; it also affects humans. The microscopic mite burrows beneath the dog's skin, causing intense itching and loss of hair, particularly on the ears, elbows, legs and face. If untreated, the dog's entire body will develop *sarcoptic mange*. Scrapings from the dog's skin, examined by the veterinarian under a microscope, will confirm their presence, and an intense treatment of insecticide and medication will relieve the itching until the mites are eradicated.

DEMODECTIC MANGE

This develops from a microscopic pest who lives in the hair follicles, causing thick, red skin; hair loss; and the eventual formation of pustules in infected hair follicles. The mites, diagnosed by the veterinarian's microscopic examination of skin scrapings and hair roots, can be destroyed by an insecticide, but the cure is more treatable before the pustules are allowed to form.

Common Problems by Area of the Body

Because the Miniature Schnauzer is a breed that requires frequent and specialized grooming, your opportunity to detect any suspicious or superficial change is maximized.

EAR PROBLEMS

Attention to the cleaning of your dog's ear canals will acquaint you with the appearance and characteristics of a normal, healthy ear, in which a slight collection of wax is normal, which has no odor and whose inside skin is light pink in color. If your dog has cropped ears, this healthy condition should be prevalent. Your Miniature Schnauzer needs veterinary care if the inside of the ear is swollen or tender, has a foul odor, has a profuse collection of wax, if a sloshing noise is heard when he shakes his head, or if the inside skin color is red.

These could all be signs of an inner ear infection, probably caused by yeast, bacteria or ear mites. Yeast and bacteria grow rapidly in dark, damp areas, which is why the inner ear is an ideal spot for them. You won't be able to tell the difference between a bacterial or a yeast infection; your veterinarian will have to perform a test to see what it is. Ear mites cause a dog to scratch at its ears frequently and shake its head. They can also cause a brown, waxy discharge. They are microscopic, so it will take your veterinarian to see them. Your vet will also need to treat the ears to flush them out.

Any ear problem will worsen if untreated. If ointment or ear drops are recommended, place the medication into the ear and vigorously massage the area just below the canal in order to channel the medication deeply into the ear's lower compartment.

You can prevent ear infections from happening by cleaning your dog's ears regularly. There are special preparations you can buy in your pet supply store that do a fine job. Follow the directions, using cotton and plastic gloves if you want. Never use cotton swabs. These can damage the ear drum if pushed in at the wrong angle.

SKIN PROBLEMS

Healthy skin is smooth and flexible with no visible scales, scabs, growths or red areas; is dandruff-free; is not excessively oily; and has no bald areas (except during the stages of a stripped coat, which is a special grooming technique).

To prevent your dog from worsening any skin problem by biting an itch or licking a wound, saturate a cloth with mouthwash, place it on the spot and rub it gently through the coat to reach the skin. Dogs hate the taste and the product contains nothing harmful.

If for any reason your dog isn't his perky, confident self, you should suspect a health problem. Keep a close eye on him so you can report anything peculiar to your vet.

Schnauzer Bumps Many Miniature Schnauzers have small wartlike nodes on their skin; these are uniquely known as Schnauzer bumps. Schnauzer bumps exude nothing, they simply exist, and typically bother the dog's owner far more than the dog; actually, she is not bothered by them at all. Much has been written about why they crop up and what to do about them, and opinions on the subject vary. Perhaps some day their mystery will be solved. Meanwhile, the logical step for a disturbed owner is to hide the bumps beneath longer hair. If you see bumps from which a fatty, oily substance is secreted, they are not just Schnauzer bumps and need medication.

Seborrhea This results from an alteration in the production of skin oils, causing a flaky, scaly skin or greasy, yellow-brown scales. A dog suffering from seborrhea will often have a rancid smell. Seborrhea in Miniature Schnauzers is sometimes incurable, but may be kept under control with a special shampoo.

Hot Spots   Skin infections that appear as patches of red, irritated skin with hair loss. The spots seem to form overnight, and are caused by the dog constantly licking or scratching at the infected spot. Hot spots can be difficult to treat, because unless the dog stops licking at the spot, it won't heal. Hot spots need to be treated with antibiotic ointment, and if they can't be bandaged, the dog should wear an Elizabethan collar to keep from licking it.

Allergies   An allergic reaction may be indicated by your dog's sneezing, coughing, watery eyes, itching and possibly vomiting and diarrhea. Just like people, dogs have or acquire allergies to all sorts of things. Various sources of allergies are dust, insect bites, carpet fibers, a new shampoo, a disagreeable inhalant and even types of food.

What is an allergy? It is a reaction to the irritating substance, called an allergen. When it comes into contact with skin or is breathed in, a complex set of events causes the body to react against it. If the allergen affects the eyes, they will tear and possibly swell; if the allergen affects the nose or respiratory system, there will be a thicker discharge, like sniffles or sneezing of mucus in people. If the skin is affected, it gets itchy, red, inflamed and even bumpy. The hair could fall out. The most common example is **flea allergy dermatitis**, which is an allergy to flea bites. Affected dogs itch all the time and get red, raw spots that may eventually cease to grow hair and get scaly and thick. Dogs with flea allergies need extra attention paid to their skin and environment to keep them flea-free.

Your veterinarian can try to determine what it is your dog is allergic to so you can first remove that substance from your home and anywhere your dog may go. Sometimes it's as simple as changing food, washing with a new cleaner or getting a different kind of bedding. Allergies are typically treated with cortisone, which can have side effects, so make sure your veterinarian explains what your dog is being treated with and what you can expect.

EYE PROBLEMS

Eyes should be bright, shiny and free from excessive tearing or discharge. The conjunctiva (the moist pink inner lining of the eyelids) should not be swollen, inflamed or have a yellow discharge. If any of these conditions are noted, the causes are widely varied.

Possibilities may be an allergic reaction, an injury, a foreign body, an irritant, or a disease whose source is parasitic, all of which may be treated with opthal-

mic medications. With extremely few exceptions, eye problems that are congenital in nature, or result from a congenital condition, are not treatable.

PRA (progressive retinal atrophy) is a genetic (inherited) eye disease in which the cells of the retina gradually degenerate, leading to loss of

Your Miniature Schnauzer's eyes, ears and mouth all need regular attention to keep them clean and clear.

sight. Initially, your dog will lose night vision, and she'll eventually go blind. PRA affects Miniature Schnauzers and many other breeds. Interestingly, however, the severity of PRA affects different breeds at different ages, causing some to lose their sight within months and others, years. While the disease itself cannot be cured, its elimination in a breed may be possible through discriminate breeding. PRA-affected dogs obviously must not be bred. Unaffected dogs (having normal eyes) may be bred, but only those who are not carriers of PRA, since one-half of their offspring would inherit the gene, thus perpetuating carriers. When two carriers are bred, the genetic expectancy is that one-fourth of the litter will be unaffected noncarriers, one-half will be carriers and one-fourth will have the disease. The agonizing problem is the inability to identify carriers.

To determine the presence or absence of the disease in a dog, her eyes must be examined annually by a board-certified veterinary opthalmologist, who sends the test findings to the Canine Eye Registration Foundation (CERF), located at Purdue University, where the results of each breed's eye tests are analyzed. Annual eye tests are necessary because a dog's early tests may find her to be unaffected, but a later test may show the disease. Through massive and costly studies, the DNA factors that identify carriers have been discovered in the Irish Setter and Miniature Poodle.

PRA is expressed in a pattern unique to the Miniature Schnauzer. One form affects puppies, who lose their sight between eight and twelve months of age. Another form affects adults, who become blind at around three years of age.

The American Miniature Schnauzer Club has made a strong commitment to raise $175,000 to fund a three-year study by the Baker Institute for Animal Health at Cornell University, hopefully to discover the DNA factors that determine PRA carriers in the Miniature Schnauzer—offering the potential to significantly benefit many breeds.

Cataracts are as common in older dogs as they are in older humans. The lens becomes clouded by an opacity that is milky gray or bluish white in color. The degree of loss of vision varies from dog to dog, and when blindness occurs, surgical removal of the lens can restore functional vision. On the other hand, **congenital juvenile cataracts (CJC)** are genetic in nature and untreatable. Like PRA, the condition is discoverable in the dog's annual eye examinations, and affects all breeds of dogs, including the Miniature Schnauzer.

MOUTH AND THROAT PROBLEMS

If something's affecting your dog's mouth, you'll notice by her actions. She will drool excessively, paw at her mouth, shake her head, cough or gag, have bad breath, have a bloody discharge from her mouth and lose her appetite (perhaps from her inability to chew or swallow).

The first thing to do is check to see if something is lodged in her mouth, like a stone or a piece of wood.

Foreign bodies may be anything from slivers of wood (from chewed sticks, twigs, furniture legs) to fabric, plastic, or whatever material to which her mischief has led her. The object may be wedged between her teeth or across the roof of her mouth. It happens!

When the object has been removed (by you or your veterinarian, if necessary), be sure to treat the injured area to avoid infection. If your dog is choking on the object, you may need to give her an abdominal thrust or the Heimlich manuever to remove it. See the section on choking under "Emergency Care and First Aid" in this chapter for instructions. Call your veterinarian right away.

Other problems include **glossitis,** an inflammation of the tongue. This condition causes the edges of the tongue to look red and swollen.

IDENTIFYING YOUR DOG

It's a terrible thing to think about, but your dog could somehow, someday, get lost or stolen. How would you get him back? Your best bet would be to have some form of identification on your dog. You can choose from a collar and tags, a tattoo, a microchip or a combination of these three.

Every dog should wear a buckle collar with identification tags. They are the quickest and easiest way for a stranger to identify your dog. It's best to inscribe the tags with your name and phone number; you don't need to include your dog's name.

There are two ways to permanently identify your dog. The first is a tattoo, placed on the inside of your dog's thigh. The tattoo should be your social security number or your dog's AKC registration number.

The second is a microchip, a rice-sized pellet that's inserted under the dog's skin at the base of the neck, between the shoulder blades. When a scanner is passed over the dog, it will beep, notifying the person that the dog has a chip. The scanner will then show a code, identifying the dog. Microchips are becoming more and more popular and are certainly the wave of the future.

Common causes are excessive tartar on the teeth, foreign bodies, cuts, burns, insect stings, or an association with other diseases present in your dog's body.

Your dog will refuse to eat, will drool and his tongue may bleed or exude a thick, brown, smelly discharge.

A **sore throat** (pharyngitis) is fairly common in dogs, causing them to cough and gag, lose appetite and possibly run a fever. As with people, the throat will appear red and inflamed. A severe condition will be complicated by swollen lymph nodes at the back of the throat and the dog's breathing will have a scratchy sound. Get a definite assessment from your veterinarian, who will probably prescribe antibiotics and a soft, bland diet.

CARING FOR TEETH AND GUMS

Like all dogs, adult Miniature Schnauzers have forty-two permanent teeth; puppies have twenty-three baby teeth with no molars. As each adult tooth emerges, any interfering baby tooth should be removed.

You should make it a habit to examine your dog's mouth several times a week. Tartar and plaque develop on dogs' teeth the same way they do on ours. Tartar is a hard yellow-brown or gray-white deposit on the teeth and cannot be removed by brushing; it must be removed professionally by your veterinarian. Tartar develops from plaque, a soft white or yellow substance.

Check your dog's teeth frequently and brush them regularly.

Buildup of either causes **gingivitis** and results in gums that are red, sensitive, swollen and sore. When rubbed, the gums may bleed. The gums separate from the sides of the teeth, allowing bacteria and food to collect inside, which invites periodontal disease.

If you want your dog to have healthy teeth all her life, and to avoid serious oral infections, the tartar on her teeth must be removed whenever it begins to accumulate. Some dogs, regardless of their diet, require less frequent tartar removal than others, who are extremely prone to an ongoing collection. The appearance of an adult dog's sparkling white front teeth is deceptive; her back teeth (and the inside of those front teeth) may have a collection of tartar, causing the gums to swell and possibly become infected, and the teeth to decay.

Dog Breath If your dog has gingivitis, what you'll probably notice first is offensive dog breath. Dog breath is a sure sign you've neglected your dog's tooth-care. If you haven't, and your dog's teeth are healthy, it's a sign of another problem. In either event, you should make an appointment to see your veterinarian.

Tartar can be easily removed by regular brushing of your dog's teeth at home. Use a toothbrush designed for dogs, a child's soft toothbrush or a gauze pad wrapped around your finger. Use toothpaste specifically formulated for dogs, *not human toothpaste, which is bad for dogs.*

"Brush" your dog's teeth by rubbing the toothpaste along the gum line and over the surface of the teeth. Do this two or three times a week (daily is preferable) as prescribed in the product's directions. There's no need to rinse. Dog toothpastes taste good to dogs, and will be rinsed and swallowed by drinking water in the course of the day.

RESPIRATORY PROBLEMS

Respiratory problems are symptomized by nasal discharge, sneezing, coughing, noisy or difficult breathing and abnormal sounds within the chest.

Kennel cough, while not life threatening, is readily spread from one dog to another and is caused by several viruses and Bordatella bronchiseptica (a bacteria). The dog will have a dry, hacking cough and may have a nasal discharge. If affected, the dog should be kept in a warm, humid environment, isolated from other dogs. The veterinarian will administer antibiotics. A vaccine has been developed to prevent the disease, and most reputable boarding kennels and canine training classes require a dog to be innoculated against the disease before he is admitted.

Bronchitis is a respiratory infection that often follows a bout of kennel cough. Your dog's dry, rough cough usually will last for days or weeks, and she may retch following a coughing spell, sometimes bringing up foamy-appearing saliva. Antibiotics must be administered.

Choking   A foreign body in your dog's windpipe is indicated by a sudden, intense fit of coughing after she has vomited or following her inhalation of foreign matter. If she can't expel the irritant, rush her to your veterinarian. (More on this in the "Emergency Care and First Aid" section of this chapter.)

Urogenital Problems

It is normal for a mature male dog to discharge a small amount of white or yellowish material from the prepuce (the skin covering the penis). Suspect infection if he frequently licks the prepuce; if the discharge is excessive, discolored or foul smelling; or if the penis is extremely red, with small bumps on it and the lining of the prepuce. The irritating infection is treatable by the veterinarian.

Anal Region   On either side of the anus is a gland that secretes a thick, liquid lubricant that enables the dog to mark his territory. If the glands, known as the anal sacs, become clogged, your dog will lick his anus and drag his rear on the ground. To relieve his discomfort, the anal sacs will need to be emptied, a procedure that you can do at home. If you find it too distasteful, inform your veterinarian so he or she can do it regularly.

To express the anal sacs, hold the tail up firmly with one hand. With a piece of gauze or tissue in the other hand, encircle the anal area with your thumb and forefinger at the eight and four o'clock positions respectively, then push in and squeeze.

The anal sac material of vile odor should exude from the two gland ducts on the anus, which you can then wipe away. The procedure should be repeated when the glandular material accumulates, or at regular weekly or monthly intervals to avoid the accumulation. If the process, when needed, is neglected, the glands become infected (evidenced by bloody or puslike discharge) and will require veterinary care.

Diseases of the Reproductive Organs Male and female dogs are susceptible to a number of diseases of their reproductive organs, such as infections of the uterus, prostatic diseases and various cancers. The best way to treat these is to prevent them from occurring. This is easily and humanely done by spaying your female Mini Schnauzer or neutering your male. A further explanation of the benefits of spay/neuter follows.

Preventive Care

SPAY AND NEUTER

This is possibly the best preventive care you can give your Miniature Schnauzer, for several reasons. Dogs can have these operations at six months of age, sometimes earlier (consult with your veterinarian). The spay operation in the female removes her uterus and ovaries. The neuter operation in the male removes his testicles. Why is it a good idea to have your pet spayed or neutered?

You may think your pet is the greatest in the world and you want another just like her, but a spayed or neutered dog is healthier and easier to care for in the long run.

First, you'll be ensuring that your dog or bitch does not become a father or mother. Though you may think your pet is the greatest Miniature Schnauzer in the world and you want another just like him or her, this is not the best reason to breed your dog. There are many wonderful pet Miniature Schnauzers out there already—too many, in fact, and there's no need to contribute to this country's serious pet overpopulation problem. Also, breeding is a risky business that more often than not results in high medical bills, more time than you imagined and heartbreak. So leave the breeding to others.

Second, as mentioned in the section on urogenital problems, there are a number of illnesses that can develop in intact animals, including uterine infection, prostatic diseases and cancers. These will not develop in spayed or neutered Miniature Schnauzers.

Third, there are practical benefits. If your female isn't coming into heat, you won't have every unfixed male in the neighborhood baying at your windows or doing whatever they can to knock down your fence to get at your girl. You also won't have the mess that comes with a female in heat, or the behavioral changes, like snappiness or whining. For your male, you won't have to worry about him roaming the neighborhood to get at someone else's female, and you'll also have to worry less about some marked male behaviors like mounting, dominance and overaggression.

About Breeding The only reason not to spay or neuter your dog is if the puppy is of show quality and you intend to show him. If you bought your puppy from a breeder, that person will probably have sold you your dog with a contract. Depending on the breeder's assessment of your puppy, the contract will either obligate you to spay or neuter the dog by a certain age or show the dog by a certain age. If the latter is the case and for some reason the dog cannot or will not be shown, then the breeder and owner can discuss spaying or neutering the dog.

Spaying or neutering your Miniature Schnauzer will prevent your dog from reproducing. Many people

Keeping Your
Miniature
Schnauzer
Healthy

ADVANTAGES OF SPAY/NEUTER

The greatest advantage of spaying (for females) or neutering (for males) your dog is that you are guaranteed your dog will not produce puppies. There are too many puppies already available for too few homes. There are other advantages as well.

ADVANTAGES OF SPAYING

No messy heats.

No "suitors" howling at your windows or waiting in your yard.

Decreased incidences of pyometra (disease of the uterus) and breast cancer.

ADVANTAGES OF NEUTERING

Lessens male aggressive and territorial behaviors, but doesn't affect the dog's personality. Behaviors are often owner-induced, so neutering is not the only answer, but it is a good start.

Prevents the need to roam in search of bitches in season.

Decreased incidences of urogenital diseases.

81

breed, or want to breed, their dogs for the wrong reasons. One of the most common is that they love their pet and want to have a puppy just like him or her. Unfortunately, a puppy from their treasured pet will not be the same. The genetic combination that created their pet was from that pet's ancestors. A puppy will be from that pet *and* from the dog they breed the pet to. If you want a dog very much like the one you have, go back to the breeder where you got your dog and get another from the same lineage.

Many people feel their dog should be allowed to reproduce because it is a purebred or because it has "papers." This, however, is no assurance of quality. If you're not showing or interested in showing, you probably have a pet-quality dog. A wonderful dog, I'm sure, but not one that should necessarily be bred. Discuss this matter with a breeder if you feel strongly about breeding your Miniature Schnauzer.

TAKING YOUR DOG'S TEMPERATURE

The normal temperature of a dog ranges from 101 to 102.5°F (38.3–39.2°C). To determine your dog's temperature, it should be taken when he is well and free from any health problems. To do it, shake down the thermometer, and lubricate the bulb with petroleum jelly, mineral or vegetable oil. With the dog standing, gently slide the thermometer into the anus as far as it will travel easily, but don't let it disappear! Hold the thermometer firmly (without pushing) for three or four minutes before taking it out, wiping it down and reading the temperature.

TAKING YOUR DOG'S PULSE

Your dog's pulse may be checked by pressing on the artery that runs along the inside of her thigh where the leg joins the body. The heartbeat can be detected by pressing yur fingers against the rib cage just below the elbow while the dog stands. Normally, the heart beats about 50 to 130 times per minute in a resting dog. The pulse, of course, is the same.

Tying a Muzzle

A simple muzzle is the best way to restrain your dog while helping him if he's been injured and is in pain. Dogs in this state tend to bite out of pain, and you should avoid being bitten by using a makeshift muzzle. Use about two feet of a narrow strip of cloth, cotton bandage or rope. Old stockings also work well. Tie a loose knot in the middle, leaving a large loop, which is slipped over the dog's nose. Tighten the knot under his chin, then pull the ends back behind his ears and tie securely. Practice muzzling him when it isn't needed to be prepared for an emergency.

Use a scarf or old hose to make a temporary muzzle, as shown.

Giving Oral Medication

Oral medication in pill or liquid form must be given with an understanding yet determined attitude. Pills and capsules are given by holding the dog's muzzle over the top of her nose, with the fingers of your left hand on her lips. Squeeze your fingers against her teeth (not her gums), and tilt her head slightly upward. Hold her still (sweet talk goes a long way) while you guide her lower teeth downward with your right

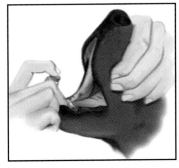

To give a pill, open the mouth wide, then drop it in the back of the throat.

fingers, and push the pill deeply, deeply into her throat. Quickly close her mouth, then, keeping it shut, blow gently into her nostrils (which induces her to swallow) and stroke her throat. If she spits it out, repeat the process until you win.

Liquid medicine is best administered from a syringe (without the needle) or an eyedropper. Spoons wiggle or may be bumped by the dog, and the amount of medicine ingested remain an unsolved mystery. With your left hand wrapped around her muzzle, elevate her head, holding her mouth shut. With your right hand, insert the syringe or eyedroper directly behind her canine teeth, pointed toward her throat, slowly squirt medication into her mouth, then gently stroke her throat.

If your dog struggles so frantically against medication that you cannot win, crush the pills or open the capsule and remove the contents; mix with creamy peanut butter. Place the mixture on the end of your finger, open the dog's mouth and stick the mixture on the roof of her mouth. After it melts, he will lick his mouth and swallow the medicine. Divide liquid medication into several parts with peanut butter to avoid an excessively runny mixture that cannot stick to his mouth.

APPLYING EYE OINTMENT OR DROPS

Ointment is most easily applied to the area of the conjunctiva (the lower eyelid). With your thumb and forefinger, roll the lower eyelid gently downward

Squeeze eye oint-ment into the lower lid.

and squeeze the ointment into the space between the eyelid and eyeball.

Drops require your Miniature Schnauzer's head to be elevated slightly. With one hand under her muzzle, hold the lower eyelid open. The other hand should be used to keep the upper lid open and drop in the medication. Prevent injury to the eye or contamination of the medication by not touching the eye with the end of the tube or eyedropper.

Other Ailments

LOSS OF APPETITE

This, in itself, may be caused by the dog's temporary disinterest in the diet you're providing. However, it is such a widely demonstrated symptom of so many illnesses and diseases that your alertness to additional symptoms is necessary.

If no other problem is indicated and the dog's normally perky behavior is unchanged, offer his usual bowl of food, remove it after twenty minutes, and repeat the process for a couple of days. If his "loss of appetite" is merely a self-imposed refusal to accept what you're offering him, he will, at that point, no doubt gratefully accept it. On the other hand, a "bad" bag of food is a possibility that merits investigation. If his refusal to eat persists, a thorough examination by the veterinarian may be necessary to determine the problem.

LAMENESS

Lameness is demonstrated by a limping dog when her limbs are painful or weak. The causes include trauma, nutritional imbalance, congenital defects, infection or Lyme disease. The source of the limp should be located by the veterinarian's palpation or X rays of the affected area, if necessary. A mild injury may heal by itself in a short time, but a more serious problem may need prompt veterinary attention and possible surgery. A serious problem would be a sprain, fracture, dislocation or bone disease.

VOMITING

Vomiting is an extremely prevalent indication of other problems. A dog who vomits once or twice presents little cause for concern. The act simply may be his way of clearing his throat. Most often, he will vomit after eating something irritating to the stomach such as garbage, grass, paper or any undigestible item. If he vomits his food and later brings up a frothy, clear or yellow liquid, do not feed him for the next twelve to twenty-four hours, and offer him ice cubes in place of water. Then offer him a bland diet of soft-boiled eggs, cottage cheese, baby food or boiled rice and boiled hamburger with the fat removed. Offer food in small portions on the first day, continuing with the ice cubes.

If the vomiting has stopped, feed bland foods the next day in normal portions, then return to the dog's regular diet. If vomiting returns, you should take him to see your veterinarian. Your veterinarian should also check your dog immediately if vomiting persists; is frequent or forceful; contains blood, fecal-type matter, worms or foreign objects; or is accompanied by other signs of illness, such as diarrhea, lethargy, weight loss or dull coat.

Run your hands regularly over your dog to feel for any injuries.

DIARRHEA

Diarrhea, another common symptom in dogs, is indicated by loose, soft and often abundant stools. A mild case is treatable at home if it is not associated with other problems. Causes may be the consumption of irritating and indigestible material, changes or upsets in the dog's normal routine, a sudden change in her diet or a switch to unfamiliar water, or her inability to tolerate certain foods. To treat diarrhea at home, do not feed her for 24 hours, restricting her to ice cubes.

The next day, offer small amounts of the bland food described to treat vomiting. Continue the procedure for three more days, even if the condition improves, then return the dog to her normal diet. She should see the veterinarian immediately if diarrhea persists for over twenty-four hours, contains blood or is accompanied by vomiting, fever or other signs of distress. Bring a specimen of the waste for your veterinarian's examination.

CONSTIPATION

This is the opposite of diarrhea. The stools become so hard and dry that it's difficult if not impossible for the dog to pass them. Constipation can be caused by dehydration, parasites, a poor diet, stress, ingestion of a foreign object, or a kidney disease. If the problem doesn't go away when you give your dog a mild laxative, more water and a more fibrous diet, your veterinarian will have to determine the cause.

Emergency Care and First Aid

When we humans are faced with an emergency involving our dogs, panic and helplessness are understandable, but dreadfully impractical. By putting emotions aside and applying first aid until the veterinarian is reached, we can alleviate the dog's pain, prevent the emergency from worsening and possibly save the dog's life. For that reason, our practice of simple procedures (like giving a fake pill, applying an unneeded muzzle, reading his normal temperature) prepares us for the moment the action becomes necessary. If we seriously arm ourselves with first-aid techniques, we may be able to face an emergency steadied with "what, why, how, when and how much to do" confidence. First aid, of course, is only preliminary action, and cannot replace professional care.

A FIRST-AID KIT

Keep a canine first-aid kit on hand for general care and emergencies. Check it periodically to make sure liquids haven't spilled or dried up, and replace medications and materials after they're used. Your kit should include:

Activated charcoal tablets

Adhesive tape
(1 and 2 inches wide)

Antibacterial ointment
(for skin and eyes)

Aspirin (buffered or enteric coated, *not* Ibuprofen)

Bandages: Gauze rolls (1 and 2 inches wide) and dressing pads

Cotton balls

Diarrhea medicine

Dosing syringe

Hydrogen peroxide (3%)

Petroleum jelly

Rectal thermometer

Rubber gloves

Rubbing alcohol

Scissors

Tourniquet

Towel

Tweezers

BE PREPARED

The first step in emergency preparedness is to expand your household emergency telephone list by adding the numbers of your veterinarian (including the emergency number and regular office hours), the animal emergency clinic (with their address) and the National Animal Poison Control Center. (This organization has both an 800 and a 900 number for callers. The numbers and more information are listed in Chapter 13). You might also record your dog's normal heartbeat and temperature. You should also have a canine first-aid kit in the house, stocked with the items listed in the sidebar in this chapter, "A First-Aid Kit.")

MOVING AN INJURED DOG

Even the gentlest dog may try to bite when he's in pain. Apply a muzzle to protect yourself, unless the dog is unconscious, vomiting, bleeding from the mouth or nose, gagging or having difficulty swallowing or breathing. A Miniature Schnauzer is small enough to be wrapped in a blanket or towel and carried. If minimized disturbance is necessary, move him onto a blanket, pulling him by the skin on his neck and over his hips. Then pull the blanket onto a board, or into a box with its side removed. Leave any injured area exposed and uppermost.

Make a temporary splint by wrapping the leg in firm casing, then bandaging it.

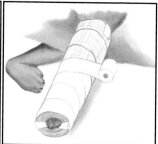

Making a splint   Use a rolled newspaper or a cardboard tube slit lengthwise to accommodate swelling and to allow easy removal. Slip the splint gently around the leg, letting the splint extend beyond the limb.

Securely (but not too tightly) wrap the splint in place with gauze, cloth strips or adshesive tape.

CHOKING—ARTIFICIAL RESPIRATION

If you notice your dog choking, gasping for air or pawing at her mouth, she may have something stuck in her mouth or throat that is preventing her from breathing. You need to act fast. First, pull her tongue forward to clean any obstruction, mucus or food from her mouth and throat.

If you can't dislodge the object this way, there are two other ways to try. (1) Lay your dog down on her side (if she's not down already), and with your fingers interlaced, place your palms against her side just below her rib cage. Give a quick, sharp thrust. Not too hard—you don't want to break any ribs. What you want to do is force air through her diaphragm sharply so the object is expelled with it. (2) If your dog is standing, you can give her the Heimlich maneuver. Stand behind her and wrap your arms around her middle, joining your hands together just under and behind her rib cage. Give a quick, sharp thrust upward.

If the object is out but your dog's not breathing or breathing irregularly, you'll have to perform artificial respiration, or mouth-to-muzzle resuscitation. Clamp your hand around her muzzle so no air can leak out. Inhale. Completely cover her nose

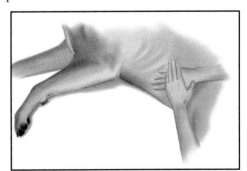

Applying abdominal thrusts can save a choking dog.

with your mouth and exhale gently every five or six seconds, or ten to twelve breaths per minute, until her chest expands. Then remove your mouth from her nose until her chest deflates.

Note: Even in respiratory arrest, a dog can close her jaws by reflex, without warning; be careful with your face is so close to hers. Call your veterinarian as soon as possible.

BLEEDING

A pressure dressing can slow or stop bleeding. Cover the wound with a clean gauze pad or cloth, and apply pressure evenly on the wound. Avoid using elasticized tape. If gauze or a pad isn't handy, place your hand on the wound and press firmly. When the bleeding slows, put on a fresh pad and hold it in place with gauze strips. If swelling of the limb is noted below the pressure pack, the dog's circulation may be blocked. Loosen or remove the bandage.

If direct pressure fails to stop the bleeding, an artery may have been severed. In addition to the pressure bandage, apply a tourniquet, realizing that it can cause greater damage than it solves; be cautious. Place a loop of rope, gauze or cloth on the extremity between the injury and the heart. Gently, but firmly, tighten it until bleeding visibly decreases at the wound site. Loosen every ten minutes or so to allow blood to return to reenter the extremity and decrease potential strangulation.

*An Elizabethan
collar keeps
your dog from
licking a fresh
wound.*

Internal bleeding, undetectable by a layperson, usually results from trauma, severe irritation or hemorrhage developed by toxins. The dog may have a painful or distended abdomen and pale or white gums, or he may cough or vomit blood; blood may be present in the urine, stool, saliva or nasal discharge. Internal hemorrhage is potentially life threatening, and a veterinarian should be consulted as soon as possible when it is suspected.

BURNS

Your Miniature Schnauzer can suffer a burn from sources as diverse as hot water pipes, fireplaces, bleach, batteries or electrical cords. There are three sources of burns, and there are three types of burns. The sources are thermal, chemical and electrical; the types are first degree, second degree and third degree. Whatever the source or type, burns hurt! Usually the skin is affected, though an electrical burn caused by chewing a cord, for example, can affect the mouth.

The degree of a burn indicates how severe it is. A first-degree burn is fairly superficial, affecting only the top layer of skin. A second-degree burn affects deeper layers. These types of burns often blister, bleed or ooze. A third-degree burn is very serious because it affects all layers of the skin, exposing muscle and tissue. They usually cause a dog to go into shock, too, making immediate veterinary attention crucial.

If your Mini Schnauzer is burned, try to flush the area with cool water and apply an ice pack. If it's a superficial burn, put antibiotic ointment on it. Anything more serious should be treated by your veterinarian.

HEAT STROKE

If you and/or your dog are in a warm place and you notice your dog panting heavily, salivating excessively and/or looking faint or weak, she's probably suffering from heat stroke.

Most cases occur when a dog is left in a car with little or no ventilation. The temperature inside soars, and the dog, who can only sweat from the pads of her feet, becomes overheated. A dog suffering from heat stroke can become permanently brain damaged after only ten minutes.

If you suspect heat stroke, quickly move your dog to a cool spot and wet him down with cool water. If he's conscious and not vomiting, give him small amounts of cool water to drink. You want to cool him down gradually. Rub his limbs to stimulate circulation. Provide plenty of ventilation en route to the veterinarian—to whose office you should be going posthaste!

SHOCK

When the cardiovascular system collapses (i.e., the heart and blood vessels fail to function), your dog goes into shock. The condition has many causes, among which are blood loss, massive injury, poisoning and kidney or liver failure. It is life threatening and requires immediate action. Your dog will be depressed and have a rapid, weak heartbeat, dilated pupils, subnormal temperature and muscle weakness. A dog in shock needs immediate attention. Wrap her in a blanket and keep her as warm and quiet as possible. If she's unconscious, position her head lower than the rest of her body. Transport her immediately to the veterinarian.

POISONING

Your Miniature Schnauzer can be poisoned by any number of things, from bad food (garbage) to house-hold cleaners. Keep the number of your veterinarian

Some of the many house-hold substances harmful to your dog.

and the National Animal Poison Control Center (listed in Chapter 13) near your telephone. Either should be contacted before administering first aid for poisoning.

If the poison can be identified, and the label on its container can be read, the veterinarian can analyze the product contents. Poisons fall into a few basic classes, and each is treated somewhat differently. Basically, treatment is to neutralize the poison and/or to eliminate it from the dog (by coating the dog's stomach with something else or inducing vomiting).

Insecticides and parasite medication are the most common type of intoxications seen in dogs. Signs of toxicosis include muscle trembling, weakness, increased salivation, vomiting and loss of bowel control, and the signs may vary depending on how badly poisoned the animal is. If these medications had been applied or administered to the dog as treatment, it is possible that the poisoning resulted from overzealous use (like using a flea or tick preparation in combination with oral deworming medications).

Oral rodenticides, such as rat poison, are usually based on a blood anticlotting factor that reacts rather slowly. Serious toxicty may be averted if the dog is induced to vomit within thirty minutes after ingestion. Some rodenticides (gopher poison, etc.) that have a strychnine base are acutely toxic, are rapidly absorbed into the dog's system and can cause convulsions and death in a short period of time.

Acids, alkalis and petroleum products cause special problems if ingested. Do not induce vomiting. Consult your veterinarian about specific treatment for the particular type of chemical to which the dog has been exposed. If you can't reach your vet, call the poison control center.

Antacids can be administered to combat acid poisoning (about two teaspoons per five pounds of body weight). To combat alkali ingestion, a mixture of one part vinegar to four parts water may be given at the same dosage. Mineral or vegetable oil may help to protect the gastrointestinal tract in petroleum distillate toxicosis (one tablespoon per five pounds of body weight). Some poisons of this type take a period of time before their clinical signs become evident, so you should consult your veterinarian as soon as possible if exposure to a chemical has occurred.

Antifreeze is very toxic to dogs, and they're very attracted to it because of its sweetness. Antifreeze can cause severe kidney damage if even a very small quantity is ingested. There are dog-safe antifreezes on the market, should you want to take extra precautions.

Caring for Your Older Dog

As your Miniature Schnauzer ages she will develop more health problems, just as people do. All of her senses may eventually be affected: sight, smell, hearing, taste—even touch.

The first thing to pay attention to is your older Mini Schnauzer's diet. The more fit she is the better she'll feel, so don't let her get fat. There are a number of "senior" and "lite" formula diets on the market. Your veterinarian will probably suggest when you should switch her food, but if you're not sure, ask.

Keep her exercising, though she won't have the endurance she once did. And be careful not to stress aging joints: don't overdo the running or jumping during playtime.

Your dog may develop cataracts, opacities of the eye lens that block vision. Alert your veterinarian if you notice a cataract forming. This is a natural part of getting older, and it may not affect how your Miniature Schnauzer gets around. Your dog knows her way around your house by smell and touch, too. Redecorating or moving will disorient an impaired dog, so if that's in your plans, take the time to help your dog get acquainted with the new lay of the land.

There are other problems of old age, including hair and tooth loss, flatulence and irregular bowel movements, a decrease in energy, sensitivity to temperature and, sometimes, moodiness. Your dog will want to sleep more and will get cold faster. She'll need you to take care of her more.

Saying Goodbye

The decision to euthanize your dog is one of the hardest you'll have to make, but it's the most humane way to say goodbye to an old friend who's in pain. Don't expect your veterinarian to make this decision for you; he or she will support and console you, but it is up to you to know when to let go. Don't let your dog suffer more than she has to. Call your veterinarian when you know it's time and let him or her know you don't want to wait in the waiting room—schedule an exact time to come in. Take your friend yourself, wrapped in her favorite blanket with a favorite toy or treat. Remember, the last sensations your dog will experience are the sound of your voice and your reassuring smell—the things she loved most during her life.

Your Happy, Healthy Pet

Your Dog's Name _____

Name on Your Dog's Pedigree (if your dog has one) _____

_____

Where Your Dog Came From _____

_____

Your Dog's Birthday _____

Your Dog's Veterinarian

    Name _____

    Address _____

    Phone Number_____

    Emergency Number_____

Your Dog's Health

    Vaccines

    type _____ date given _____

    type _____ date given _____

    type _____ date given _____

    type _____ date given _____

    Heartworm

    date tested _____ type used_____ start date _____

Your Dog's License Number_____

Groomer's Name and Number _____

Dogsitter/Walker's Name and Number _____

Awards Your Dog Has Won

    Award _____ date earned _____

    Award _____ date earned _____

part three

Enjoying
your
Dog

chapter 8

Basic
Training

by Ian Dunbar, Ph.D., MRCVS

Training is the jewel in the crown—the most important aspect of doggy husbandry. There is no more important variable influencing dog behavior and temperament than the dog's education: A well-trained, well-behaved and good-natured puppydog is always a joy to live with, but an untrained and uncivilized dog can be a perpetual nightmare. Moreover, deny the dog an education and she will not have the opportunity to fulfill her own canine potential; neither will she have the ability to communicate effectively with her human companions.

Luckily, modern psychological training methods are easy, efficient, effective and, above all, considerably dog-friendly and user-friendly.

Doggy education is as simple as it is enjoyable. But before you can have a good time play-training with your new dog, you have to learn what to do and how to do it. There is no bigger variable influencing the success of dog training than the *owner's* experience and expertise. *Before you embark on the dog's education, you must first educate yourself.*

Basic Training for Owners

Ideally, basic owner training should begin well *before* you select your dog. Find out all you can about your chosen breed first, then master rudimentary training and handling skills. If you already have your puppy-dog, owner training is a dire emergency—the clock is ticking! Especially for puppies, the first few weeks at home are the most important and influential days in the dog's life. Indeed, the cause of most adolescent and adult problems may be traced back to the initial days the pup explores her new home. This is the time to establish the *status quo*—to teach the puppydog how you would like her to behave and so prevent otherwise quite predictable problems.

In addition to consulting breeders and breed books such as this one (which understandably have a positive breed bias), seek out as many pet owners with your breed as you can find. Good points are obvious. What you want to find out are the breed-specific *problems,* so you can nip them in the bud. In particular, you should talk to owners with *adolescent* dogs and make a list of all anticipated problems. Most important, *test drive* at least half a dozen adolescent and adult dogs of your breed yourself. An 8-week-old puppy is deceptively easy to handle, but she will acquire adult size, speed and strength in just four months, so you should learn now what to prepare for.

Puppy and pet dog training classes offer a convenient venue to locate pet owners and observe dogs in action. For a list of suitable trainers in your area, contact the Association of Pet Dog Trainers (see chapter 13). You may also begin your basic owner training by observing

other owners in class. Watch as many classes and test
drive as many dogs as possible. Select an upbeat, dog-
friendly, people-friendly, fun-and-games, puppydog pet
training class to learn the ropes. Also, watch training
videos and read training books. You must find out what
to do and how to do it *before* you have to do it.

Principles of Training

Most people think training comprises teaching the dog
to do things such as sit, speak and roll over, but even a
4-week-old pup knows how to do these things already.
Instead, the first step in training involves teaching
the dog human words for each dog behavior and activity and for each aspect of the dog's environment. That
way you, the owner, can more easily participate in the
dog's domestic education by directing her to perform
specific actions appropriately, that is, at the right time,
in the right place and so on. Training opens communication channels, enabling an educated dog to at least
understand her owner's requests.

In addition to teaching a dog *what* we want her to
do, it is also necessary to teach her *why* she should do
what we ask. Indeed, 95 percent of training revolves
around motivating the dog *to want to do* what we want.
Dogs often understand what their owners want; they
just don't see the point of doing it—especially when
the owner's repetitively boring and seemingly senseless
instructions are totally at odds with much more pressing and exciting doggy distractions. It is not so much
the dog that is being stubborn or dominant; rather, it
is the owner who has failed to acknowledge the dog's
needs and feelings and to approach training from the
dog's point of view.

THE MEANING OF INSTRUCTIONS

The secret to successful training is learning how to use
training lures to predict or prompt specific behaviors—
to coax the dog to do what you want *when* you want.
Any highly valued object (such as a treat or toy) may be
used as a lure, which the dog will follow with her eyes

and nose. Moving the lure in specific ways entices the dog to move her nose, head and entire body in specific ways. In fact, by learning the art of manipulating various lures, it is possible to teach the dog to assume virtually any body position and perform any action. Once you have control over the expression of the dog's behaviors and can elicit any body position or behavior at will, you can easily teach the dog to perform on request.

Teach your dog words for each activity she needs to know, like down.

Tell your dog what you want her to do, use a lure to entice her to respond correctly, then profusely praise and maybe reward her once she performs the desired action. For example, verbally request "Tina, sit!" while you move a squeaky toy upwards and backwards over the dog's muzzle (lure-movement and hand signal), smile knowingly as she looks up (to follow the lure) and sits down (as a result of canine anatomical engineering), then praise her to distraction ("Gooood Tina!"). Squeak the toy, offer a training treat and give your dog and yourself a pat on the back.

Being able to elicit desired responses over and over enables the owner to reward the dog over and over. Consequently, the dog begins to think training is fun. For example, the more the dog is rewarded for sitting, the more she enjoys sitting. Eventually the dog comes to realize that, whereas most sitting is appreciated, sitting immediately upon request usually prompts especially enthusiastic praise and a slew of high-level rewards. The dog begins to sit on cue much of the time, showing that she is starting to grasp the meaning of the owner's verbal request and hand signal.

WHY COMPLY?

Most dogs enjoy initial lure-reward training and are only too happy to comply with their owners' wishes. Unfortunately, repetitive drilling without appreciative feedback tends to diminish the dog's enthusiasm until she eventually fails to see the point of complying anymore. Moreover, as the dog approaches adolescence she becomes more easily distracted as she develops other interests. Lengthy sessions with repetitive exercises tend to bore and demotivate both parties. If it's not fun, the owner doesn't do it and neither does the dog.

Integrate training into your dog's life: The greater number of training sessions each day and the *shorter* they are, the more willingly compliant your dog will

become. Make sure to have a short (just a few seconds) training interlude before every enjoyable canine activity. For example, ask your dog to sit to greet people, to sit before you throw her Frisbee and to sit for her supper. Really, sitting is no different from a canine "Please."

To train your dog, you need gentle hands, a loving heart and a good attitude.

Also, include numerous short training interludes during every enjoyable canine pastime, for example, when playing with the dog or when she is running in the park. In this fashion, doggy distractions may be effectively converted into rewards for training. Just as all games have rules, fun becomes training . . . and training becomes fun.

Eventually, rewards actually become unnecessary to continue motivating your dog. If trained with consideration and kindness, performing the desired behaviors will become self-rewarding and, in a sense, your dog will motivate herself. Just as it is not necessary to reward a human companion during an enjoyable walk in the park, or following a game of tennis, it is hardly necessary to reward our best friend—the dog—for walking by our side or while playing fetch. Human company during enjoyable activities is reward enough for most dogs.

Even though your dog has become self-motivating, it's still good to praise and pet her a lot and offer rewards once in a while, especially for a good job well done. And if for no other reason, praising and rewarding others is good for the human heart.

PUNISHMENT

Without a doubt, lure-reward training is by far the best way to teach: Entice your dog to do what you want and then reward her for doing so. Unfortunately, a human shortcoming is to take the good for granted and to moan and groan at the bad. Specifically, the dog's many good behaviors are ignored while the owner focuses on punishing the dog for making mistakes. In extreme cases, instruction is *limited* to punishing mistakes made by a trainee dog, child, employee or husband, even though it has been proven punishment training is notoriously inefficient and ineffective and is decidedly unfriendly and combative. It teaches the dog that training is a drag, almost as quickly as it teaches the dog to dislike her trainer. Why treat our best friends like our worst enemies?

Punishment training is also much more laborious and time consuming. Whereas it takes only a finite amount of time to teach a dog what to chew, for example, it takes much, much longer to punish the dog for each and every mistake. Remember, *there is only one right way!* So why not teach that right way from the outset?!

To make matters worse, punishment training causes severe lapses in the dog's reliability. Since it is obviously impossible to punish the dog each and every time she misbehaves, the dog quickly learns to distinguish between those times when she must comply (so as to avoid impending punishment) and those times when she need not comply, because punishment is impossible. Such times include when the dog is off leash and 6 feet away, when the owner is otherwise engaged (talking to a friend, watching television, taking a shower, tending to the baby or chatting on the telephone) or when the dog is left at home alone.

Instances of misbehavior will be numerous when the owner is away, because even when the dog complied in the owner's looming presence, she did so unwillingly. The dog was forced to act against her will, rather than molding her will to want to please. Hence, when the owner is absent, not only does the dog know she need not comply, she simply does not want to. Again, the trainee is not a stubborn vindictive beast, but rather the trainer has failed to teach. Punishment training invariably creates unpredictable Jekyll and Hyde behavior.

Trainer's Tools

Many training books extol the virtues of a vast array of training paraphernalia and electronic and metallic gizmos, most of which are designed for canine restraint, correction and punishment, rather than for actual facilitation of doggy education. In reality, most effective training tools are not found in stores; they come from within ourselves. In addition to a willing dog, all you really need is a functional human brain, gentle hands, a loving heart and a good attitude.

In terms of equipment, all dogs do require a quality buckle collar to sport dog tags and to attach the leash (for safety and to comply with local leash laws). Hollow chew toys (like Kongs or sterilized longbones) and a dog bed or collapsible crate are musts for housetraining. Three additional tools are required:

1. specific lures (training treats and toys) to predict and prompt specific desired behaviors;

2. rewards (praise, affection, training treats and toys) to reinforce for the dog what a lot of fun it all is; and

3. knowledge—how to convert the dog's favorite activities and games (potential distractions to training) into "life-rewards," which may be employed to facilitate training.

The most powerful of these is *knowledge*. Education is the key! Watch training classes, participate in training classes, watch videos, read books, enjoy play-training with your dog and then your dog will say "Please," and your dog will say "Thank you!"

Housetraining

If dogs were left to their own devices, certainly they would chew, dig and bark for entertainment and then no doubt highlight a few areas of their living space with sprinkles of urine, in much the same way we decorate by hanging pictures. Consequently, when we ask a dog to live with us, we must teach her *where* she may dig, *where* she may perform her toilet duties, *what* she may chew and *when* she may bark. After all, when left at home alone for many hours, we cannot expect the dog to amuse herself by completing crosswords or watching the soaps on TV!

Also, it would be decidedly unfair to keep the house rules a secret from the dog, and then get angry and punish the poor critter for inevitably transgressing rules she did not even know existed. Remember: Without adequate education and guidance, the dog will be forced to establish her own rules—doggy rules—and most probably will be at odds with the owner's view of domestic living.

Since most problems develop during the first few days the dog is at home, prospective dog owners must be certain they are quite clear about the principles of housetraining *before* they get a dog. Early misbehaviors quickly become established as the *status quo*—

becoming firmly entrenched as hard-to-break bad habits, which set the precedent for years to come. Make sure to teach your dog good habits right from the start. Good habits are just as hard to break as bad ones!

Ideally, when a new dog comes home, try to arrange for someone to be present as much as possible during the first few days (for adult dogs) or weeks for puppies. With only a little forethought, it is surprisingly easy to find a puppy sitter, such as a retired person, who would be willing to eat from your refrigerator and watch your television while keeping an eye on the newcomer to encourage the dog to play with chew toys and to ensure she goes outside on a regular basis.

POTTY TRAINING

To teach the dog where to relieve herself:

1. never let her make a single mistake;
2. let her know where you want her to go; and
3. handsomely reward her for doing so: "GOOOOOOOD DOG!!!" liver treat, liver treat, liver treat!

Preventing Mistakes

A single mistake is a training disaster, since it heralds many more in future weeks. And each time the dog soils the house, this further reinforces the dog's unfortunate preference for an indoor, carpeted toilet. *Do not let an unhousetrained dog have full run of the house.*

When you are away from home, or cannot pay full attention, confine the dog to an area where elimination is appropriate, such as an outdoor run or, better still, a small, comfortable indoor kennel with access to an outdoor run. When confined in this manner, most dogs will naturally housetrain themselves.

If that's not possible, confine the dog to an area, such as a utility room, kitchen, basement or garage, where elimination may not be desired in the long run but as an interim measure it is certainly preferable to doing it all around the house. Use newspaper to cover the floor of the dog's day room. The newspaper may be used to soak up the urine and to wrap up and dispose of the feces. Once your dog develops a preferred spot for eliminating, it is only necessary to cover that part of the floor with newspaper. The smaller papered area may then be moved (only a little each day) towards the door to the outside. Thus the dog will develop the tendency to go to the door when she needs to relieve herself.

Never confine an unhouse-trained dog to a crate for long periods. Doing so would force the dog to soil the crate and ruin its usefulness as an aid for housetraining (see the following discussion).

Teaching Where

In order to teach your dog where you would like her to do her business, you have to be there to direct the proceedings—an obvious, yet often neglected, fact of life. In order to be there

to teach the dog *where* to go, you need to know *when* she needs to go. Indeed, the success of housetraining depends on the owner's ability to predict these times. Certainly, a regular feeding schedule will facilitate prediction somewhat, but there is nothing like "loading the deck" and influencing the timing of the outcome yourself!

The first few weeks at home are the most important and influential in your dog's life.

Whenever you are at home, make sure the dog is under constant supervision and/or confined to a small area. If already well trained, simply instruct the dog to lie down in her bed or basket. Alternatively, confine the dog to a crate (doggy den) or tie-down (a short, 18-inch lead that can be clipped to an eye hook in the baseboard near her bed). Short-term close confinement strongly inhibits urination and defecation, since the dog does not want to soil her sleeping area. Thus, when you release the puppydog each hour, she will definitely need to urinate immediately and defecate every third or fourth hour. Keep the dog confined to her doggy den and take her to her intended toilet area each hour, every hour and on the hour.

When taking your dog outside, instruct her to sit quietly before opening the door—she will soon learn to sit by the door when she needs to go out!

Teaching Why

Being able to predict when the dog needs to go enables the owner to be on the spot to praise and reward the dog. Each hour, hurry the dog to the intended toilet area in the yard, issue the appropriate instruction ("Go pee!" or "Go poop!"), then give the dog three to four minutes to produce. Praise and offer a couple of training treats when successful. The treats are important because many people fail to praise their dogs with feeling . . . and housetraining is hardly the time for understatement. So either loosen up and enthusiastically praise that dog: "Wuzzzer-wuzzer-wuzzer, hoooser good wuffer den? Hoooo went pee for Daddy?" Or say "Good dog!" as best you can and offer the treats for effect.

Following elimination is an ideal time for a spot of play-training in the yard or house. Also, an empty dog may be allowed greater freedom around the house for the next half hour or so, just as long as you keep an eye out to make sure she does not get into other kinds of mischief. If you are preoccupied and cannot pay full attention, confine the dog to her doggy den once more to enjoy a peaceful snooze or to play with her many chew toys.

If your dog does not eliminate within the allotted time outside—no biggie! Back to her doggy den, and then try again after another hour.

As I own large dogs, I always feel more relaxed walking an empty dog, knowing that I will not need to finish our stroll weighted down with bags of feces!

Beware of falling into the trap of walking the dog to get her to eliminate. The good ol' dog walk is such an enormous highlight in the dog's life that it represents the single biggest potential reward in domestic dogdom. However, when in a hurry, or during inclement weather, many owners abruptly terminate the walk the moment the dog has done her business. This, in effect, severely punishes the dog for doing the right thing, in the right place at the right time. Consequently, many dogs become strongly inhibited from eliminating outdoors because they know it will signal an abrupt end to an otherwise thoroughly enjoyable walk.

Instead, instruct the dog to relieve herself in the yard prior to going for a walk. If you follow the above instructions, most dogs soon learn to eliminate on cue. As soon as the dog eliminates, praise (and offer a treat or two)—"Good dog! Let's go walkies!" Use the walk as a reward for eliminating in the yard. If the dog does not go, put her back in her doggy den and think about a walk later on. You will find with a "No feces—no walk" policy, your dog will become one of the fastest defecators in the business.

If you do not have a backyard, instruct the dog to eliminate right outside your front door prior to the walk. Not only will this facilitate clean up and disposal of the feces in your own trash can but, also, the walk may again be used as a colossal reward.

CHEWING AND BARKING

Short-term close confinement also teaches the dog that occasional quiet moments are a reality of domestic living. Your puppydog is extremely impressionable during her first few weeks at home. Regular confinement at this time soon exerts a calming influence over the dog's personality. Remember, once the dog is housetrained and calmer, there will be a whole lifetime ahead for the dog to enjoy full run of the house and garden. On the other hand, by letting the newcomer have unrestricted access to the entire household and allowing her to run willy-nilly, she will most certainly develop a bunch of behavior problems in short order, no doubt necessitating confinement later in life. It would not be fair to remedially restrain and confine a dog you have trained, through neglect, to run free.

When confining the dog, make sure she always has an impressive array of suitable chew toys. Kongs and sterilized longbones (both readily available from pet stores) make the best chew toys, since they are hollow and may be stuffed with treats to heighten the dog's interest. For example, by stuffing the little hole at the top of a Kong with a small piece of freeze-dried liver, the dog will not want to leave it alone.

Remember, treats do not have to be junk food and they certainly should not represent extra calories. Rather, treats should be part of each dog's regular daily diet: Some food may be served in the dog's bowl for breakfast and dinner, some food may be used as training treats, and some food may be used for stuffing chew toys. I regularly stuff my dogs' many Kongs with different shaped biscuits and kibble.

Make sure your puppy has suitable chew toys.

The kibble seems to fall out fairly easily, as do the oval-shaped biscuits, thus rewarding the dog instantaneously for checking out the chew toys. The bone-shaped biscuits fall out after a while, rewarding the dog for worrying at the chew toy. But the triangular biscuits never come out. They remain inside the Kong as lures, maintaining the dog's fascination with her chew toy. To further focus the dog's interest, I always make sure to flavor the triangular biscuits by rubbing them with a little cheese or freeze-dried liver.

If stuffed chew toys are reserved especially for times the dog is confined, the puppydog will soon learn to enjoy quiet moments in her doggy den and she will quickly develop a chew-toy habit— a good habit! This is a simple *autoshaping* process; all the owner has to do is set up the situation and the dog all but trains herself— easy and effective. Even when the dog is given run of the house, her first inclination will be to indulge her rewarding chew-toy habit rather than destroy less-attractive household articles, such as curtains, carpets, chairs and compact disks. Similarly, a chew-toy chewer will be less inclined to scratch and chew herself excessively. Also, if the dog busies herself as a recreational chewer, she will be less inclined to develop into a recreational barker or digger when left at home alone.

Stuff a number of chew toys whenever the dog is left confined and remove the extra-special-tasting treats when you return. Your dog will now amuse herself with her chew toys before falling asleep and then resume playing with her chew toys when she expects you to return. Since most owner-absent misbehavior happens right after you leave and right before your expected return, your puppydog will now be conveniently preoccupied with her chew toys at these times.

Come and Sit

Most puppies will happily approach virtually anyone, whether called or not; that is, until they collide with adolescence and

develop other more important doggy interests, such as sniffing a multiplicity of exquisite odors on the grass. Your mission, Mr./Ms. Owner, is to teach and reward the pup for coming reliably, willingly and happily when called—and you have just three months to get it done. Unless adequately reinforced, your puppy's tendency to approach people will self-destruct by adolescence.

Call your dog ("Tina, come!"), open your arms (and maybe squat down) as a welcoming signal, waggle a treat or toy as a lure and reward the puppydog when she comes running. Do not wait to praise the dog until she reaches you—she may come 95 percent of the way and then run off after some distraction. Instead, praise the dog's *first* step towards you and continue praising enthusiastically for *every* step she takes in your direction.

When the rapidly approaching puppy dog is three lengths away from impact, instruct her to sit ("Tina, sit!") and hold the lure in front of you in an outstretched hand to prevent her from hitting you midchest and knocking you flat on your back! As Tina decelerates to nose the lure, move the treat upwards and backwards just over her muzzle with an upwards motion of your extended arm (palm-upwards). As the dog looks up to follow the lure, she will sit down (if she jumps up, you are holding the lure too high). Praise the dog for sitting. Move backwards and call her again. Repeat this many times over, always praising when Tina comes and sits; on occasion, reward her.

For the first couple of trials, use a training treat both as a lure to entice the dog to come and sit and as a reward for doing so. Thereafter, try to use different items as lures and rewards. For example, lure the dog with a Kong or Frisbee but reward her with a food treat. Or lure the dog with a food treat but pat her and throw a tennis ball as a reward. After just a few repetitions, dispense with the lures and rewards; the dog will begin to respond willingly to your verbal requests and hand signals just for the prospect of praise from your heart and affection from your hands.

Instruct every family member, friend and visitor how to get the dog to come and sit. Invite people over for a series of pooch parties; do not keep the pup a secret— let other people enjoy this puppy, and let the pup enjoy other people. Puppydog parties are not only fun, they easily attract a lot of people to help *you* train *your* dog. Unless you teach your dog how to meet people, that is, to sit for greetings, no doubt the dog will resort to jumping up. Then you and the visitors will get annoyed, and the dog will be punished. This is not fair. *Send out those invitations for puppy parties and teach your dog to be mannerly and socially acceptable.*

Even though your dog quickly masters obedient recalls in the house, her reliability may falter when playing in the backyard or local park. Ironically, it is *the owner* who has unintentionally trained the dog *not* to respond in these instances. By allowing the dog to play and run around and otherwise have a good time, but then to call the dog to put her on leash to take her home, the dog quickly learns playing is fun but training is a drag. Thus, playing in the park becomes a severe distraction, which works against training. Bad news!

Instead, whether playing with the dog off leash or on leash, request her to come at frequent intervals—say, every minute or so. On most occasions, praise and pet the dog for a few seconds while she is sitting, then tell her to go play again. For especially fast recalls, offer a couple of training treats and take the time to praise and pet the dog enthusiastically before releasing her. The dog will learn that coming when called is not necessarily the end of the play session, and neither is it the end of the world; rather, it signals an enjoyable, quality time-out with the owner before resuming play once more. In fact, playing in the park now becomes a very effective life-reward, which works to facilitate training by reinforcing each obedient and timely recall. Good news!

Sit, Down, Stand and Rollover
Teaching the dog a variety of body positions is easy for owner and dog, impressive for spectators and

extremely useful for all. Using lure-reward techniques, it is possible to train several positions at once to verbal commands or hand signals (which impress the socks off onlookers).

Sit and ***down***—the two control commands—prevent or resolve nearly a hundred behavior problems. For example, if the dog happily and obediently sits or lies down when requested, she cannot jump on visitors, dash out the front door, run around and chase her tail, pester other dogs, harass cats or annoy family, friends or strangers. Additionally, "Sit" or "Down" are the best emergency commands for off-leash control.

It is easier to teach and maintain a reliable sit than maintain a reliable recall. *Sit* is the purest and simplest of commands—either the dog is sitting or she is not. If there is any change of circumstances or potential danger in the park, for example, simply instruct the dog to sit. If she sits, you have a number of options: Allow the dog to resume playing when she is safe, walk up and put the dog on leash or call the dog. The dog will be much more likely to come when called if she has already acknowledged her compliance by sitting. If the dog does not sit in the park—train her to!

Stand and ***rollover-stay*** are the two positions for examining the dog. Your veterinarian will love you to distraction if you take a little time to teach the dog to stand still and roll over and play possum. Also, your vet bills will be smaller because it will take the veterinarian less time to examine your dog. The rollover-stay is an especially useful command and is really just a variation of the down-stay: Whereas the dog lies prone in the traditional down, she lies supine in the rollover-stay.

As with teaching come and sit, the training techniques to teach the dog to assume all other body positions on cue are user-friendly and dog-friendly. Simply give the appropriate request, lure the dog into the desired body position using a training treat or toy and then *praise* (and maybe reward) the dog as soon as she complies. Try not to touch the dog to get her to respond. If you teach the dog by guiding her into position, the dog will quickly learn that rump-pressure means sit, for example, but as yet you still have no control over your dog if she is just 6 feet away. It will still be necessary to teach the dog to sit on request. So do not make training a time-consuming two-step process; instead, teach the dog to sit to a verbal request or hand signal from the outset. Once the dog sits willingly when requested, by all means use your hands to pet the dog when she does so.

To teach **down** when the dog is already sitting, say "Tina, down!," hold the lure in one hand (palm down) and lower that hand to the floor between the dog's forepaws. As the dog lowers her head to follow the lure, slowly move the lure away from the dog just a fraction (in front of her paws). The dog will lie down as she stretches her nose forward to follow the lure. Praise the dog when she does so. If the dog stands up, you pulled the lure away too far and too quickly.

When teaching the dog to lie down from the standing position, say "Down" and lower the lure to the floor as before. Once the dog has lowered her forequarters and assumed a play bow, gently and slowly move the lure *towards* the dog between her forelegs. Praise the dog as soon as her rear end plops down.

After just a couple of trials it will be possible to alternate sits and downs and have the dog energetically perform doggy push-ups. Praise the dog a lot, and after half a dozen or so push-ups reward the dog with a training treat or toy. You will notice the more energetically you move your arm—upwards (palm up) to get the dog to sit, and downwards (palm down) to get the dog to lie down—the more energetically the dog responds to your requests. Now try training the dog in silence and you will notice she has also learned to respond to hand signals. Yeah! Not too shabby for the first session.

To teach **stand** from the sitting position, say "Tina, stand," slowly move the lure half a dog-length away from the dog's nose, keeping it at nose level, and praise the dog as she stands to follow the lure. As soon

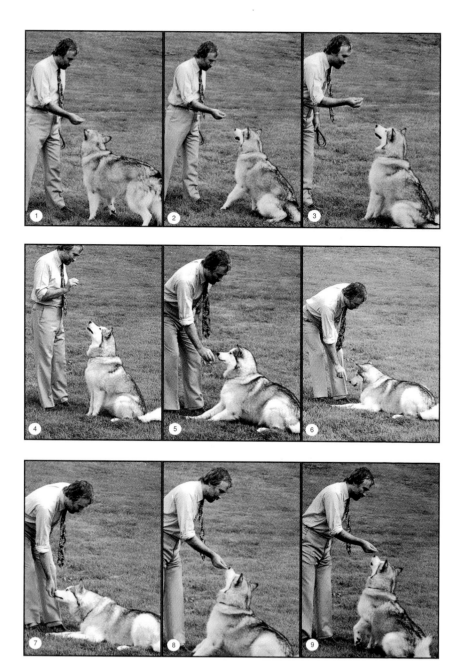

Using a food lure to teach sit, down and stand. 1) "Phoenix, sit." 2) Hand palm upwards, move lure up and back over dog's muzzle. 3) "Good sit, Phoenix!" 4) "Phoenix, down." 5) Hand palm downwards, move lure down to lie between dog's forepaws. 6) "Phoenix, off. Good down, Phoenix!" 7) "Phoenix, sit!" 8) Palm upwards, move lure up and back, keeping it close to dog's muzzle. 9) "Good sit, Phoenix!"

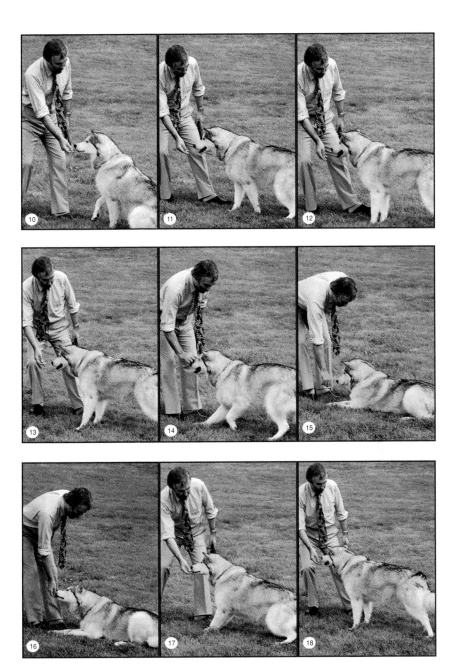

10) *"Phoenix, stand!"* 11) *Move lure away from dog at nose height, then lower it a tad.* 12) *"Phoenix, off! Good stand, Phoenix!"* 13) *"Phoenix, down!"* 14) *Hand palm downwards, move lure down to lie between dog's forepaws.* 15) *"Phoenix, off! Good down-stay, Phoenix!"* 16) *"Phoenix, stand!"* 17) *Move lure away from dog's muzzle up to nose height.* 18) *"Phoenix, off! Good stand-stay, Phoenix. Now we'll make the vet and groomer happy!"*

as the dog stands, lower the lure to just beneath the dog's chin to entice her to look down; otherwise she will stand and then sit immediately. To prompt the dog to stand from the down position, move the lure half a dog-length upwards and away from the dog, holding the lure at standing nose height from the floor.

Teaching **rollover** is best started from the down position, with the dog lying on one side, or at least with both hind legs stretched out on the same side. Say "Tina, bang!" and move the lure backwards and alongside the dog's muzzle to her elbow (on the side of her outstretched hind legs). Once the dog looks to the side and backwards, very slowly move the lure upwards to the dog's shoulder and backbone. Tickling the dog in the goolies (groin area) often invokes a reflex-raising of the hind leg as an appeasement gesture, which facilitates the tendency to roll over. If you move the lure too quickly and the dog jumps into the standing position, have patience and start again. As soon as the dog rolls onto her back, keep the lure stationary and mesmerize the dog with a relaxing tummy rub.

To teach **rollover-stay** when the dog is standing or moving, say "Tina, bang!" and give the appropriate hand signal (with index finger pointed and thumb cocked in true Sam Spade fashion), then in one fluid movement lure her to first lie down and then rollover-stay as above.

Teaching the dog to **stay** in each of the above four positions becomes a piece of cake after first teaching the dog not to worry at the toy or treat training lure. This is best accomplished by hand feeding dinner kibble. Hold a piece of kibble firmly in your hand and softly instruct "Off!" Ignore any licking and slobbering *for however long the dog worries at the treat*, but say "Take it!" and offer the kibble *the instant* the dog breaks contact with her muzzle. Repeat this a few times, and then up the ante and insist the dog remove her muzzle for one whole second before offering the kibble. Then progressively refine your criteria and have the dog not touch your hand (or treat) for longer and longer periods on each trial, such as for two seconds, four seconds, then six, ten, fifteen, twenty, thirty seconds and so on.

The dog soon learns: (1) worrying at the treat never gets results, whereas (2) noncontact is often rewarded after a variable time lapse.

Teaching *"Off!"* has many useful applications in its own right. Additionally, instructing the dog not to touch a training lure often produces spontaneous and magical stays. Request the dog to stand-stay, for example, and not to touch the lure. At first set your sights on a short two-second stay before rewarding the dog. (Remember, every long journey begins with a single step.) However, on subsequent trials, gradually and progressively increase the length of stay required to receive a reward. In no time at all your dog will stand calmly for a minute or so.

Relevancy Training

Once you have taught the dog what you expect her to do when requested to come, sit, lie down, stand, roll-over and stay, the time is right to teach the dog *why* she should comply with your wishes. The secret is to have many (*many*) extremely short training interludes (two to five seconds each) at numerous (*numerous*) times during the course of the dog's day. Especially work with the dog immediately *before* the dog's good times and *during* the dog's good times. For example, ask your dog to sit and/or lie down each time before opening doors, serving meals, offering treats and tummy rubs; ask the dog to perform a few controlled doggy push-ups before letting her off leash or throwing a tennis ball; and perhaps request the dog to sit-down-sit-stand-down-stand-rollover before inviting her to cuddle on the couch.

Similarly, request the dog to sit many times during play or on walks, and in no time at all the dog will be only too pleased to follow your instructions because she has learned that a compliant response heralds all sorts of goodies. Basically all you are trying to teach the dog is how to say please: "Please throw the tennis ball. Please may I snuggle on the couch."

Remember, it is important to keep training interludes short and to have many short sessions each and every day. The shortest (and most useful) session comprises asking the dog to sit and then go play during a play session. When trained this way, your dog will soon associate training with good times. In fact, the dog may be unable to distinguish between training and good times and, indeed, there should be no distinction. The warped concept that training involves forcing the dog to comply and/or dominating her will is totally at odds with the picture of a truly well-trained dog. In reality, enjoying a game of training with a dog is no different from enjoying a game of backgammon or tennis with a friend; and walking with a dog should be no different from strolling with a spouse, or with buddies on the golf course.

Walk by Your Side

Many people attempt to teach a dog to heel by putting her on a leash and physically correcting the dog when she makes mistakes. There are a number of things seriously wrong with this approach, the first being that most people do not want precision heeling; rather, they simply want the dog to follow or walk by their side. Second, when physically restrained during "training," even though the dog may grudgingly mope by your side when "handcuffed" on leash, let's see what happens when she is off leash. History! The dog is in the next county because she never enjoyed walking with you on leash and you have no control over her off leash. So let's just teach the dog off leash from the outset to *want* to walk with us. Third, if the dog has not been trained to heel, it is a trifle hasty to think about punishing the poor dog for making mistakes and breaking heeling rules she didn't even know existed. This is simply not fair! Surely, if the dog had been adequately taught how to heel, she would seldom make mistakes and hence there would be no need to correct the dog. Remember, each mistake and each correction (punishment) advertise the trainer's inadequacy, not the dog's. The dog is not stubborn, she is not stupid and she is not bad. Even if she were, she would still require training, so let's train her properly.

Let's teach the dog to *enjoy* following us and to *want* to walk by our side off leash. Then it will be easier to teach high-precision off-leash heeling patterns if desired. Before going on outdoor walks, it is necessary to teach the dog not to pull. Then it becomes easy to teach on-leash walking and heeling because the dog already wants to walk with you, she is familiar with the desired walking and heeling positions and she knows not to pull.

FOLLOWING

Start by training your dog to follow you. Many puppies will follow if you simply walk away from them and maybe click your fingers or chuckle. Adult dogs may require additional enticement to stimulate them to follow, such as a training lure or, at the very least, a lively trainer. To teach the dog to follow: (1) keep walking and (2) walk away from the dog. If the dog attempts to lead or lag, change pace; slow down if the dog forges too far ahead, but speed up if she lags too far behind. Say "Steady!" or "Easy!" each time before you slow down and "Quickly!" or "Hustle!" each time before you speed up, and the dog will learn to change pace on cue. If the dog lags or leads too far, or if she wanders right or left, simply walk quickly in the opposite direction and maybe even run away from the dog and hide.

Practicing is a lot of fun; you can set up a course in your home, yard or park to do this. Indoors, entice the dog to follow upstairs, into a bedroom, into the bathroom, downstairs, around the living room couch, zigzagging between dining room chairs and into the kitchen for dinner. Outdoors, get the dog to follow around park benches, trees, shrubs and along walkways and lines in the grass. (For safety outdoors, it is advisable to attach a long line on the dog, but never exert corrective tension on the line.)

Remember, following has a lot to do with attitude—
your attitude! Most probably your dog will *not* want to
follow Mr. Grumpy Troll with the personality of wilted
lettuce. Lighten up—walk with a jaunty step, whistle a
happy tune, sing, skip and tell jokes to your dog and
she will be right there by your side.

BY YOUR SIDE

It is smart to train the dog to walk close on one side or
the other—either side will do, your choice. When walking, jogging or cycling, it is generally bad news to have
the dog suddenly cut in front of you. In fact, I train my
dogs to walk "By my side" and "Other side"—both very
useful instructions. It is possible to position the dog
fairly accurately by looking to the appropriate side and
clicking your fingers or slapping your thigh on that
side. A precise positioning may be attained by holding
a training lure, such as a chew toy, tennis ball or food
treat. Stop and stand still several times throughout the
walk, just as you would when window shopping or
meeting a friend. Use the lure to make sure the dog
slows down and stays close whenever you stop.

When teaching the dog to heel, we generally want
her to sit in heel position when we stop. Teach heel

*Using a toy to teach sit-heel-sit sequences: 1) "Phoenix, sit!" Standing still, move lure up and back over dog's
muzzle . . . 2) to position dog sitting in heel position on your left side. 3) Say "Phoenix,heel!" and walk ahead,
wagging lure in left hand. Change lure to right hand in preparation for sit signal. Say "Sit" and then . . .*

122

position at the standstill and the dog will learn that the default heel position is sitting by your side (left or right—your choice, unless you wish to compete in obedience trials, in which case the dog must heel on the left).

Several times a day, stand up and call your dog to come and sit in heel position—"Tina, heel!" For example, instruct the dog to come to heel each time there are commercials on TV, or each time you turn a page of a novel, and the dog will get it in a single evening.

Practice straight-line heeling and turns separately. With the dog sitting at heel, teach her to turn in place. After each quarter-turn, half-turn or full turn in place, lure the dog to sit at heel. Now it's time for short straight-line heeling sequences, no more than a few steps at a time. Always think of heeling in terms of sit-heel-sit sequences—start and end with the dog in position and do your best to keep her there when moving. Progressively increase the number of steps in each sequence. When the dog remains close for 20 yards of straight-line heeling, it is time to add a few turns and then sign up for a happy-heeling obedience class to get some advice from the experts.

4) use hand signal to lure dog to sit as you stop. Eventually, dog will sit automatically at heel whenever you stop. 5) "Good dog!"

No Pulling on Leash

You can start teaching your dog not to pull on leash anywhere—in front of the television or outdoors—but regardless of location, you must not take a single step with tension in the leash. For a reason known only to dogs, even just a couple of paces of pulling on leash is intrinsically motivating and diabolically rewarding. Instead, attach the leash to the dog's collar, grasp the other end firmly with both hands held close to your chest, and stand still—do not budge an inch. Have somebody watch you with a stopwatch to time your progress, or else you will never believe this will work and so you will not even try the exercise, and your shoulder and the dog's neck will be traumatized for years to come.

Stand still and wait for the dog to stop pulling, and to sit and/or lie down. All dogs stop pulling and sit eventually. Most take only a couple of minutes; the all-time record is 22½ minutes. Time how long it takes. Gently praise the dog when she stops pulling, and as soon as she sits, enthusiastically praise the dog and take just one step forward, then immediately stand still. This single step usually demonstrates the ballistic reinforcing nature of pulling on leash; most dogs explode to the end of the leash, so be prepared for the strain. Stand firm and wait for the dog to sit again. Repeat this half a dozen times and you will probably notice a progressive reduction in the force of the dog's one-step explosions and a radical reduction in the time it takes for the dog to sit each time.

As the dog learns "Sit we go" and "Pull we stop," she will begin to walk forward calmly with each single step and automatically sit when you stop. Now try two steps before you stop. Wooooooo! Scary! When the dog has mastered two steps at a time, try for three. After each success, progressively increase the number of steps in the sequence: try four steps and then six, eight, ten and twenty steps before stopping. Congratulations! You are now walking the dog on leash.

Whenever walking with the dog (off leash or on leash), make sure you stop periodically to practice a few position commands and stays before instructing the dog to "Walk on!" (Remember, you want the dog to be compliant everywhere, not just in the kitchen when her dinner is at hand.) For example, stopping every 25 yards to briefly train the dog amounts to over 200 training interludes within a single 3-mile stroll. And each training session is in a different location. You will not believe the improvement within just the first mile of the first walk.

To put it another way, integrating training into a walk offers 200 separate opportunities to use the continuance of the walk as a reward to reinforce the dog's education. Moreover, some training interludes may comprise continuing education for the dog's walking skills: Alternate short periods of the dog walking calmly by your side with periods when the dog is allowed to sniff and investigate the environment. Now sniffing odors on the grass and meeting other dogs become rewards which reinforce the dog's calm and mannerly demeanor. Good Lord! Whatever next? Many enjoyable walks together of course. Happy trails!

THE IMPORTANCE OF TRICKS

Nothing will improve a dog's quality of life better than having a few tricks under her belt. Teaching any trick expands the dog's vocabulary, which facilitates communication and improves the owner's control. Also, specific tricks help prevent and resolve specific behavior problems. For example, by teaching the dog to fetch her toys, the dog learns carrying a toy makes the owner happy and, therefore, will be more likely to chew her toy than other inappropriate items.

More important, teaching tricks prompts owners to lighten up and train with a sunny disposition. Really, tricks should be no different from any other behaviors we put on cue. But they are. When teaching tricks, owners have a much sweeter attitude, which in turn motivates the dog and improves her willingness to comply. The dog feels tricks are a blast, but formal commands are a drag. In fact, tricks are so enjoyable, they may be used as rewards in training by asking the dog to come, sit and down-stay and then rollover for a tummy rub. Go on, try it: Crack a smile and even giggle when the dog promptly and willingly lies down and stays.

Most important, performing tricks prompts onlookers to smile and giggle. Many people are scared of dogs, especially large ones. And nothing can be more off-putting for a dog than to be constantly confronted by strangers who don't like her because of her size or the way she looks. Uneasy people put the dog on edge, causing her to back off and bark, only frightening people all the more. And so a vicious circle develops, with the people's fear fueling the dog's fear *and vice versa.* Instead, tie a pink ribbon to your dog's collar and practice all sorts of tricks on walks and in the park, and you will be pleasantly amazed how it changes people's attitudes toward your friendly dog. The dog's repertoire of tricks is limited only by the trainer's imagination. Below I have described three of my favorites:

SPEAK AND SHUSH

The training sequence involved in teaching a dog to bark on request is no different from that used when training any behavior on cue: request—lure—response—reward. As always, the secret of success lies in finding an effective lure. If the dog always barks at the doorbell, for example, say "Rover, speak!", have an accomplice ring the doorbell, then reward the dog for barking. After a few woofs, ask Rover to "Shush!", waggle a food treat under her nose (to entice her to sniff and thus to shush), praise her when quiet and eventually offer the treat as a reward. Alternate "Speak" and "Shush," progressively increasing the length of shush-time between each barking bout.

PLAY BOW

With the dog standing, say "Bow!" and lower the food lure (palm upwards) to rest between the dog's forepaws. Praise as the dog lowers

her forequarters and sternum to the ground (as when teaching the down), but then lure the dog to stand and offer the treat. On successive trials, gradually increase the length of time the dog is required to remain in the play bow posture in order to gain a food reward. If the dog's rear end collapses into a down, say nothing and offer no reward; simply start over.

BE A BEAR

With the dog sitting backed into a corner to prevent her from toppling over backwards, say "Be a bear!" With bent paw and palm down, raise a lure upwards and backwards along the top of the dog's muzzle. Praise the dog when she sits up on her haunches and offer the treat as a reward. To prevent the dog from standing on her hind legs, keep the lure closer to the dog's muzzle. On each trial, progressively increase the length of time the dog is required to sit up to receive a food reward. Since lure-reward training is so easy, teach the dog to stand and walk on her hind legs as well!

Teaching "Be a Bear"

Getting
Active
with your Dog

by Bardi McLennan

Once you and your dog have graduated from basic obedience training and are beginning to work together as a team, you can take part in the growing world of dog activities. There are so many fun things to do with your dog! Just remember, people and dogs don't always learn at the same pace, so don't be upset if you (or your dog) need more than two basic training courses before your team becomes operational. Even smart dogs don't go straight to college from kindergarten!

Just as there are events geared to certain types of dogs, so there are ones that are more appealing to certain types of people. In some

128

activities, you give the commands and your dog does the work (upland game hunting is one example), while in others, such as agility, you'll both get a workout. You may want to aim for prestigious titles to add to your dog's name, or you may want nothing more than the sheer enjoyment of being around other people and their dogs. Passive or active, participation has its own rewards.

Consider your dog's physical capabilities when looking into any of the canine activities. It's easy to see that a Basset Hound is not built for the racetrack, nor would a Chihuahua be the breed of choice for pulling a sled. A loyal dog will attempt almost anything you ask him to do, so it is up to you to know your

All dogs seem to love playing flyball.

dog's limitations. A dog must be physically sound in order to compete at any level in athletic activities, and being mentally sound is a definite plus. Advanced age, however, may not be a deterrent. Many dogs still hunt and herd at ten or twelve years of age. It's entirely possible for dogs to be "fit at 50." Take your dog for a checkup, explain to your vet the type of activity you have in mind and be guided by his or her findings.

You needn't be restricted to breed-specific sports if it's only fun you're after. Certain AKC activities are limited to designated breeds; however, as each new trial, test or sport has grown in popularity, so has the variety of breeds encouraged to participate at a fun level.

But don't shortchange your fun, or that of your dog, by thinking only of the basic function of her breed. Once a dog has learned how to learn, she can be taught to do just about anything as long as the size of the dog is right for the job and you both think it is fun and rewarding. In other words, you are a team.

To get involved in any of the activities detailed in this chapter, look for the names and addresses of the organizations that sponsor them in Chapter 13. You can also ask your breeder or a local dog trainer for contacts.

You can compete in obedience trials with a well trained dog.

Official American Kennel Club Activities

The following tests and trials are some of the events sanctioned by the AKC and sponsored by various dog clubs. Your dog's expertise will be rewarded with impressive titles. You can participate just for fun, or be competitive and go for those awards.

OBEDIENCE

Training classes begin with pups as young as three months of age in kindergarten puppy training, then advance to pre-novice (all exercises on lead) and go on to novice, which is where you'll start off-lead work. In obedience classes dogs learn to sit, stay, heel and come through a variety of exercises. Once you've got the basics down, you can enter obedience trials and work toward earning your dog's first degree, a C.D. (Companion Dog).

The next level is called "Open," in which jumps and retrieves perk up the dog's interest. Passing grades in competition at this level earn a C.D.X. (Companion Dog Excellent). Beyond that lies the goal of the most ambitious—Utility (U.D. and even U.D.X. or OTCh, an Obedience Champion).

AGILITY

All dogs can participate in the latest canine sport to have gained worldwide popularity for its fun and excitement, agility. It began in England as a canine version of horse show-jumping, but because dogs are more agile and able to perform on verbal commands, extra feats were added such as climbing, balancing and racing through tunnels or in and out of weave poles. Many of the obstacles (regulation or homemade) can be set up in your own backyard. If the agility bug bites, you could end up in international competition!

For starters, your dog should be obedience trained, even though, in the beginning, the lessons may all be taught on lead. Once the dog understands the commands (and you do, too), it's as easy as guiding the dog over a prescribed course, one obstacle at a time. In competition, the race is against the clock, so wear your running shoes! The dog starts with 200 points and the judge deducts for infractions and misadventures along the way.

All dogs seem to love agility and respond to it as if they were being turned loose in a playground paradise. Your dog's enthusiasm will be contagious; agility turns into great fun for dog and owner.

FIELD TRIALS AND HUNTING TESTS

There are field trials and hunting tests for the sporting breeds—retrievers, spaniels and pointing breeds, and for some hounds—Bassets, Beagles and Dachshunds. Field trials are competitive events that test a dog's ability to perform the functions for which she was bred. Hunting tests, which are open to retrievers,

---

TITLES AWARDED BY THE AKC

Conformation: Ch. (Champion)

Obedience: CD (Companion Dog); CDX (Companion Dog Excellent); UD (Utility Dog); UDX (Utility Dog Excellent); OTCh. (Obedience Trial Champion)

Field: JH (Junior Hunter); SH (Senior Hunter); MH (Master Hunter); AFCh. (Amateur Field Champion); FCh. (Field Champion)

Lure Coursing: JC (Junior Courser); SC (Senior Courser)

Herding: HT (Herding Tested); PT (Pre-Trial Tested); HS (Herding Started); HI (Herding Intermediate); HX (Herding Excellent); HCh. (Herding Champion)

Tracking: TD (Tracking Dog); TDX (Tracking Dog Excellent)

Agility: NAD (Novice Agility); OAD (Open Agility); ADX (Agility Excellent); MAX (Master Agility)

Earthdog Tests: JE (Junior Earthdog); SE (Senior Earthdog); ME (Master Earthdog)

Canine Good Citizen: CGC

Combination: DC (Dual Champion—Ch. and Fch.); TC (Triple Champion—Ch., Fch., and OTCh.)

spaniels and pointing breeds only, are noncompetitive and are a means of judging the dog's ability as well as that of the handler.

Hunting is a very large and complex part of canine sports, and if you own one of the breeds that hunts, the events are a great treat for your dog and you. He gets to do what he was bred for, and you get to work with him and watch him do it. You'll be proud of and amazed at what your dog can do.

Fortunately, the AKC publishes a series of booklets on these events, which outline the rules and regulations and include a glossary of the sometimes complicated terms. The AKC also publishes newsletters for field trialers and hunting test enthusiasts. The United Kennel Club (UKC) also has informative materials for the hunter and his dog.

Retrievers and other sporting breeds get to do what they're bred to in hunting tests.

HERDING TESTS AND TRIALS

Herding, like hunting, dates back to the first known uses man made of dogs. The interest in herding today is widespread, and if you own a herding breed, you can join in the activity. Herding dogs are tested for their natural skills to keep a flock of ducks, sheep or cattle together. If your dog shows potential, you can start at the testing level, where your dog can earn a title for showing an inherent herding ability. With training you can advance to the trial level, where your dog should be capable of controlling even difficult livestock in diverse situations.

LURE COURSING

The AKC Tests and Trials for Lure Coursing are open to traditional sighthounds—Greyhounds, Whippets,

Borzoi, Salukis, Afghan Hounds, Ibizan Hounds and Scottish Deerhounds—as well as to Basenjis and Rhodesian Ridgebacks. Hounds are judged on overall ability, follow, speed, agility and endurance. This is possibly the most exciting of the trials for spectators, because the speed and agility of the dogs is awesome to watch as they chase the lure (or "course") in heats of two or three dogs at a time.

TRACKING

Tracking is another activity in which almost any dog can compete because every dog that sniffs the ground when taken outdoors is, in fact, tracking. The hard part comes when the rules as to what, when and where the dog tracks are determined by a person, not the dog! Tracking tests cover a large area of fields, woods and roads. The tracks are

laid hours before the dogs go to work on them, and include "tricks" like cross-tracks and sharp turns. If you're interested in search-and-rescue work, this is the place to start.

This tracking dog is hot on the trail.

EARTHDOG TESTS FOR SMALL TERRIERS AND DACHSHUNDS

These tests are open to Australian, Bedlington, Border, Cairn, Dandie Dinmont, Smooth and Wire Fox, Lakeland, Norfolk, Norwich, Scottish, Sealyham, Skye, Welsh and West Highland White Terriers as well as Dachshunds. The dogs need no prior training for this terrier sport. There is a qualifying test on the day of the event, so dog and handler learn the rules on the spot. These tests, or "digs," sometimes end with informal races in the late afternoon.

Here are some of the extracurricular obedience and racing activities that are not regulated by the AKC or UKC, but are generally run by clubs or a group of dog fanciers and are often open to all.

Canine Freestyle This activity is something new on the scene and is variously likened to dancing, dressage or ice skating. It is meant to show the athleticism of the dog, but also requires showmanship on the part of the dog's handler. If you and your dog like to ham it up for friends, you might want to look into freestyle.

Lure coursing lets sighthounds do what they do best—run!

Scent Hurdle Racing Scent hurdle racing is purely a fun activity sponsored by obedience clubs with members forming competing teams. The height of the hurdles is based on the size of the shortest dog on the team. On a signal, one team dog is released on each of two side-by-side courses and must clear every hurdle before picking up its own dumbbell from a platform and returning over the jumps to the handler. As each dog returns, the next on that team is sent. Of course, that is what the dogs are supposed to do. When the dogs improvise (going under or around the hurdles, stealing another dog's dumbbell, and so forth), it no doubt frustrates the handlers, but just adds to the fun for everyone else.

Flyball This type of racing is similar, but after negotiating the four hurdles, the dog comes to a flyball box, steps on a lever that releases a tennis ball into the air, catches the ball and returns over the hurdles to the starting point. This game also becomes extremely fun for spectators because the dogs sometimes cheat by catching a ball released by the dog in the next lane. Three titles can be earned—Flyball Dog (F.D.), Flyball Dog Excellent (F.D.X.) and Flyball Dog Champion (Fb.D.Ch.)—all awarded by the North American Flyball Association, Inc.

Dogsledding The name conjures up the Rocky Mountains or the frigid North, but you can find dogsled clubs in such unlikely spots as Maryland, North Carolina and Virginia! Dogsledding is primarily for the Nordic breeds such as the Alaskan Malamutes, Siberian Huskies and Samoyeds, but other breeds can try. There are some practical backyard applications to this sport, too. With parental supervision, almost any strong dog could pull a child's sled.

Coming over the A-frame on an agility course.

These are just some of the many recreational ways you can get to know and understand your multifaceted dog better and have fun doing it.

Your Dog
and your
Family

by Bardi McLennan

Adding a dog automatically increases your family by one, no matter whether you live alone in an apartment or are part of a mother, father and six kids household. The single-person family is fair game for numerous and varied canine misconceptions as to who is dog and who pays the bills, whereas a dog in a houseful of children will consider himself to be just one of the gang, littermates all. One dog and one child may give a dog reason to believe they are both kids or both dogs. Either interpretation requires parental supervision and sometimes speedy intervention.

As soon as one paw goes through the door into your home, Rufus (or Rufina) has to make many adjustments to become a part of your family. Your job is to make him fit in as painlessly as possible. An older dog may have some frame of reference from past experience, but to a 10-week-old puppy, everything is brand new: people, furniture, stairs, when and where people eat, sleep or watch TV, his own place and everyone else's space, smells, sounds, outdoors—everything!

Puppies, and newly acquired dogs of any age, do not need what we think of as "freedom." If you leave a new dog or puppy loose in the house, you will almost certainly return to chaotic destruction and the dog will forever after equate your homecoming with a time of punishment to be dreaded. It is unfair to give your dog what amounts to "freedom to get into trouble." Instead, confine him to a crate for brief periods of your absence (up to three or four hours) and, for the long haul, a workday for example, confine him to one untrashable area with his own toys, a bowl of water and a radio left on (low) in another room.

Lots of pets get along with each other just fine.

For the first few days, when not confined, put Rufus on a long leash tied to your wrist or waist. This umbilical cord method enables the dog to learn all about you from your body language and voice, and to learn by his own actions which things in the house are NO! and which ones are rewarded by "Good dog." House-training will be easier with the pup always by your side. Speaking of which, accidents do happen. That goal of "completely housetrained" takes up to a year, or the length of time it takes the pup to mature.

The All-Adult Family

Most dogs in an adults-only household today are likely to be latchkey pets, with no one home all day but the dog. When you return after a tough day on the job, the dog can and should be your relaxation therapy. But going home can instead be a daily frustration.

Separation anxiety is a very common problem for the dog in a working household. It may begin with whines and barks of loneliness, but it will soon escalate into a frenzied destruction derby. That is why it is so important to set aside the time to teach a dog to relax when left alone in his confined area and to understand that he can trust you to return.

Let the dog get used to your work schedule in easy stages. Confine him to one room and go in and out of that room over and over again. Be casual about it. No physical, voice or eye contact. When the pup no longer even notices your comings and goings, leave the house for varying lengths of time, returning to stay home for a few minutes and gradually increasing the time away. This training can take days, but the dog is learning that you haven't left him forever and that he can trust you.

Any time you leave the dog, but especially during this training period, be casual about your departure. No anxiety-building fond farewells. Just "Bye" and go! Remember the "Good dog" when you return to find everything more or less as you left it.

If things are a mess (or even a disaster) when you return, greet the dog, take him outside to eliminate, and then put him in his crate while you clean up. Rant and rave in the shower! *Do not* punish the dog. You were not there when it happened, and the rule is: Only punish as you catch the dog in the act of wrongdoing. Obviously, it makes sense to get your latchkey puppy when you'll have a week or two to spend on these training essentials.

Family weekend activities should include Rufus whenever possible. Depending on the pup's age, now is the time for a long walk in the park, playtime in the backyard, a hike in the woods. Socializing is as important as health care, good food and physical exercise, so visiting Aunt Emma or Uncle Harry and the next-door neighbor's dog or cat is essential to developing an outgoing, friendly temperament in your pet.

If you are a single adult, socializing Rufus at home and away will prevent him from becoming overly protective of you (or just overly attached) and will also prevent such behavioral problems as dominance or fear of strangers.

Babies

Whether already here or on the way, babies figure larger than life in the eyes of a dog. If the dog is there first, let him in on all your baby preparations in the house. When baby arrives, let Rufus sniff any item of clothing that has been on the baby before Junior comes home. Then let Mom greet the dog first before introducing the new family member. Hold the baby down for the dog to see and sniff, but make sure some-

one's holding the dog on lead in case of any sudden moves. Don't play keep-away or tease the dog with the baby, which only invites undesirable jumping up.

The dog and the baby are "family," and for starters can be treated almost as equals. Things rapidly change, however, especially when baby takes to creeping around on all fours on the dog's turf or, better yet, has yummy pudding all over her face and hands! That's when a lot of things in the dog's and baby's lives become more separate than equal.

Dogs are perfect confidants.

Toddlers make terrible dog owners, but if you can't avoid the combination, use patient discipline (that is, positive teaching rather than punishment), and use time-outs before you run out of patience.

139

A dog and a baby (or toddler, or an assertive young child) should never be left alone together. Take the dog with you or confine him. With a baby or youngsters in the house, you'll have plenty of use for that wonderful canine safety device called a crate!

Young Children

Any dog in a house with kids will behave pretty much as the kids do, good or bad. But even good dogs and good children can get into trouble when play becomes rowdy and active.

Teach children how to play nicely with a puppy.

Legs bobbing up and down, shrill voices screeching, a ball hurtling overhead, all add up to exuberant frustration for a dog who's just trying to be part of the gang. In a pack of puppies, any legs or toys being chased would be caught by a set of teeth, and all the pups involved would understand that is how the game is played. Kids do not understand this, nor do parents tolerate it. Bring Rufus indoors before you have reason to regret it. This is time-out, not a punishment.

You can explain the situation to the children and tell them they must play quieter games until the puppy learns not to grab them with his mouth. Unfortunately, you can't explain it that easily to the dog. With adult supervision, they will learn how to play together.

Young children love to tease. Sticking their faces or wiggling their hands or fingers in the dog's face is teasing. To another person it might be just annoying, but it is threatening to a dog. There's another difference: We can make the child stop by an explanation, but the only way a dog can stop it is with a warning growl and then with teeth. Teasing is the major cause of children being bitten by their pets. Treat it seriously.

Older Children

The best age for a child to get a first dog is between the ages of 8 and 12. That's when kids are able to accept some real responsibility for their pet. Even so, take the child's vow of "I will never *ever* forget to feed (brush, walk, etc.) the dog" for what it's worth: a child's good intention at that moment. Most kids today have extra lessons, soccer practice, Little League, ballet, and so forth piled on top of school schedules. There will be many times when Mom will have to come to the dog's rescue. "I walked the dog for you so you can set the table for me" is one way to get around a missed appointment without laying on blame or guilt.

Kids in this age group make excellent obedience trainers because they are into the teaching/learning process themselves and they lack the self-consciousness of adults. Attending a dog show is something the whole family can enjoy, and watching Junior Showmanship may catch the eye of the kids. Older children can begin to get involved in many of the recreational activities that were reviewed in the previous chapter. Some of the agility obstacles, for example, can be set up in the backyard as a family project (with an adult making sure all the equipment is safe and secure for the dog).

Older kids are also beginning to look to the future, and may envision themselves as veterinarians or trainers or show dog handlers or writers of the next Lassie best-seller. Dogs are perfect confidants for these dreams. They won't tell a soul.

Other Pets

Introduce all pets tactfully. In a dog/cat situation, hold the dog, not the cat. Let two dogs meet on neutral turf—a stroll in the park or a walk down the street—with both on loose leads to permit all the normal canine ways of saying hello, including routine sniffing, circling, more sniffing, and so on. Small creatures such as hamsters, chinchillas or mice must be kept safe from their natural predators (dogs and cats).

Festive Family Occasions

Parties are great for people, but not necessarily for puppies. Until all the guests have arrived, put the dog in his crate or in a room where he won't be disturbed. A socialized dog can join the fun later as long as he's not underfoot, annoying guests or into the hors d'oeuvres.

There are a few dangers to consider, too. Doors opening and closing can allow a puppy to slip out unnoticed in the confusion, and you'll be organizing a search party instead of playing host or hostess. Party food and buffet service are not for dogs. Let Rufus party in his crate with a nice big dog biscuit.

At Christmas time, not only are tree decorations dangerous and breakable (and perhaps family heirlooms), but extreme caution should be taken with the lights, cords and outlets for the tree lights and any other festive lighting. Occasionally a dog lifts a leg, ignoring the fact that the tree is indoors. To avoid this, use a canine repellent, made for gardens, on the tree. Or keep him out of the tree room unless supervised. And whatever you do, *don't* invite trouble by hanging his toys on the tree!

Car Travel

Before you plan a vacation by car or RV with Rufus, be sure he enjoys car travel. Nothing spoils a holiday quicker than a carsick dog! Work within the dog's comfort level. Get in the car with the dog in his crate or attached to a canine car safety belt and just sit there until he relaxes. That's all. Next time, get in the car, turn on the engine and go nowhere. Just sit. When that is okay, turn on the engine and go around the block. Now you can go for a ride and include a stop where you get out, leaving the dog for a minute or two.

On a warm day, always park in the shade and leave windows open several inches. And return quickly. It only takes 10 minutes for a car to become an overheated steel death trap.

Motel or Pet Motel?

Not all motels or hotels accept pets, but you have a much better choice today than even a few years ago. To find a dog-friendly lodging, look at *On the Road Again With Man's Best Friend,* a series of directories that detail bed and breakfasts, inns, family resorts and other hotels/motels. Some places require a refundable deposit to cover any damage incurred by the dog. More B&Bs accept pets now, but some restrict the size.

If taking Rufus with you is not feasible, check out boarding kennels in your area. Your veterinarian may offer this service, or recommend a kennel or two he or she is familiar with. Go see the facilities for yourself, ask about exercise, diet, housing, and so on. Or, if you'd rather have Rufus stay home, look into bonded petsitters, many of whom will also bring in the mail and water your plants.

chapter 11

Your Dog
and your
Community

by Bardi McLennan

Step outside your home with your dog and you are no longer just family, you are both part of your community. This is when the phrase "responsible pet ownership" takes on serious implications. For starters, it means you pick up after your dog—not just occasionally, but every time your dog eliminates away from home. That means you have joined the Plastic Baggy Brigade! You always have plastic sandwich bags in your pocket and several in the car. It means you teach your kids how to use them, too. If you think this is "yucky," just imagine what the person (a non-doggy person) who inadvertently steps in the mess thinks!

Your responsibility extends to your neighbors: To their ears (no annoying barking); to their property (their garbage, their lawn, their flower beds, their cat—especially their cat); to their kids (on bikes, at play); to their kids' toys and sports equipment.

There are numerous dog-related laws, ranging from simple dog licensing and leash laws to those holding you liable for any physical injury or property damage done by your dog. These laws are in place to protect everyone in the community, including you and your dog. There are town ordinances and state laws which are by no means the same in all towns or all states. Ignorance of the law won't get you off the hook. The time to find out what the laws are where you live is now.

Be sure your dog's license is current. This is not just a good local ordinance, it can make the difference between finding your lost dog or not.

Dressing your dog up makes him appealing to strangers.

Many states now require proof of rabies vaccination and that the dog has been spayed or neutered before issuing a license. At the same time, keep up the dog's annual immunizations.

Never let your dog run loose in the neighborhood. This will not only keep you on the right side of the leash law, it's the outdoor version of the rule about not giving your dog "freedom to get into trouble."

Good Canine Citizen

Sometimes it's hard for a dog's owner to assess whether or not the dog is sufficiently socialized to be accepted by the community at large. Does Rufus or Rufina display good, controlled behavior in public? The AKC's Canine Good Citizen program is available through many dog organizations. If your dog passes the test, the title "CGC" is earned.

The overall purpose is to turn your dog into a good neighbor and to teach you about your responsibility to your community as a dog owner. Here are the ten things your dog must do willingly:

1. Accept a stranger stopping to chat with you.
2. Sit and be petted by a stranger.
3. Allow a stranger to handle him or her as a groomer or veterinarian would.
4. Walk nicely on a loose lead.
5. Walk calmly through a crowd.
6. Sit and down on command, then stay in a sit or down position while you walk away.
7. Come when called.
8. Casually greet another dog.
9. React confidently to distractions.
10. Accept being left alone with someone other than you and not become overly agitated or nervous.

Schools and Dogs

Schools are getting involved with pet ownership on an educational level. It has been proven that children who are kind to animals are humane in their attitude toward other people as adults.

A dog is a child's best friend, and so children are often primary pet owners, if not the primary caregivers. Unfortunately, they are also the ones most often bitten by dogs. This occurs due to a lack of understanding that pets, no matter how sweet, cuddly and loving, are still animals. Schools, along with parents, dog clubs, dog fanciers and the AKC, are working to change all that with video programs for children not only in grade school, but in the nursery school and pre-kindergarten age group. Teaching youngsters how to be responsible dog owners is important community work. When your dog has a CGC, volunteer to take part in an educational classroom event put on by your dog club.

Boy Scout Merit Badge

A Merit Badge for Dog Care can be earned by any Boy Scout ages 11 to 18. The requirements are not easy, but amount to a complete course in responsible dog care and general ownership. Here are just a few of the things a Scout must do to earn that badge:

Point out ten parts of the dog using the correct names.

Give a report (signed by parent or guardian) on your care of the dog (feeding, food used, housing, exercising, grooming and bathing), plus what has been done to keep the dog healthy.

Explain the right way to obedience train a dog, and demonstrate three comments.

Several of the requirements have to do with health care, including first aid, handling a hurt dog, and the dangers of home treatment for a serious ailment.

The final requirement is to know the local laws and ordinances involving dogs.

There are similar programs for Girl Scouts and 4-H members.

Local Clubs

Local dog clubs are no longer in existence just to put on a yearly dog show. Today, they are apt to be the hub of the community's involvement with pets. Dog clubs conduct educational forums with big-name speakers, stage demonstrations of canine talent in a busy mall and take dogs of various breeds to schools for class-room discussion.

The quickest way to feel accepted as a member in a club is to volunteer your services! Offer to help with something—anything—and watch your popularity (and your interest) grow.

Therapy Dogs

Once your dog has earned that essential CGC and reliably demonstrates a steady, calm temperament, you could look into what therapy dogs are doing in your area.

Therapy dogs go with their owners to visit patients at hospitals or nursing homes, generally remaining on leash but able to coax a pat from a stiffened hand, a smile from a blank face, a few words from sealed lips or a hug from someone in need of love.

Nursing homes cover a wide range of patient care. Some specialize in care of the elderly, some in the treatment of specific illnesses, some in physical therapy. Children's facilities also welcome visits from trained therapy dogs for boosting morale in their pediatric patients. Hospice care for the terminally ill and the at-home care of AIDS patients are other areas where this canine visiting is desperately needed. Therapy dog training comes first.

Your dog can make a difference in lots of lives.

There is a lot more involved than just taking your nice friendly pooch to someone's bedside. Doing therapy dog work involves your own emotional stability as well as that of your dog. But once you have met all the requirements for this work, making the rounds once a week or once a month with your therapy dog is possibly the most rewarding of all community activities.

Disaster Aid

This community service is definitely not for everyone, partly because it is time-consuming. The initial training is rigorous, and there can be no let-up in the continuing workouts, because members are on call 24 hours a day to go wherever they are needed at a moment's notice. But if you think you would like to be able to assist in a disaster, look into search-and-rescue work. The network of search-and-rescue volunteers is worldwide, and all members of the American Rescue Dog Association (ARDA) who are qualified to do this work are volunteers who train and maintain their own dogs.

Physical Aid

Most people are familiar with Seeing Eye dogs, which serve as blind people's eyes, but not with all the other work that dogs are trained to do to assist the disabled. Dogs are also specially trained to pull wheelchairs, carry school books, pick up dropped objects, open and close doors. Some also are ears for the deaf. All these assistance-trained dogs, by the way, are allowed anywhere "No Pet" signs exist (as are therapy dogs when properly identified). Getting started in any of this fascinating work requires a background in dog training and canine behavior, but there are also volunteer jobs ranging from answering the phone to cleaning out kennels to providing a foster home for a puppy. You have only to ask.

Making the rounds with your therapy dog can be very rewarding.

part four

Beyond
the
Basics

chapter 12

Recommended Reading

Books

ABOUT HEALTH CARE

Ackerman, Lowell. *Guide to Skin and Haircoat Problems in Dogs.* Loveland, Colo.: Alpine Publications, 1994.

Alderton, David. *The Dog Care Manual.* Hauppauge, N.Y.: Barron's Educational Series, Inc., 1986.

American Kennel Club. *American Kennel Club Dog Care and Training.* New York: Howell Book House, 1991.

Bamberger, Michelle, DVM. *Help! The Quick Guide to First Aid for Your Dog.* New York: Howell Book House, 1995.

Carlson, Delbert, DVM, and James Giffin, MD. *Dog Owner's Home Veterinary Handbook.* New York: Howell Book House, 1992.

DeBitetto, James, DVM, and Sarah Hodgson. *You & Your Puppy.* New York: Howell Book House, 1995.

Humphries, Jim, DVM. *Dr. Jim's Animal Clinic for Dogs.* New York: Howell Book House, 1994.

McGinnis, Terri. *The Well Dog Book.* New York: Random House, 1991.

Pitcairn, Richard and Susan. *Natural Health for Dogs.* Emmaus, Pa.: Rodale Press, 1982.

ABOUT DOG SHOWS

Hall, Lynn. *Dog Showing for Beginners.* New York: Howell Book House, 1994.

Nichols, Virginia Tuck. *How to Show Your Own Dog.* Neptune, N. J.: TFH, 1970.

Vanacore, Connie. *Dog Showing, An Owner's Guide.* New York: Howell Book House, 1990.

ABOUT TRAINING

Ammen, Amy. *Training in No Time.* New York: Howell Book House, 1995.

Baer, Ted. *Communicating With Your Dog.* Hauppauge, N.Y.: Barron's Educational Series, Inc., 1989.

Benjamin, Carol Lea. *Dog Problems.* New York: Howell Book House, 1989.

Benjamin, Carol Lea. *Dog Training for Kids.* New York: Howell Book House, 1988.

Benjamin, Carol Lea. *Mother Knows Best.* New York: Howell Book House, 1985.

Benjamin, Carol Lea. *Surviving Your Dog's Adolescence.* New York: Howell Book House, 1993.

Bohnenkamp, Gwen. *Manners for the Modern Dog.* San Francisco: Perfect Paws, 1990.

Dibra, Bashkim. *Dog Training by Bash.* New York: Dell, 1992.

Dunbar, Ian, PhD, MRCVS. *Dr. Dunbar's Good Little Dog Book,* James & Kenneth Publishers, 2140 Shattuck Ave. #2406, Berkeley, Calif. 94704. (510) 658–8588. Order from the publisher.

Dunbar, Ian, PhD, MRCVS. *How to Teach a New Dog Old Tricks,* James & Kenneth Publishers. Order from the publisher; address above.

Dunbar, Ian, PhD, MRCVS, and Gwen Bohnenkamp. Booklets on *Preventing Aggression; Housetraining; Chewing; Digging; Barking; Socialization; Fearfulness; and Fighting,* James & Kenneth Publishers. Order from the publisher; address above.

Evans, Job Michael. *People, Pooches and Problems.* New York: Howell Book House, 1991.

Kilcommons, Brian and Sarah Wilson. *Good Owners, Great Dogs.* New York: Warner Books, 1992.

McMains, Joel M. *Dog Logic—Companion Obedience.* New York: Howell Book House, 1992.

Rutherford, Clarice and David H. Neil, MRCVS. *How to Raise a Puppy You Can Live With.* Loveland, Colo.: Alpine Publications, 1982.

Volhard, Jack and Melissa Bartlett. *What All Good Dogs Should Know: The Sensible Way to Train.* New York: Howell Book House, 1991.

ABOUT BREEDING

Harris, Beth J. Finder. *Breeding a Litter, The Complete Book of Prenatal and Postnatal Care.* New York: Howell Book House, 1983.

Holst, Phyllis, DVM. *Canine Reproduction.* Loveland, Colo.: Alpine Publications, 1985.

Walkowicz, Chris and Bonnie Wilcox, DVM. *Successful Dog Breeding, The Complete Handbook of Canine Midwifery.* New York: Howell Book House, 1994.

ABOUT ACTIVITIES

American Rescue Dog Association. *Search and Rescue Dogs.* New York: Howell Book House, 1991.

Barwig, Susan and Stewart Hilliard. *Schutzhund.* New York: Howell Book House, 1991.

Beaman, Arthur S. *Lure Coursing.* New York: Howell Book House, 1994.

Daniels, Julie. *Enjoying Dog Agility—From Backyard to Competition.* New York: Doral Publishing, 1990.

Davis, Kathy Diamond. *Therapy Dogs.* New York: Howell Book House, 1992.

Gallup, Davis Anne. *Running With Man's Best Friend.* Loveland, Colo.: Alpine Publications, 1986.

Habgood, Dawn and Robert. *On the Road Again With Man's Best Friend.* New England, Mid-Atlantic, West Coast and Southeast editions. Selective guides to area bed and breakfasts, inns, hotels and resorts that welcome guests and their dogs. New York: Howell Book House, 1995.

Holland, Vergil S. *Herding Dogs.* New York: Howell Book House, 1994.

LaBelle, Charlene G. *Backpacking With Your Dog.* Loveland, Colo.: Alpine Publications, 1993.

Simmons-Moake, Jane. *Agility Training, The Fun Sport for All Dogs.* New York: Howell Book House, 1991.

Spencer, James B. *Hup! Training Flushing Spaniels the American Way.* New York: Howell Book House, 1992.

Spencer, James B. *Point! Training the All-Seasons Birddog.* New York: Howell Book House, 1995.

Tarrant, Bill. *Training the Hunting Retriever.* New York: Howell Book House, 1991.

Volhard, Jack and Wendy. *The Canine Good Citizen.* New York: Howell Book House, 1994.

General Titles

Haggerty, Captain Arthur J. *How to Get Your Pet Into Show Business.* New York: Howell Book House, 1994.

McLennan, Bardi. *Dogs and Kids, Parenting Tips.* New York: Howell Book House, 1993.

Moran, Patti J. *Pet Sitting for Profit, A Complete Manual for Professional Success.* New York: Howell Book House, 1992.

Scalisi, Danny and Libby Moses. *When Rover Just Won't Do, Over 2,000 Suggestions for Naming Your Dog.* New York: Howell Book House, 1993.

Sife, Wallace, PhD. *The Loss of a Pet.* New York: Howell Book House, 1993.

Wrede, Barbara J. *Civilizing Your Puppy.* Hauppauge, N.Y.: Barron's Educational Series, 1992.

Magazines

The AKC GAZETTE, The Official Journal for the Sport of Purebred Dogs. American Kennel Club, 51 Madison Ave., New York, NY.

Bloodlines Journal. United Kennel Club, 100 E. Kilgore Rd., Kalamazoo, MI.

Dog Fancy. Fancy Publications, 3 Burroughs, Irvine, CA 92718

Dog World. Maclean Hunter Publishing Corp., 29 N. Wacker Dr., Chicago, IL 60606.

Videos

"SIRIUS Puppy Training," by Ian Dunbar, PhD, MRCVS. James & Kenneth Publishers, 2140 Shattuck Ave. #2406, Berkeley, CA 94704. Order from the publisher.

"Training the Companion Dog," from Dr. Dunbar's British TV Series, James & Kenneth Publishers. (See address above).

The American Kennel Club produces videos on every breed of dog, as well as on hunting tests, field trials and other areas of interest to purebred dog owners. For more information, write to AKC/Video Fulfillment, 5580 Centerview Dr., Suite 200, Raleigh, NC 27606.

chapter 13

Resources

Breed Clubs

Every breed recognized by the American Kennel Club has a national (parent) club. National clubs are a great source of information on your breed. You can get the name of the secretary of the club by contacting:

The American Kennel Club
51 Madison Avenue
New York, NY 10010
(212) 696-8200

There are also numerous all-breed, individual breed, obedience, hunting and other special-interest dog clubs across the country. The American Kennel Club can provide you with a geographical list of clubs to find ones in your area. Contact them at the above address.

Registry Organizations

Registry organizations register purebred dogs. The American Kennel Club is the oldest and largest in this country, and currently recognizes over 130 breeds. The United Kennel Club registers some breeds the AKC doesn't (including the American Pit Bull Terrier and the Miniature Fox Terrier) as well as many of the same breeds. The others included here are for your reference; the AKC can provide you with a list of foreign registries.

American Kennel Club
51 Madison Avenue
New York, NY 10010

United Kennel Club (UKC)
100 E. Kilgore Road
Kalamazoo, MI 49001-5598

American Dog Breeders Assn.
P.O. Box 1771
Salt Lake City, UT 84110
(Registers American Pit Bull Terriers)

Canadian Kennel Club
89 Skyway Avenue
Etobicoke, Ontario
Canada M9W 6R4

National Stock Dog Registry
P.O. Box 402
Butler, IN 46721
(Registers working stock dogs)

Orthopedic Foundation for Animals (OFA)
2300 E. Nifong Blvd.
Columbia, MO 65201-3856
(Hip registry)

Activity Clubs

Write to these organizations for information on the
activities they sponsor.

American Kennel Club
51 Madison Avenue
New York, NY 10010
(Conformation Shows, Obedience Trials, Field
Trials and Hunting Tests, Agility, Canine Good

Citizen, Lure Coursing, Herding, Tracking,
Earthdog Tests, Coonhunting.)

United Kennel Club
100 E. Kilgore Road
Kalamazoo, MI 49001-5598
(Conformation Shows, Obedience Trials, Agility,
Hunting for Various Breeds, Terrier Trials and
more.)

North American Flyball Assn.
1342 Jeff St.
Ypsilanti, MI 48198

International Sled Dog Racing Assn.
P.O. Box 446
Norman, ID 83848-0446

North American Working Dog Assn., Inc.
Southeast Kreisgruppe
P.O. Box 833
Brunswick, GA 31521

Trainers

Association of Pet Dog Trainers
P.O. Box 385
Davis, CA 95617
(800) PET–DOGS

American Dog Trainers' Network
161 West 4th St.
New York, NY 10014
(212) 727–7257

**National Association of Dog Obedience
Instructors**
2286 East Steel Rd.
St. Johns, MI 48879

Associations

American Dog Owners Assn.
1654 Columbia Tpk.
Castleton, NY 12033
(Combats anti-dog legislation)

Delta Society
P.O. Box 1080
Renton, WA 98057-1080
(Promotes the human/animal bond through
pet-assisted therapy and other programs)

Dog Writers Assn. of America (DWAA)
Sally Cooper, Secy.
222 Woodchuck Ln.
Harwinton, CT 06791

National Assn. for Search and Rescue (NASAR)
P.O. Box 3709
Fairfax, VA 22038

Therapy Dogs International
6 Hilltop Road
Mendham, NJ 07945